The White Coat Diaries

MADI SINHA

BERKLEY
New York

BERKLEY
An imprint of Penguin Random House LLC
penguinrandomhouse.com

Library of Congress Cataloging-in-Publication Data

Names: Sinha, Madi, author.
Title: The White Coat Diaries / Madi Sinha.
Description: First edition. | New York: Berkley, 2020.
Identifiers: LCCN 2019059340 (print) | LCCN 2019059341 (ebook) |
ISBN 9780593098196 (trade paperback) | ISBN 9780593098202 (ebook)
Subjects: GSAFD: Love stories.
Classification: LCC PS3619.I57624 W45 2020 (print) | LCC PS3619.I57624 (ebook) |
DDC 813/.6—dc23
LC record available at https://lccn.loc.gov/2019059340
LC ebook record available at https://lccn.loc.gov/2019059341

First Edition: September 2020

Printed in the United States of America
1 3 5 7 9 10 8 6 4 2

Cover art and design by Vikki Chu
Book design by Ashley Tucker

For my girls

CHAPTER ONE

I just want to help people, I just want to help people, I just want to help people. . . .

I crouch on the floor in an Emergency Department supply closet, wedged in between boxes of adult diapers and pregnancy tests. The door swings open, and a nurse pokes her head in.

"Are there any linens left in here?" she asks.

"I'm not sure." I stare into my lap, letting my hair fall across my face like a curtain. Hopefully she doesn't notice my puffy eyes.

"Are you the intern that just stuck herself?"

"Yes." I discreetly wipe my nose with the back of my hand. I try to sound less panicked than I feel. "Yup, that was me. I just took the needle out of the patient and accidentally stuck myself in the hand with it. Like an idiot." I attempt to laugh ironically, but it comes out sounding more like a desperate whimper.

"Well, when you're done doing whatever it is you're doing, you need to report to Employee Health. They'll test you and give you medication." She peers down at me through her tiny bifocals. Her voice sympathetic, she asks, "Have you ever had a needle stick before?"

My chest is so tight I can barely get the word out. "No."

"Well, I've had four in my career, and it's not that big a deal."

"Really?" I'm buoyed by a surge of hope. "Did you—"

"Make sure to get yourself together before coming back out here. It's unprofessional to cry in front of the patients." She closes the door abruptly.

The motion-sensor light goes off, and I am left in near–pitch darkness.

I just want to help peo— Oh fuck everyone!

I spend probably fifteen minutes sitting in the dark supply closet, too exhausted and depleted to move. I've been awake for over twenty-four hours. During that time, I've peed twice, eaten once, and asked myself, *How did it come to this?* eighteen times. I thought I'd be good at this. Why am I not good at this? I reach into the pocket of my white coat for my inhaler, and the lights flick back on. From the corner of my eye, I see something tiny and brown scurry across the floor and dive behind a box of gauze pads. I spring to my feet, and my head strikes the shelf above me. Pain sears through the back of my skull. I yelp, and as my hand flies up to my scalp to check for bleeding, I knock over a box, causing a million little Band-Aids to come fluttering down all around me like ticker tape, as if to say, *Congratulations! You're a twenty-six-year-old loser hiding in a closet.*

It wasn't supposed to be like this. I graduated at the top of my class—Alpha Omega Alpha honor society, in fact—from medical school. I beat out hundreds of other applicants for a coveted internal medicine residency spot at Philadelphia General Hospital. *The* Philadelphia General, my first choice. I could have easily gone to the Cleveland Clinic or Mass General or Mayo, but I chose to go where I knew the training was rigorous and unmatched because I was certain, beyond a doubt, that I could handle it, probably with one arm tied behind my back.

I can recite the name of every bone, muscle, and nerve in the adult human body the way other people can recite song lyrics (and, just for reference, there are 206 bones in the human body). I can diagram, from memory, the biochemical pathway by which the liver converts squalene into cholesterol. I can list the top twenty medications for hypertension *and* the side effects of each, without using a mnemonic device. I've studied. My God, have I studied. I've studied to the point of self-imposed social isolation. To the point of obsession. I've prepared for this for years, decades, my whole life. I wrote an essay in third grade titled "Why Tendons Are Awesome!" that not only earned me an A, but was prominently displayed for months on the classroom bulletin board. I mean, I was *meant* for this.

I've been an intern for twenty-four hours, and that arm that's tied behind my back? I'm ready to rip it off this instant.

Sighing, I crouch down, pick up all the Band-Aids, and cram them back into their box. Then I emerge from the closet sheepishly, expecting to find at least one of the several ED nurses waiting for me, ready to comfort me in that stern-but-understanding, maternal way of theirs. The only person at the nurses' station is a disinterested janitor on his cell phone.

A balding man wearing large, square wire-rimmed glasses and an angry expression barks at me from the hallway. "Excuse me! Miss, do you work here?"

I nod, and he approaches. "My wife is still waiting for a bed." He indicates a woman in a hospital gown lying on a stretcher that's been pushed to one side of the bustling ED hallway. "When is she going to be moved to her room?"

"I'm not sure . . . ," I say, uncertain if I can help him but desperately wanting to do something, anything, right. "Has she been admitted?"

"Obviously, yes. She's being admitted for observation for pneumonia. Her name is Tally. Lenore Tally. Do you have any information on her?"

The name means nothing to me. "I'm sorry, she's not one of my patients, but I can try to find her nurse for you," I offer. The few nurses in sight look busy, drawing blood and taking vital signs. "It might take a few minutes, but—"

The man throws up his hands in frustration. "None of you people have any answers! Oh, for God's sake, I'll find her nurse myself!" He storms off, and I can hear his voice echoing down the hall: "Excuse me? Do you work here?"

My shoulders sag. So much for doing something right. At this point, it's clear: the gaping black hole of despair that has consumed my being can be filled by only one thing. I need baked goods, and I need them *stat*. I hurry to the vending machine in the ED waiting room, eat two and a half bags of mini chocolate chip cookies while waiting for the elevator, and find, to my great disappointment, that my mood is only marginally brightened.

It had never occurred to me—until the moment I drew the needle out of my patient's vein, popped off the test tube full of his blood, crossed my hands to reach for the gauze pad, and jabbed the end of the needle into the back of my hand—that I might be putting myself at risk by spending my days and nights tending to sick people. Well, then again, that's not true. It *had* occurred to me, but before it became an actual possibility, the idea of contracting a potentially lethal disease from a patient had a noble, romantic, Victorian sort of feel to it: the selfless, waistcoated doctor carrying a leather satchel and a jar full of leeches, sacrificing herself at the bedside of her patient—that sort of thing.

I know the chances of actually getting sick are extremely slim, especially if I take prophylactic antiviral medication, but I worry nonetheless. I worry with a fervor that I both recognize as irrational and embrace as inevitable. Worry out of proportion with reality is kind of my *thing*.

"Is this your first needle stick?" The nurse at the tiny Employee Health office next to the hospital pharmacy—her name tag identifies her as "Rhonda"—looks irked and preoccupied. When I walked in a moment ago, she was engaged in a heated phone conversation with someone named Hank about getting his lazy ass off the couch and maybe, for once in his worthless life, cleaning up the cat's vomit. It was quite a few minutes of this sort of thing before she turned around and realized I was sitting right in front of her desk, awkwardly trying to decide whether to wait for her to notice me or just interrupt her. When she hung up the phone, it was with one eye fixed suspiciously on me. "Can I help you?"

I told her what had happened and, in doing so, triggered another bout of panicky tears. Rhonda kindly, if impatiently, handed me a box of Kleenex. Then she proceeded to fish out from a filing cabinet no less than eight different questionnaires, each of which she now seems determined to methodically complete in its entirety.

"No. This is my first needle stick," I answer, twisting the damp Kleenex around my fingers.

"Do you have any risk factors for HIV or hepatitis C?" Rhonda asks.

"No."

"Have you ever been tested for either?"

"No."

"Are you currently sexually active?"

"Nope."

"When was the last time you were sexually active without barrier protection?"

"Um . . . never."

"As in you've never had unprotected intercourse?"

"As in . . . I've never had intercourse."

Rhonda pauses, her pen hovering above the paper.

"It's cultural," I add quickly. "I'm Indian. Premarital sex is frowned upon. Like, a lot. You've seen *Bend It Like Beckham*, right?"

"That's . . . fine," Rhonda says, scratching one raised eyebrow.

I sigh inwardly. *Whatever, Rhonda.*

She asks me for my medical history (*None, except a mild case of asthma*), list of allergies (*None, except cats*), and social history (Do I smoke? *No*. Drink? *No*. Do I use illicit drugs? *Obviously not.*). Then she asks me to put my arm on her desk, ties a tourniquet around my biceps, and draws four vials of blood.

As she tapes a wad of gauze over my skin, she says, "You'll need to come in for another blood test in six weeks and again in three months." She hands me a slip of paper. "And this is for the antiviral tablets. Pick them up at the pharmacy next door. You'll take them three times a day for the next six weeks."

I look at the prescription. "Lamivudine? A nucleoside reverse transcriptase inhibitor?" I say, aghast.

Rhonda stares at me. "That's the protocol."

"But the potential side effects of this are nausea, diarrhea, abdominal pain, headaches, pancreatitis, and liver failure."

She regards me skeptically. "If you say so."

"Isn't there anything else I could take instead?" I plead. "I'm an intern. I can't afford to have headaches and go into liver failure. I have patients to round on. I have a lot to do."

"That's the protocol." She enunciates each word in a way that indicates that she has fulfilled the duties laid out in her job description and, therefore, our interaction must come to an immediate close.

I turn toward the door. "You don't think didanosine or even efavirenz would be a better—"

Rhonda puts her phone to her ear. "Have a nice day, Doctor!"

I'm sitting at one of a cluster of long tables near a picture window. A curt little sign in a metal stand nearby reads: *Reserved for PGH Doctors and Staff.* It's early, a half-moon still visible in the dawn sky, and the only other patron in the cafeteria dining room is an elderly man connected to an oxygen tank that he carries in a cloth duffel bag. He shuffles in my direction, notices the sign, then shuffles away. A plastic tray appears across the table from me, and a slender young man with round glasses says, "Hi. Stuart Ness, Harvard Med." He begins to vigorously dissect a grapefruit.

"Yes, I remember. We met at orientation." Where you introduced yourself as Stuart Ness from Harvard Med. Twice.

"Being on call is great!" he enthuses without prompting. "I admitted eleven patients, started fourteen IV lines, and still had time to watch a movie. I'm not even tired. I think I'll go for a run when our shift is over."

I wonder if it's possible that I'm so fatigued I'm hallucinating this entire interaction with this gratingly peppy Harry Potter lookalike. "That's dynamite," I say.

"I'm so psyched to finally be here. I can't wait to meet Dr. Portnoy. The man, the legend, am I right?"

"Yup."

"And *the* Dr. V. Did you hear that we get to work with him? Like, actually round with him and everything?" His eyes gleam. "So awesome!"

"It's pretty awesome." I manage a thin smile.

"What was your name again?"

"Norah Kapadia."

"Hey, any relation to Dr. Kapadia, the head of Pediatrics at UPenn? The one that came up with the Kapadia criteria for Kawasaki disease? I mean, I don't know how common a last name of Kapadia is, but—"

I blow a puff of air through my pursed lips. I've lost track of how many times I've answered this question over the years, but it always comes from someone eager to show off that they're well-versed in rare pediatric disorders. "That's my father."

"No way! Is he still practicing?"

"He passed away." I tuck a strand of hair behind my ear.

Stuart shifts in his seat. "Oh, wow. I'm really sorry."

I nod tersely and shrug. "It's fine. It was a long time ago."

"His paper on the diagnosis of Kawasaki is epic. It's practically biblical."

I smile at the compliment.

Having finished dismembering his grapefruit, Stuart starts in on an enormous bowl of oatmeal. "He must have been an amazing doctor."

"That's what I've heard." And I'm sure he never spent a night on call crying in a supply closet. I stare at my plate and silently count exactly twenty-three little sugarcoated doughnut crumbs.

Stuart clears his throat. His tone is forcefully bright. "So, how was your night?"

"I got a needle stick."

His eyes widen in a way so cartoonish I almost expect a honking sound to accompany his stunned facial expression. "Seriously? Yikes. Did the patient have any . . . you know . . . communicable diseases?"

"HIV."

"Oh, boy. Well, the rate of HIV infection from a needle stick is like one in one hundred thousand. I wouldn't even worry about it. Now, hep C, that's the scary one. That's more like one in forty."

I jab my index finger at the crumbs. "He had hepatitis C, too."

He takes this in. "Wow. You were that kid in elementary school that ran with scissors, right?"

A tray slams onto the table, silverware rattling. Clark, an acquaintance of mine from medical school who has the soulful eyes and determined jawline of a young Ernest Hemingway—as well as the tendency to crack each of his ten knuckles one at a time, loudly and repetitively—drops into a chair. Wearing a faded white T-shirt over bloodstained green scrub pants, he looks as if he's narrowly survived some sort of natural disaster. Sections of his black hair project from his head at varying sharp angles. "Good morning." His voice is a low growl that reminds me of a lawn mower. "This place should be burned to the ground."

Stuart puts out his hand, grinning. "Whoa! Another rough first night. Hi! I'm Stuart Ness, Harvard Med."

Clark glances at Stuart's hand and takes a slow breath. A vein bulges in his left temple. "Norah," he says without looking at me, "I'm going to put my head down on the table. I want you to take this fork and jam it into my carotid."

"Ha! I like this guy!" Stuart laughs, clapping him on the back.

I smile sympathetically at Clark, though I'm fairly sure my night was worse than his.

"Let me ask you," Clark says. "Is it too late to get off this crazy train? What if we quit now, before it gets any worse?"

I sigh and rub my forehead, the beginnings of a migraine coalescing somewhere deep in the frontal cortex of my brain. "I can't quit. I've put too much time and work into getting *on* this crazy train. I can't bail out now. What about student loan debt?"

"Sallie Mae. That heartless bitch," Clark grumbles, rubbing his eyes with the heels of his hands.

"Easy there, buddy. It's only the first day," Stuart says, smiling encouragingly. He's about to clap Clark on the back again when Clark shoots him a look so menacing that Stuart's hand freezes in midair.

A moment passes before I realize that a female voice is commenting, dispassionately, from the loudspeaker overhead: "Code blue, room 512. Code blue, room 512."

A fork clatters to the floor.

We run.

CHAPTER TWO

Sprinting up the stairs would be easier if my white coat didn't weigh fifteen pounds. Senior residents like to joke that interns carry their lives around in their pockets. Mine are filled with two miniature textbooks, three pens, a stethoscope, a reflex hammer, a hospital ID badge, a penlight, a laminated map of the hospital, and a protein bar. A wearable emergency preparedness kit. Unlike the embarrassingly short medical students' white coat, which projects nothing but bewilderment and the deflection of responsibility (*Me? Oh no, I'm not the doctor. I'm a student. I'm just here to observe. Although once they let me catch a baby as it came shooting out of a woman's birth canal. It was a beautiful experience.*), the long doctor's coat radiates confidence and capability: *Throw anything at me, I'm ready.*

In a code blue, the first doctor to arrive at the bedside gets to "run" the code—be the leader and make treatment decisions—at least until the senior resident or attending arrives. I've seen codes run before, but this is my first opportunity to be at the helm. This is my chance, *finally*, to prove my abilities.

The first thing I lose from my coat pockets is a miniature pharmacopeia, a medication reference book. It bounces away down the stairwell, but I keep going, taking the stairs two at a time. I'll be damned if I can't beat Stuart Ness from Harvard Medical School to room 512. If I can't compete with him academically, I'm determined to at least outrun him. I've met people like Stuart. There was always one in every class in college and medical school, someone for whom everything seemingly came easy, the curve-breaker, the guy who thought organic chemistry would be great if only it were a *little* more challenging.

Which is why I'm not entirely surprised when I see a blur of brown, perfectly groomed hair and green scrubs flash past me somewhere between room 485 and room 502. I arrive—perspiring excessively and panting—to see a breathless, ruddy-cheeked nurse standing over an elderly male patient. The nurse chews her lip and adjusts and re-adjusts her reading glasses, while Stuart, at her elbow, stares at the heart monitor above the bed. The tracing shows a heart rate dangerously fast and erratic, and the words "Critical Value" blink angrily on the screen. The patient, his skin pale and clammy, his eyes wide with panic, speaks in a soft whimper. "What's happening?"

"Your heart is beating too fast," the nurse says, fiddling with the wires taped to the man's chest. Her movements are confident, but worry ripples through her voice.

"He's in A-fib," Stuart announces, anxiously clutching his stethoscope with both hands. "Unstable A-fib. Maybe we should try a medication? Maybe diltiazem?"

The patient's blood pressure is falling due to his heart arrhythmia. If his heart rate isn't slowed down, right now, he'll go into cardiac arrest. Every cardiology textbook I've read clearly outlines the appropriate next steps for this exact scenario.

Why are they just standing around?

A crash cart with a defibrillator is next to the bed. I grab the electrical paddles as the heart monitor emits an ear-splitting alarm. The patient's blood pressure reads 80 over 35 and is falling by the second. The nurse, the patient, and Stuart all turn to me and speak at once.

"Maybe let's wait for the resident," Stuart says.

"Are you sure that's what you want to do?" the nurse says.

"What are those for, Doc?" the patient says, his voice barely a whisper. His eyes drift closed.

I shock him. The sound is like a candle being extinguished. "Clear!" I remember to shout, moments too late.

The patient's limbs jerk and waggle; then he is still, and the heart monitor is silent. No one moves. The nurse clutches her chest, steadying herself against a chair.

Oh my God. What have I done? That should have worked. Why didn't it work?

The patient's eyes snap open. "WHHHAAAAAAT THE FUUUUUUCK!!!" He tries to crawl out of the bed.

The nurse struggles to restrain him. "Mr. Leeds, I'm very sorry about that, I—"

"What did you do to me? What in the name of God, you mother—"

It occurs to me that I should have warned him, said something to prepare him, probably, before shocking him. But, with the heart monitor now beeping a jaunty, steady rhythm, I'm giddy with relief. "Look, Mr. Leeds, you're not in atrial fibrillation anymore!" I smile at him triumphantly. *I saved you. I pulled you back from the brink of death.*

Mr. Leeds has a wild look in his eyes. "Get away from me! Get her away from me!"

I'm taken aback. Maybe he's confused. After all, he's just had a near-death experience. Then I catch Stuart's eye. He's gawking at me, his mouth agape.

A dozen residents and medical students have crowded into the doorway, craning their necks this way and that to peer over one another's shoulders like a flock of curious, wide-eyed birds. Among them is Clark, holding a steaming cup of coffee.

"What's happening? What'd you guys do?" he asks.

Stuart turns to stare at him, his mouth still hanging open. "Dude. You stopped for *coffee*?"

A gangly man with a ponytail wearing a long, tattered white coat, his lips pursed as if he's just tasted something rancid, squeezes into the room, shouting, "You people need to move, now! I need to get in here." He is followed by a petite young woman in scrubs who has secured her hair around a pencil. Their name badges identify them as General Surgery residents.

"Terry! Thank goodness!" The nurse seizes the man's arm.

Terry pushes his wire glasses up the bridge of his nose while drawing in a deep breath, the whistling sound produced hinting that he likely has either a chronic sinus obstruction or really, really tiny nasal passages. "Tell me what's going on," he says.

Mr. Leeds clutches the bed rails. "These people are trying to kill me!"

"That intern just defibrillated the patient." The nurse's tone is accusatory. "He was wide awake!"

Honestly, I don't understand what she's so upset about. The patient was moments away from death, and now he's alert and talking. Full of vim and vigor, in fact. Yes, *technically*, you're supposed to sedate the patient with something like Valium before shocking them, because having your heart electrocuted while you're awake is probably as unpleasant as being unexpectedly struck by lightning, but—

"The intern did what?" Terry's voice becomes increasingly shrill, like a teakettle coming to a boil. He turns to me menacingly. "What do you think you're doing?"

My heart pounds against my ribs as I drop the paddles and cross my arms over my chest. "His heart rhythm was irregular," I say, unable to quell the tremor in my voice. "And his blood pressure—"

"Are you incompetent?"

"He was unstable—"

"This is *my* patient!" Terry paces back and forth, seething. "You don't do anything to *my* patient! What department are you from?" He grabs my arm and twists it forcefully—not enough to hurt, but enough to knock me slightly off balance—to look at my coat sleeve, where the words *Internal Medicine House Staff* are embroidered in blue thread near the shoulder. "Internal Medicine? Who's your senior resident?"

I open my mouth but can't form any coherent words. Humiliation pricks at the corners of my eyes. *Don't cry in front of the patient.*

"That's me." A young man in his late twenties with a rakish smile and tousled brown hair saunters past the crowd at the door. Ethan Cantor, a senior resident. I remember him from orientation; he was disarmingly friendly and not nearly as intimidating as the senior residents I'd worked with on clinical rotations in medical school. "What's the problem, Terrance?" Ethan asks casually.

"You need to supervise your interns, Ethan!" Terry says. "This genius just shocked my patient! Without sedating him!"

Ethan glances at the heart monitor, then nods with the air of a surfer admiring a particularly impressive wave. "Nice. It's Norah, right? What was it, unstable atrial fibrillation?"

I nod nervously. "His blood pressure was really low, eighty over thirty-five."

"Sir, sorry we had to do that to you." Ethan places his hand on Mr. Leeds's shoulder. "But the young doctor here probably just saved your life."

I lift my chin righteously but avoid making eye contact with Terry.

Terry snorts. "You don't shock for an irregular heart rhythm!"

"If the patient's unstable, yes, you do." Ethan listens to Mr. Leeds's chest with his stethoscope.

"Do you two guys know what you're doing?" Mr. Leeds asks, helplessly scanning the room for reassurance. The residents and students in the doorway adjust their white coats and look away.

Terry glances at Mr. Leeds as if he's surprised Mr. Leeds is still there. "I'm a chief resident of Surgery!" His face reddens.

"And I'm a chief resident of Internal Medicine and a Visa Gold card member," Ethan replies dismissively, still listening to Mr. Leeds's chest. He pulls the stethoscope out of his ears and loops it around his neck. "Sir, I need to get you transferred to the Intensive Care Unit."

Terry balks. "You're not transferring him! We're taking him to surgery in an hour. His gallbladder needs to come out."

Ethan shrugs. "Sorry, the gallbladder will have to wait. We need to figure out why he got unstable. When's the last time he had lab work?"

The nurse flips through a chart. "Yesterday."

"What was the anion gap?" Ethan asks.

She squints at him. "The what?"

He takes the chart from her. "The bicarbonate level plus the chloride level, subtracted from the sodium level plus the potassium level. Quick, what's ninety plus fifteen, subtracted from one-twenty-six?"

"Twenty-one," Stuart and I both say immediately. Maybe he says it a fraction of a second before me. *Show-off.*

"Redraw labs, and let's get ready for the transfer, please," Ethan says.

"Ethan, you need to back off." Terry puts his hands on his hips. "Mr. Leeds, we're going ahead with your surgery as planned."

It's like I'm ringside at a boxing match between two brains. It's unexpectedly exciting. I silently root for Ethan's cerebral cortex to beat Terry's to a bloody, ineffectual pulp.

"Okay, guys, we need one decision here," the nurse says.

Ethan sighs impatiently. "Terry, let me explain this to you. He has a high anion gap. That means too much acid. Too much acid is bad for the heart. You operate, you cause more acid. More acid, more bad. You follow?"

"I'm calling the attending!" Terry seizes the bedside phone. "You can explain to him why you're hijacking his patient."

Ethan shrugs. "You guys can call your mommy from the hallway. We have work to do here."

Terry glowers at Ethan for a moment, one side of his face making little twitching movements, then slams the phone down and turns to the tiny female Surgery resident with the pencil bun.

"Why are you still standing there?" he thunders. "Get Dr. Brenner on the phone, now! Move, all of you!"

The tiny Surgery resident raises her eyebrows at Ethan, suppressing a smile, and follows Terry as he jostles past the smirking crowd in the doorway.

Ethan gives them a parting salute, and it's just as satisfying as if he'd punched Terry into unconsciousness. The crowd at the door recedes.

Ethan turns to me. "Norah, what medication do you want to start Mr. Leeds on to make sure he doesn't go back into atrial fibrillation?"

"What do *I* want to start him on?" I shake my head, confused. Why is he asking *me*?

"He's your patient. What are you going to do next, Doctor?"

The word "doctor" echoes in my head, clouding my thoughts. *Focus. I know this*. "The treatment for atrial fibrillation is—"

"Amiodarone. An amiodarone drip," Stuart says, twitching like a cocker spaniel ready to bound off its leash.

My lips pressed together, I blow a puff of air out of my nostrils. "Amiodarone. That's what I was about to say."

"Good work, you guys." Ethan scribbles a note in the chart and hands it to the nurse. "You're going to be fine, Mr. Leeds. The ICU team is going to look after you."

There's considerably less fanfare going on than I would have expected. I mean, I just *saved a life. On my first day. Maybe I'm good at this after all.*

"I don't ever want that done again!" Mr. Leeds's eyes haven't lost their panicked sheen. "What she did to me, that shock treatment. Not ever again!"

Ethan nods reassuringly. "We won't have to do that to you again. I promise."

In the hallway outside the room, eager to make the most of this learning opportunity, I turn to Ethan. "Dr. Cantor, what's the dose of amiod—"

His face has fallen. "What the hell were you thinking?" he hisses, glancing around to make sure no one else is in earshot.

Stunned, I step backward. "What?"

"You shocked a patient without sedating him?"

"I thought—"

"Listen, Norah," he says, his eyebrows knitted together. "You have to wait for a senior resident for this kind of thing. Just because you read in a textbook that one of the treatments for unstable A-fib is an electric shock doesn't mean you just do it without checking with a senior first. Do you have any idea how traumatic and painful that is for a patient? A dose of IV diltiazem would have worked just as well."

Stuart, appearing behind us, folds his arms and grins smugly.

Ethan shakes his head, disappointment in every crease around his eyes. "You don't use a fire hose when a water gun would do the job. I covered for you this time, but I'm not going to do that again, got it? This isn't med school. This is residency at PGH. You can't make mistakes like that."

I nod repeatedly, my neck and ears burning with shame. I look, I imagine, like a terrified bobblehead doll.

Ethan turns toward the stairwell, glancing at his pager. As he walks away, he mumbles, "It's gonna be a long year. Jesus."

CHAPTER THREE

All around me is serene darkness, a blissful cocoon of nothingness. Then, suddenly, I'm falling, plummeting through space. My head drops and snaps back, and I'm awake. An attending—Dr. Something-or-Other from the Pulmonary Medicine department—is saying, "And that's the most important thing to remember about ventilators. All right. Any questions?"

Vinegar stings my nasal passages. My salad, half-eaten, sits in front of me. The dim room is filled with rickety metal desks that creak loudly with every muscle twitch or shift of weight. These lunchtime lectures will occur several times a week, we've been told, and attendance is mandatory.

Seated next to me, Clark picks at the remnants of a plastic-wrapped ham sandwich. "Let . . . me . . . the hell . . . out," he mutters, his eyes fixed on the wall clock above the door.

My voice is thin and desperate. "Only thirty more minutes," I say. At 12:00 p.m., those of us who were on call last night can go home. I haven't slept in twenty-seven-and-a-half hours. I'm shivering, and my head throbs. My limbs feel as though they're only partially under my control, and my left eye is twitching.

At the back of the room, several second- and third-year residents whisper among themselves. They're like the clique of popular high school upperclassmen that sits together in the lunchroom and rates the newbies on looks and, in this case, likelihood to accidentally kill a patient. I'm not positive, but I think I hear one of them mumble my name—"Kapadia"—and snicker. When I turn around, several of them avert their eyes. I wonder if they've made the connection to my father. *There she is—the great Dr. Kapadia's daughter, the one who defibrillated a man for no reason! Obviously she's only here because of her last name.* I shrink into my seat.

Ethan is scrolling through the news feed on his phone. Next to him, evidently engrossed in the lecture, is the other Internal Medicine chief resident, Francesca. A stout, robust woman with a frosted pixie haircut and a fervent gaze, Francesca strikes me as the type of person who approaches even mundane tasks—grocery shopping or ordering from a restaurant menu, for example—with the same level of intensity that most people reserve for crisis situations.

The lecturer says, "And one last word of advice for the new interns: remember to document everything. If you give the patient a packet of graham crackers, write a note about it in the chart. If you didn't document it, it didn't happen. Good note-keeping equals good doctoring. All right, good luck to you all this year. Make Philly General proud."

The audience applauds, and the lecturer leaves the conference room.

"All right, everyone, listen up," Ethan says, standing. "Our esteemed director of medical education, Dr. Fancy Forks, wants you all to know that Jake-O is visiting this week, so remember not to leave your uncapped needles lying around or wear open-toed shoes or do anything else to get us fined."

The upperclassmen laugh. Francesca rolls her eyes at Ethan and chuckles. I look around the room in confusion and catch the other interns doing the same.

Ethan continues. "And, I'm sure this goes without saying, but if anyone asks if you're working over eighty hours a week, remember the correct answer is, 'No. Never. What the hell are you suggesting, you government clown?'"

More laughs from the upperclassmen.

Francesca stands. "Some housekeeping stuff: The call schedules are done and posted. Make sure you have your vacation requests in to Barbara by tomorrow. Interns, don't get your hopes up about vacation requests; seniority rules, and you'll get days off when it's convenient for the rest of us. On a social note, Genetiks Pharma is sponsoring a dinner for us next Friday. Seven o'clock at Akira Hibachi on Walnut Street. Hope to see you all there, unless you're on call, in which case you don't get to go, sucks to be you. Any questions? No? Okay, class dismissed, then."

I have so many questions. As the upperclassmen file out of the room, I tap Stuart on the shoulder. "Why do they call him Fancy Forks? And who's Jake-O?"

Stuart shrugs and turns back to his pocket-size copy of *Harrison's Principles of Internal Medicine*. A young woman with lustrous waist-length brown hair, perfect eye makeup, and an Italian accent leans over from her seat behind me. "And why can't we wear open-toed shoes?"

Clark looks over his shoulder at her, does a double take, spins around in his chair, and grins toothily. "I have no idea, but . . . hello." He extends his hand. "I'm Clark." His usual gruff demeanor has evaporated, replaced by a leering intensity that, I think, he believes is charming.

The young woman is unaffected. "I'm Bianca. And I'm married."

Clark retracts his hand, nods in acknowledgment, and wordlessly turns back around in his seat.

"J-C-H-O, not Jake-O. It's the Joint Commission of Hospitals." A twitchy young woman with red-rimmed glasses is sitting next to

Bianca. She speaks at nearly three times the average rate of words per minute. "They inspect hospitals to make sure they're following the rules. Hospitals are terrified of JCHO. Open-toed shoes mean that a needle or something could fall on your toe and injure you and then—watch out! Lawsuit. I'm Imani, by the way. I'm from Wisconsin. Yup, the land of cheese. I'm going to Mass General for an ophthalmology residency next year. I'm just here for my intern year. I had no idea it gets so hot in Philadelphia!" She turns to me, wide-eyed with admiration. "Is it true you shocked a patient on your first day? That's amazing!"

Taken off guard, I stare at her blankly for a moment before replying, "Thanks. I guess."

"Diltiazem would have worked just as well," Stuart, without looking up from his book, mutters resentfully.

Clark leans in to interrupt. "So, fellow interns, where are we drinking tonight?"

Before anyone can reply, Ethan and Francesca approach our group. We straighten in our seats.

"Okay, newbies," Ethan says. "You five are the few, the proud, the bottom of the totem pole. Your job is to admit patients from the Emergency Department, round on them every day, attend to their every need, and keep the nurses from bothering us."

Francesca nods. "Your pager should never, ever leave your side, even when you're not on duty."

"Call is every third night, give or take. The schedule is in the residents' lounge," Ethan says. "No, you don't get to choose when you're on call. Also, you'll be assigned to a different service every two and a half months. No, you don't get to choose where you're assigned."

"You'll round with your assigned attending every morning," Francesca says. "You'll be either on time or early to rounds. Those are the two choices."

"Don't trust the ED attendings."

"Don't trust the nurses."

"Double-check everything yourself."

"Don't take shortcuts."

"Don't kill anyone. That's an important one. And stay hydrated."

"Coffee is not a good replenishment fluid."

"And try not to defibrillate anyone unnecessarily." Ethan winks at me, and my face burns with humiliation again. "Any questions?"

My head is spinning. My fellow interns are silent and subdued.

Francesca makes aggressive eye contact with each of us in turn. "Most important, remember that your work reflects on me and Ethan, on our attendings, and on the reputation of this hospital. You're all members of the Team now. The Team saves lives. The Team has each other's backs. The Team rises and falls together and is only as strong as its weakest link. And right now, you guys are all the weakest links." She pauses, and for a moment it seems as though she might finish her thought with an encouraging word or a bit of motivational wisdom. Instead, abruptly cheerful, she says, "Okay. Don't just sit there! Let's get to work!"

We stand in unison, causing a cacophony of screeching desks. Clark leans over to Stuart, his eyes sunken and bewildered. "Seriously, dude. Where are we drinking?"

At 12:00 p.m., I step out of the hospital lobby and into the midday sunshine, blinking. The scent of Philadelphia in the summertime—something not unlike the scent inside a portable toilet—envelops me in a steamy fog. I dodge lunch trucks and idling taxis to cross the street, then turn back and look up at the dual soaring, sand-colored hospital towers. A circular drive leads to the sleek sliding doors of the Emergency Department. Overhead, a glass-enclosed walkway connects the parking garage to the second floor of the hospital. On the side of the building, the words *Philadelphia General Hospital, est. 1875* are carved into the limestone facade in stately script.

Standing on the sidewalk amid the ebb and flow of wheelchairs and white coats, sweat drenching my collar, I sigh. If I didn't come back here tomorrow, I doubt anyone would miss me. Just another intern who couldn't handle the grind, a frightening, cautionary tale for future classes of interns: Look to your left, look to your right. Do you see Norah Kapadia? No. Because she was a terrible doctor and shocked a man for no reason and stuck herself and contracted hepatitis C and quit. Don't be like her.

I reach into my pocket for my phone. Seven missed calls. *Crap.*

I set off toward home, the phone pressed to my ear.

"I've been trying to call you since last night." Her tone is vexed and resentful. How dare I worry her.

"I know," I say. "I'm sorry. It was my first night on call, and it was really busy—"

"Whole night, Norah. I didn't sleep whole night." Articles don't factor strongly into my mother's speech pattern. In her native Gujarati, there's no grammatical equivalent of "the" or "a."

"I'm sorry I didn't pick up. But I didn't sleep the whole night either."

"One text! You couldn't send one text? Did you know—I saw it on *Dateline*—criminals are more likely to attack woman with glasses and ponytail? And what do you have? Glasses and ponytail! I was so worried about you. I tried calling hospital, but they wouldn't page you, and then I called Paul, and he came over at two a.m. to sit with me because I couldn't sleep and my blood sugar was 345. It was terrible!"

I pinch the bridge of my nose. "You called Paul? Why didn't he text me?"

"He didn't want to bother you, of course," she says impatiently. "I was going to send him to hospital to look for you, but then Nimisha said—"

"Whoa, wait," I say, panic rising in my chest. "When did you talk to Nimisha Auntie?"

"Last night."

"Since when are you talking to her again?"

She makes a clicking noise with her tongue, the way she always does when she's annoyed about having to explain something to me that should be obvious. "She's my oldest friend. Of course I talk to her."

I hesitate, choosing my words carefully. "Ma, remember, you agreed the last time. You said yourself, Nimisha isn't your friend—"

"*Besharam!* Have some respect, Norah!"

"Sorry." I roll my eyes. "Nimisha *Auntie* isn't your friend."

There is a long silence, and I glance at my phone to make sure she hasn't hung up. Then, her tone indignant, she says, "When I came to this country in 1986, twenty-two years old, new bride, not speaking word of English, with one suitcase and ten dollars, after your father's family turned their backs on us, you know who was there for me? You know who taught me English and took me to Woolworth and bought me my first winter coat?"

"I know." I sigh. "I know. She's been lording that coat over you for decades. But that was in the past. Now she's—"

"Honest. She is honest."

I shake my head. "No. Nope. She's the opposite of honest."

She sighs, and I can tell she's shaking her head, too. We've hit an impasse. As usual. "Talk to Paul."

Before I can say a word, my brother's voice on the other end says, "Hey, Nor. How was your first night?"

"Ma is talking to Nimisha Auntie again."

"I know. It's been for a few weeks."

"Weeks?" I stop in the middle of the sidewalk, and a woman behind me nearly collides with me. She shoots me a glare and steps around me. "What do you mean, weeks? Paul, you know what happened the last time she let that horrible woman back into her life. She's toxic. Why didn't you tell me?"

"I didn't find out until I came over here today. She's also started shopping again."

I groan. "Oh God. How bad is it?"

"Well, from what I can see, it's mostly handbags this time." His voice echoes, and I can tell he's stepped into the garage, where my mother usually hoards her purchases. The entire floor and two racks of tall shelves are covered with the spoils of her past shopping sprees: handbags, shoes, clothes, hats, three giant Costco thirty-five-packs of tennis balls and an economy-size crate of Hawaiian coffee. She doesn't play tennis or drink coffee. "About six Michael Kors and a couple Coach."

"Six?" I'm still stopped in the middle of the sidewalk. Two streams of foot traffic flow by on either side of me. "Jesus, Paul. Are the tags still on?"

"Yeah," he says. "I'll return them."

I find his preternatural calm in stressful situations both admirable and annoying. I hate being the hysterical one. "What's her blood sugar?"

"Right now? It's fine. Down to 120. I made her take her insulin. I think she's been binge-eating chocolate croissants again, though. I found an empty family pack in the trash."

In the background, my mother's voice approaches. "Paul, what are you doing in here? These are my things; you can't just take them!"

"Ma, you can't afford all this stuff," Paul says.

"How do you know what I can and can't afford?"

"You know what Dr. Kendra says. You shop when you're depressed and feel bad about yourself—"

Now he's done it. Ma refuses to let us refer to her as "depressed," even though every mental health professional she's ever seen (and there have been quite a few) has told her she is. "I'm not depressed! I'm not some crazy old lady! Is that what you think of me? Shame on you! I'm your mother!"

She continues in this vein while I say, "Paul, put her back on. Can you hear me? Put her back on!"

"Jesus, the two of you!" Paul says, his frustration breaking through. "Fine, yell at each other. I have to go to work."

I realize that it's a Tuesday afternoon. Has Paul been there all day? I cringe with guilt. Paul is always the one missing work when Ma goes into one of her moods. "Sorry, Paul. Just let me talk to her." I hear him hand the phone to my mother, and she grunts into the receiver. "Ma, please go see Dr. Kendra. I'll come drive you to the appointment, if you want."

"Dr. Kendra!" She fumes. "I have nothing to say to her, that *Dr.* Kendra. I'm not going to take more medicine." Her voice becomes muffled as she pulls the receiver away from her mouth. "Paul! There's chana masala in freezer! I made it for you! Take it home!"

"Ma, Dr. Kendra thinks your depre—I mean, your nerves would be calmer if you tried taking the Zoloft again. Can you just talk to her about it? Please?" I'm running out of energy to argue with her. This is how she wins. She wears me down, every time.

"Norah, I've told you million times. This Kendra doesn't know anything. I told her how my in-laws treated me, how I came to America with nothing, how they took my wedding jewelry—gifts from my family, meant for me—and gave it to my sister-in-law. Such insult! Such slap in face! And you know what this Kendra said to me? She said I should find hobby. She said, 'You should take up knitting or macramé.' I don't know even what macramé is! Why would I waste my time doing crafts?"

"Ma, she didn't mean that literally." I duck under the shade of a storefront awning. "She meant just find something to occupy your mind, so you don't keep dwelling on how Dad's family hurt you."

"I need Indian lady doctor. Someone who understands."

"I know, Ma, but there aren't any female Indian psychologists who take your insurance in all of north Jersey. We've looked. And you need someone local that you can see when you're . . . when you need help."

"I am widow, Norah." Her voice drips with melodrama. Every muscle fiber in my body twists into a knot. Here we go again. "Widow with unmarried daughter. Do you know what people think?"

I take a calming breath. *Don't react, Norah. You always react.* "What people, Ma? Who are these people?"

"Everyone! I can't show my face at community center, let alone at temple!"

"Is that what Nimisha Auntie said? Let me guess: Did she tell you that everyone's judging you because you're a widow with an unmarried daughter? Because that's super original of her." I'm like a train charging downhill, picking up speed. "Did she tell you that in India your in-laws all think you're a curse on the family and that you're at the bottom of the social ladder, you're practically an outcast? Did she tell you any other respectable widow would wear a white sari and shave her head and never leave her house? And that all of this would magically be reversed if I would just find a rich Indian husband from a respectable family and pop out a couple of Indian boy-children?" I say it all in one breath.

My mother's voice is steadier now, probably because we've performed this exact routine dozens of times before. We know all our lines by heart. "When Nimisha says those things—"

"When she says those things, she's trying to upset you. She gets a charge out of knocking you down. It makes her feel better about herself."

"You think you understand, but you grew up here. You don't know."

"Ma, I *do* know. I *do* understand. But you don't live in India anymore. It's not 1986 anymore. You don't talk to Dad's family. Why do you care what they think, anyway?"

"If you understood, you wouldn't have to ask that, *beti.*" She sighs. "I'm going to go take nap, since I didn't sleep whole night. I only called to make sure you were safe."

And, just like that, it's over.

"Okay, Ma. Don't forget to take your afternoon dose of insulin."

"I won't. I love you, *beti.*"

A familiar, volatile mix of guilt and anger threatens to blow me apart. I've lost again. I know I have, and so does she. "I love you, too." I hang up and press my hands to my forehead.

Smells waft toward me from the open door of the shop. Lavender, cherry, lemon, all swirling together, light and soapy.

"Would you like to try our new hibiscus perfume? Or our organic chamomile hand cream?" A woman with a denim apron and a silver tray covered with little apothecary bottles approaches when I step inside. I raise the bottle of perfume to my nose and breathe in the calming floral scent. I tell myself to walk out of the store because I'm not my mother. I tell myself that this is a pattern, and I'm going to regret this later. I tell myself that there is a psychological term for this, and it's called "maladaptive coping," and it's triggered by increased blood levels of the stress hormone cortisol.

"How much is this?" I ask.

"For the little bottle, it's $49.95, and for the big bottle, it's $65. It's on sale today."

"I'll take the big bottle," I say. "And the hand cream, and two lip balms. And whatever this one is." I hand her a little amber bottle of something called pomade that smells wonderful.

She smiles happily as I offer her my credit card. "Okay. Sure, okay, great! I'll just ring them up for you."

I walk back out to the sidewalk, a pretty fabric shopping bag on one arm, having never caught the name of the store. I should go back and return all this. But I can't do that now without looking like a crazy person. No, I'll return it all tomorrow, or this weekend. No harm done.

I walk four blocks to my apartment building, which is sandwiched between a store that sells knockoff watches and a threading salon called Karma Eyebrow Emporium, climb three flights of stairs, open the door, and collapse on the foyer carpet. It's wonderfully dark, cool, and silent, with no beeping heart monitors or loudspeaker announcements. I consider falling asleep right here, my face pressed against the welcome mat.

"You're out of milk," a strange man's matter-of-fact voice says.

I scream and spring to my feet. A wiry man, naked except for tiny yellow boxer shorts, is sitting at the kitchen table, eating a bowl of Lucky Charms.

"Who are you?" I back toward the door.

"Um . . . I'm Albert Moosally," the man says, after a period of contemplation. I wait for him to elaborate, but, based on his expression, he has no plans to do so. He spoons cereal into his mouth and chews it noisily. With his aquiline nose and broad ears, he has a distinctly rodent-like appearance.

"How did you get in here?" I have one hand on the doorknob.

His chewing slows. After what feels like a very long time, he says, "Beth let me in. Yesterday. Before we had coitus. I used the last of the milk." He has a dreamy look in his eyes, as if he's just recited a haiku. I sniff the air. No, I don't smell weed.

I hear the bathroom door down the hall open, and my roommate, Beth, appears, dressed in a bathrobe with a towel wrapped around her head. Beth and I have been living together in this tiny two-bedroom, one-bathroom apartment for the past three weeks. A resident in her second year, Beth is placid and humorless in a way that makes me think her ancestors were the sturdy Germanic sort.

"Oh, hey, Norah," she says, breezing past me. "Was that you screaming?" She opens the refrigerator and roots around inside like an animal making a burrow. "There's no milk."

Albert says nothing but pours more cereal into his bowl. Beth switches on the coffee maker and begins to leaf through a newspaper. I stare at them both with my mouth slightly agape. "Beth!" I say. "Who is this?"

"Hm?" She looks up. "Oh sorry, this is Al, my boyfriend."

"You didn't tell me you had a boyfriend who would be staying over here," I say, smiling and crossing my arms as if this information is a delightful surprise.

"Al is a Neurology resident." She beams at him proudly.

"Okay, but when we discussed rooming together, you never said anything about having a boyfriend who might stay overnight or"—I glance at my watch—"well into the late afternoon."

Beth's smile is patronizing. She sits, folding her hands on top of the table. "People have boyfriends, Norah. I'm a twenty-eight-year-old woman. Of course I have relationships."

"Of course," I say defensively. I glance over my shoulder into the living room, where a yellowed pair of men's socks and one muddy sneaker sit on the sofa cushions. "But in the housing questionnaire there was a section about having visitors over to the apartment on a regular basis. I answered 'No,' and so did you. That's part of the reason we were matched as roommates."

"A boyfriend is not a visitor," Beth says. "A boyfriend is more like a pet that lives with you. If Al were a cat, would you object to him living here?"

"Wait, Al is living here?" I'm thrown. "And yes, I would object to you having a cat. I'm allergic to cats."

She nods. "Mm-hm. So, then, this has worked out perfectly."

"What has?"

"Al is very handy. He's going to install shelves in the bathroom. And this morning he killed a roach."

"Wait, we have roaches?"

"This is Philadelphia," Beth says pointedly. "People have roaches, Norah. Now, I need to talk to you about this electric bill that's been sitting here on the table for the last *three* days." She hands me an envelope with a plastic window. "I put my half of the money in. I don't see your half in here yet."

I peek into the envelope: the bill is $225. "Oh, wow. That's more expensive than I thought it would be." I quickly calculate the sum of rent, plus groceries, plus cell-phone bill, plus this astronomical electric bill, plus other utilities and realize the meager paycheck I'm expecting in two weeks will barely cover it all, even after I return the things I bought today. I try not to panic.

Beth unwraps her towel turban and starts to braid her thick blond hair. "I like to pay my bills two weeks in advance of the due date. I hope, since we're all living together, you'll keep that in mind and try to be a little more responsible from now on." She turns back to her newspaper. Al reaches across the table for the crossword puzzle. I feel like a toddler who's been scolded by her mother.

"Okay." I drift toward my room. "Sorry about that."

"Two percent," Al says.

"What?"

He looks up from the crossword. He squints, his expression strained, as if formulating a complete thought requires extreme effort. "I prefer two percent milk."

I've never been one for confrontation, at least not with anyone other than Ma. I know I should be more assertive, not just with Beth, but in my life in general. My usual coffee order is something like "mediumish coffee with some creamer, or not, whatever." I've read that standing with your hands on your hips and your shoulders squared—a "power pose"—can help foster confidence. I take a deep breath, look Al straight in the eye, assume the power pose, and prepare to let fly the long string of expletives that's racing through my mind. I immediately lose my nerve and settle on sighing loudly and walking away instead. Clearly, this power-pose theory is unfounded, pseudoscientific garbage.

My bedroom is so tiny that the foot of the bed blocks the door from opening completely. I squeeze in and collapse on the pink comforter, only to jump up immediately and check the sheets and pillow for cockroaches. Then I collapse again, kick at the door, and am asleep before it slams shut.

CHAPTER FOUR

It's my second night on call.

"Wait!" I yell to the nurse.

She looks back.

"Would you mind staying?" I try to calm the nervous trill in my voice. "I've never done one of these."

She nods and stands patiently in the doorway, leaning against the jamb, her hands in the pockets of her polka-dot scrub shirt. A fluorescent light flickers overhead. This room is like all the other patient rooms in the hospital: closet-like bathroom just past the door, television mounted high in a corner, gray-and-beige laminate tables flanking the bed, and a dusky pink vinyl recliner chair near the window. On the wall behind the head of the bed is a speaker connected to the nurses' station and a little red button, the code button, that summons the medical team in case of emergency. The name of the nurse on shift is written in dry-erase marker on a whiteboard on the wall. *Mandi*, with a heart over the *i* instead of a dot.

And the smell. It's hard to nail down what the hospital smell *is*, exactly, and easier to identify what it's *not*: a home smells like washed laundry and open windows and coffee and sunlight. The hospital smells like none of those things. It smells like hair and skin and sweat and urine and bile. The sweet dankness of disease and the institutional citrus of Clorox wipes. Bodies and bleach, close together.

Pulling vinyl gloves over my hands, I step to the bedside and try not to gasp. Skin pale and taut, with thick eyebrows that meet on the bridge of his nose and incisors that protrude from beneath his upper lip, the patient looks like a sleeping vampire. His mouth and both eyes are slightly open, his forehead creased as if he's concentrating. I recognize the characteristic facial features immediately: porphyria.

I hold my breath to quiet the sound of my own lungs and put my stethoscope on the man's chest. Nothing. I take the penlight from my pocket, use my thumb and index finger to lift both of his crusted eyelids, and shine the light into his eyes. His glassy pupils stare straight ahead without reacting. Then I make a fist with one hand and, after a moment of hesitation, vigorously rub my knuckles over his breastbone as hard as I can. I know I won't hurt him, but I flinch anyway.

"Okay," I say to the nurse.

At the nurses' station down the hall, I write in the chart: *Called by nurse to pronounce patient. Patient examined, no heart or lung sounds, pupils fixed and dilated, unresponsive to tactile stimuli. Patient pronounced dead at 3:55 a.m.*

A slow, protracted march toward death is what the senior residents like to call "circling the drain." According to the chart, this patient had been doing so for quite some time. A genetic form of porphyria caused his kidneys to fail, then his liver. Weeks ago, his family decided that no heroic measures were to be taken to revive him should he stop breathing—DNR status. There would be no alarm bells, no CPR, no ventilators.

Ferri's *Practical Guide to the Care of the Medical Patient*—a copy of which I carry in my coat pocket—states that when notifying the patient's next of kin, you should "identify yourself to the family in a humble and caring manner and inform them that their next of kin has expired . . . and always try to comfort them that their relative died peacefully."

I find the phone number for the patient's emergency contact, his mother, in the chart. After five rings, a muffled voice answers.

"Hello, this is Dr. Kapadia calling from Philadelphia General Hospital," I say.

"What?"

"Hi, it's Dr. Kapadia, Philadelphia General. I'm sorry about the hour."

"Yes. What do you want?"

"I'm so sorry to have to inform you that John Potts passed away a short time ago."

Silence.

"I'm very sorry. He died peacefully," I say, cringing. I have no idea whether he died peacefully or not. How could anyone know what someone else's experience of death was like? Maybe he went happily toward a white light. Maybe he ran screaming from the light. Maybe there was no light at all, just a disorienting, frigid darkness.

Still silence. Tears sting at the corners of my eyes. This poor woman. She must have known this was coming, but it probably doesn't feel real to her. Like when my father died. I remember only bits and pieces, sounds, smells. Samosas frying in the kitchen, the doorbell, Nimisha Auntie sobbing on the doorstep, my mother shrieking, then silence and whispering and Paul looking up from his math homework in the study, the only time I've ever seen him look afraid. I was reading a library book about frogs. It all replays in my mind, sometimes unexpectedly, like the stuttering reels of an old home video.

My voice quivers with emotion. "Ma'am, I'm so very sorry. Is there anything I can do? Anyone I can call for you?"

"You have the wrong number."

"What?"

"Miss, you have the wrong number."

"You're not the next of kin of John Potts? Phone number three-one-six, five-four-seven-eight?"

"Nine. Five-four-seven-*nine*."

"Oh my gosh, I'm so—"

The dial tone hums in my ear. I hang up and hear a muffled noise behind me. The nurse is resting her head on her arms, her body shaking. She glances up at me and staggers off, shrieking into her cupped hands with delight.

My face flushed, I dial again, carefully this time.

"Yes?"

"Hi. Sorry for the hour. It's Dr. Kapadia from Philadelphia General Hospital? I'm looking for Mrs. Potts?"

"Speaking. Is this about John?"

"Yes, ma'am. I'm very sorry, but he passed away a short time ago. He died peacefully. . . ."

"Peacefully? Who are you?"

"I'm Dr. Kapadia, the intern."

"Where is Dr. Herring? Where is John's doctor?"

"He's not . . . I don't think he's in the hospital right now—"

"He's at home asleep, is that what you're telling me?" I can almost feel the heat of her angry breath through the receiver. "And they asked some student to call me? I want to talk to Dr. Herring. You have him paged right now."

I motion to a passing nurse and relay the request. She shakes her head.

"Ma'am, Dr. Herring won't be available until tomorrow morning," I say, flustered but trying to affect as professional a tone as possible. "I can have my supervising resident paged for you, if you would like."

"What is your name? Spell it," she demands.

I spell my name.

"Well, I'll be calling the president of the hospital tomorrow. This is completely inappropriate. You are a student. You do *not* call me to tell me anything about my son. I want to speak to Dr. Herring, nobody else, you hear me?" She hangs up.

I find nothing in Ferri's guidebook regarding what to do next in this situation. Shaken, I page the on-call resident, one of the third-years. Ten minutes later, the phone rings. "Internal Medicine resident," a woman's voice says.

"Hi, it's the intern."

"What do you need? Talk fast," she says.

I rapidly explain what happened.

"Listen, I have two patients who are both simultaneously having strokes right now, so you're going to have to handle that yourself. Good luck." She hangs up before I can apologize for bothering her.

After a moment's hesitation, I page the attending. I wait twenty minutes before paging him again. I stare at the phone and listen to the steady ticking of the clock on the wall. Every now and then, a nurse passes by, but otherwise it is eerily silent.

The phone rings loudly. I grab the receiver.

"Dr. Herring!" a booming voice with a British accent announces. "Dr. Herring! It's Dr. Herring!"

"Yes, yes, hello, Dr. Herring, this is the intern. Sorry to page you at this hour," I say.

"This is Dr. Herring!" He is shouting now.

"Yes, sir. Can you hear me?"

"Bloody hell, stop shouting. What do you want?"

I explain what happened, then say, "I think, sir, that the patient's mother would like you to call her personally."

There is a long silence. This is followed by an unusual guttural sound. He's snoring.

"Dr. Herring?" I whisper.

I hear him startle and snort. "Who is this?"

"It's the intern."

He replies with a selection of colorful, decidedly British-sounding expletives. Then he says, "Don't ever bother me with this drivel again," and hangs up.

I sit there for a long while, stunned and thinking about the moment I graduated from medical school two months ago: the heady sense of accomplishment, striding buoyantly across the stage to seize my diploma from the dean, as if nothing could stop my ascent. Now it's as if I've deflated and crashed into a heap on the pavement. I've failed a dead man. What if I'm not meant for this type of work? I was very good at school, at forcing myself to sit in a library cubicle for days or weeks at a time and commit facts to memory—what if that's my maximal potential? What if I've already accomplished everything I can hope to accomplish in life, and I've just struck the ceiling of my natural abilities?

Finally, I write another note in the chart: *Next of kin called and informed*. I sign my name underneath: *Norah Kapadia, MD*. I write the two letters of my degree in microscopic print. I consider adding the words "kind of" after them.

The first rays of morning light streak in through a window. A wave of fatigue hits me all at once. I drag myself to the vending machine in the hallway and buy a can of diet Sprite and a roll of Oreos. Then I rest my back against the warm, humming machine and slide down it until I'm sitting on the floor. I can't help picturing the dead man's waxen face, his vacant brown eyes under hanging eyelids. I've been around dead people before, of course. The anatomy lab in medical school was filled with dead bodies, rows of them. But they were long dead. Preserved in formaldehyde, wrapped in plastic, and stripped of identity. This was different. This man was newly dead. His name was John Potts, and he had a mother who cared about him.

I lean my head back and close my eyes.

"Intern!"

I spring into a crouch position. The soda can rolls away, clattering.

Ethan smiles down at me. "Hi." His scrubs are rumpled, and he has more scruff than usual. He looks like a rugged mountain man just back from splitting wood or otherwise maintaining the homestead. He wears his stethoscope around his neck, and the sleeves of his white coat are rolled up to his elbows. My heart jumps into my throat.

Squinting up at him, I manage to wheeze, "Hi."

"Norah, it's way too early in your intern year to be spooning with the vending machine." He extends his hand. "Come on, I'll buy you breakfast."

I hesitate. Then, I take his hand.

Pulling me to my feet, he says, "Cookies and soda at dawn, huh? I'm guessing it was a rough night?"

I meet his gaze, and his expression is so warm and sympathetic, it catches me off guard. A tear threatens to form at the corner of my eye and, panicked, I blink it back. "It's nothing. I just got yelled at by an attending for calling to tell him his DNR patient died."

"Who's the attending?"

"Dr. Herring."

He chuckles ruefully. "I'm not surprised. Herring's an asshole. And an idiot. Either Herring or the nurses will kill the patient when you're not looking. Remember that. Do you like waffles?"

"Waffles?" My head spins from the sudden pivot to breakfast foods.

"They make the best waffles at the caf, but you have to know Lionel."

"Lionel?"

"Keep up, newbie," he says, smiling, as he heads for the elevator. "I'm about to blow your mind."

Lionel looks like he might have been cast off a pirate ship at one point in his life for being too surly. When we approach the grill station, he's muttering angrily to himself, clutching a spatula with both hands as if he might try to snap it in half.

A demure man with *Endocrinology* embroidered on the sleeve of his white coat is attempting to order. "Belgian waffle, please?"

"Nope," Lionel says, looking him in the eye steadily.

The man adjusts his necktie. "No?"

"Nope," Lionel says.

The man stares at him, waiting for some explanation, but none is forthcoming. I watch with a mix of fascination and terror as a subtle rage builds in Lionel's face, as if he may completely lose control and start smashing all the glass objects in his immediate vicinity if this fellow doesn't vanish from his line of sight this instant. Sensing danger, the man nods and quickly moves on toward a display of bagels.

"Lionel!" Ethan says cheerfully. "Morning, buddy."

Lionel's expression of barely controlled contempt is unchanged.

"Did you work the overnight?" Ethan asks.

Lionel makes a low grunting sound and turns around to tend to a puddle of eggs that has been bubbling and congealing on the enormous grill.

"Yeah," Ethan says, "me too. I'm beat. This hospital sucks."

"It's sucked for years," Lionel says, directing his bitterness at the eggs, pulverizing them into a scramble.

"Yeah, I hear you. I caught the end of *When Harry Met Sally* on TV, though."

Without turning around, Lionel asks, "When he runs to the party to tell Sally he loves her?"

Ethan glances at me knowingly, as if we are sharing a confidence, but I have no idea what's going on.

"Yup. When you realize you want to spend the rest of your life with somebody—"

"You want the rest of your life to start as soon as possible!" Lionel turns to us, his face aglow, looking like he might burst into happy song. "That's one of my favorites."

"Great movie, right?" Ethan says. "Hey, are you making the waffles today?"

Lionel frowns. "It's such a pain in the ass, making the batter, keeping it the right temperature so it doesn't get goopy, cleaning the waffle iron. I hate those damn waffles." For a moment, it seems like we'll be moving along to the bagel station too, but apparently bolstered by the thought of Harry and Sally, Lionel smiles reluctantly and adds, "But I'll hook you guys up. Should take about ten minutes."

"Thanks, buddy. You're the man."

Ethan pays for us at the cash register, and ten minutes later, we are each carrying a tray with an enormous, golden-brown, pillowy work of heartbreaking perfection to a table in the staff-only section.

"*When Harry Met Sally*?" I ask, inhaling the heady scent of maple syrup and vanilla. "That's the secret?"

Ethan grins proudly. "Yup. He loves romantic comedies. As long as you can drop a quote or two from one of the greats—*Princess Bride*, *You've Got Mail*, *Sleepless*—you'll get waffles." He takes a bite, and his face glows with the kind of bliss that can come only from the consumption of cooked dough.

"*Sleepless*?"

"*In Seattle*," he says, as if it shouldn't require explanation.

"Right. And you happen to know all these movies well enough to quote them?"

"I actually do. My fiancée—well, ex-fiancée—would force me to watch all these chick movies, so I've seen them all. My mind's filled with drug dosages and useless movie quotes."

I take a bite of my waffle, and suddenly everything seems right and beautiful in the world. My mouth half-full, I mutter, "Oh my God."

Ethan nods. "I know. It's kind of life-changing."

"My mind is blown. You were right," I say. His comment about his ex-fiancée is just kind of hanging there in that awkward conversational space between revealing something personal and elaborating on it. I wonder if I should ask him about it, or at least offer my condolences on his failed engagement (which seems like a pretty big deal, even though he mentioned it like it was an afterthought). I decide to keep quiet, not wanting to be rude and pry.

"My ex, Heather, is an Anesthesia resident at UPenn," he says.

Oh. All righty then.

I'm grateful that my mouth is full, saving me from having to reply right away. I raise my eyebrows and nod instead. I've found that nodding while raising one's eyebrows is a good, generic way to respond to almost any awkward social situation. In the right context, it can convey interest, acceptance, acknowledgment, even sympathy. It's a catchall, as far as facial expressions go.

"We're still friends," Ethan says, seemingly more to fill in the silence created by my chewing than for any other reason.

"Oh, that's good." My mouth is still half-full. "Sorry to hear it didn't work out."

He shrugs. "Better to find out now than after we get married, right?"

I wish I had something meaningful to say in response. Instead, I say, "Ugh, relationships."

"Exactly. Residency isn't conducive to healthy relationships."

I frown, thinking of the adorable couple from medical school—Tyler and Lynn—who, immediately after our commencement ceremony, mutually decided to part ways. The breakup of LynnLer was discussed and dissected at length by the rest of our class for days afterward, and it was generally agreed that, had they stayed together during residency, the relationship would have ended anyway, and probably badly. The prophylactic split was the smart thing to do. My thoughts shift immediately to Ma; every year that goes by with me still single adds weight to the anchor dragging her down toward a social abyss. If I'm not married in the next several years, she may never resurface. "Do you really think that?" I ask.

"Didn't you just pronounce someone dead? And call their family and tell them that person was dead? Think about it. That's not normal." He smiles a broad, plastic smile, and his voice deepens an octave. "'How was your day at work, honey?'" He shrugs and continues breezily, answering himself, "'Oh, standard. Someone died, their family was devastated, let's make dinner and watch a movie.'"

I nod. "I'm supposed to carry on like it's all standard procedure. Meanwhile, if I let myself think about it . . ."

He finishes my thought. "People in other, normal jobs might have their computer crash or someone take their hole puncher—that's their day-to-day office crap. Our day-to-day office crap is death and human suffering."

"I don't know if I made the right career choice. I feel so incompetent," I say. I immediately wonder if admitting incompetence in front of your supervisor is a workplace blunder, but he smiles kindly.

"Everyone feels incompetent at the beginning," he says. "If you don't feel like an idiot at least some of the time, you're doing something wrong."

"Okay, but what if you feel like an idiot *all* of the time?"

"That means it's working," he says with a laugh. He glances at his pager.

"What's working?"

"It. The process. Making you into a doctor. Preparing you for the awesome responsibility of holding life in your hands." He stands suddenly. "Gotta run. Bianca has a pancreatitis that's going south. Don't mess with the pancreas; there's another pearl of wisdom for you."

"I'll have that embroidered on a pillow," I say.

He laughs again, and dimples momentarily appear at both corners of his smile. I've noticed them before, probably when we first met, and registered it in some neglected recess of my mind: *He's handsome.*

"See you at rounds, Norah," he says.

I watch him leave, his stride confident, ready to deal with whatever this wayward pancreas is going to try to throw at him. I wonder if I'll ever feel that way—cool, competent, prepared for anything—instead of feeling like a bumbling, emotional mess. *What if I miss a diagnosis? What if I accidentally hurt someone?*

I'm not used to this type of doubt. I like certainty. I'm truly comfortable only when things are logical, the outcomes predictable, the evidence and limits well-defined and irrefutable. I remember finding out from Paul, when I was six, that Santa Claus isn't real, and being relieved instead of disappointed, because it all finally made sense. *Ah, a magical bearded man doesn't break into millions of children's homes over a twenty-four-hour period. It's all an elaborate hoax that, oddly, is the only explanation I hadn't already considered.* It was satisfying, like the final piece of a puzzle snapping into place.

I like that distance divided by time is always equal to velocity. It scratches some subconscious itch of mine that one carbon molecule attached to two oxygen molecules is always carbon dioxide. Science makes sense. X plus Y equals Z. I love everything about X and Y and the fact that the two of them can be consistently relied upon to produce Z.

Human anatomy is consistent and logical: the biceps muscle is always controlled by the musculocutaneous nerve. The hip bone is always connected to the thigh bone (technically, the *acetabulum* is always connected to the *femur*).

Human behavior, on the other hand, is neither consistent nor logical. I was ten when my father died, and my mother went to pieces in a way no one could have predicted. There's nothing scientific about the way a person's mind falls apart. Ma's periods of rationality are punctuated by random bouts of destructive self-negligence and spending. Long before we were old enough to know what was happening, she frittered away Dad's life insurance money on trinkets and clothes and furniture we didn't need. Now, Paul and I take turns being her parental figure and therapist, reminding her to take her insulin, balancing her checkbook, making her doctors' appointments, and—when she's really at her lowest—filling her refrigerator and reminding her to eat. We both went to college locally and lived at home. I went to medical school in New York, a twenty-minute drive from Ma's house in north Jersey. For over a decade, this is how it's been. Paul and I dedicate every spare moment to keeping Ma from lapsing into a diabetic coma or spiraling into a depressive void.

So it follows that, for a person in my midtwenties, there are a lot of things I've never done. I've never ice-skated, attended a college sporting event, or spent New Year's Eve doing anything other than watching fireworks on my television, flanked by Paul and my mother. I've never traveled by myself. Other than a sip here or there, I've never had an alcoholic beverage. I've never gone to a school dance (I spent my senior prom night with two other dateless friends, watching *Friends* reruns), attended a fraternity party, or been part of a large group of girls without coats wearing cocktail dresses and high heels and cramming themselves into a taxi in the dead of winter.

I envy confident people who can befriend anyone with an easy smile or a quick joke. At parties, I'm the bespectacled girl drinking orange juice and carefully studying the wall art. I can only think of clever things to say *days* after the occasion. I've been on a total of two dates in my life: once with a fellow medical school classmate who spent the whole evening talking about professional wrestling, and the other in sixth grade when I sat at a table in the lunchroom with Jeremy Corkie, who tried to hold my hand and then stole my sandwich.

* * *

I met my best friend, Meryl, at Lenape Day Camp in sixth grade, and I've always been grateful for her; if I'm a social island, she's my tether to the mainland. A week later, on Friday night, she stops by my apartment on her way home from studying at Barnes & Noble.

"Wear something skanky," she calls from inside my closet.

"I don't have anything skanky. Besides, it's a work event." I pull a plain black blouse over my head.

"It's a pharmaceutical dinner. It's business-skanky." Her hand appears, dangling a pair of silver pumps, from behind a row of hanging clothes. "These still have the price tag on them. When did you buy these? They were expensive!"

I grab the shoes from her and sheepishly clear my throat. "I've been meaning to return them."

"Is that guy Ethan going to be there?"

"Ethan, my chief resident? I don't know. Why?"

Meryl laughs and rolls her eyes. "Come on! Why? Because all you've done is talk about him for the past week." She does a terrible impression of my voice. "'Oh, Ethan made the greatest diagnosis! Ethan said the funniest thing! Ethan is the most gifted doctor the world has ever seen!'"

I cross my arms defensively. "So? He's a good career role model. Like the way Ruth Bader Ginsburg is to you."

"Yeah, but I've never mentioned RBG's dimples to you."

I wave her off but wonder if she has a point. I'm in the habit of suppressing my romantic feelings. When I was growing up, there was an understanding in our Indian community that dating was strictly forbidden. Ma and the other aunties would talk about marriage, certainly—the implication being that the perfect Indian professional would appear from thin air or via arranged meeting when their children came of age—but romance and courtship have little to do with traditional Indian matrimony. Meet-cutes are reserved exclusively for Bollywood movies, and no respectable family would allow their daughter to consort with a man for the purpose of "getting to know him." I internalized this mind-set as a teenager, believing my self-shaming to actually be a very discerning taste in men: there just weren't any guys smart enough or interesting enough for me. The wrestling fan and Jeremy Corkie were one-offs—I enjoyed their brief attention but wasn't particularly interested in either of them—and the thought of actually developing significant feelings for someone, now that I'm an adult and can consort with whomever I wish, makes me acutely, cringingly anxious.

Still, I try on the shoes.

"Didn't he just break up with his fiancée? Better jump on that."

Meryl has lived a life very different from mine. For years now, I've tried to explain to her that most women can't assume that every heterosexual man they cross paths with will be interested in dating them, but, bless her heart, she has no understanding of how the rest of the world lives. Ever since college, after she shed the awkward teenage visage that I never quite managed to shake, Meryl's been the type of woman who makes a Barbie doll look average. And she's not even trying. She hates shopping, never exercises, and gets a haircut maybe twice a year. She basically rolls out of bed each morning looking like a cross between Megan Fox and the sunrise. As exasperating as this is, I have to admit I love walking into a room with her and silently counting all the heads that turn in her direction. It's like a game, one I've been playing now for almost a decade.

"Mer, even if I was interested in him—and I'm definitely not, because he's basically my boss—it's way too early to jump on anything. His fiancée broke up with him two months ago. She called it off a week before their wedding. They'd already paid for the caterer and the band and everything."

The details of Ethan's breakup with Heather are widely known throughout the hospital, since gossip, not unlike meningitis, spreads rapidly wherever people are in close quarters. I've overheard some of the other residents talking about it. Not that I'm interested in gossip, but sometimes you can't help but overhear things.

"That witch! He must have been heartbroken," Meryl says. Then she grins. "Which makes this the perfect time to try to get into his pants."

As if on cue, there is a passionate moan from the other side of the wall. Meryl recoils. "Ugh, gross! How's life going here in hospital-subsidized housing, by the way?" She gives my desk chair a skeptical look before tentatively perching on top of the desk. "Kill any roaches?"

"I'm not here very much," I say. "Fortunately."

"Can I just say, again, that I can't believe you're letting that naked mole rat live here?"

"I can't believe I didn't realize it would be a mistake to room with a Psychiatry resident. Beth is like the gatekeeper to an alternate universe."

Meryl gestures to the wall. "Doesn't that bother you? You know, given your"—her voice drops to a whisper—"*situation*?"

I shake my head. Meryl refers to my virginity like a judgmental elderly woman gossiping about her neighbor's unemployed son's marijuana use; she finds it distasteful but not entirely surprising. "Yes, as much as it bothers you. Mer, it's not like I'm that unusual. Lots of people haven't had intercourse yet."

"And the people who have had intercourse don't call it 'intercourse.'"

"I've been busy," I say, peeling the price tag off the bottom of one pump. "It's hard to meet guys in the library. They don't have happy hour there."

"Well, I've been to the hospital, and it's floor-to-ceiling men in that place. Beth cannot be the only one having relations in this apartment. Oh my God, just the thought of the two of them over there—"

She clutches her hair and squeezes her eyes shut. "My mind's eyes! My mind's eyes!"

I laugh. "Go home, Meryl. Save yourself."

She pulls on her backpack. "All right, yeah, I have to run. You look great. But it wouldn't kill you to put some makeup on."

"You don't even wear makeup."

"Yes," she says, her tone matter-of-fact, "because I'm broke and jobless. But if I had a business-skanky work event to go to, you'd best believe I'd have a faceful of foundation right now."

I roll my eyes at her. "Go home, Meryl. And take your annoyingly flawless complexion with you."

"Call me later. I'll be up, studying for the bar. Again."

Meryl has taken and failed the ridiculously, maddeningly, stupidly difficult Pennsylvania bar exam multiple times. At this point, I feel like I have, too. I've helped her run flash cards and slog through practice tests so many times I think I may qualify for an honorary law degree. We've opened each of her results envelopes together, cried together, then picked ourselves up and dragged ourselves back to studying together. "This is gonna be the one," I say. "I feel it in my bones. You'll pass it." I say it like I can will it into reality; I want it for her so badly.

She sighs. "Right. Fourth time's the charm. You have no idea how much I'd kill for your genius brain."

"You definitely don't want my brain, believe me."

"But I do. It holds so much more information than mine. Yours is like one of those giant beach totes, and mine's a teensy evening bag that barely fits a tampon and a piece of gum. Those tiny bags are worthless shit. The shoes look super cute, by the way. Better run or you'll be late."

I'm late. I follow a kimono-clad hostess across the crowded restaurant, teetering in the silver pumps, my face itching under a layer of foundation (the bottle of which I discovered in a makeup bag I hadn't touched in over two years). A group of residents is crowded around a hibachi table. I push my glasses up the bridge of my nose and notice one empty seat next to Ethan. His coat is draped over the chair.

"Are you saving this for anyone, Dr. Cantor?" I ask.

"Norah, call me Ethan." He pulls the chair out for me. "It's all yours. I was pretending to save it because I didn't want to sit next to Byron."

Byron is one of the second-year residents, a glistening behemoth of a man with the personality of an aged frat boy. He is seated across the table, a cup of sake in one hand, a skewer strung with knots of chicken in the other. He appears to be singing righteously to the bewildered young man with a bun and goatee sitting next to him.

"Man-bun over there is Gabe, Byron's medical student," Ethan says. "Poor bastard has to follow Byron all over the hospital and pretend to be interested in everything he says. I feel bad for the guy."

I shrug. We've all been that med student before. When I was a student, I once had a resident who made me follow her into the bathroom and listen, outside the stall, while she lectured me about various diseases of the kidney while peeing.

A flushed man in an ill-fitting suit appears behind me. "Hello, hello, hello! Thanks for joining us! I'm Jim, Genetiks Pharmaceuticals. What year are you?"

I shake his hand and find it is unpleasantly moist. "Intern."

"A newbie! Good, good, good. I promote Zynexa. Are you familiar with it? It's a new antibiotic, the new gold standard for drug-resistant pneumonia. Great, great medication. I have a lot of studies I can bore you with later. Can I get you a drink?"

I shake my head.

"You gotta have something," he says. "Glass of wine?" He beckons a waiter. "Order anything you like. I want you guys to have a great time tonight."

"Are there any side effects?" I ask.

"Side effects of wine? Tons!" He laughs, then is abruptly serious. "Minimal. Minimal. Studies showed some nausea, some increased bleeding after minor trauma, some acid reflux. It comes in oral and IV form. It's also covered by Medicare, which translates to 'No need to spend hours on the phone with the insurance company!'" He mimes air quotation marks and slaps Ethan on the shoulder. "Remember, Zynexa for pneumonia. The *next* big thing in pneumonia treatment." He staggers toward Clark, a few chairs away, and slaps him on the shoulder as well. "Having a good time, boss?"

Ethan leans toward me. He smells like warm apple cider. And cucumbers. And the ocean. It makes my legs feel oddly gelatinous. "He's trashed. He was doing shots with the other guys when I got here." A waiter places a plate of sushi in front of Ethan. In the middle of the hibachi table, a chef wearing a bandana over his hair is brandishing a knife in each hand. He yelps, then suddenly and furiously minces an onion into a million tiny pieces.

"This is the first one of these I've been to," I say. "A pharmaceutical dinner, I mean. It's a little weird, some random salesman buying us dinner."

"It's the only way you're going to get a decent meal during residency," Ethan says. "I try not to overthink it. The food at the hospital cafeteria gets old fast." He smiles and takes a sip of his beer.

The ground starts to rattle and shake. Across the table, several other residents are pounding their fists on the table, chanting, "By-ron! By-ron!" Sweating profusely, his eyes squeezed shut, Byron is trying to consume—in one breath—the towering cocktail listed on the menu as the Mount Fujiyama. He nearly falls off his chair twice before slamming the glass on the table in triumph. The other residents hoot and applaud as Jim from Genetiks Pharmaceuticals high fives each of them in turn. When he reaches the end of the line, he squeals, "Zynexa!" and thrusts his fist into the air.

"That guy's an idiot." Two bronze bare legs cross and uncross in the seat next to Ethan.

"Hello, Elle," Ethan says.

An impossibly petite young woman with cascading black hair leans her elbows on the table. "I haven't been here five minutes and he asked for my phone number." She smooths her tiny, one-shoulder dress. "Hi, I'm Elle."

I recognize her as the Surgery resident with the pencil bun who accompanied Terry into Mr. Leeds's room after I defibrillated him. She's stunning, all delicate wrists and feline eyes and angular cheekbones.

"I'm Norah," I say, noticing how frumpy I look next to her. I wish I'd worn the skanky skirt Meryl picked out.

Elle's eyes light up. "Oh, I remember you! The nurses call you Dr. Shocks-a-lot."

The last remaining scrap of my self-confidence withers and dies on the spot. I consider hiding under the table.

"We won't mention what the nurses call Elle," Ethan says, winking.

She smacks him on the arm playfully. "Knock it off, Cantor." She turns back to me. "I hope Terry didn't scare you. He's harmless. He's just a pissy old lady sometimes."

Ethan nods. "Yeah, just ignore him. Terry's like a goat with a urinary tract infection."

"That's probably unfair to goats," I say.

Elle smirks approvingly. "I knew I liked you."

"I didn't think you came to these drug dinners, Elle," Ethan says. "Don't you object to them on moral grounds?"

"Girl's gotta eat." She takes a sip of his beer, then runs her finger around the rim of the glass. "And I like this restaurant."

"The power of free sushi," he says with a wry smile.

Elle straightens defensively. "Hey, just because I'm enjoying their food doesn't mean I'm prescribing their drug. I'm not a sellout." She turns to me. "You're not eating, Norah?"

Her question catches me off guard. I have an embarrassingly narrow palate. I can't tolerate seafood or anything even remotely spicy. I hate trying new foods, preferring the comfortable safe space of buttered pasta and peanut butter sandwiches and prepackaged baked goods. "I don't really like hibachi. Or sushi." I shrug my shoulders nonchalantly.

Elle cocks her head to one side. "You don't? Then why'd you come?"

I cringe inwardly. *I'm here trying to be social, and it's just as uncomfortable as I thought it would be. I wish I'd stayed home.*

The waiter deposits a towering piece of chocolate cake covered in strawberry sauce before me. "Your chocolate volcano cake, miss."

Elle grins. "How cute are you? You definitely need a glass of milk to go with that."

I laugh weakly. It's impossible not to notice Elle's minuscule, sophisticated-looking seaweed salad, positioned in front of her like a value judgment: here is someone who makes good choices, in food and, we can extrapolate, in life.

Warmth sneaks up the back of my neck. My sympathetic nervous system has been kicked into overdrive and is causing the hundreds of tiny blood vessels in my face to dilate. In 1.3 seconds, I'll be as red as a baboon's sunburned backside.

"That cake looks amazing," Ethan says. "Hey, do you mind?" He motions with his fork, and I nod, not wanting to be rude. He tastes a bite. "Yup. It's amazing. I'm totally ordering one of these to go."

The heat recedes from my face. I smile at him gratefully and tuck into my chocolate volcano with zest while Elle, after a longing glance at my plate, picks at her salad with a pair of chopsticks.

"How was your first week?" Ethan asks.

I consider this. "It was like one long nightmare, actually."

He shrugs. "Only three more years to go."

"Did it go by fast for you?" I wipe chocolate from the side of my mouth with a napkin.

"Actually, it was like having all my teeth pulled, one at a time."

I laugh. "Terrific. Thanks."

"Happy to help." He smiles. Dimples again.

"What will you do next year?" I ask. "After you graduate from residency?"

"Hopefully another year of indentured servitude. I'm applying for Portnoy's oncology fellowship."

"I still haven't met him. The man, the legend, right?"

"He wrote the book on oncology. Literally."

"Why did you choose oncology?"

He spins a drink coaster between his thumb and index finger. "Cancer is the height. The baddest of the bad guys. If I'm gonna treat disease, I'm not wasting my time on strep throat and pneumonia, the small fries. I'm going after the big fish."

"I've never heard anyone analogize medicine and sportfishing."

He laughs at himself. "I'm gonna reel in that sarcoma." He mimes throwing out a fishing line and reeling it back in.

I find this hysterical. The little flick of his wrist, the sincere expression on his face, the reference to the rare type of cancer. I laugh so hard that I convulse, seizure-like, in complete silence. After a moment, Ethan glances at me in concern, as if he's considering that I might actually be having a seizure.

I gasp loudly.

"You okay?" he asks, bemused.

I hold up my index finger, trying to suppress the peals of laughter bubbling up from my insides. Once I've composed myself, Ethan raises his eyebrows at me. "You sure you're okay? Can I get you something? Glass of water?"

"No. Nope. I'm fine. Thanks." I smile.

"Okay. Good. Glad you're okay. Because I was going to get medical attention for you like—" He mimes the fishing motion once more, and, like paper snakes popping out of a can, I burst out laughing again.

"What's so funny, you guys?" Elle leans toward Ethan.

"Sportfishing," Ethan says, and Elle's mouth twists into a puzzled frown as I grin at our new inside joke.

A microphone somewhere yawns to life, and a voice says, "Welcome, everyone, to karaoke night at Akira Hibachi! We already have a volunteer for our first performance. Please give it up for Francesca!"

Across the table, Francesca is stretching her arms and loosening her jaw muscles by shaking her head back and forth like a dog after a bath. I look at Ethan, concerned.

"Oh, you're not going to want to miss this," Ethan says. "Believe me."

Elle is cringing as if she already has a headache. The opening bars of Celine Dion's "Power of Love" blast out of the speaker system, and someone hands Francesca a microphone. My phone buzzes in my pocket.

On the sidewalk outside, I press the phone to my ear.

"Norah, I don't want to worry you, but my left arm is numb. Do you think it's heart attack?"

"What? Oh my God, Ma, how long has this been?"

"About one hour, *beti*." Her voice is thready. "And some chest pressure. Not much, but some. It was venti before, but now it's grande chest pressure."

"Ma, you don't rate medical symptoms by comparing them to Starbucks drink sizes! I'm calling an ambulance to take you to the hospital."

"I don't want to go to hospital and wait for hours in emergency room for nothing. Chest pain is tall now."

"What about your blood pressure?"

"One-sixty over sixty-eight. My vision is getting blurry."

I sigh up at the starless city sky. "I'm on my way. I'll stay on the phone with you."

"But you're probably busy. I don't want to bother you." She coughs weakly, then whimpers.

"It's fine. I'll be there in an hour and a half."

I race home to get my car out of the lot, the line still connected.

"Where are you now?" Ma asks.

"I just got to the parking lot."

"Is it dark?"

"Of course it's dark. It's nine o'clock."

"Do you see any muggers?"

"No. I don't see anyone who is identifying themselves as being a mugger."

"I mean anyone suspicious. You have ponytail? You should take it out."

I groan in frustration. "Ma, that's ridiculous." I wiggle the key into the car door while yanking the ponytail holder out of my hair. As I pull the car onto the highway entrance ramp, I ask, "Have you checked your blood sugar?"

"I haven't felt like eating all day." I can hear her leafing through the pages of *Stardust*, a Bollywood tabloid. It's the only thing she ever reads. "My sugar has been so low all day."

"So, why don't you eat something?"

"My stomach."

"What's wrong with your stomach?"

"It has bubbles. Feeling like bubbles. What is that in soda? When you open soda bottle?"

"Bubbles."

"No. Another English word."

"Gas."

"Right. My stomach has gas bubbles. I don't feel like eating."

"Ma, you have to eat or your blood sugar gets too low. Remember what happened last time?"

"I'm checking my blood pressure again." I hear the sound of her automated blood pressure cuff inflating.

She checks her blood pressure four times during my drive to her house. I pull the car into the driveway of her duplex. "I'm coming inside. You can hang up now."

When I walk into the kitchen, she's sitting in her usual spot, the tabloid open on the table in front of her.

"How was your drive?"

"Ma, I talked to you the whole way here."

"You need haircut." She eyes my wild, curly hair, unsecured by a hair elastic.

"I don't have time for a haircut. How's your chest pressure and arm numbness?"

She goes to the stove to pour herself a cup of tea. "Better. I just took Valium, and that made me feel much better."

Dr. Kendra thinks Ma's many medical symptoms are manifestations of anxiety, a fact Ma ostensibly contends, though she carries a bottle of Valium in her purse at all times. She refuses to take antidepressants but grudgingly agrees to the antianxiety medication, probably because the pill is so tiny that it looks harmless.

"Sit down and have some tea." She pours a cup for me and returns to the table. "You should make time for haircut."

"There *is* no time."

"No time for haircut, no time for sleeping, no time for anything." She shakes her head pityingly. "Just like your father. He had no time. Not even for us."

"Ma, please don't start."

"Start what? I'm telling truth."

"You've told me all of this before."

"Norah, you're smart, you've studied. That's fine. But I have life knowledge."

"And I won't ever be happy until I'm married and blah, blah. Yes, I know." Under my breath I mutter, "Thank you for your profound life knowledge."

She frowns, annoyed. "One day, you'll understand. This job. This *job*, not life, takes everything from you. That's what it did to your father. It took him from us."

The powder keg forms in my chest again. "A car accident took him from us. Dad loved his work. I would think you'd be proud that I'm following in his footsteps."

Her voice becomes louder and higher-pitched. "Who said you have to follow in his footsteps? Who is making you?"

"No one! I want to. Why is that so hard to understand?" I say. "You know, some Indian mothers *want* their children to become doctors."

Ma rolls her eyes. "Norah, you want to be doctor, fine. But you should be *married* doctor."

"I don't have time to look for a husband right now, Ma. And no, I'm not signing up for Shaadi-dot-com."

"Why not? Paul met Reena on Shaadi-dot-com."

Not true. My brother didn't meet his wife on an Indian matrimonial website; he met her at a bar in the East Village called Flaming Dick's, but they've never told Ma that. She still thinks Paul doesn't drink.

"It's just not for me."

"You will be old woman," she says, her eyes narrowed with bitter intensity. "You will be old and unmarried with no children, and what will people think?"

"That's a little dramatic. I'm in my twenties."

She makes a clicking noise with her tongue. "You are losing your prime years!"

"Prime years? I'm not an aging horse."

"Once you turn thirty, no good Indian boys will want to marry you. They'll all be taken. Look at what happened to Brinda Auntie's daughter, Mona, the lawyer."

The parable of Ma's second-cousin's daughter, Mona the Lawyer, is as follows: Mona went to Harvard Law and, by the age of thirty-one, was a partner in the most prestigious law firm in Boston. But she was never able to find a suitable Indian husband, so she ended up marrying someone she met at a speed-dating event when she was forty. He turned out to have a girlfriend and kids in Connecticut, and it was several months before Mona learned the truth and filed for divorce. Her vile husband dragged out the proceedings for years, and now he gets alimony and lives in a mansion in Miami on her dime, while she is doomed to eternal spinsterhood and her family is forever shunned by Indian society because, obviously, none of this would have happened if she had just focused less on her career and gotten married before the age of thirty, the way you're supposed to do.

I push away my teacup. "Maybe I don't want to marry a good Indian boy. Maybe I don't want to get married, period. Or have kids. I don't even really like kids."

Her eyes widen, her head recoiling as if I've slapped her. She stares at my teacup for a moment. Then she raises her eyes and says, "Fine. You want to shame your whole family? You want to make my life miserable? Nimisha has two wonderful son-in-laws and six grandchildren. What do I have?" Tears stream down her face. "What do I have, Norah? Your father is gone, and I have nothing."

Guilt tears at my insides like a thing with talons. "It's okay, Ma. You have me and Paul. You have Kai and Reena."

"Nimisha's daughters, their husbands, and all her grandchildren live with her. They live all together, how it should be. I'm alone. Paul and Reena are busy with Kai, and you have"—she waves her hand—"your *job*."

"Ma . . ." I'm not sure I want to go down this road, but I do anyway. "You have to take some ownership. You have to *do* something. You can't just sit around here all day dwelling on your problems and stress-eating chocolate croissants and sending your blood sugar through the roof. What about that online class Reena was telling you about?"

"My eyes get blurry when I look at computer screen."

"Well, then, what about going to the community center? They have bingo and card games. It would get you out of the house."

"I told you, Norah. I can't go to community center. I always run into Devika Auntie and Smita Auntie there, and they ask me when you're getting married, and I have to make excuses, and it's too stressful for me."

"Ma, that's an excuse—"

"Besides, I don't have anyone to drive me. Reena goes to work and can never drive me."

"You know how to drive, Ma."

"I have to cross bridge to go to community center. I can't drive across bridge. I have phobia of bridges. You know that."

"What about cooking? You used to love to cook."

"I can't hold utensils. My carpal tunnel syndrome would make my hands numb, and I'd drop them."

I go through all the usual suggestions, and she responds with all the usual excuses. It's past midnight when I back the car out of Ma's driveway after checking her blood pressure, drawing up her evening dose of insulin, folding her laundry, and taking out the trash. I leave with a brown paper bag full of Ma's chocolate croissants that I found hidden in the garage. I stress-eat them all by the time I get home.

CHAPTER FIVE

"What do people do for fun in Italy, Bianca?" Stuart, red-eyed and fighting back a yawn, is paging through an ancient copy of *Gray's Anatomy* usually used to prop up a table leg in the residents' lounge.

"Sex," Bianca says.

Clark looks over his shoulder at her. She winks at him.

After three weeks, the residents' lounge—despite its dated wood paneling and threadbare orange upholstery—has started to feel like home. I grab a slice of cold pizza out of a box on the floor and drop onto a couch.

"Why'd you move to the US?" Stuart asks. "Didn't you have your own practice in Milan?"

"Yes. I moved for love," Bianca says, as if it were obvious.

"Of course. Because all the rampant sex just wasn't enough," Clark mutters. He flips through television channels.

"Is it pretty similar, medicine here and over there?" I ask.

She chuckles. Even her laugh has an accent. "No, nothing is the same. First of all, in Italy no one pays to go to the doctor. It's all paid for by the government. And if you have a pain or an infection, your doctor gives you the name of a medicine and you go to the store and buy a little vial of liquid and a syringe and you give yourself an injection. No prescriptions. No pills."

"Do doctors get sued in Italy?" Stuart asks, wide-eyed.

"No, never."

"So, you give the patient a needle and, when he accidentally buys the wrong medication and injects it into his eyeball, for example, that person doesn't try to sue you?"

"Why would he sue me? It's not my fault he is too stupid to follow my instructions."

Clark shakes his head in wonder. "That's just . . . un-American."

Imani rushes in, and we groan in unison.

"Come on, guys, give me a break." She sits and opens a small notebook, her knee bouncing up and down nervously.

"How many are there?" Bianca asks.

Imani hesitates, tugging at the end of her ponytail. "Five."

We groan again.

"How is that possible?" Clark asks. "How can there be any more patients to admit when we've already admitted the entire population of southeastern Pennsylvania?"

Imani holds up her hands and, in her usual breathless, rapid-fire way, says, "I'm sorry, guys, I'm just the messenger. Blame the ED. There's one for each of us: Clark, you have bed 11—might be a heart attack or indigestion. Bianca, bed 9—cellulitis. Norah, bed 12—shortness of breath. I got bed 2—stroke. And, Stuart, special just for you, bed 5—rectal bleeding."

Stuart rubs the sleep out of his eyes, then claps his hands and springs to his feet. "Go, team! Let's save some lives, people."

Clark claps his. "Let's try to avoid litigation, people."

Together, we file into the bright light of the hallway. Stuart, Clark, and Imani wait for the elevator. I decide to take the stairs so I can stop off at the second-floor pantry for a soda. A few days ago, Ethan told me about the hidden pantry located between the Interventional Cardiology procedure suite and the Physical Therapy gym. Twice as big as pantries on other floors, the second-floor pantry contains a wide selection of tiny, squat cans of Shasta soda as well as packaged graham crackers and, on occasion, peanut butter Ritz sandwiches. It also has a freezer that is sometimes stocked with extra ice cream from the Pediatrics wing. It's the Shangri-la of hospital pantries. The senior residents pride themselves on not just knowing where food is stashed throughout the hospital but having adapted physiologically to sustaining themselves on minimal nutrition. If needed, they like to brag, they could all live for days on nothing but Jell-O cups and miniature cans of ginger ale. I gather that adapting to dearth of all kinds—of sleep, of comfort, of time, of emotion—is going to be necessary to survive the next three years.

At the top of the stairwell, Bianca takes my elbow. "You two make a nice couple." She smiles knowingly.

"What?" I look at her in alarm. "Who makes a nice couple?"

"You and Clark," she says. "You two know each other from med school, right?"

I laugh. "Yes, but we're definitely not a couple."

Bianca furrows her brow. "Really? Well, there's a rumor going around about the two of you, just so you know." She starts down the stairs.

"About me and *Clark*? Seriously?" I follow her. Our voices echo in the stairwell.

Bianca shrugs. "You know how hospitals are. Like high schools. I heard that you guys used to date in med school, then you broke up, and now you're on-again, off-again. It's not true?"

"No, not true. None of that is even remotely true. We're barely friends. I never even hang out with Clark, except when we're on call together."

"Well then, in a way, you *do* sleep together," she says, chuckling.

"Right." I roll my eyes. "We sleep together all the time."

"You have a boyfriend?" she asks over her shoulder.

"Me? No. I'm way too boring to have a love life."

She laughs. "I don't believe that. I think you'll find a boyfriend here in no time. There *are* a few attractive men. And lots of unattractive ones with money."

This makes me laugh, too.

The second-floor pantry has just been stocked with ice-cream sandwiches. It's like I've won the lottery.

I hate the Emergency Department. I hate the squeaky linoleum flooring and the bare, incessantly flickering fluorescent lights overhead. I hate that the steady, maddening beeping of monitors is punctuated by sudden Munchian screams of agony, or inebriation, or "I've been waiting here for over four hours!" at irregular intervals and from any direction. Yes, if there is a hell, it must look and sound—and, certainly, smell—a lot like this.

I throw the wrapper of my ice-cream sandwich in the trash and furtively wipe my hands on my scrub pants. Then I find bed 12 and step through the curtain surrounding it.

"Hi. I'm—"

"The intern. She has pneumonia," says a man in large, square wire-rimmed glasses. I've seen this man before. Here, in the ED, three weeks ago. I glance at the chart, looking for the patient's name: Lenore Tally.

Mr. Tally motions to his wife, who is recumbent on a stretcher. "It's bacterial. She needs to be admitted to a telemetry unit and started on Rocephin and Zithromax. Stat, please."

His wife nods in agreement. I notice that the two of them share an oddly similar short hairstyle, plump body habitus, and narrow range of sour facial expressions. I smile and mention that it's nice to meet them. They regard me sternly.

"Listen, we've been through this before, so if you could just move this along," Mr. Tally says.

"Certainly, sir." Sometimes I feel like a waitress. *Let me check with the chef. Our specials tonight are saltine crackers and enemas.* "I just have a few questions. It says in your chart that you're short of breath. Can you tell me more about that?"

Tell me more about that. A magical little phrase. Quite a lot of time in medical school is spent learning how to conduct a proper patient interview. The key precept of this training is as follows: you, the physician, have limited time. They, the patient, have a colorful life history that has nothing to do with their current medical condition but that they will, nonetheless, want to share with you in its excruciating entirety. The most efficient way to get to the relevant information, while still maintaining the illusion that you are captivated by every glorious detail, is to coax the patient into what is commonly referred to as the Cone.

The Cone—really more of a funnel—consists of an open-ended statement that invites conversation (*Tell me more about that*), quickly followed by a series of questions, each more focused than the last (*Are you vomiting? Is there blood in your vomit? Does the blood resemble coffee grounds, or is it bright red?*).

"I'm always a little short of breath; it's just worse now," Mrs. Tally says.

"Can you describe the shortness of breath? Does it feel like you can't catch your breath or more like a pressure in your chest?"

"Like I can't catch my breath."

"Do you have any other symptoms? Like coughing or a fever?"

"I'm coughing more than usual."

"Are you coughing up mucus?"

"Yes, some."

"Does it have a color?"

"No, it's just clear."

"And when you cough, do you get chest pain?"

"Chest pain?" she says. "Once, about four months ago, I had a pain. No, not a pain, but a burning, you know? After eating. I can't eat spicy foods. I never could. Or tomatoes—I'm severely allergic to tomatoes."

Riveting stuff, but her tangent out of the Cone must be stopped.

"It might have been a fish bone," she continues. "Remember that, honey? I think it got stuck on the way down—"

"So, let me ask you a question," I say. "Have you had any chest pain recently?"

"My God, could the fish bone still be in there?"

No, no, no. Get back in the Cone!

"Once, in 1974, my sister swallowed a chicken bone. Did I mention I'm severely allergic to tomatoes?"

I sigh. "So, no chest pain recently, then?"

"We've already answered all these questions." Mr. Tally folds his arms across his chest. "All you people ask the same questions."

It's true. They've probably told their story to half a dozen people. The ED staff uses a simpler version of the Cone designed to sort patients into two groups: 1) Those for whom death is imminent; and 2) Everyone else. Fall into category 2, and chances are you'll be waiting several hours for medical attention and then detailing your long list of nonurgent symptoms to someone who doesn't have time to write them down.

This patient's chart simply reads, "Fifty-eight-year-old female. History of pneumonia. Short of breath. Chest X-ray ordered."

"Yes, I'm sorry about that. I'll just go look at your chest X-ray. Should only be a minute," I say.

Mr. Tally exhales loudly. "The ED doc already looked at it. He said it was pneumonia. Like I told you."

Ethan's advice rings in my ears. *Don't trust the ED attendings.*

"Yes, sir, but I'll have to look at it myself. It shouldn't take long."

He huffs. "This is a joke."

A woman screams from the neighboring curtain. "Someone, help him! Doctor!"

"I have to go," I say, my voice full of righteous impatience. I swipe the curtain aside with more vigor than is necessary.

Eyes closed and mouth agape, the elderly man on the next gurney is as blue as his hospital gown. A frantic young woman stands on the far side of the bed. "Please, help him!" she says.

My heart jumps into my mouth, and I look around, panicked. I notice a stunned-looking medical student with a short white coat at the nurses' station. There are no doctors or nurses in sight, and the patients in the hallway are watching in helpless, slack-jawed horror. For a moment I stand there, unable to move under the weight of the tremendous responsibility that has just been lowered onto my shoulders.

It's up to me.

I spring into the kind of action for which years of medical school have prepared me. I grab the man's shoulders and shake his limp body. "Sir! Sir!" I shout. I put my ear to his mouth to listen for breathing. I hear nothing. I press two fingers into his neck to feel his carotid pulse. Again, nothing. I exchange a glance with the young woman, who regards me anxiously.

The heart monitor on the wall shows a flat line. Two nurses rush to the bedside.

"Asystole!" I say.

The nurses look at each other.

"Asystole!" I say, louder. The nurses exchange nervous glances again. They seem confused. "His heart has stopped. Call a code blue!" I say. I am impressed by my own capacity for definitive leadership. I clamp a breathing mask over the patient's mouth and begin pumping air into him. "Start chest compressions!" I command.

The young woman makes a guttural sound and says, "He's dead."

"We have to try to restart his heart," I say, breathless, drops of sweat beginning to form on my brow.

"No, he's dead," she says again. "He's been dead for hours. Help *him.*" She points to the floor. I sweep the bed linens aside to look under the gurney. Lying at the young woman's feet, sprawled out on his back, is an unconscious man in skinny jeans and a T-shirt. He stirs and moans.

"What the hell?" he says, his voice cracking.

The young woman sighs impatiently. "You fainted. Again."

"A little overwhelmed, huh?" one of the nurses says. She helps the young man to his feet.

"I don't feel well," the man says, holding his head. "Is there a doctor?"

The nurse casts a quick glance over her shoulder at me, and I'm swallowed whole by a wave of humiliation.

"We'll find you one," she says.

The smell of canola oil and garam masala hits me like a wave of unwelcome nostalgia when I step into Ma's foyer two weeks later. The scent of my childhood. I take off my sneakers and place them under the hall table, next to a pair of smart-looking Franco Sarto leather pumps and a pair of ratty loafers. Obviously, Paul and Reena are already here.

"Look, Norah! Reena made full Gujarati dinner." Ma smiles proudly as I poke my head into the kitchen.

Reena, wearing cheetah-pattern leggings and a blousy T-shirt that reads *#MomLife*, is pan-frying paratha on the stove. She holds a metal spatula in one hand and her six-month-old son, my nephew, Kai, on her opposite hip.

"While holding a baby!" Reena says cheerfully, though the strained way she smiles suggests she's not really enjoying the experience as much as Ma is.

Paul is standing at the counter, opening and closing his mouth, his hand on his chin. "Norah, I have a sore throat," he says. "How do I know if it's strep?" Paul is calm and clearheaded about Ma's medical problems but the opposite when it comes to his own health.

"It's not strep," I say.

"But are you sure?" He rubs his shaved head. "Shouldn't I be on antibiotics, just in case?"

"Do you have a fever?" I say.

"No."

"Then it's not strep."

"But I think my glands are swollen." He massages his ears.

"Your glands are in your neck."

"Seriously, you are such a drama queen," Reena says, shifting Kai to her other hip. The baby blows a spit bubble while trying to insert all of his fingers into one of her nostrils. "You should just see my Reiki master. It helps maintain your immune system." The baby attempts to dislodge her nose ring. She seems unaffected. "That's why I'm never sick. Antibiotics are poison."

I look at the ceiling. How the two of them—my brother, the raging hypochondriac, and his wife, the most misinformed individual in the history of humankind—ever got together is a question that will haunt me forever.

Paul and Reena lived here with Ma until a few months ago, when they moved into their own place just two miles away. Paul still comes over several times a week to take out the trash, go through the bills, and make sure Ma is taking her insulin. Ma wasn't happy about living by herself but reluctantly agreed after we all promised to come to dinner once a week. Reena always does the cooking. I've missed the last few dinners because of work, a fact Ma points out every time she calls.

I set the kitchen table, and Ma, Reena, and I fill the dinner plates with sticky basmati rice, paratha, baingan bharta made from eggplant, and sweet yogurt shrikhand. Meanwhile, Paul sits at the head of the table—in what I refer to in my mind as his "Paul is the only one who gets to sit here because he has a penis" chair—and does nothing. Ma is traditional like that. She likes to dote on her only son and likes to see her daughter-in-law and daughter doing the same. Reena and I have an unspoken understanding that we go along with this "Paul is king" routine for Ma's sake, but if Paul ever started to expect our servitude outside Ma's house, one of us would kill him in his sleep.

Reena deposits Kai in his high chair, and I, scowling resentfully, present Paul with his dinner plate. Ma mumbles a Sanskrit prayer for wisdom and insight under her breath. "Did you check your blood sugar, Ma?" Paul asks.

"Of course, *beta*." She nods and puts a heaping spoon of shrikhand into her mouth. I cringe. Shrikhand is yogurt seasoned with saffron and sweetened with sugar. A *lot* of sugar. I draw my breath in through my teeth, determined to keep my thoughts to myself and avoid another argument.

"Did you tell Norah we picked a date for the *havan*?" Reena asks Paul. He shakes his head in reply, his mouth full.

"A *havan*? Like a housewarming?" I ask.

"I'm so glad it's going to finally be done," Ma says, licking shrikhand off her spoon. "You've been living in that unblessed house for too long. You can't live in house that hasn't been blessed."

"And it's a good excuse to have a big Diwali party," Reena adds blithely. "It's November second. You can make it, right, Norah?"

"I'll have to check with work."

"It's like two months away. I'm sure they'll give you the evening off." Reena's smile is steely.

"Usually interns don't get to choose their days off," I say.

"But you'll ask," Ma says quickly, noticing the looks Paul and Reena are exchanging now.

"Sure." I tear off a piece of paratha. "I'll ask, but I can't promise anything."

There's an awkward silence, then Ma asks, "How's Meryl? We haven't seen her in so long. Did she pass her bar exam yet?"

"Not yet," I say. Paul and Reena are still giving each other looks. "What, you guys?"

Paul clears his throat. "Nothing. Later. It can wait."

Reena shoots him a death stare that he pretends not to notice.

"Hon, could you get me some more rice?" he asks, holding his plate out to her.

Ma looks at Reena expectantly. Reena slowly and deliberately pushes away from the table, stands up, carries Paul's plate to the stove, and begins to dump one spoonful after another of fragrant ecru grains onto it, malice in her every movement.

I help wash and dry the dinner dishes.

"I have to get going." I slip my shoes back on. "I have to be at work early tomorrow."

Ma is drying her hands on a dish towel. "I don't like that girl, Beth, your roommate. She doesn't have boyfriend, does she? She's not one of these loose girls who bring boys to their apartment, right? Shameful." She shakes her head. "I don't know how people raise their children these days. No decency."

Do not engage. Repeat. Do not engage. "I have to run," I say.

"Take this box with you. I made chana masala. Put it in your freezer." She indicates a large yellow cardboard box on the floor that used to contain baby diapers and now is filled with freezer bags of spiced chickpeas in a tomato base. It's a staple, an easy recipe that Ma prepares by mixing canned garbanzo beans with prepackaged spices. The Indian equivalent of Kraft mac and cheese.

"Ma, that box is bigger than my freezer."

She waves her hand dismissively. "You can make room. Just cram it in. You need to eat. You're getting too skinny. You look malnourished."

Paul hoists the box, saying, "I'll help you out to the car with it. It's heavy."

Reena is trying to keep Kai from pulling out her earring. "Say goodbye to Norah *Faiba*. Bye, Norah *Faiba*. Buh-bye!" She waves the baby's plump little arm against his will.

"Bye, everyone." I pull the door shut behind me. Paul has managed to wrestle open the trunk of my aging Honda Civic without dropping the box. "Need a hand with that?"

"Nope. I got it." He closes the trunk and buries his hands in his pockets. He glances toward the house. Reena peeks through the curtains at us, then disappears.

"Norah," Paul says, and I can tell this isn't going to be good, "Reena and I need help with Ma."

"Help? Like we need to find a different psychologist? I totally agree, but—"

He sighs and shakes his head. "No, Nor. We need help managing her. After she ended up in the hospital this past winter . . . we just can't. We have a baby now."

I try to stay calm. I dig around in my handbag for my inhaler. "I know."

"Reena and I both work, and I travel. We can't drop everything and be here every time she needs us."

"I know." My mind races. "We could hire someone. Like an aide to check on her a few times a week."

"We already looked into that. It's way too expensive. Reena even tried to see if her medical insurance would cover it." He shakes his head. "We need help, Nor. We need *you* to help."

I draw in my breath. It's not like Paul to be so direct. This, obviously, is something Reena put him up to. "I do help, Paul. I was just over here three weeks ago when she called me like she was having a heart attack and—"

"I'm over here every day, Nor. Either me or Reena is over here every day. For hours. And thank goodness we are. Who knows how long she would have been lying there the last time, if Reena hadn't checked on her. It's not fair to Reena to ask her to take care of Ma *and* Kai. She didn't sign up for this."

The idea that Reena thinks of my mother as a *this*—an onerous nuisance, a burdensome *thing*—is infuriating. "She didn't sign up for this? Sign up for what?"

Paul looks at the sky and rubs his chin. "To be Ma's daughter. You're Ma's daughter. Not her."

You're Ma's daughter. Three efficient little words that confer a lifetime's worth of guilt and obligation.

"You think I should quit. You both think I should quit so I can move back in here and help out more with Ma. That's what she wanted you to say to me, right? This is all Reena's idea, I know it."

"Nor, come on. This isn't about Reena. It's about us taking care of Ma. She's getting worse."

The pitch of my voice jumps a full octave. "It's only three years. Three years and I'll be done with residency."

"And then what? You'll be a doctor and still busy, and nothing will change. Nor, we understood when you were in med school, but you have your MD now and you could get a job—maybe with Vikram Uncle—and live here with Ma. You could save up money and—"

"And you and Reena and Kai could get on with your lives."

His shoulders sag with frustration. "I don't want you to have to quit. I really don't. Maybe you could take a year off or something, just until Kai is older."

"It doesn't work that way, and you know it." Hurt and bitterness build behind my sternum. "I'm doing this for Dad, Paul. To carry on his legacy. Doesn't that mean anything to you?"

He is quiet for a moment. "There's legacy, and there's responsibility. Dad would want us to fulfill our responsibilities."

"I'm not moving back in here. And I'm definitely not working for Vikram Uncle. I'm not quitting, Paul. I've come too far." He's about to reply when I quickly add, "But I'll help more. I'll be here more."

"How?"

"I'll manage. If you guys need me, I'll be here. I promise. Okay?"

He sighs. He looks unconvinced, but he says, "Okay," nods, and puts his fist out for me to bump.

I tap my knuckles lightly against his, my intestines twisting themselves into knots. "Okay."

CHAPTER SIX

I've stopped keeping track of how many times I've been on call. At least a dozen, probably more. My pager is like a nagging child tugging at my shirtsleeves. It beeps almost incessantly:

Doctor, this patient fell out of bed. She's fine, but you need to come check on her. It's the protocol.

Doctor, can I get an order for Maalox for my patient? The cafeteria served spicy tacos today.

Doctor, bed 816 can't sleep. No, he doesn't want a sleeping pill; he just wants me to tell you he can't sleep.

Doctor, bed 432 is short of breath.

Bed 617 has a headache.

Bed 712 hasn't had a bowel movement in four days.

Do you think this wound looks infected?

This EKG looks weird. You need to get up here, *right now*.

Sometimes, there's a lull between 3:00 a.m. and 4:00 a.m. If I make it all the way to the South Wing—where the residents' lounge and call rooms are located—without my pager beeping again, I either watch television in the lounge or sit on the bed in an empty call room and lean my head against the wall to nap. I don't lie down or take off my shoes; doing either practically guarantees another page. Not that I could sleep, even if I tried. I might doze off for a few minutes here or there, but I'm always too wound with anxiety and adrenaline to sleep deeply.

Some of the other interns have their own unique call superstitions. Bianca has lucky "call socks"—they're bright orange and have the words "Fuck this shit" embroidered around the cuff. Imani sleeps only on the sofa in the residents' lounge, nowhere else. Clark never brushes his teeth, which is absolutely foul, but he swears by the protective power of poor dental hygiene.

I'm dozing on the bed, huddled under a blanket in the dark and trying to ignore the chill seeping in through the drafty call room window, when there is a knock.

"Anyone in here?"

It's Ethan. I smooth my hair to make sure it's not sticking straight up and open the door. Squinting, I raise a hand to my eyes to block the bright hallway lights.

"Oh, hey, Norah," Ethan says, disappointed. His eyes are ringed in red, his chin covered in stubble. "I was looking for an empty room. I wanted to try to sleep for a minute."

In my semi-somnolent state, it takes me a moment to process this information. "There are no empty call rooms?"

He shakes his head. "There must have been a mistake with the schedule. Even the rooms with two beds are filled."

"Did you try the lounge?"

"Imani is asleep on the sofa in there."

"She snores," I say sympathetically.

"Yeah, loud." He sighs. "You wouldn't think someone so small could make that much noise. Anyway, sorry to wake you. I'll just wait until a bed frees up."

He turns to go. He looks so worn and tired, his usually strong shoulders sagging, his chin practically on his chest. "You're welcome to have one side of the bed in here," I say before I can think it through.

He looks at me skeptically, then at the twin bed.

"I sleep sitting up," I say quickly. "It's a call superstition. So, half the bed is free, regardless. If you don't need to lie down, there's pillows and an extra blanket, so . . ."

"You sure you don't mind?"

"I'm probably going to get paged again in a minute, so no, I don't mind. You don't snore, do you?"

He grins. "No, I swear I don't. Thanks, Norah."

He props a pillow against the wall and settles in at the foot of the bed, his long legs folded under him, his back to me. I pass him one of my wafer-thin hospital-issue blankets, and he tucks it around himself. I climb back into my spot at the head of the bed.

"You usually sleep like this?" Ethan asks, rubbing his neck. "How?"

"I don't know. I just do. You're saying you're not comfortable?"

He laughs. "Listen, I'm not complaining. I appreciate you sharing your room. Good night."

I smile. He looks so comically huge, balled up at the end of the bed like a turtle retreating into its shell. "Good night."

I can't sleep. Ethan keeps moving around, shifting this way and that. He's so close, I can feel the heat radiating off his body.

"Dr. Cantor?" I whisper.

"Ethan," he says without lifting his head, his voice muffled by his pillow. "Norah, call me Ethan."

"Ethan . . . are you awake?"

"Yeah, I'm awake. It's freezing in here."

"I know. We should burn these blankets to make a fire."

He laughs. "Great idea. We can throw our pagers into the fire, too, and then just go home."

"Dr.—I mean—Ethan, can I ask a question?"

"Sure."

"What would happen if I—and by 'I,' I mean 'someone'—dropped out of residency? What would they do next?"

Ethan is quiet for a moment. Then he says, his face still pressed against the pillow, "I wouldn't do that. First of all, you spent years in medical school just to get here, and it would be a waste to quit now. And you could get a job with a drug company, but most of them want doctors who've finished their residencies. Other than that, the job options are really limited. Why do you ask?" He turns to face me, and his eyes are two shining points in the darkness.

I'm suddenly aware of my heart thrumming against my rib cage. There's something unexpectedly intimate about this conversation, the late hour, the dark, the bed, Ethan's two shining eyes. I can barely see his face, which, I suppose, is why I feel comfortable enough to say, "I have some family stuff going on."

"What kind of stuff? You don't have to tell me if you don't want to."

"My dad." I chew the inside of my lip. This isn't something I talk about with anyone, ever. I'm not the type to readily share personal information, even with friends. "My dad was a doctor. A great one. Ever since he passed away, I've wanted to follow in his footsteps, carry on his legacy. Turns out the rest of my family doesn't care about his legacy as much as I do."

"But it's important to you, right?" Ethan's gaze is intent.

"He died when I was ten. And even before that, I barely saw him. I remember wanting to know him, to know what he was like. To understand what was important to him. Being a doctor is all I have left of him."

Ethan sighs and runs his hand through his hair. "Norah, that sucks. I'm sorry. I lost someone when I was a kid, too. I get it. This is your connection to him. You can't just give that up."

"I have a stethoscope. His stethoscope, engraved with his name. He used it every day. He'd let me play with it sometimes to hear my own heartbeat."

"That's awesome." Ethan's voice is quiet. "Do you use it?"

"I don't. I keep it on a shelf at my mom's house. I don't feel worthy of it yet, you know? I feel like I have to earn the right to use it. Is that weird?"

He shakes his head. "No. Makes perfect sense. My dad has a tuba—a high-end one, like concert-hall-quality because he used to be a musician—and he wouldn't let me touch it until I had seven years of tuba lessons under my belt. I had to earn the right to play it."

"Wait. You play the tuba?"

"I do."

"I don't even know what to say to that."

"No one ever does."

Our laughter fills the dark room. A lightness, an expansive calm, spreads from my chest into the rest of my body. I'm hyperaware of my breath moving in and out of my lungs and of the fact that the same air is moving through Ethan's. An intimacy of shared oxygen molecules.

"How long have you played the tuba?"

"I started playing when I was eight, and then I joined marching band. . . ."

Somewhere in the middle of his tuba story, feeling warm and relaxed, I fall asleep. When I suddenly snap awake again, horrified and hoping I haven't been drooling, I notice Ethan asleep, too. His blanket is on the floor. I grab it and carefully tuck him in again, then curl up at my end of the bed. She must be a fool, the woman who broke this man's heart.

When I wake up at 4:45 a.m., feeling remarkably rested, a note written on a paper towel is in Ethan's spot on the bed: *Good morning! Thanks again for letting me crash with you. If you have time for breakfast, meet me in the caf at 5am. E.*

I quickly wash my face and brush my teeth at the tiny, yellowed porcelain sink in the corner of the room, grab my hoodie, and dash downstairs to the cafeteria.

Ethan is waiting for me with waffles.

The glow that spreads across my face and turns my ears pink is a result, I know, of the reflexive release of the hormone norepinephrine from my adrenal glands in response to a strong emotional stimulus. Suddenly, though, when Ethan spots me and waves, the physiology of it all seems irrelevant.

Historically, medicine has always been problematic for women.

When Elizabeth Blackwell, America's first female physician, attended medical school, she was asked to excuse herself from lectures regarding reproductive anatomy. When Dr. Harriot Hunt applied to Harvard Medical School in 1843, the all-male student body tried to block her admission by drafting a letter that argued "no woman of true delicacy" would willingly participate in the scientific study of male genitalia. In fact, the entire academic establishment of the time seemed convinced that a female was too dainty and fragile a creature for the gritty practice of medicine. I like to think that I salute all the women who came before me by standing here, right now, with my gloved finger inserted up this elderly man's rectum.

"What're you doing back there, Doc?" he asks, shouting as if I were in another room.

"Still disimpacting you, Mr. Rose," I say.

"I haven't taken a dump in two weeks!"

"Yes, sir. That's common after surgery."

"So, you're just fishing the poop right outta there, eh?"

"That's right."

"With your finger?"

"With my finger."

"You're a good doctor."

It's been ten weeks since I started my intern year. This is my first week on the General Surgery service, and the third disimpaction I've performed in the last forty-eight hours. The weeks, days, and hours of my life have never moved more slowly.

"Done with this one?" Terry's peevish face appears through a gap in the bedside curtain.

In my short time under Terry's tutelage, I've learned two critical things: all of his questions are rhetorical, and he thinks my name is Nadine.

"Wrap this up, Nadine," he says, drawing back the curtain. "Who takes more than ten minutes to do a disimpaction?" He glances at the bedpan containing the small mountain of fecal material I've extracted from Mr. Rose. He raises his eyebrows. "That's all you've gotten out of him?" He scoffs. "Are you serious? What have you been doing?"

I stare at him, agog. A very primal part of me wants desperately to hurl the feces at him.

"Do you always have so much trouble with simple—"

He's still talking, but his voice fades away. Suddenly, everything moves in slow motion, and my knees go weak beneath me.

Dr. V has arrived.

As usual, an entourage of deferential residents trails behind him like ducklings shadowing their mother. Dr. V takes off his sunglasses, and his dazzling blue eyes lock with mine. "That is a lot of shit," he says. He flashes a gleaming-white smile at the patient, then holds out the sunglasses. Three residents reach for them at once. They jostle one another, and the winner, giddy with delight, gingerly folds them and places them in his breast pocket. "You're an intern, right?" Dr. V asks.

I nod, unable to speak. *The* Dr. V is talking to me. The Dr. V who authored *Principles of Cardiothoracic Surgery* Volumes I–IV, counts Oprah among his personal friends, looks like George Clooney, and invented the Vandroogenbroeck vein grafting technique that revolutionized cardiac bypass surgery. There's a 64 percent chance of my fainting. Approximately.

"Great! I've been looking for you," he says. "I need your help with something. It's very important."

"If you need help with a case, Dr. V, I'd be happy to assist," Terry says, stepping in front of me eagerly.

Dr. V waves him off. "No, Terry, I need the intern. Why don't you finish up here, and she can come with me."

I hand the bedpan to Terry. He looks at me incredulously, then at the bedpan, then at me again. I flash a vengeful smile over my shoulder as I toss my gloves in the trash bin marked *Biohazard* and join the throng following Dr. V down the hall. Elle, wearing scrubs and a surgical bonnet over her ponytail, appears at my elbow.

"What does he want your help with?" she asks, her voice a whisper.

"I have no idea," I whisper back. I hurry to keep up with her quick pace.

"You know, he never asks interns to assist with surgeries. He never even lets them *watch* the surgeries."

"I know. I've heard."

At the front of the rapidly moving pack, Dr. V is looking at X-ray films, holding them up to the fluorescent lights while dodging stretchers with extrasensory precision.

Without turning around, he says, "Who knows the treatment for transient constrictive pericarditis after cardiac bypass surgery?"

An uncertain murmur ripples through the crowd of residents.

"Come on, you guys," Dr. V says, his pace becoming increasingly brisk to the point where I'm half jogging to keep up. "You should all know this."

The resident next to me fumbles with his phone, attempting to Google the answer.

"Henderson, put your phone away!" Dr. V says. He still hasn't turned around.

Henderson sheepishly puts the phone back into his pocket. The other residents snicker like boys in a schoolyard.

"Prednisone," I say, under my breath.

Elle nudges me. "Say it louder."

"Prednisone," I say, louder.

Dr. V glances over his shoulder. "Correct. What dosage?"

"Five milligrams per kilogram per day for ten days," I say. I remember reading about this that night Meryl and I went to Barnes & Noble to study and the barista, who is secretly in love with Meryl, kept giving us free cupcakes and trying to strike up a conversation with her.

"Also correct. Well done, intern," Dr. V says.

I blush and look at my shoes, feeling several pairs of disdainful eyes on me. "Lucky guess," someone grumbles.

Dr. V's cell phone rings. "Doctor V," he answers, still moving at top speed. "No, I will not fly business class. Just charter a plane. Hold on a minute. I need a red pencil." He holds one hand aloft. Books and instruments clatter to the floor as the residents tear at their pockets. Finally, someone produces a wax pencil and places it in Dr. V's open palm. He makes lines on the X-ray films and says into the phone, "Economy class? Cancel the whole trip."

"You must have made an impression on him," Elle whispers, without taking her eyes off Dr. V. "Why else would he ask for your help?"

"This is the first time I've ever talked to him," I say, bewildered.

"There are junior residents here who would kill to scrub in on one of his surgeries. And *you're* not even a Surgery resident."

"Maybe he has me mistaken for someone else."

"Dr. V doesn't make mistakes," she says, as definitively as if it were the sum of two numbers.

Dr. V stops suddenly, and we all collide with one another. "This is a blue pencil," he says. "Who handed me this?" There is silence and fidgeting. "Who handed me this?"

"Um, that's mine, Dr. V," one of the residents says, raising his hand.

Dr. V approaches him. He holds the pencil at the tip of the resident's nose. "What color is this, Doctor?"

The resident opens his mouth and produces a low, whining sound.

Dr. V regards him. "Is this red? Is. This. Red?"

"No, sir," the resident says.

"No! It's blue. Don't ever hand me this again!" He throws the pencil to the floor, and it ricochets into a passing nurse's leg.

The resident averts his eyes meekly and mumbles an apology.

"Here you go, Dr. V," Elle says, handing him one of four identical red wax pencils lined up neatly in her breast pocket.

Dr. V's cell phone rings again. "Elle, meet me in OR 3 in five minutes, and bring the intern. You'll be assisting me with my next case. The rest of you will go refamiliarize yourselves with the color wheel." As he strides away, we hear him say into the phone, "Yes, I realize our son is only going to graduate from college once—what the hell is JetBlue?"

"You just contaminated yourself. Scrub again," Elle says. A mask covers her nose and mouth, but I can tell she's scowling.

Given the prominence of antibiotics and vaccinations in modern medicine—not to mention the presence of pump bottles of disinfecting goop every fifteen feet in the hospital—it's easy to forget that there was a time when the leading scientific minds believed that illness was caused by amorphous vapors and when no one was required to wash their hands before returning to work. The modern practice of surgery takes germ theory to its inevitable extreme.

"What did I do?" I stand at the metal sink with my hands raised in front of me, water dripping down my arms and into the sleeves of my scrub shirt.

"You dropped your arms below your waist."

"I did?" Washed hands and arms must be held above waist level at all times, as the volume of air below the waist is considered to be contaminated.

"You did. You'll have to start again, from the beginning." She walks away, toward the OR, her wet hands clasped together in front of her as if she were praying.

I grab a little silver packet from the shelf above the sink. Inside is a bar of soap attached to a plastic brush. Just like I learned in medical school, I push a lever below the sink with my knee to turn on the faucet. I lather up, then run the brush over the outside surface of my right index finger ten times, then over the palm side of my right index finger ten times, then over the inside surface of my right index finger ten times, then over the back of my right index finger ten times. I repeat this process with the other nine fingers, then with each hand, and finally with each arm up to the elbow. Then I rinse each arm, taking care that the water flows from my hands to my elbows. This way, any microorganisms that still happen to be stubbornly clinging to my elbows won't make their way to my fingertips and, from my fingertips, to the patient. I clasp my dripping hands together and am careful not to let them touch my shirt, the sink, or anything else in my vicinity.

The idea that Dr. V has asked me, an Internal Medicine intern with no surgery experience, to assist on one of his operations is thrilling. After a week of disimpactions and practicing how to tie a proper surgical knot on my sneaker laces five thousand times, I'm elated at the chance to prove I'm capable of more. *Wait until Stuart hears about this*. An enjoyably smug satisfaction stretches my mouth into an elfish grin.

I back into the operating room, nudging the door open with my hip. Immediately, there is a ten-degree drop in ambient temperature and an icy, anxious pit in my stomach. Operating rooms are always uncomfortably cold; the frigid temperature, in theory, slows bleeding and, if nothing else, keeps the surgeons from overheating and sweating to death. The room is silent except for the rhythmic hissing of the ventilator. A body, covered in blue drapes, lies on the table. Dr. V and Elle are hunched over it, scalpels in hand. An enormous spotlight on an adjustable metal arm is positioned just over Dr. V's shoulder, shining onto a bloody incision in the center of the patient's chest. At the head of the table, an anesthesiologist sits on a stool, adjusting the several IV lines that are dripping medications into the patient's veins. At the foot of the table, a stone-faced nurse dressed in a surgical gown and mask presides over a vast array of scalpels, retractors, and other instruments, all neatly laid out on sterile green towels. I approach her with trepidation, shivering with cold and nerves. She fixes her gaze on me.

I smile and whisper, "Hi. I'm—"

"Hemostat!" Dr. V says.

Like a flash, the nurse's hand shoots out, grabs an instrument that looks like a small pair of pliers, and claps it into Dr. V's open palm. She looks at me again.

I whisper, "Hi. I'm—"

In one fluid motion, she towels off my hands, yanks a huge paper gown over my arms, knocks me around with her elbow, and pulls the gown closed behind me, expelling the air from my lungs. Then she smacks a latex glove over each of my hands. Wordlessly, she turns back to the instruments.

A turbulent whirring noise fills the room, and bits of powdery bone spray into the air in a fine mist. I crane my neck to look over Elle's shoulder. Dr. V is sawing the patient's breastbone in half with a circular blade. I hold my breath. This is it. Any second now, he and Elle will pull the two halves of the bone apart and expose the patient's chest cavity—lungs, heart, and all. My eyes widen, and beneath my face mask, I smile with rampant excitement. The whirring stops.

"Intern!" Dr. V says, without looking at me. "Finally. I'm glad you're here. I have something very important I need you to do."

If my father could see me now. "Yes, sir," I say, drawing myself up to my full height. I know Dad would be so proud of what his little girl has accomplished, here at the elbow of this great and famous surgeon, carrying on the Kapadia legacy in medicine.

"Go get my car inspected and then bring it back," Dr. V says. "My keys are over there."

I look at Elle. She raises her eyebrows and shrugs sympathetically.

"Scut," I mutter into my mask.

Scut. Scut. Scut. This is a huge, steaming pile of scut.

Scut is the menial work that attendings and residents task to their inferiors. There are an infinite variety of prosaic tasks that might be regarded as scut: hunting for old patient medical records, making photocopies, shuttling charts or X-ray films or patients from one department to another, that sort of thing. It's an integral part of the medical school and residency experience, and I've come to grudgingly accept that some scut is unavoidable. This, however, is the most humiliating trivial errand on which I've ever been sent and the first time scut has involved my leaving hospital property. Still, it's Dr. V who's asking. I have a nagging feeling that the future of my entire career is hanging on whether I can successfully get his car out of the parking deck, across downtown, and back without scratching it or allowing a bird to poop on it.

I cross the second floor of the hospital parking deck until I find reserved parking spot number 5. *You've got to be kidding me.* It's an Aston Martin. A tiny, silver space-pod-like coupe. The interior looks like it was designed by a steampunk watchmaker with a James Bond obsession; the polished mahogany dashboard is covered with intricate gold dials of varying sizes and at least a dozen mysterious gauges and buttons. *One of these probably turns it into a submarine.*

I slide behind the steering wheel. The cream leather seat conforms to my body. It's like a plush cocoon. *Oh my God, I could sleep in this car. I could live out the remaining decades of my life in this car.*

I press the ignition button carefully, and a screen in the center console glows, displaying the words "Welcome Back, Geoff" and playing a sprightly Vivaldi concerto evocative of skipping, carefree, through vast fields of money.

I coax the car out of the garage and onto Broad Street, the main thoroughfare through downtown. I drive so slowly that elderly pedestrians on the sidewalk overtake me. All the way to the inspection station, I'm trailed by a chorus of horns that erupts when I glide to a complete stop at every intersection.

An attendant asks for the car's registration. It tumbles out of the glove box along with an autographed CD of Neil Diamond's greatest hits (*To Dr. V, Looking forward to wiping the tennis court with your ass again real soon. Regards, Neil*), a little placard that reads, *Philadelphia Heliport VIP Parking*, and a pen embellished with *Mandarin Oriental Hotel—Dubai* in gold script. Quickly, I put all the items back in place. I wait for my turn behind a long line of other, less impressive vehicles.

My phone rings. "I was going to leave a message," Meryl says, happily surprised. "I thought you'd be at work, you know, saving lives and whatnot."

I'm too embarrassed to admit what I'm actually doing. "I have a minute. What's up?"

"I feel like I barely see you. I know you're busy, but you looked at the website for that youth hostel in Maui, right? Because I'm going to book our room. It's a popular place, and I don't want it to sell out. We can worry about the flight later."

Meryl and I have decided to celebrate the end of my intern year this June and her (hopefully) passing the bar by treating ourselves to a weeklong trip to Hawaii this summer because Meryl's never been to Hawaii and, well, I've never been anywhere. We've been planning and saving up the money for the trip for the past year, justifying the expense by reassuring each other that having something to look forward to in life is the key to success and achievement.

"Yes! The Banana Bungalow, right? It looks great." I open and close the leather sun visor. "The summer seems so far away."

"Nine months." She sighs miserably. "People literally grow an entire human in their uterus in that amount of time. I hope you know, I'm going on this trip whether I pass the bar or not. And if I don't pass, I'm planning to stay in Hawaii and live there forever in a van on the beach and forget this whole lawyer thing. I'll sell weed and my wardrobe will consist entirely of bikinis. I might change my name to 'Starlight.' Dirk supports my plan."

I laugh. "Stop talking nonsense. Of course you'll pass. How's Dirk?" I flick the turn signal on and off.

"Meh. I'm debating breaking up with him."

"Oh no. Why?" I try to affect a tone of genuine disappointment, but honestly, I've never much liked Meryl's current boyfriend, Dirk.

"I don't have time for his drama. I posted a picture of us on Instagram and he got all weird because he didn't like his hair in the picture and he was all like, 'You should have checked with me first before posting that' and I'm like, 'What are you talking about?' and he's like, 'My social media persona is vital to my career.' I mean, how pretentious is that? I think all the success has gone to his head."

Dirk, an aspiring Broadway actor, is currently starring in a community theater production of *Bye Bye Birdie* at Burlington County College in New Jersey.

"You're right. You don't have time for that drama." There is an unlabeled button in the dashboard that I debate pushing. Instead, I open the console in the armrest and find a pair of Cartier sunglasses and a receipt for an $850 dinner at Morimoto.

"Pull forward, miss!" The attendant waves me toward him. I inch Dr. V's car forward, shift into park, and step out, letting the attendant slide behind the wheel with his clipboard. He whistles, impressed. "This your car?"

I shake my head, covering the receiver with my hand. "No, it's my boss's."

"What's your boss's?" Meryl asks.

I sigh. "One of the attendings is making me get his car inspected."

"What? No. That's ridiculous!"

"I know."

"Then why are you doing it?"

"It's complicated, Mer."

There is a pause. Then she says, "Dirk is texting me. 'Hey, babe, you still mad?' Ugh, what is wrong with him? Of course I'm still mad. And he knows I hate that he calls me 'babe.'"

The attendant hands me his phone. "Could you get a picture of me in the car?"

"I have to let you go," I say to Meryl while trying not to drop either phone. "But let's catch up over brunch Sunday, okay?"

We agree on where and when to meet and hang up. The attendant poses for his picture with a broad grin and his arm draped over the steering wheel while wearing what I'm pretty sure are Dr. V's sunglasses.

An hour later, I drive Dr. V's car—which not only passed inspection but was photographed by three other attendants—back into the hospital parking deck.

When I return to the OR, Elle is gone, and Dr. V is operating on a different patient. I place his car keys on a table near the door and turn to leave. Suddenly, without looking up, he says, "Intern! Finally, you're back. Go scrub. I need your help with something."

What does he want me to do now? Wash his delicates? I swear under my breath as I scrub the skin off my raw hands, march back into the OR, get batted about by the same humorless nurse, and step up to the operating table to await my next meaningless assignment.

The patient's heart is exposed. It is ruddy and purple like a bruise, covered in a lattice of bulging blue veins, pulsating and quivering and surrounded by glistening pebbles of golden fat. On either side, a pink, iridescent lung gently expands and contracts.

"This is what the chest cavity looks like in a living person," Dr. V says. "Not much like the cadaver lab, right?"

I shake my head in wonder, recalling the brown, leathery organs dripping with formaldehyde that I dissected in medical school.

"Right," he says. "So, reach in there and pick up the heart."

"Do what?"

"Go ahead." He grabs my wrist, yanks it into the chest cavity, and I am suddenly cradling a man's beating heart in the palm of my hand. "That's what normal sinus rhythm feels like."

Behind my mask, my mouth hangs open and my breath has stopped completely. The rhythmic pounding of the heart rockets through my fingertips, up my arm, and into my chest. I feel powerful in a heady way totally foreign to me. It's thrilling.

"Okay, that's enough." Dr. V pushes my hand aside. "Go help Terry. He's on the third floor. I think he's doing another disimpaction."

I am still hardly breathing when I leave the OR. I toss my mask, gown, and gloves into the trash and practically float to the elevator. When it stops at the next floor, Elle steps inside. "How'd it go?" she asks.

I can barely form the words. "There was a heart . . . and I was . . . holding it. . . ."

Elle smiles. "Welcome to the entourage."

CHAPTER SEVEN

I have just lapsed into a dreamless sleep in the call room when my pager sounds. It's set to vibrate and rattles on the desk next to my head, then plummets to the floor. After a moment, it starts buzzing about under the bed like an insect in its death throes. I struggle to find it in the darkness, then grab for the phone.

"Hi. It's the intern." I rub my eyes and glance at the clock: 2:00 a.m.

A meek voice replies, "Hi! Um . . . so sorry to bother you but . . . this patient . . . could you please come look at him?"

"What's going on?"

"His . . . penis."

"Yes?"

A nervous pause. "It's . . . not normal."

"Not normal?"

"No."

"What specifically is abnormal about it?"

"It's huge."

"I'm sorry? You're saying his penis is abnormally huge?"

"Yes."

"I'll be right there."

Without question, it is huge. Elephantine, really. Its owner is a pleasantly demented elderly gentleman who seems unperturbed that three women are standing over him at this late hour, gawking at his genitals. The nurses, who look young enough to have just arrived from cheerleading practice, are bright pink. One of them says, "The nurse who had the shift before me didn't say anything about this. I came in here to put a catheter in his bladder because he hasn't peed in, like, seventeen hours."

Clearly, something is amiss. The Brobdingnagian organ lies limply between the patient's legs.

"Sir, do you have any pain . . . in this area?" I gesture vaguely.

"My sister, Gert, once went swimming with Margaret Thatcher," he replies, smiling.

"Oh? Okay. That's nice." I smile at him and nod. "Is he on any new medications?" I ask the nurse.

"Metoprolol, for his blood pressure," she says. "And an antibiotic, Zynexa."

I ask the patient for permission to perform an examination. He shrugs. "If you'd like to have coffee with the prime minister, I imagine that'd be all right." I palpate the penis, move it back and forth, pick it up, let it drop. The patient looks around the room serenely. "They were rich, the prime minister's family," he says. "They had bicycles!"

My coffee with the prime minister complete, I page the attending assigned to the patient, a doctor I've never met. He calls back fifteen minutes later. I take the call at the nurses' station.

"What?" His voice is a weary croak.

"Sorry to bother you, sir. This is the intern. Your patient, Mr. Foster, he hasn't urinated in several hours—"

"So put a catheter in him," he says curtly.

"Yes, sir, but his penis is . . ."

"Is what?"

"Abnormally huge."

"Is it painful? Is it priapism?" Priapism is a sustained erection, a painful medical emergency.

"I don't think so. . . ."

"Well, what is it, then?"

I hesitate. Then I say helplessly, "I don't know."

"Well, I don't know either. Just put the catheter in him." He hangs up.

Great. Thanks for the help. Awesome mentoring, jerk.

In the hallway outside the patient's room, I recap the phone call for the nurses. "So, I guess we're putting a catheter in him," I say. It has to be done. If any more urine builds up in his bladder, the patient's kidneys could be damaged. We return to the room, where the nurses sterilize the unfortunate phallus by dousing it with iodine, then offer me a catheter the size of a child's drinking straw.

There isn't an orifice in the human body into which a physician cannot or will not readily insert a catheter. The technique is simple: cover one end of the plastic tubing in a viscous lubricant, then feed it through the aperture of interest. I've done this before, several times. As far as body parts go, penises, in particular, are ridiculously easy to catheterize.

Feeling confident, I pull sterile gloves over my hands, then easily thread a few inches of the catheter into the patient's penis. It quickly gets stuck. I twist and turn the tubing but can neither advance it further, nor draw it out. The patient groans in pain. I look at the nurses. I sense that they expect me to be familiar with the appropriate course of action in this situation. Thinking fast, I decide that the only logical strategy is to try to force the catheter past whatever is obstructing it. The tubing is flexible and should be able to squeeze through even a tiny opening. I push on the catheter firmly, and suddenly, to my relief, the resistance gives way and it slides into place. Urine flows through the tubing and into a collection bag. The nurses exclaim in delight.

Then, there is a faint rumbling, and—not unlike lava from a volcano—two jets of blood explode out around the catheter and spray several feet into the air. The nurses scream. The patient yelps in surprise. I clamp my thumbs over the end of the penis, but this just directs the stream of blood onto the far wall. In the several moments before the bleeding stops, I reflect on what a pathetic and disturbing way this would be for this kindly old man to meet his demise.

The flow of blood slows to a trickle, then stops. I look around. There is blood on the floor, my glasses, and both of the nurses. I look at the patient. He grins at me like a child with a secret.

"Bicycles!" he says.

"Are you okay, sir?" I ask, still clinging to his penis with both hands.

He squints up at me, as if he's just noticing my presence. "Are you Indian? My sister, Gert, was a personal friend of Indira Gandhi. She taught Mrs. Gandhi how to fly an airplane in 1954 at the Delhi airport."

I look desperately at the nurses. "I have to call a resident," I say.

I know the resident on call tonight must be busy and probably doesn't have time for something as non-life-threatening as a bladder catheter, but I dial the number anyway. I pace the hallway between the patient's room and the nurses' station while the patient regales the nurses with stories about his sister, Gert, whom, I have to admit, if she's real, sounds like quite the badass.

When the resident calls back ten minutes later, I nearly knock the phone off the counter as I grab for the receiver. It's Francesca.

"Hey, Norah. This better be good. I have four patients all circling the drain right now, and I'm the only one keeping them alive."

I describe the situation as succinctly as I can. I try to think of a way to avoid using the words "abnormally huge." I give up and use the words "abnormally huge."

"Is it still bleeding?" she asks.

"No. But there was a lot of blood. *A lot.*"

"It's probably fine. Just order a Urology consult and they'll sort it out tomorrow."

It's probably fine? Probably?

"Okay, but you don't think—"

"Sounds good! Gotta run!" she says, her tone friendly even as she hangs up on me midsentence.

Blood pounds in my ears, an anxious thought clamoring at the edges of my mind: What if something dangerous is going on with this patient? I chide myself for not studying penile pathophysiology more carefully in medical school. I stare at my phone. I could Google "abnormally huge penis," which probably would just produce a list of porn websites, or I could try calling the only other person I can think of who might be able to help me, even though he's not on duty tonight.

"Hey, Norah. What's up?" Ethan says when he answers on the first ring.

"Ethan, I'm really sorry to wake you."

He yawns. "It's fine. What's going on?"

I quickly explain what's happened over the past hour. "Francesca's too busy to come examine the patient. She says it's probably fine, but—"

"But you just don't feel right about it."

"Right." I smile with relief. He always understands perfectly what I mean to say, even if I haven't said the words aloud.

"Well, I'm not sure what's going on with your patient, but I'll come over and take a look."

"Wait, what? You'd come to the hospital?"

"Yeah, I live, like, two blocks away. It's just easier for me to see this giant penis for myself."

"But it's three a.m."

"Do you want my help or not?"

I hesitate. Then I say, "I want your help."

"See you soon, then."

Fifteen minutes later, the nurses, Ethan, and I are gathered at the bedside, staring at Mr. Foster's privates.

"Yeah, that's a penile implant," Ethan says, unimpressed.

"A what?" I whisper, hoping the patient won't overhear me. "I've never even heard of that."

"Yeah, it's not something they cover much in med school," Ethan says in a normal tone of voice. A day or two's worth of stubble covers his chin, and he is wearing a hoodie and jeans. He looks like he could use a cup of coffee, or several. He leans down so his mouth is next to Mr. Foster's ear and says loudly, "Sir, when did you have this penile implant put in?"

Mr. Foster regards him for a moment before replying, "My sister, Gert, was Miss Pennsylvania 1962!"

"It's a treatment for erectile dysfunction," Ethan says, turning his back to Mr. Foster. "It's supposed to inflate and deflate by pushing a button in the scrotum, but sometimes the buttons break, especially on older models."

I find this information profoundly disturbing. "So the patient just walks around with . . ."

"Yup. With a prosthetic erection in his pants for the rest of his senile years."

I glance at Mr. Foster, who seems blithely unconcerned about what's being said, right in front of him, about his faulty penile apparatus and his obvious caducity.

"Should we go into the hallway?" I ask.

Ethan doesn't hear me. He continues. "It's not painful and usually not a problem, but sometimes the inside of the penis can scar, and that blocks the flow of urine. When the scar tissue is messed with—like with a catheter—it bleeds. Sometimes a lot."

I'm still whispering. "Do you think the catheter could have . . . you know, caused any serious damage?"

Ethan shakes his head and says, again without lowering his voice, "Nah. This guy has end-stage liver disease. His penis is the least of his problems."

I clamp a hand over my mouth and glance anxiously at Mr. Foster.

Ethan shakes his head at me, bemused. "What? He's eighty-six and demented. He's not going to remember any of this tomorrow."

"I know, but . . ."

As if to confirm Ethan's statement, Mr. Foster calls out, "Bicycles!" and yawns and stretches and promptly falls asleep, snoring softly.

I'm relieved to know nothing serious is going on with the patient, but I'm also riddled with guilt about dragging my senior resident in from home and embarrassed that I worked myself into knots over nothing.

"Ethan, thank you," I say. "I'm so sorry you had to come in here for this."

He shrugs and rubs his eyes. "Don't mention it. I'm glad it wasn't anything major. You owe me a coffee later today, though." He waves, grinning, as he heads for the door. "See you in a few hours, Norah."

"Bye! See you in a few!" I call after him, my voice higher-pitched and more girlish than I intend for it to sound. How does he always have that effect on me? "Thank you again!"

One of the nurses whistles. "Wow. I've never seen a resident come in from home to help out like that."

Her colleague nods, saying, "He's a good one. Some of them are real jerks."

I smile in agreement, wondering if she's crossed paths with Terry. The nurses leave the room, and I stand there for a moment, watching Mr. Foster sleeping. Then, gingerly, I lift up his sheets. Everything appears to be in order: still abnormally huge, but the catheter is in place, and there's no bleeding. *A penile implant? Who'd have thought?* I consider the immeasurable vastness of the body of knowledge I have yet to learn and am momentarily overwhelmed.

Then it occurs to me that I am scrutinizing a sleeping stranger's privates and that the most remarkable thing about this situation is how utterly normal it seems.

Meryl takes a sip of her Bloody Mary to steady herself, then says impassively, "Well. That's the most horrific story I've ever heard, and I'm pretty sure I'm scarred for life now." She shakes her head in confusion while waving her hands. "Wait, wait. So, it's just broken and no one fixes it?"

I rest my chin in my hand and say, with authority because I've just finished reading an extensive chapter on the subject in the textbook *Principles and Practice of Urology*, which I borrowed from the hospital library, "In an older patient with other, more pressing medical problems, they might just leave it alone." I shrug and add, with a dismissive wave of my hand, "The guy has end-stage liver disease. His penis is the least of his problems."

Meryl's glass freezes in midair. "Whoa. That's how you talk about your patients?" Her eyes widen reproachfully.

I'm suddenly defensive. "He's super demented. He doesn't know what's going on."

"So what?" Meryl demands. "My grandpa had dementia before he died, and I wouldn't have wanted anyone to say something like that about him. What's up with you? I've never heard you talk about your patients like that before."

"I'm just tired," I say, which I know sounds like a pathetically thin excuse, so I add, "And that's how everyone talks in the hospital. It's not out of disrespect or anything, it's just . . . how we talk."

Meryl frowns skeptically. "If you say so."

Of course I can't expect her to understand. She's never pulled a night on call or pronounced someone dead or saved a patient who was on the cusp of death. She doesn't have any idea what it's like.

A waitress brings us both cheese omelets, and I use the opportunity to change the subject. "I still can't believe Ethan came in from home to help me out. Residents usually don't sacrifice sleep for anyone."

"Oh, that's the best part of the story," Meryl says, nodding in agreement. She tucks into her omelet. "I'm telling you, you should jump on that."

I smile hesitantly. "Well, on that topic, I kind of have news."

She raises her eyebrows and leans forward in her chair.

I explain that a group of the senior residents has been planning, for months, to go to a VIP Halloween party at a club downtown. Ethan had an extra ticket (one that I'm pretty sure was originally intended for his ex-fiancée, though I didn't ask) and offered it to me yesterday afternoon, while we were waiting in line at the hospital coffee cart together, saying, "If you're not doing anything, you should come. It'll be fun. Doctors behaving badly."

"Oh. My. God." Meryl's mouth is half-full. "He asked you out? This is huge!"

"I don't think it's a date."

"Are you meeting at the party, or are you going there together?"

"We're meeting at his apartment and walking over to the party together."

"Oh, it's a date, my friend."

"It's more like a two-work-colleagues-slash-friends-go-to-a-party-together-on-Halloween type of situation."

"Wait." Meryl's smile fades. "It's on Halloween? What about my Booze-o-Rama?" Meryl has been throwing her annual Halloween party since we were in college.

"Well, yeah. They're the same night."

Meryl hesitates as if she's waiting for me to say something else, then frowns. "This is a special occasion, so I guess I understand."

I shake my head, one eyebrow raised. "What are you talking about? I'm not about to miss Booze-o-Rama. I haven't missed one in seven years. But I might have invited Ethan to your party. Is that okay?"

Meryl's mouth drops open in amazement. "I'm sorry, what now? A guy asked you out to a party, and then *you* asked *him* out to a party? It's like I don't even know who you are. The universe is imploding."

My face reddens. "I didn't ask him out. It's not a date! He said, 'Hey, let's go to this resident party,' and I said, 'I have to go to my friend's party that night,' and he said, 'We can go to the resident party and then go to your friend's party afterward.' That's it. Just two acquaintances going to two parties. Together."

Meryl taps her index finger against her chin. "Were those his exact words? *We* can go to your friend's party? You know what that means? He thinks of the two of you as a *we*. That's huge."

"It's not huge. It just means he knows how to use pronouns correctly."

Meryl stirs the stick of celery in her Bloody Mary while nodding at me sagely. "Oh, it's huge, my friend."

Something under the table is buzzing.

"What's that noise?" Meryl asks.

I grab my pager out of my handbag. It's set to vibrate and blinks a hospital extension on its screen. "It's the hospital. Hold on a sec."

I dial the number, and a male voice answers. "OR three."

"It's the intern. Norah? I was paged to this number."

"Hey, this is Henderson, the Surgery resident. Dr. V wants you to pick up his dry cleaning and drop it off at the doctor's lounge on the fourth floor."

"But . . . I'm not on call today. And it's a weekend."

There is a brief silence. "Yeah. So the dry cleaners is on Fourth and Spruce, and he needs it before he leaves the hospital at two o'clock, so . . ."

Meryl is watching me carefully. "What's going on?"

I motion for a pen, and she hands me one out of her bag.

"What's the name of the dry cleaners?" I ask.

"City Cleaners. His stuff is under his wife's name, Penny Vandroogenbroek."

I write down the name and address of the cleaners on a napkin while Meryl looks on.

"Hold on a second," she hisses. "Is he having you *pick up dry cleaning*?"

I shrug helplessly. "Okay, I'll have it there by two," I say into the phone. Henderson grunts in reply and hangs up.

"Oh, no way." Meryl shakes her head in disgust. "Is this the car inspection guy? That bastard is calling you on your day off to pick up his laundry? Isn't he super rich? Doesn't he have people for that?"

"I think I'm his people for that." I bitterly jab my fork at my eggs.

"Why didn't you tell him to go fuck himself?"

"It's not that simple, Mer. There's a totem pole, and at this point I'm lucky to even be on it. Interns get evaluated at the end of each rotation, and if you get a bad review from an attending, it can affect your whole career."

"You're not his personal assistant, Nor. He's abusing his power. You need to stand up for yourself."

"I know, but—"

"But you don't do confrontation."

"I don't do confrontation."

Meryl sighs. "That's probably why he picked you to do his dirty work in the first place. He knows you won't fight back." She waves over the waitress and hands her some cash. Then she stands and slings her bag over her shoulder, looking at me expectantly. "Let's go."

"Let's go? Where?"

"You only have until two to pick up his dry cleaning, right? That place is all the way across town. So, let's go."

That's the type of friend Meryl is. Your problems are her problems, no questions asked. "You don't have to come with me, Mer," I say. "I can go on my own."

She waves me off. "You could. But it'll suck less if we go together."

In the end, it takes both of us, Meryl's collapsible shopping cart, and an obliging Uber driver to get Dr. V's thirty-five dress shirts, three suits, and one tuxedo from Fourth and Spruce to the hospital. We make it there just before 2:00.

I'm in the bathroom of Ethan's apartment wearing a brown paper bag with the word "Skippy" written in blue marker across the front. The bag is upside down, with a hole for my head in the bottom, and one for each arm in the sides. I pull on leggings and sneakers and complete my ensemble with a powder blue pillbox hat. I check my reflection in the mirror. I look ridiculous. And my thick black hair is doing that half-curly, half-straight frizzy thing that it does in humid weather, which is definitely not helping. I throw it back into a ponytail. *Terrific, now I look twelve. All I'm missing is a backpack and acne.*

I hear Ethan in the hallway outside and marvel at the fact that even his footsteps have become familiar. If I'm sitting behind a nurses' station looking over a chart, I can always tell when Ethan is approaching, just from the faint squeak of his sneakers against the vinyl floor. Like a reflex, my pulse quickens and my breath catches before my conscious self even recognizes why.

This isn't a date. Obviously. Two people wearing coordinating costumes doesn't imply anything more than mutual esteem or a chummy sort of camaraderie, like dogs and their owners wearing matching sweaters.

Meryl's party is costume-required, a fact that I had forgotten until this morning, when, in a panic, I texted Ethan.

Nothing like a last-minute costume. Any ideas? was his reply.

None, I'd sent back.

Well, I have this goofy T-shirt.

And it sort of spiraled from there. After work today, we visited the secondhand shop across the street from the hospital, and here we are. Right. Now I'm going to have to go out in public dressed like this.

I step out of the bathroom.

Ethan's apartment is small and modern. In the 1800s, the building was a hoopskirt factory (I learned this from one of the very chatty front desk attendants while I was waiting for Ethan to buzz me in), manufacturing restrictive undergarments for women to make their skirts look fuller and their waists look smaller. Renovated after decades of neglect, the building is now home to sleek studios with exposed-brick walls and metal piping. The front door to Ethan's place opens right into the kitchen, which is too small to fit a proper table but has a high-top poured-concrete island with two copper bar stools. From there, a narrow hallway runs past the powder room and the bedroom and into the living room, where a slip-covered IKEA sofa sits in front of a coffee table covered with neat stacks of medical journals. An industrial-size window takes up one wall, offering a sweeping view of the Delaware River.

I'm comfortable here, I notice. I feel none of my usual social anxiety, even though I'm about to go to a party dressed, literally, in a paper bag. Ethan peeks into the kitchen, and my heart skips a few beats, as if it were giddily clicking its heels.

"Lookin' good!" he says. He's wearing jeans, a purple T-shirt emblazoned with the word "Smuckers," and a fedora with plastic grapes decorating the brim.

"Didn't I see that outfit in this season's Banana Republic catalog?" I ask.

He laughs and reaches out to gently adjust my hat, his hand lingering on my hair slightly longer than necessary. "Let's go, gorgeous."

In the elevator, we are joined by a smartly dressed couple on their way to dinner. As we descend in silence, they glance at us curiously. I shift my weight, and my brown paper dress crinkles loudly. Ethan chortles under his breath.

Outside, we walk quickly. The turtleneck I'm wearing underneath the paper bag is no match for the biting wind, and I stretch the sleeves over my hands. Ethan thrusts his hands into his pockets and, when we stop at a corner to wait for the light to change, hops from one foot to the other, grinning, trying to stay warm. I laugh at him through chattering teeth.

I'm looking forward to spending time with Ethan outside of work, but I'd much rather we were going to a cozy, quiet coffee shop by ourselves to talk about our favorite books or discuss which historical figures we most admire (mine's Darwin, naturally). I can't keep that night in the call room out of my mind: I ache for another hushed, intimate moment with him.

Suddenly, Ethan wraps one arm around my shoulders and draws me in, rubbing my upper arm, trying to warm me up. "We're almost there!" he says reassuringly. I want desperately to curl into him, to stay tucked under his arm, but the crosswalk sign blinks, and he releases me. We jog across the intersection. I try to catch my breath.

A line is already stretched down the sidewalk by the time we arrive at Pompeii, one of those aggressively trendy clubs with negligible lighting and bored-looking waitresses wearing copious eyeliner.

"We should be on the guest list," Ethan says. He gives our names to a hulking man at the door, who lifts a red velvet rope and waves us underneath. I follow Ethan through a throng of happy people in costumes. We duck past a vampire, a flapper, and a pair of disturbingly sexy clowns before we stumble on our party.

"Hey, Peanut Butter and Jelly!" someone yells. Ethan waves. I recognize Elle and some of the other second- and third-year residents. One of them is dressed in hospital scrubs dotted with crimson paint splotches and carries a fake butcher knife.

"Psychotic surgeon?" I shout over the music. He nods.

"Grocery bag?" he asks. I shake my head and turn to point at Ethan. Elle is saying something that's evidently hilarious into his ear. Ethan beckons to me. I hurry over, and he crosses his arms and says, "Okay, here's my other half. Now guess."

"Oh, PB and J! That's so cute!" Elle coos. She takes a sip of what is clearly not her first drink of the evening. She's wearing a form-fitting red strapless dress with a prominent zipper up the back and knee-high black boots with a spiked heel.

"What are you, Elle?" I ask.

"Me? I'm a hot girl!" She raises her glass to a group of girls on a couch nearby, all of who, it seems, have chosen a similar costume. They cheer.

What Elle says next is inaudible to me over the din of voices and dance music; however, it would appear that she's launched into some fascinating story. Ethan is leaning in close, and her hand rests on his chest.

My glasses are sliding down the bridge of my nose. I try to push them back into place without calling attention to them. I check my phone, fidget with my hair, adjust my hat. I wonder how much longer

Elle's story can go on. Based on her hand motions, there seems to be no end in sight, but I'm determined not to leave my other half; his costume makes no sense without me.

My phone rings. "I'll be right back," I say. Neither of them hears me. On the sidewalk outside, I can just make out Meryl's desperate voice.

"Should I go to the ER?"

"What happened?" I ask.

"Weren't you listening? I cut my finger! It's bleeding everywhere! What should I do? You're a doctor—come help me!"

"How did you cut yourself?"

"I was reaching into a drawer, and there must have been something sharp in there. Oh my God, am I going to bleed out?"

"No, you're not going to bleed out," I say, glancing skyward. "Just put pressure on it. I'll be right there." I go back inside, where Elle now has her arm draped across Ethan's shoulders.

"Ethan, my friend Meryl just called," I say, trying to sound buoyant. "I think we should head over there. She's having some sort of medical emergency."

His brow furrows. "Is it serious?"

"Meryl is kind of dramatic, so probably not. But I feel obligated to check on her." I motion to the exit.

"You're leaving already?" Elle asks, clutching Ethan's arm. "You just got here!" She sways a bit, and he grabs her by the shoulders to keep her from tipping over.

"We have another party to go to, one of Norah's friends," Ethan says.

"But you haven't even seen Blood Clot or Chandelier Sign or Strep-Z yet." Elle pouts. "They just texted. They're on their way over."

I wonder what the embarrassing backstory is behind all the seniors' nicknames. I imagine I'll be Shocks-a-lot at least until I graduate, if not for the rest of my life.

"Norah, why don't you go on ahead and I'll meet you there?" Ethan says. "You can text me if you need help with the medical emergency."

"Okay. Sure." I struggle to sound nonchalant.

"You can handle it. Just use what we've taught you," he says encouragingly.

"Go make us proud!" Elle waves her drink, sending it sloshing over the rim of her glass.

"I'll do my best," I say. "See you a little later, then?"

"Definitely." He smiles and nudges me with his elbow. "Just don't run off with anyone dressed as a marshmallow, okay?"

I could be wrong, but I think he holds my glance a few seconds longer than expected. It's impossible to tell for sure in the dark.

A light rain has started to fall as I set out for Meryl's apartment. "Hey, look, a bag lady!" someone yells from across the street. I keep my head down and walk quickly. I cross South Street, where an adult video store with neon signage shares a wall with a taxidermist on one side and a colorful eatery serving nothing but meatballs on the other. Revelers in costume are everywhere, spilling out of bars, blocking traffic. Car horns blare. It's faster to walk than to try to call an Uber in this mayhem.

By the time I reach Meryl's building several blocks away, the rain has become a downpour, and my costume and I are soaked through. I wait an eternity for the tiny elevator, and when it finally arrives, slump against the back wall, grateful to have it all to myself.

"Hold the elevator!" someone calls.

I pretend not to hear. Just as the doors are sliding closed, a young man with dark, slicked-back hair tied into a bun and wearing sunglasses and a black leather jacket squeezes through them. He shakes the water off his clothes and the plastic shopping bag he's carrying, then turns to me with an irked expression.

"I said, 'Hold the elevator.'"

"I didn't hear," I say.

"Is that a costume?"

"No."

"Are you supposed to be peanut butter?"

"Yes."

"You don't look like peanut butter."

"My friend dressed like jelly. It makes more sense when he's standing next to me."

"Where is he?"

"He's at another party."

"You probably should have planned that better."

"And what are you supposed to be?"

"I'm Bono."

"You don't look like Bono."

"I look exactly like him."

"You look nothing like him."

"Maybe you don't know what Bono looks like."

"Maybe you can't see because it's the middle of the night and you're wearing sunglasses."

"I can see well enough to know you don't look like peanut butter."

We ride the rest of the way in silence.

At Meryl's floor, I step out and hasten down the hallway without glancing back.

"I guess this is goodbye," he calls after me.

"Weirdo," I mutter under my breath.

"Oh, is it raining?" Meryl asks when she swings open the door. The sound of raucous laughter erupts from somewhere inside the apartment.

I smile wearily before asking, "How's your finger?"

"Oh, it's fine. Gabe helped me."

"Who's Gabe?"

A familiar voice behind me says, "I have Band-Aids!" Bono appears, steps around me, and hands Meryl the shopping bag.

"Norah," Meryl says, "this is Gabe, my friend from yoga. He's a medical student. He held pressure on my finger and got it to stop bleeding. He's so awesome."

"I'm awesome," Gabe says, glancing at me smugly, "and so is my costume."

So that's why he looks vaguely familiar. I remember seeing Gabe at the Zynexa dinner a few months ago. He's Man-bun.

I follow them into the kitchen. "Let me see it," I say, taking Meryl's hand. Other than a little speck of dried blood on the tip of her ring finger, it seems uninjured.

With profound gravity, Gabe nudges me aside and places a tiny bandage over the cut. "There you go," he says proudly.

"Thank you so much!" Meryl sighs with relief. "I need a drink. Thank goodness you were here, Gabe." She rushes off toward the living room.

"Yes, thank goodness you were here for the paper cut," I mutter, crossing my arms resentfully.

Gabe grins. "Actually, it was an index card laceration."

"Was that a nerdy doctor joke? That was terrible," I say.

"It was terrible." He nods somberly. "I've embarrassed myself."

I shake my head, looking down at my outfit. "I'm wearing a wet paper bag. If either of us has embarrassed ourselves, it's me."

"Just ditch the bag," he says.

"I can't. My friend—"

"Who, Jelly?"

"Yes. He'll be here any minute."

"And you two are a set."

"Yes." I like the way that sounds. "We're a set."

In the living room, Meryl is passionately recounting her harrowing medical emergency to a roomful of guests I don't recognize. Her circle of friends changes frequently, due to her tendency to annex whatever social group belongs to the guy she's dating. When the relationship ends and her former beau's friends are forced to choose sides, they inevitably choose Meryl. She remains close with these people until she starts dating someone else. Then, she gradually supplants the old circle with the new one. Meryl split up with Dirk last week, and I gather, from the lively conversation about *Pippin* that has just begun, that these are his former friends. Not surprisingly, considering most of them are theater-folk, their costumes are amazing. One girl has spray-painted her hair in rainbow colors and wears a white fur unicorn suit. She clasps a beer bottle in between two disconcertingly realistic-looking hooves.

I settle into a chair in a corner and pretend to be interested in the finer points of musical theater. I'm secretly smug; as one of Meryl's oldest friends, I'll never have to worry about being replaced. At next year's Halloween party, I'll be the only one of us in the room invited back.

Nearby, a young man carrying two beer bottles and dressed as the Queen of Hearts from *Alice in Wonderland* (complete with powdered face, caked-on blue eye shadow, and curly scarlet wig) struggles to right himself after nearly falling over. He points at me and trills, "I don't see a drink in your hand! Off with her head!"

Meryl looks over her shoulder. "Norah doesn't drink," she says. "She's never had a drink in her life."

The young man lets this abomination sink in. Then, "Like, never?" he says. "Like, not even in college?"

I shake my head. A sea of costumed faces gawks at me as if I were some exotic zoo animal.

"Wait, are you super religious?" the young man asks, slurring his words. "Are you one of those, like, Jehovah Buddhists?"

Meryl scowls dismissively. "Shut up, Topher."

As he staggers away, the young man commands over his shoulder, as if by royal decree, "You should have a drink. Life is short!"

I glance at my watch. It's been forty minutes, and still no sign of Ethan. I reassure myself that he's probably on his way over here right now.

A bottle of Mendocino Coast pinot grigio is leaving a water ring on the coffee table. Its label features a pencil sketch of an hourglass-shaped woman running down a beach in the surf, presumably naked, her hair blowing freely in the wind.

A guy dressed as some sort of cowboy merman (ten-gallon hat, green fishnet tights, mesh shirt, fish tail waving behind him) perches on the arm of my chair, invading my personal space by at least a foot. "Hey," he says, leering. "Sup, beautiful?"

I don't suffer from any grand delusions about my looks. I'm an objective person who believes in unbiased observation. And, objectively speaking, I'm reasonably attractive. Not alluring like a Hollywood starlet, obviously, but cute the way you'd expect the starlet's homely, non-famous older cousin to be. I have a symmetrical face, well-groomed eyebrows (facilitated by living upstairs from a threading salon), clear skin, and an acceptable nose-to-face ratio. At Lenape Day Camp, I was rated by the boys' barracks as a solid 6.5 (for reference, Meryl was rated a 12). I occasionally get hit on, but not nearly frequently enough that I find it annoying; it's still novel to me. I'm flattered by the cowboy merman's attention, but I think it's better if I don't lead him on only to have to ditch him when Ethan gets here.

"Thanks," I say, smiling politely. "Nothing. Just reading this fascinating tome on"—I grab one of the oversize coffee table books and read the title—"*Cats and Plants*." *Really, Meryl?*

"That's cool," the rodeo merman says, clearly not getting the hint. "I like cats. And plants."

"Yeah," I say. "Me too. I'm not sure anyone doesn't like plants, though. Like, what kind of person hates plants?"

The merman considers this carefully. "I dunno."

"Maybe a person with a really severe ragweed allergy," I offer. "Or a bad prior experience with poison ivy."

He furrows his brow in frustration, clearly disappointed with the direction our conversation has taken, then says, "Do you wanna ride my dolphin?"

"Your what?" I say, taken aback. Then I notice that he's holding a child's hobbyhorse with a stuffed dolphin head on the end where the horse's head should be. "Oh," I say. Because I'm not really sure what else to say to a grown man carrying a marine animal on a stick. "No, thanks. I'm good."

His shoulders sag dejectedly. "Do you want a drink? I'm going to the kitchen." I shake my head, and he mounts his dolphin stick and gallops off at a slow, sad pace.

After thirty minutes, the bottle of Mendocino Coast is sitting in a puddle of condensation, and Ethan still hasn't arrived. I text him a casual You're missing a fun party! and wait.

An hour later, after I've finished the entirety of *Cats and Plants*, I reflect on the idea that maybe life *is* short. I've avoided alcohol up to this point because, logically, it doesn't make sense to consume a known neurotoxin. But everyone else in the room seems to be blithely enjoying themselves without worrying about this or any of the other potential long-term pathophysiologic effects of their beverage choices. Maybe trying just one glass, without overthinking it, is what I need to do. I certainly can't keep sitting here, obsessively checking my watch every two minutes. That's just unhealthy.

I discreetly drink a glass of lukewarm Mendocino Coast. It tastes like grape juice and floor cleaner and burns the lining of my esophagus in a way that feels entirely self-destructive but is still, somehow, enjoyable. As I start my second glass, Meryl is describing how her finger was nearly amputated. An hour after that, I've had two more glasses, and Meryl is explaining how her finger fell off and Gabe reattached it with a bit of dental floss. I can't feel my tongue.

Sometime after 3:00 a.m., I stumble home wearing someone else's coat. I don't recall quite how I got there, but I do know that I vomited into the kitchen sink upon my arrival and had some sort of freewheeling conversation with Al about either communism or hummus—I can't remember which—before I collapsed into my bed. I am asleep, still in my tattered paper bag costume, when my phone beeps with a text message from Ethan that reads, Hey Peanut Butter. Sorry lost track of time. Dead tired. Going home. Sorry I missed your friend's party. See you at work. Happy Halloween!

I sit up like a bolt, enraged and affronted into sobriety. *What? He can't be serious. There had better be a more robust apology coming or—*

Another text from Ethan: a kissy-face emoji followed by a smiley-face emoji.

I gasp. *Well, now.* I let myself fall back onto my pillow, clutching my phone to my chest, grinning. Considering the evidence—the way his hand brushed against my hair, his arm around my shoulder, the elbow nudge, the prolonged glance—it's logical to conclude that Ethan and I have a connection. More than that, though, I feel it. I feel it in a way I've never felt anything before, a way that feels like proof, like fact. I feel it in my bones. All 206 of them.

CHAPTER EIGHT

"Nadine!" The phone does little to mitigate the chafing quality of Terry's voice. I search for the volume button on the lounge telephone. "There's a trauma patient down in the ED who needs an EJ line. Some drugged-up jackass. Go put it in."

"An EJ line?" I say. "I've never done one by myself before." The dial tone hums in my ear. I stare at the receiver.

"You've never done one what by yourself?" Stuart's head appears from behind a large volume of *Harrison's Principles of Internal Medicine*. He seems on edge, as if he's already had too much caffeine, even though it's only 10:00 a.m.

"An external jugular line."

"Awesome! I've never done one either," he says. "I'll come."

A young ED nurse with what appears to be seasonal allergies looks harried when we arrive at the nurses' station. "You guys here for bed 7? Good luck with that. Can't wait till they get him out of here." She blows her nose into a tissue.

"Angry drunk?" Stuart asks her.

"His alcohol screen was negative," the nurse says, showing us the chart. "And we're waiting for the rest of his tox screen to come back from the lab. Probably cocaine. He's got the crazy coke eyes."

We find bed 7. The patient seated on the stretcher has just

vomited into a basin that he clutches on his lap. A black fracture boot is strapped around his right leg.

He groans. "I have a head punch." He leans back against the pillows and drapes his heavily tattooed forearm over his eyes. A bruise covers his left temple and cheek.

"Dude, what?" Another man, keeping him company, is teetering precariously on the rear two legs of a chair. He laughs giddily and adjusts and readjusts his baseball hat. "What are you talking about?"

The patient grins at the ceiling, slurring his words together. "Shutupyoufuckingbastard." Frothy, bile-tinged vomitus sloshes out of the basin and onto the floor.

"Excuse us, we're here to place your IV line," I say, minding where I step.

The patient squints at us. "What are you guys? Students? I got no veins. Nurses stuck me like a hundred times already."

"That's why we're here," Stuart says. He pulls on a pair of gloves and hands me a packet of alcohol swabs and an IV needle. "We're going to use the vein in your neck."

"You can try," he says, smiling and lifting his chin. "But I've shot drugs into those, too."

"Your vein will be easier to see if we lay you flat," I say. As Stuart and I lower the head of the stretcher, I ask, "What happened to you?"

His friend in the chair erupts in laughter again. "Dude, tell them what you did. Tell them."

The patient smiles through clenched teeth. "I made this ramp out of wood planks. Big ramp. Then, I tried to drive the car over it. You know, like *Dukes of Harvard*."

"*Dukes of Harvard*? *Harvard*?" His friend snorts with merriment. "It's *Dukes of* Hazzard."

The patient regards him. "That's what I said."

"He's been mixing words up. It's fucking hilarious," his friend says.

I ready the IV needle by removing it from its plastic sheathing while Stuart swabs one side of the man's neck with alcohol.

"Okay, ready? Here's the pinch." Gingerly, I push the IV needle through the man's skin, just behind his earlobe.

"Holy shit!" the patient says. "That shit hurts!"

He flinches, and I release the needle and jump back.

"Is that needle still in my neck? Holy shit!" He clutches the bedsheets with both hands.

"Holy shit!" his friend says.

"Norah, what are you doing?" Stuart hisses.

I shudder, my palms sweating. *I can't get stuck again. I just can't.*

"Norah?" Stuart's voice sounds far away. I can't even turn my head to look at him.

He nudges me aside, grasps the needle, wiggles it about, and says, "There. Got it." I help him tape the IV catheter in place while avoiding his skeptical gaze.

The patient groans again. "I have a splitting head punch."

"You mean headache?" Stuart asks.

"Right. That's what I said." He laughs. "Shit."

At the nurses' station, Stuart raises his eyebrows at me. "Froze up, huh? You all right?"

I nod. "Fine. Thanks for jumping in."

He grins. "Whatever that guy's on, I want some."

I open the chart. A printed sheet of lab results is clipped inside.

"Stu," I say, "his tox screen is normal. He's not on anything."

We exchange a glance and turn around to see the patient's head quivering violently.

"Hey! Something's happening to him," his friend says, pointing.

The man's arms and legs begin to tremble, then thrash.

"Seizure! Help!" I shout.

Several nurses and a doctor rush to him, inject sedatives through the IV line in his neck, and ferry him away to the CT scanner.

An hour later, he is dead.

"And the Darwin Award goes to . . . Bo Duke."

Stuart and I sit in the near-total darkness in a vast room filled with cubicles, looking over the shoulder of a mustachioed bald man who is slowly making his way through a family-size bag of Poppin' Jalapeño Doritos. In the glow from the computer monitor, I can see the fluorescent orange cheese powder he's leaving on his keyboard as he clicks through a series of CT scan images.

"Thanks for reviewing the CT films with us, Dr. Gill," Stuart says. "We have no idea what we're looking at."

Dr. Gill shrugs. "Sure. You guys have to learn from cases like this. Next time some patient drives his car over a homemade ramp and dies. . . . Wow, this guy really hit his head hard. He lacerated his middle meningeal artery." He taps the side of his head. "It's right here. The blood rushes out and fills up the epidural space just beneath the skull, then it just crushes the brain like a tidal wave taking out a house. That's too bad."

"Could he have had surgery? Could that have saved him?" I ask. I desperately want him to say no, to confirm that this patient was doomed regardless of whether we made the diagnosis or not.

"Yup. Neurosurgery can fix this, if they get it early," Dr. Gill says, licking cheese powder off his fingers. "But don't beat yourself up. It's tricky. There's usually a window of time after the trauma when the patient feels fine; then suddenly they just tank and die."

I'm sick to my stomach, and I know it shows on my face. I glance at Stuart, who, if he's upset, is doing a much better job of maintaining a professional demeanor than I am. I excuse myself, flee to the nearest ladies' room, and splash cold water onto my face. Ethan was right—there's nothing normal about this job. There's nothing normal about casually eating a bag of chips while discussing a man's crushed brain.

I stare at my wet reflection in the mirror. I don't look like a doctor. I look nothing like the wizened, old, kindly men in white coats who populate Norman Rockwell paintings. They always seem so self-assured, so unaffected. From what I remember, my father was like that, too.

As I dry my face, I push away thoughts of the dead man and his jocular friend. Instead, I focus on the science—the uniquely tortuous anatomy of the arteries of the skull and the singular fragility of brain tissue, which has the consistency of lukewarm butter. Then, bolstered—for the moment—by scientific objectivity, I turn off the tap and step back out into the hallway.

The next morning, I join the other interns at a table in the cafeteria in time to hear Stuart saying, his mouth full, "The blood builds up in there and—boom! Squashes the brain like a grape."

"That's so awesome," Imani says. "I mean, not for the patient, obviously. But you guys get all the interesting cases. All I ever see in this place is heart attacks and strokes."

My phone rings.

"Is this Norah Kapadia?" a woman's voice asks. "This is Rhonda from Employee Health. Good news, your labs came back, and they all look good."

Without thinking I say, "So, I definitely don't have HIV or hep C?"

The other interns stare at me.

"No, you don't," Rhonda says.

I breathe in relief. "Thank you."

I hang up, and Bianca asks, "Is that an American thing? You just publicly announce the results of your STD checks?"

"I got a needle stick a few months ago. I had to get tested a few times, just to make sure."

Stuart points his fork at me. "You freaked out doing the EJ line on Bo Duke. Is that why?"

I nod. Then I say, aloud but really to myself, "I'm not sure I'm cut out for this doctor thing."

Imani laughs ruefully. "Please. I think about quitting every other day. If I didn't have so much student loan debt, I'd run away and join the circus or become a psychic medium for dogs or do something else that I'd be more competent at."

"You know," Bianca says, "I have a lot more experience than all of you, but I still make mistakes. You'll improve, you'll see."

"Bee," I say, "I knew the patient had HIV and hep C, and I still managed to stick myself. I put the needle in his vein, he flinched, and then I jabbed myself right in the hand. Who does that?"

"Lots of people," Stuart says. "It happens, literally, all the time. It's just a matter of time before we all do it, too."

"I was so tired one night I wrote an order for metoprolol instead of for Mylanta," Imani says.

Clark gapes at her. "No way. You ordered a blood pressure med to treat gas?"

Stuart chortles. "Imani is very aggressive about treating gas."

"Imani treats gas by putting the patient into a coma," Clark says.

This makes him and Stuart laugh so hard that they pound the table and gasp for breath. Bianca, Imani, and I exchange glances of quiet exasperation.

"Shut up, guys," Imani says. "A nurse caught it, so nothing bad happened."

Bianca nods sympathetically. "Thank goodness for the nurses. It's easy to make mistakes, especially on no sleep."

Stuart sighs loudly. "Well, there was that time I accidentally did a rectal exam on a patient who didn't really need one."

It's suddenly very quiet.

"I was in med school," Stuart says, his cheeks flushed with embarrassment, "and the attending in the outpatient clinic said, 'Go in the room and give the patient a complete examination.' So, I did what I was taught, a full physical exam."

"Including a rectal exam?" Bianca's eyes are wide.

Stuart crosses his arms defensively. "Doesn't a full physical examination include a rectal exam?"

"What was the patient being seen for?" I ask.

"Cataracts," Stuart says. "The attending meant a complete *eye* examination."

We all dissolve into laughter as Stuart's face goes flame red.

"I think we need to toast," Clark says, clearing his throat. He raises his glass of orange juice. "To Norah not contracting hepatitis from her patient. Well done, Shocks-a-lot."

We toast with our juice and coffee cups. I look around the table at our matching starched white coats and smile. For the first time in my life, I have a group of friends, a clique, a squad. What I feel is more than just a sense of belonging; it's a thrill of momentum, like being swept up in a wild current. Our shared purpose is to help one another stay afloat, and everything else seems secondary and unimportant. The world outside the hospital is on the shoreline, quickly shrinking out of sight.

Suddenly I remember that Diwali is next week.

I stare at my reflection in the gilt rococo mirror over the vanity in Paul and Reena's new powder room. This mirror is more visually interesting than I am. I'm wearing a black knee-length dress and a gray cardigan. *It probably wouldn't kill me to wear more makeup.*

Paul and Reena purchased this sensible three-bedroom, split-level house in need of renovation earlier this year and have just finished remodeling the kitchen and bathrooms. The gilt mirror is typical of Reena, whose decorating style is solidly at the intersection of Liberace and a Dollar Store.

When I open the door, a silver-haired woman wearing a glittery red sari and a gold headband is waiting for the powder room. "Norah? Hello, *beti*! Don't you look adorable!" She squeezes my face between her hands.

I wince, my stomach dropping to the floor. "Hi, Nimisha Auntie."

"What's different?" She takes a step back to better see me. "The hair? No. Have you gained weight? That must be it. Oh, thank goodness, because you were far too skinny last year. What an improvement."

"Thank you," I say, unsurprised. The backhanded compliment is Nimisha Auntie's forte.

"Have you seen my Dimple? She's expecting again!" Nimisha Auntie smiles, her eyes wide, her nostrils flaring, her lips pressed tightly together. She looks like a cartoon lizard.

"That's so great." I glance at my phone. "Another grandchild? Good for you. How many does that make now? A full half dozen?"

She cackles merrily, unfazed by my attempt at passive aggression. "And Dimple's husband is taking our whole family on an all-expenses-paid trip to Bermuda to celebrate! Your ma needs a son-in-law, Norah. She has too much stress. Ever since your papa died in that car accident, I've been telling her, 'Rupali, you need to get Norah married. A widow with an unmarried daughter is a curse on the family.' It sounds harsh, but you know I say this to her out of love. Who bought her first winter coat for her, after all?" She makes a clicking sound with her tongue, and her voice drops to a loud whisper. "You should hear the ladies at the community center talk about her. She used to have so many friends, but now . . ." She shakes her head. "No one wants to associate with a cursed widow."

Ma would be livid if I ever dared to speak rudely to Nimisha Auntie. She's lectured me before about the way I greet her and the other aunties with "Hi" instead of—as she would prefer—pressing my hands into an obeisant namaste while bowing. Ma is fervent about the Indian tradition of showing deference where it's due, and because Nimisha Auntie is older than me and a cherished family friend, no matter what ridiculous garbage spews from her mouth, I have no choice but to respect her. And she knows it. I stay silent, my lips pressed together, my hands clasped in front of me.

"I know some very nice boys I could introduce you to, Norah. My cousin has a family friend, and they have an engineer son. He's a very nice boy. He's not what you would call good-looking, but at your age a girl can't be picky. And everyone eventually gets ugly, right? Right?" She cackles again.

"Some of us more so than others," I mumble as she disappears into the powder room.

Paul and Reena come down the hall, sprinkling holy water from a copper pot onto the floor. A priest from the Hindu temple dressed in a white tunic and khaki trousers follows them, chanting in Sanskrit.

"Excuse us," Paul says. "Just blessing our house here."

Reena shoots him a look. "Can you take this seriously, please?"

"Paul!" I hiss under my breath. "What is Nimisha Auntie doing here?"

Paul shrugs helplessly. "Ma invited her."

"Why didn't you stop her?"

"I can't just kick her out."

Reena scowls at us both. "You guys, can you discuss this later?"

I follow them back into the living room, which is filled with guests who, for the most part, are feigning interest in the ceremony while eagerly awaiting the arrival of appetizers. Paul, Reena, and the priest sit on a blanket spread over the hardwood floor, in front of a gold altar decorated with tea-light candles and a statuette of Ganesha, the god of good fortune. The scent of sandalwood wafts from a burning incense stick. They place flowers at the feet of the tiny deity, then press their hands together in prayer as the priest concludes his chant with a deep and resounding "Om."

The guests congratulate Paul and Reena, the priest is dismissed, and someone switches on a television channel featuring Bollywood music videos. Kai is passed from person to person, having his cheeks pinched and squeezed by dozens of doting, cooing aunties. He tolerates this patiently, sucking his thumb and then wiping the saliva on each woman's sari.

A stentorian laugh comes from the direction of the kitchen, momentarily drowning out everything, even the music videos. Vikram Uncle.

"High-heel shoes are idiotic!"

"I like how they look," Reena says, glancing at me in exasperation as I enter the kitchen. She's sliding a tray of naan out of the oven. Ma is seated at the kitchen table, her blood pressure cuff inflating around her arm. Across the table from her, Paul picks over a platter of crudités.

"You'll be in a wheelchair by the time you're my age!" Vikram Uncle loads a cocktail napkin with mini pakoras on toothpicks. He smooths his mustache, an unruly handlebar-type thing that's always getting food caught in it. "Reena, as a scientist, I am telling you that Boyle's law says that volume and pressure are inversely proportional. Small shoe, lots of pressure on your toes. It's simple physics." He scoffs and gestures at the air.

Reena tosses her dark hair over one shoulder. "Norah, I don't believe in doctors, but will wearing heels give me bunions?"

"I think," I say, "that it depends on the type of shoe—"

"Norah's not really a doctor yet," Vikram Uncle says, waving me off. "She's still in school."

I bristle. "I graduated from medical school, actually." Under my breath I add, "Several months ago." I take a seat at the table.

"She's officially Dr. Kapadia now," Paul chimes in.

Vikram Uncle shrugs. "Well, whatever, but she's still learning. She's a *trainee*." He says it like he assumes my job is to deliver flowers while dressed in a pink-and-white-striped outfit with a matching hat.

"Eat something, Noonie," my mother says, the blood pressure cuff still around her arm. "You know how we both get light-headed when we don't eat."

"I don't get light—"

"You're so tired. You work too hard. Look at you, bags under your eyes." She pushes my bangs off my forehead. "Vikram, couldn't you hire Norah to come work for you?"

"Thanks, but I'm going to practice medicine," I say. "You know, I'm going to actually be a doctor. Like we've discussed."

Vikram Uncle snorts his disapproval. "Eh, doctors. They're ten cents a dozen. When I came to this country in 1972, the doctor was king." He raises his pointer finger into the air and waves it about. "All the immigrants wanted their kids to become doctors. I went to my doctor last week, and you know who I saw? A nurse practitioner. A nurse! And she calls herself 'Doctor.' They let any Tom, Dick, or Jimmy practice medicine these days."

"Harry," I say. "It's Tom, Dick, or Harry."

"Eh, whatever." Vikram Uncle shrugs. "Harry, Jimmy, Barbara. English expressions make no sense."

Paul smiles at me sympathetically. "You know, you all may be surprised to learn that, in some circles, being a doctor is considered very prestigious."

I smile back and mouth, *Thank you.* I catch Reena rolling her eyes.

"Utpal, I am aware that being a doctor is prestigious," Vikram Uncle says pointedly, using Paul's given name. "But there's no *money* in it anymore. It's a dying profession. Pun intended." He grins with satisfaction.

"What do you mean, dying profession?" Paul says. "People will always need doctors."

"Insurance companies!" Vikram Uncle motions as though he were throwing dollar bills into the wind. "Everyone knows the doctors are all on the leash of the insurance companies. The doctor is an employee, not the boss. You can have all the prestige you want, but if you're not the boss, pffft." The gesture he makes to accompany this sound is, I presume, supposed to mimic air being let out of a balloon and the balloon shooting off at a tangent, lost and directionless.

My mother hasn't been listening. "Did you see Meryl?" she says. "She looks so nice. She brought her friend." She lowers her voice conspiratorially. "He's boy."

I head for the living room, weaving through a throng of guests until I find Meryl. She's wearing a perfectly draped pink chiffon sari, her hair in a neat topknot.

"Happy Diwali!" she says, hugging me. She takes a step back. "Where's your Indian outfit?"

I'm the only woman here not wearing a sari. "I came straight from work. I didn't have time to drape my sari properly. It always takes me forever. Did you put that on yourself?"

She nods. "I remembered how to do it from Paul's wedding. It's easy once you get the hang of it. So, you remember Gabe, right?" She points across the room to where Gabe, dressed in a blue kurta top and jeans, a plastic cup of soda in hand, is engaged in animated conversation with several men. He claps one of them on the back and laughs enthusiastically.

"Oh, I remember him." I raise my eyebrows at her.

"I know, I know," she says, waving me off. "It's very new. I left you a message a few days ago but—"

"I'm sorry, I've been so busy with work—"

"He's really great, I promise." She beckons to him, and he saunters over.

"Who are those guys?" Meryl asks.

Gabe shrugs. "No idea. Hello, Norah," he says casually. "Great party."

"I'm getting some mango lassi," Meryl says. "You guys want any?"

I shake my head. Meryl mouths the words "Be nice" in my direction and is gone.

"You have my coat," Gabe says.

"No, I don't," I say.

"Yes, you do."

I sigh quietly. "Did you wear it here today?"

"No. Because you have it."

"I don't have your coat." A moment later it occurs to me that I might. "Halloween . . ."

"Halloween."

"That was your coat I wore home?"

He smiles.

"I'm sorry," I say. "I didn't realize."

"That's okay. You were upset about Jelly not showing up. Did he ever tear himself away from—what did you call her—the Surgery Whore?"

"I said that?" My voice is increasingly panicked. "Out loud? To you?"

"All the way home."

"You walked me home?"

"So where is he?"

"Who?"

"Who? Jelly. I want to meet him."

"I wasn't myself, you know. I don't really ever drink alcohol. And I shouldn't have said that about the Surgery . . . individual. She's actually a very nice person and not a sex worker, and even if she were, that's not something I would judge her for because as women we're economically—"

"Ah, he's not here. Is he with her?" He crosses his arms over his chest.

"What? No. I don't know. No."

"You keep looking at your phone."

I cross my arms and tuck the phone under my elbow. "So?"

"Slept with him yet?"

I suck in my breath, setting off a coughing fit.

"Right. I didn't think so," he says.

"He just broke up with his fiancée," I say between coughs. "He's not really ready to be in a relationship right now."

"Not ready? He told you that?" Gabe flashes a smile at Meryl, across the room at the buffet table.

"He was with his fiancée for two years. Of course he's not ready. It's obvious."

"Uh-huh. So this is a Florence Nightingale type of thing you're doing?"

"A what?"

"You know, he's wounded, you heal him, he falls for you. Women love the rescue fantasy."

"Do they?" I say, my tone saccharine. "You sure do know a lot about women."

"You're saying I'm wrong?"

"I'm saying you don't know anything about me."

"I know you're a person who will wear a wet paper bag for someone who doesn't bother showing up for you."

I make an offended tsking sound while squinting. "That is *not* what happened!"

"You're someone who lets people walk all over you. You're doormat-ish."

"I am *not* a doormat."

"Doormat-*ish*. You have some doormat-like qualities."

"Well, you're asshole-ish. You have some asshole-like qualities. And you look ridiculous in that kurta. Stop appropriating my culture."

"Nice cardigan," he replies.

My mother appears at my elbow, smiling gratuitously. "Oh, hello. Norah, is this Meryl's friend?"

"No," I say, staring at Gabe, wishing I could vaporize him with my eyes.

"Mrs. Kapadia, it's a delight to meet you." Gabe smiles charmingly. "The house-blessing ceremony was beautiful. Happy Diwali."

My mother looks pleased. "Happy Diwali to you, too. You look nice in kurta." She turns to me, her smile vanishing. "Norah, there's someone I want you to meet." Under her breath, she implores, "Keep open mind."

A lanky young man with a ponytail and a black turtleneck sweater appears at her side, smiling eagerly. "Hi, Norah! I've heard a lot of nice things about you." He extends his hand.

Oh no. No no no no no no.

I shake his hand. "Hi."

"This is Ketan." My mother beams at the young man and squeezes his arm. "He has master's degree in biology and wonderful job. He wants to talk to you."

My cheeks flush. I can't believe she's doing this, without my permission, right in the middle of the living room with all these people watching. I bet this was Nimisha Auntie's idea. I glance at Gabe, swaying back and forth on his heels smugly.

Ketan smiles again and is about to say something when I hold up my hand. "Listen, I'm going to have to stop you right there. I'm sorry." I clear my throat. *Sorry is something a doormat would say in this situation*. "Actually, I'm *not* sorry. I can't talk to you."

Ketan shakes his head, confused. "You can't? Okay, maybe I can give you my phone number and—"

"No. Nope. I don't want your number."

Ma laughs uncomfortably, then glares at me. "Norah! Don't be rude!"

A few of the other guests are now watching us with interest. Meryl appears next to Gabe, balancing a plate of appetizers atop a plastic cup of mango lassi. I steel myself. I won't let Ma walk all over me.

"Ma, I've told you a million times. I don't want to get married. Not now, maybe not ever. And I certainly don't want to get arrange-married. I can't believe you would ambush me like this!"

Ma stares at me as if she has no idea what I'm talking about. I turn to Ketan. "I'm sure you're great, but I don't want to be set up, okay? So, it was nice meeting you, but this"—I gesture between the two of us—"is a dead end." There is a long silence during which Ketan gawps at me, his chin retracted as if he's deciding whether to turn and run.

"I don't want to marry you," he says.

"What?" My mouth goes dry. I'm acutely aware of every head in the room swiveling toward us. No one wants to miss the unfolding of a train wreck.

"Yeah, I'm already engaged. So . . . I definitely don't want to get married . . . to you." He turns to Ma, whose mouth contorts so much that one side of it practically makes contact with her eyebrow.

"Norah, Ketan works at Vikram Uncle's company." Ma rubs her forehead. "I wanted him to talk to you about how great his job is."

"Oh, it's an awesome place to work. I love it," Ketan says quickly, looking around for an escape. "I'm going to just . . . food." He dissolves into the crowd.

My entire body cringes. My fingers and toes curl, and my head drops into my shoulders. I wish I could collapse in on myself and vanish, leaving only a dull gray cardigan crumpled on the floor to remember me by. "Ma, I'm sorry—"

Ma turns away, shaking her head, muttering angrily in Gujarati, and the guests turn back to their conversations. A few of them snicker quietly. I catch Meryl's eye, and she gives me a pained smile.

"I kind of want to kill myself," I whisper.

"Maybe just hide in the kitchen instead," she suggests, her hand on my shoulder.

When I duck back into the kitchen, Vikram Uncle has moved on to a tray of paneer tikka, and his mustache is tinged with bright orange sauce.

"So, Norah," he says, rolling the "r" in my name, "your ma says you need a job. Did you meet Ketan? First-class fellow. He works for me. He just bought a Mercedes."

"I have a job, Uncle."

He waves his hand. "You could have a first-class job at Shastri BioLabs: nine-to-five, a five-minute commute from your ma's house—you could live here! Plus health benefits, a 401(k) plan, paid vacation, and plenty of time for family life. What's more important than family life, right?"

"I don't know. Job fulfillment? Doing something meaningful with my life?" I'm skirting the edge of disrespectful behavior. I'm sure the Indian community gossip machine is already buzzing with news of my shameful outburst in the living room five minutes ago.

Vikram Uncle explodes into acerbic laughter. "Job fulfillment? You young people are hilarious. A job is for making money. When you're tired of all that *fulfillment*, let me know. I have a great *job* for you in my company." He laughs all the way into the living room, the cloying scent of his cologne trailing behind him.

Alone in the kitchen, I open the freezer door and lean in, letting the painfully cold air blast me in the face. I watch my breath turn to mist. I wonder if Gabe is right. Am I deluding myself about Ethan? I think there's something between us, but do I really *know* that? How do I prove it? I wish the scientific method could be applied to human attraction. I wish there were a randomized, controlled trial that could definitively determine if my crush likes me back.

My phone buzzes in the pocket of my cardigan. A text from Ethan: Hey, saw on the schedule that neither of us is on call this Friday. Any plans yet?

I hold my breath and text back, None.

Dinner? 7pm? There's a new place in Old City I want to check out.

I manage to resist the urge to squeal girlishly. Reena comes into the kitchen, her arms full of empty plates and teacups that she deposits in the sink. She glances at me.

"Looking for something?"

I shut the freezer door but keep hold of the handle. I'm afraid I might lift off the ground. "Nope. I'm good."

"Could you make another pot of chai?" she asks. "The aunties are going through it like water. You know how to make chai, right?" She arches an eyebrow skeptically and adjusts her sari.

Reena speaks fluent Gujarati and goes to India at least every other year. I, on the other hand, haven't been to India since I was five, and while I understand the language, can't speak it at all. It's been obvious for years that Reena judges me for being insufficiently Indian.

"Of course I do." I grab an enormous pot from the counter, rinse it out enthusiastically, and fill it with a gallon of milk. Then I set it to boil on the stove. "I've got this." I smile, barely able to control my glee and eager for Reena to leave the kitchen so I can reply to Ethan's text.

Reena nods slowly, doubtfully. "Okay, then. Let me know if you need help with it. The spices are in the cabinet above the microwave."

She goes back into the living room, looking over her shoulder at me as she does.

"I won't. I'm good. I'm golden!" I wave my hand reassuringly.

Once she's disappeared, I squeal giddily and text Ethan: Sure. Meet there?

I'll pick you up, he replies. We can share an Uber.

I text back a thumbs-up emoji and bite my lip, grinning. *This time, it's definitely a date,* I think. *Okay, focus and organize. First, Google how to make chai. Then, plan what I'm going to wear.*

CHAPTER NINE

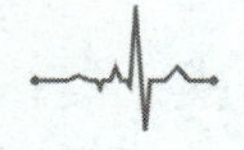

ASAP to 4th Floor Nursing Station, reads the text on my pager. I run up four flights of stairs to the ward.

"Intern!" a nurse says. A dark crescent of skin underlines each of her eyes, and a pack of cigarettes peeks out of the breast pocket of her scrubs. "You ordered urine output measurements on bed 19."

"Yes, I did," I say. "Dr. V wanted them."

"Well, I don't have time for that. You're going to have to get them yourself."

"The collection bag has to be emptied and measured every two hours."

"Right. You just pour the pee into a little cup and read off the volume." She folds her arms.

"But . . . I have a bunch of other patients I need to go check on, two patients in the ED to admit for Dr. V, and I have to go to the mandatory afternoon lecture." I smile and shrug helplessly. "There's no way I can get up here every two hours."

"Well, that's not my problem." She starts to walk away.

"Wait!"

She turns back.

"You're the nurse for bed 11, too, right?"

"So?"

"One of the other interns, Clark, asked you for urine outputs on bed 11 yesterday," I say.

"And?"

"I'm just asking for the same thing on my patient. I'm sorry . . . you know, Dr. V. . . ."

"Like I told you, I don't have time for that today." As she lumbers off, she mutters under her breath, "Get over it."

I watch her go.

A rhythmic clicking begins behind me, grows exponentially louder, then stops suddenly. I turn around to see Elle wearing knee-high black boots and, under her white coat, a V-neck cashmere sweater-dress.

"Come with me." Striding down the hallway, her heels striking the floor tiles loudly, she calls, "Excuse me!"

The nurse looks over her shoulder, and Elle, never slowing her pace, says, "Who do you think you're talking to?"

"This is between her and me," the nurse says. With a huff, she sinks into a padded office chair at the nurses' station and rests one elbow on the counter. "You're not involved here, honey."

Elle lifts the nurse's ID badge off her chest with one finger. "I can either give your name to the head of your department, Lydia, or you can decide to do your job. Your choice."

"That's not my job—"

"Yes, it is." Elle's voice is steady, almost pleasant, like an automated phone message. "Your problem is you don't want to get off your lazy ass and do it. So either get off your lazy ass, or I will see that it is handed to you on a plate. Honey."

I hold my breath. With a loud grunt, Lydia heaves herself from the chair and totters off toward bed 19, muttering. Elle smiles with satisfaction.

"You didn't have to do that," I say, grateful and impressed.

"Believe me, it was my pleasure. If you were a man, she would've been all, 'Right away, Doctor.'" As she turns to go, she says, "We women docs have to stick together, right?"

"Who do you think she's sleeping with?" Bianca twirls her fork, a sprig of lettuce waving from its prongs.

"Who?" Stuart says, looking up from his pocket version of Moore's *Neuroanatomy*. Bianca nods toward a table where Elle is having lunch surrounded by a throng of attentive male Surgery residents.

"You mean she's not sleeping with you?" Clark says. "Thanks for ruining that for me, Bee."

Bianca kicks him under the table. Then she says, "She's wearing the same outfit today as yesterday."

"They're scrubs," I say. "How can you tell?"

She nods knowingly. "I can tell."

"I hear she's . . . friendly," Stuart says.

Clark's expression is wistful. "I'd like to be her friend."

Bianca passes him a napkin. "Here. For your drool."

"You know, she's an excellent surgeon," I say, tapping a carrot stick on the table.

Bianca rests her chin in her hand. "I always see her hanging around Ethan. I bet the two of them are an item."

I break the carrot stick in half. "She's in the running for chief resident next year."

"I thought he was engaged," Stuart says.

Bianca waves her hand. "Ancient history. The fiancée left him."

"Right before the wedding," Clark says. "He's on the rebound."

"That was months ago," I say. "I'm sure he's moved on."

"No way," Bianca says. "He was with that Anesthesia girl for two years."

"You know what they say," Clark says, leaning back in his chair and putting both hands on his chest. "Nothing heals a broken heart like boobies." He jiggles his hands up and down. "Great big boobies."

"In medicine, we refer to those as 'pendulous breasts,'" Stuart says.

Clark points his fork at him. "Right you are, my friend. Great, big, pendulous mammary glands." He and Stuart snicker like naughty ten-year-old boys.

Bianca, ignoring them, purses her lips. "Ethan needs a fun, spontaneous girl. Elle's perfect for him."

"You think so?" I say. "You don't think she seems a bit intense? Maybe Ethan needs someone milder-mannered and more, you know . . . analytical."

"Analytical? That sounds boring." Bianca shakes her head. "Ethan's getting over a broken heart. He needs a firecracker, not a sedative."

I mutter something about having to check on a patient and flee to the gift shop. Ducking behind a row of greeting cards, I press my phone to my ear.

"What?" Meryl's voice is a high-pitched whine. "I can hardly hear you. Who's a firecracker?"

"Do you think I'm being paranoid?"

"About the Surgery chick? Probably not. What time is it?"

"Noon. Are you still in bed?"

She groans. "I was out late with Gabe last night. I don't think I'm going to see him anymore."

"Really?" I try to hide the relief in my voice. I'm not sure what Meryl ever saw in Gabe to begin with. "Why?"

"He told me"—she pauses for effect—"his SAT scores."

"I'm sorry?" I try to stifle a laugh.

"He's like, 'I got a 1500 on my SATs, what'd you get?'"

"Oh my goodness. That is . . . unusual."

"It's ridiculous. I mean, who even remembers their SAT scores? How is that relevant?"

"What did you say to him?"

"Well, I said that I think I got around 1250, and then he just sat back in his chair, all smug, like he'd accomplished something. I mean, is he serious?"

"He might be."

She sighs reluctantly. "I have to break up with him, right? I can't date someone who thinks he's better than me because he scored higher on his SATs."

"I'm sorry, Mer, I really am," I say.

She sighs again. "Tell me again why you're worried about the Surgery chick? You think she's dating your guy?"

"Ethan. His name's Ethan. But let's talk about it later. You have a lot going on."

"I probably shouldn't see him again, right?"

"I don't know," I say. "I'm going to dinner with Ethan tomorrow, and I'm not sure anymore if it's even a date or—"

There is a click, then, "Oh crap. That's Gabe on the other line," Meryl says.

"Go. I'll call you later."

"Are you sure?"

"Yes, go," I say, urging her off the line. She promises to call back later and hangs up.

A teddy bear holding a heart-shaped box of chocolates smirks at me from a shelf. I glare at it. *What are you looking at, you commercial product designed to make single women feel like garbage? Just so you know, I got a 1550 on my SATs . . . not that that's important. But still, I did.*

My feet hurt.

"I think it's down this alley here," Ethan says.

Loathe to drive on the cobblestoned side streets of Old City out of fear they might damage his car's shock absorbers, our splenetic Uber driver let us out at the major intersection nearest our destination.

An icy blast whips over my bare legs as I pick my way around a puddle of melting snow and cross the street, following Ethan. My cashmere V-neck sweaterdress ends at my mid-thigh, something that—along with my long-standing conviction that stockings are an extraneous piece of useless fashion—I deeply regret. Still, I affect what I'm pretty sure is a confident, breezy stride—the kind ebullient women in shampoo and feminine hygiene product commercials are always managing—until a sharp pain in my left ankle alerts me that the spiked heel of my knee-high black boot has become firmly wedged between two cobblestones. Ethan has disappeared around a corner.

Headlights flash in the shiny street, and I briefly consider the tragic headline "Outrageously Stylish Woman Crushed by Philadelphia Taxicab," while yanking desperately at my calf. Finally, I slip my foot out of the boot, wriggle the heel about to dislodge it, and hop madly to the curb.

"Found it!" Ethan reappears, his left eyebrow raised the way it always is when he's bemused. "What happened to you?"

I take a few careening steps. "I'm having technical difficulties with my footwear," I say. I smile and shrug. Confident and breezy. I cram my damp foot back into the boot, the heel of which has snapped off and now dangles from a thin strip of pleather.

"I think I found the place. Looks like it's a block up," he says, glancing at his watch. "We'd better hurry."

I nearly topple over, and Ethan grabs my elbow to steady me. "Whoa, technical difficulties? Norah, the heel's broken. You'll sprain your ankle."

Damn that discount shoe store on Chestnut Street. That's the last time I buy shoes from a store that purveys knockoff designer footwear *and* refurbished television sets.

"Should I get us a cab?" he asks. "Or carry you? To the nearest shoe store?"

I think for a moment. "No," I say, pulling off both of my boots. "You said it was only a block up. I'll sprint it."

"What? Barefoot? Are you sure?"

But I'm already trotting down the sidewalk on tiptoe. "Hurry! We'll miss our reservation!" I say buoyantly, just as I plunge ankle-deep in a frigid pool of runoff, the thought of athlete's foot and waterborne parasites flashing through my mind. I imagine Ethan, several paces behind, shaking his head and thinking, *She's so fun and spontaneous! So breezy!* Being with me is probably like a breath of fresh air after that awful breakup with his horrible fiancée. And why not? Why couldn't I be that effervescent type? The type that drinks to excess, doesn't consider the weather when selecting her clothing, is unexpectedly nonchalant about the necessity of footwear? I'm enjoying this new, vivacious persona, this side of me I've never allowed myself to have.

When I look back, Ethan is jogging to keep up. I grin at him. "It's cold!"

"You think?" He smiles, shaking his head, and I am momentarily lighter, and freer and happier with myself than I've ever been.

We miss our reservation.

The restaurant is, in fact, *several* blocks up, and by the time we arrive, my toes are dusky and stinging and I am fairly certain at least one of them will require amputation. The hostess gives us a look of disbelief and pity when we ask how long the wait might be for a table.

"It's Friday night," she says, before turning away.

I should probably be upset. I'm barefoot, my feet are wet and cold, and I'm hungry. But Ethan takes my hand, his fingers warm and strong around mine, and says, "I'm really sorry about this. Should we just get pizza?" and I grin as if he'd just suggested a trip to Disney World. Maybe we'll tell the story of this misadventure at our wedding someday.

At a hole-in-the-wall pizzeria across the street—the storefront sign of which features a buxom woman eating a slice of pizza, a string of melted cheese dripping into her cleavage—we stand at a high-top table surrounded by inebriated college students. I pull my boots back on and teeter back and forth on one heel.

"You sure you're okay? I could fight one of these guys for a booth," Ethan offers.

"No need. I'm great. I have the equilibrium of a mountain goat," I say.

"A mountain goat?"

"You know, on the mountains, they balance . . . so they don't fall off . . ." My voice fades. It's unlikely that confident, breezy women spend their evenings watching the National Geographic Channel.

"Sorry about this," he says. "This wasn't what I had in mind at all when I asked you to dinner."

"It's not so bad. And it's comforting to know that if one of these guys stops breathing due to alcohol poisoning, you're here to save him."

He smirks. "I'd probably call 911 and run in the other direction."

"No you wouldn't. Would you?"

"I never tell anyone what I do for a living. As soon as people find out, it's like, 'Hey, do you mind looking at this boil on my ass?'"

"That's probably awkward at parties," I say.

"That doesn't happen to you?"

"I get asked for advice every once in a while." The thought of Ma with her blood pressure cuff around her arm flashes through my mind. "Maybe more than once in a while."

He shakes his head. "The minute I set foot outside the hospital, I stop being a doctor. You have to have boundaries. Otherwise, it takes over your life. Heather would get so attached to her patients. She'd bring home all the stress, worrying about how this or that one did after their surgery. You can't function that way."

Wait. He just mentioned his ex-fiancée. On a date. Is *this a date?*

I hesitate for a moment, then ask casually, "So, what happened with you and Heather?"

He shrugs. "We met in med school, and I guess we just changed over the years. At the end we weren't the same people we started out as. You know how it is. Everything's great at the beginning, then you settle into a groove, then things just fizzle out. Just how it goes sometimes, right?"

I've been a distant witness to the ups and downs of romantic relationships by virtue of having been Meryl's friend for many years, but otherwise, I have a very limited frame of reference for this sort of thing. But I get it. I really do. It's like what happened between Rachel and Ross in the third season of *Friends*. Heartbreaking.

"That must have been really hard," I say sympathetically. "Kind of makes me glad I've never been in a serious relationship." I realize that throwing in the word "serious" is a little misleading, considering that I've never been in anything close to a romantic relationship, serious or otherwise, unless you count my many years of fervent devotion to Dakshesh McDermott, the imaginary boyfriend I created for myself when I was thirteen. For reference, all the seventh-grade girls were inventing imaginary boyfriends that year; it was a trend on par with butterfly clips and sweat pants with vague adjectives bedazzled across the butt. Dakshesh was, like me, Indian, not an athlete, interested in science. He thought I was beautiful and clever and would tell me so all the time. He was also a Jedi. He still pops up from time to time, arising from my subconscious to give me an encouraging shot on the arm or share my excitement over the latest issue of *Smithsonian* magazine. I'll always love Dakshesh.

"Never? Really?" Ethan looks surprised. "Why not?"

I hesitate, panicked. It's too much to explain, too awkward, too non-breezy: *I've had a very limited range of social experiences, for cultural reasons and because, to this point, I've been singularly focused on caring for my depressed mother while maintaining academic excellence, the result being that I've spent every Friday night for the past eight years in a library conversing with an imaginary boyfriend.*

"I don't like complicated relationships," I say, shrugging.

He nods in agreement. "I'm with you. You don't strike me as a high-maintenance kind of girl."

"Oh God, no," I say vehemently. "I'm like the polar opposite of high-maintenance. I'm like no-maintenance." It's the truth. If I had a boyfriend (a real one), I wouldn't be clingy or needy. I wouldn't expect flowers on Valentine's Day or a phone call every night. I wouldn't insist on being the center of his attention all the time. Just being the girlfriend of someone wonderful would be enough.

Ethan smiles. "I like that about you," he says.

There's an expectant pause, and I wonder if he's going to kiss me. I'm not even remotely religious, but this seems like a good time for a rapid, silent prayer: *God, please let him kiss me. I promise to be a good human being and contribute all I can to humanity if you'll just let him kiss me. Amen and namaste.* I lean toward him slightly, just as a drunk hipster with a flannel shirt careens into our table.

"Dude, watch your table," he slurs, then stumbles off.

The spell is broken.

Damn hipsters. If one of you stops breathing, I'm not helping save you either.

Two slices and a Diet Coke later, we summon another Uber, the back seat of which smells like garlic. A light snow has started to fall.

Ethan squeezes my knee. "That was fun."

"Yous guys new to Philly?" the driver, a man with sparse dentition, says.

Ethan and I exchange a glance. "Yes," we reply in unison.

"Well, over to your right is Independence Hall," the driver says. "Where the Founding Fathers signed the Declaration of Independence."

"Giving us freedom from the Japanese," Ethan says, grinning.

"From the British," the driver says, glancing over his shoulder at us. "The British."

"Ah, right," Ethan says. "My mistake."

We speed along Walnut Street toward City Hall.

"And on the other side of Independence Hall," the driver says, pointing, "is the Liberty Bell."

"One if by land, two if by sea," Ethan says.

"Boston Tea Party," I say, suppressing a smile.

"No, no," the driver says, his voice increasingly agitated. "That was in Boston. This bell had nothing to do with Boston or Paul Revere."

"Really? You sure?" Ethan asks.

"Am I sure? Yes, I'm sure," the driver says, twisting nearly the entire way around in his seat. "Now if you go this way for another mile or so, you'll be at the art museum. Worth a visit. Best art museum on the East Coast, hands down."

"Somebody famous ran up the steps, right?" I say. "In that movie . . . *Hercules*?"

"I think it was Clint Eastwood," Ethan says. "Yeah, definitely Eastwood."

"Sylvester Stallone!" The driver nearly swerves into a lamppost as he screeches to a halt in front of my building. "In *Rocky*! Stallone! Geez, Christ almighty."

I climb out, holding my breath, weighing my options: I could say good night. Or I could do something a confident, spontaneous person would do.

I turn to Ethan and say, "So, do you want to come up—"

"Thomas Jefferson lived on the next block!" the driver says, as the car lurches ahead and the door slams shut, narrowly missing Ethan's fingers. They speed away.

"Right," I say aloud.

I am putting my key in the lock when my phone rings. I smile. "Hi."

"Hi."

I can hear the driver shout, "Seventeen seventy-six!" in the background.

"Want to see a movie tomorrow night?" Ethan says. "I hear they're showing all six *Rocky*s at the Ritz."

"Perfect."

I am soaking my feet in the tub, blissfully indulging in a minute-by-minute review of the evening's events, when my phone rings again.

"Norah!" Clark's voice is thin and desperate. He groans, and the sound echoes.

"Clark? Where are you?"

"The can." He groans again. "It's a beast!"

"What's a beast?"

"I'm dying! Could I have cholera?"

"I don't think so. You sound awful."

"I don't know which end to point at the toilet."

I cringe. "That's . . . more vivid than I needed it to be. Do you need meds? Do you need to go to the ED?"

"No, but I'm on call tomorrow. Can you cover for me?"

"I wish I could, but—"

"You're my last hope, Norah. Bianca's in New York, and Stuart's grandmother is celebrating her bicentennial or something. Imani is on tonight, so that just leaves you. I would owe you, big-time."

"It's just that . . . I have something important tomorrow, you know?"

"I guess I'll survive." He sighs weakly.

I try to ignore the guilt needling at my chest from the inside, like something sharp lodged in my esophagus. Then I hear myself say, "You know, it's okay, I can reschedule." I smack myself on the forehead. *Stupid, stupid, stupid.*

"You sure? Great! Thanks a million, Norah."

"No problem," I say. "Hope you—"

He hangs up.

I text Ethan—sorry! covering for clark tomorrow. stomach virus—and am settling into bed when he replies, hmm . . . virus or hangover? night, peanut butter. xo jelly.

Thirty-six hours later, I stand, gloved and gowned, at the foot of an operating table.

"Nadine! How many times do I have to page you?"

"Once, Terry," I say. "You only have to page me once."

He scowls behind his surgical mask. "Then why did I have to page you four times before you responded?"

"I was in the ICU. A patient coded and I was doing chest compressions."

"Well, in that case, you should have told a nurse to return your pages."

I'm scowling now. "I'm sorry, but that didn't occur to me, since I was preoccupied with the impending death of my patient."

A bead of sweat drips from Terry's forehead into the open body cavity on the table.

"Terry! Goddamn it, why do you sweat so much?" Dr. V says. "Go towel off. If this patient dies of an infection, you're fired."

Terry slinks away from the table with a shamed expression. He stands silently, his gloved hands clasped in front of him and dripping blood onto the floor, while a tiny nurse with a hand towel climbs a step stool and begins mopping sweat off his face and neck.

"Intern," Dr. V says, without looking up, "I need you to do something for me. It's very important."

I sigh quietly while clenching my fists. I only have two more weeks to go on this service. *I can do this.*

Forty minutes later, I pull Dr. V's Aston Martin up to the towering wrought iron gates that mark the entrance to his driveway. A little gold plaque is engraved with the words *Le Cœur*. The Heart.

"You have arrived," the British female voice of the navigation system says.

I certainly have.

The gates swing open, and two conspicuous security cameras peer down and rotate to follow the car as I steer it into the long, tree-lined driveway. Carefully, I maneuver around a tiered stone fountain, coming to a stop in front of a brick-faced Georgian mansion with a sprawling portico. A red Toyota Rav4 is parked there, too. *Probably the cleaning lady*. A little painted sign on a footpath nearby reads *Pool and Courts*, with an arrow pointing off into the distance.

I climb the front steps and try several keys on Dr. V's key chain before I find the one that fits the door lock. Dark hardwood floors line the entryway, which is decorated with tall potted palm trees and a white leather chaise. I glance at my palm, where I have scrawled *left up stairs, second right, 3rd closet, side pocket*. I climb the gracefully curving staircase, pass a landing with a nondescript bust on a pedestal, turn left at the top, and make my way to the second door on the right. Stepping into the master suite, I notice that the delicate, Caribbean-style canopy bed is unmade. I imagine that Mrs. V awoke at a leisurely hour this morning and flitted downstairs in her robe for crepes and café latte, prior to heading out for her twice-weekly spa appointment. *Must be nice*.

On the dresser is a collection of family photographs in silver frames. In one, a stunning woman I assume is Mrs. V smiles at an adorable girl and boy in matching sailor outfits. I'm careful not to touch anything. On a shelf in the third closet along the wall I find a brown briefcase, and in its side pocket, a USB drive. Now for the forty-minute drive back to the hospital.

I spot a framed wedding picture on one of the nightstands and am admiring it when a woman appears from the adjoining bathroom, wearing a silk robe and slippers. She recoils and steps back into the doorway, then realizes I've spotted her.

"Norah! What are you doing here?"

It's Elle.

I fumble for words, any words, to make this less mortifying. "He forgot this," I say, holding up the thumb drive. I realize my mouth is open. I clamp it shut.

Elle sweeps her hair over one shoulder and crosses her arms, her expression worried and sheepish. "Listen, don't mention this to anyone, okay? You know how rumors get around."

"Oh, don't worry about it." I do my best to feign insouciance while quickly calculating the implications: Elle, whom I've regarded as a role model to this point, is sleeping with an attending, presumably to get ahead. Is this why Dr. V always seems to choose her, out of all the Surgery residents, to assist on his cases? Is this why she was nominated for chief resident? Do the other Surgery residents know?

"Really, please don't say anything," she says. "This isn't what it looks like. We've talked about marriage and everything."

"Oh." I nod while raising my eyebrows. The catchall expression. "That's nice. I won't say anything. Who would I tell, anyway?"

"Thank you. For not saying anything. Thank you in advance."

She glances at me with hesitation, then disappears into the bathroom.

Back behind the wheel of the car, I dial Meryl's number.

"Elle is sleeping with an attending!" I'm relieved and confused at the same time. "Not with Ethan, with an attending. I just caught her at his house wearing a bathrobe."

"The Surgery girl?" Meryl says. "Wow. Isn't that an ethics violation? It's one thing to date another resident, but the attending is the doctor in charge of everyone, right? Wait, is this Dr. Dry Cleaning we're talking about?"

"It is."

"That son of a bitch. He really thinks he can get away with anything, doesn't he? You should report him. He should be fired."

"I don't know. . . . Elle said something about them getting married. . . ."

"Isn't he already married?"

"Yeah, but—"

"Both of them should be fired."

"I promised Elle I wouldn't say anything. Besides, it's not my business." I pull the car onto the highway.

Meryl sighs, disappointed that I don't share her righteous outrage. After a moment, she says, "How do you know this Elle isn't sleeping with Dr. Dry Cleaning *and* with Ethan?"

This is an idea I hadn't considered. The thought makes me queasy. "How much free time could she have? That's a lot of work, carrying on secret affairs with two men."

"All I know," Meryl says, "is that people will always make time for sex."

I weigh the validity of this statement all the way back to the hospital. By the time I pull Dr. V's car into the parking deck, I've dismissed it as baseless nonsense.

CHAPTER TEN

My ten weeks with General Surgery completed, I start my rotation on the Oncology service.

"Intern," a nurse says as soon as the elevator doors slide open. "Room 12 wants to see a doctor. She was admitted last night. You're late, by the way."

I drop my bag at the nurses' station, don my white coat, drain my coffee cup, and find room 12. My eyes adjust to the dim light.

"Finally," a man says. "We've been waiting to see someone all morning."

His voice sounds familiar, but I can't place it. As they come into focus, I realize it's the dour look-alike couple from the ED three months ago, the Tallys. Mrs. Tally is propped up in bed, pillows supporting every extremity, a tray of food on the bedside table in front of her. Her husband crosses his arms.

"You're the doctor?" he says.

"Yes, we met in the Emergency Department a few months ago," I say.

"Okay. So, the last time we were here, my wife must have told you her medical history."

"Yes, she did."

"So how do you explain this?" He points to the tray. Mrs. Tally looks at me expectantly.

"How do I explain . . . what?" I ask.

"This. *This*," Mr. Tally says, pointing with increased vigor.

"The breakfast tray?"

"Right. What is on the breakfast tray?"

"It's bacon . . . and an egg sandwich."

"An egg sandwich with what?"

"I'm sorry, I'm not sure what we're talking about."

"What is on the egg sandwich, Doctor?" he says. His wife's expression has not changed.

"It looks like cheese and tomato."

"Tomato. TOMATO!" says Mr. Tally.

"TOMATO!" says Mrs. Tally.

"Tomato," I say, nodding slowly.

"I'm severely allergic to tomatoes!" Mrs. Tally says. "I told you that. I've told everyone that."

"What happens when you eat tomatoes?" I ask.

She leans forward and enunciates each word. "Severe . . . acid . . . reflux."

I take a deep breath through my nose. "I understand why you're upset, but a true medical allergy means you go into anaphylaxis or get a rash or hives or something like that. Acid reflux isn't considered an allergy."

Her expression is blank.

"Medically speaking," I say.

"I'm allergic to tomatoes," she says.

"And what about her biopsy results?" her husband asks.

"Biopsy?"

"Of the thing in her lung."

"What thing?"

Mr. Tally throws up his hands in frustration. "None of you people have any answers! Why isn't she on an antibiotic for her pneumonia?"

There is a flurry of activity at the door, and a diminutive man with a prominent bald spot enters, followed by Ethan, two second-year residents, and several medical students.

"*Here's* the intern," the small man says, somehow regarding me without looking directly at me. "Glad you decided to join us, Doctor. On my service we start rounds at exactly six a.m."

One of the students hands him a chart. I glance at my watch. It is 6:08.

"Are you always this late?" the small man asks.

"No, sir," I say. "I'm sorry. I was speaking with this patient—"

"Either come in on time, or don't come in at all, understand?"

I nod, my face burning. Ethan smiles at me sympathetically.

"All right." He tucks the chart under his arm and turns to the Tallys. "I'm Gaylord Portnoy, head of Oncology. You have cancer. Non-small-cell carcinoma of the lung, according to the biopsy. This is a very treatable form of lung cancer. We'll begin chemotherapy immediately." He walks out of the room, his gaggle trailing behind him.

Mrs. Tally's mouth opens. Her husband stoops forward, leaning against the bed rail for support. He looks up at me, his expression pleading. "They said it was just a mass. They told us it probably wasn't dangerous."

"We're going to take good care of her," Ethan says, smiling encouragingly from the doorway.

"It's *cancer*?" Mr. Tally continues, his voice increasingly panicked. "They told us it was a growth. They didn't say it was cancer. No one ever said the word 'cancer.'"

Ethan takes a few steps back into the room. "I know this is a lot to process right now. But your wife is in excellent hands. I'll have one of the residents come back after rounds to explain the chemotherapy to you and answer any questions you have." He smiles again and turns to go, saying over his shoulder, "Norah, keep up."

My mind reels. *What the hell just happened? That* was the man, the legend? That petulant, heartless leprechaun? I glance at the Tallys, then hurry to catch up with Ethan and the rest of the group making its way to the next room.

We round on seventeen other patients. As we move from one bedside to the next, Dr. Portnoy quizzes us about chemotherapy regimens and patterns of metastatic spread of different types of cancer. The other residents answer eagerly. They seem grateful to be at the feet of a master. I, however, can't manage to produce, from my addled mind, the correct answer to even one of Portnoy's questions. I keep picturing Mrs. Tally sitting in bed, her mouth agape, stunned. *Cancer*, and her whole life tilted on its axis and fell apart.

It's still weighing on my mind later that day, as Ethan and I wait in line on the sidewalk at a lunch truck, watching as a sweaty man with a prominent belly threads meat onto skewers. "What was that this morning?" I ask. "With the lady with the non-small-cell lung cancer? Portnoy just dropped that bomb on them and left."

"That's why they call him Lord Portnoy." Ethan studies the chalkboard menu posted on the side of the truck. "The Lord giveth the diagnosis. He doesn't have time to coddle."

"She thought she had pneumonia."

He shrugs. "She hit the cancer lottery. She has the most treatable form of lung cancer there is, and the best oncologist in the country. She's gonna be fine."

"You really want to spend another year working for that guy?"

"I know he doesn't have the warmest personality," Ethan says, "but the man's a legend, and for good reason. If I had to trim his dog's toenails every weekend for a year in exchange for being his fellow, it'd be worth it."

"I'm guessing it's a pretty competitive fellowship?"

"Last year there were 250 applicants for two spots."

"But you've worked with him for three years as a resident, so you have an advantage, right? As opposed to a resident applying from a different hospital."

"Not necessarily. He's easy to piss off. I'm just praying I stay on his good side. That's kind of how it works. The better you are at your job, the more of a prima donna you can be. And Portnoy's the most prima of prima donnas. What do you want to eat? I'm buying."

"Anything. A sandwich. Maybe something with cheese. Or whatever you're having," I say.

He orders us both grilled cheese and, as we wait, nudges me playfully with his elbow. "So, I've been thinking. How would you feel about me taking you out someplace that doesn't involve drunk college guys and pizza?"

I shrug nonchalantly and say, "Sure, sounds good," but can't stop my face from lighting up. How would you feel about *me taking you out*? This time, he's definitely asking me out on a date. I'm almost certain. I don't ask for clarification; that doesn't strike me as consistent with my new casual, confident attitude. Instead, I decide to let the evidence speak for itself.

Lately, I've been thinking about Baltimore. Ethan's whole family lives there, and he plans to move back there to practice after Portnoy's fellowship. I've been to Baltimore only once, on a middle school field trip, but—if the quality of its aquarium is any indication—I'm certain I would love it there. I daydream about the future: a charming little house in a quaint neighborhood walking distance from shops and restaurants, Ethan and I maybe commuting to work together. I'd drive up on alternate weekends to help out with Ma, of course. I've mapped the route online and, as long as we live north of the Washington Beltway, the trip would take less than three hours during off-peak traffic times. I know it's just a fantasy, but I think it's important that even fantasies be well-researched.

"Norah?" Ethan's voice is an intimate whisper in the darkness.

I don't open my eyes. "Yes?" My mouth curls into a coy half smile.

"Fat Dan has no blood pressure."

My shins hit the wooden coffee table, the pain nearly knocking the wind out of me, and I grope about the chair cushions for my glasses. Across the room, Ethan is illuminated by the light from the lounge vending machine. We're both covering the Intensive Care Unit tonight. This is my first time assigned to ICU call.

Ethan glances at his pager, stretches, and scratches his chin. "Break's over." He springs to his feet.

Fat Dan has been in ICU bed 7 for months. No one really remembers the circumstances surrounding his admission to the hospital. The residents who looked after him in those first few weeks—before he was placed on a ventilator in a chemically induced coma—have graduated, and most of the nurses who were assigned to him have been transferred to other departments. As a result, Fat Dan has become something of a legend at Philadelphia General, mythic in his ability to skirt death at every juncture. Like all mythical heroes, however, he has one great, tragic flaw: Samson had his hair, Achilles had his heel, Fat Dan has gangrene. The surgeons have been amputating different bits and parts of his infected foot every week: the black, shriveled toes went first, then a piece of the swollen forefoot, then a necrotic chunk out of his heel. While that was happening, his kidneys failed, a piece of his large intestine died and had to be surgically removed, and he had a stroke that rendered him paralyzed on one side. There's no question that he won't survive for much longer but, according to the senior residents, that's entirely beside the point.

"Norah, Fat Dan can't die on our watch," Ethan says as we sprint up the stairwell. "I bet Isaac a thousand bucks he wouldn't croak until after I graduate."

The glass doors of the Intensive Care Unit slide open, and a familiar, fetid odor wafts over us. "Has that gotten stronger? You can smell that foot infection from the elevator," I say, wrinkling my nose.

"You can smell it from the parking lot. As of this morning, he has the holy triad. That's never a good sign."

"What's the holy triad?"

"Pacemaker, feeding tube, colostomy," Ethan says, tracing a triangle over his torso.

A group of nurses, like a well-organized guard in formation, has surrounded the bed. Dan's turgid, protuberant belly—a lattice of tortuous blue veins stretched across taut and nearly translucent skin—is all that is visible. His body shudders with the ebb and flow of oxygen from the ventilator, making him look like a giant, quivering jellyfish.

The ICU head nurse is a man with silver hair wearing scrubs and a hoodie with the Philadelphia General logo—two doves joined at their beaks to form a heart—embroidered on the front. "Hi, Ethan," he says, smiling apologetically. "His blood pressure tanked all of a sudden."

Ethan pulls gloves over his hands. "You've checked all the usual suspects?"

"Several times."

"EKG?"

"They did one about two hours ago. It was normal."

"New medicines?"

"Zynexa and Levophed."

"Let me see the stump."

The nurse draws back the sheet and unwraps the gauze bandages. I gasp. All that remains of the foot is a dusky knob of flesh dotted with white droplets of pus.

"I see the surgeons are still trying to save the foot," Ethan says, placing his stethoscope on Dan's chest.

The head nurse sighs. "Yes, they are. Even though that's the leg that's paralyzed." The heart monitor beeps more rapidly. "What do you think?" His tone is casual, but his eyes dart between the bed and the monitors.

"Shhh." Ethan's brow is furrowed.

The beeping becomes erratic, and the heart monitor emits warning chimes.

"Where's the EKG?" he asks.

"It's on the electronic chart," the nurse says. "But the system is down."

Ethan pulls the stethoscope from his ears. "You're kidding."

"It's been hit or miss since this afternoon. The IT department is working on it."

"I need to see that EKG. There's no time to do another one."

"They store the hard copies in the Cardiology department."

Ethan's shoulders drop. The Cardiology department is on the other side of the hospital. The heart monitor alarms loudly.

"V-tach, v-tach!" the head nurse announces urgently. He hands Ethan a pair of electrical paddles.

"Clear!" Ethan shouts. Dan's chest recoils and shudders with the jolt.

"Start chest compressions and give epinephrine," Ethan says. "Norah, do you know where Cardiology is?"

A lone nurse making rounds watches with raised eyebrows as I come flying down the corridor, sneakers squeaking, coat trailing behind me.

"EKGs, I need current-patient EKGs! It's an emergency," I say to the night clerk at the desk. He points to a towering filing cabinet in a corner. I yank open the drawer marked *ICU* while dialing Ethan's phone number.

"You found the hard copy?" His voice is nearly drowned out by the alarms.

"Yes," I say, my pulse pounding as I scan the undulating lines of the EKG. The automatic computer readout—*NORMAL STUDY*—is printed across the top of the pink-and-white graph paper.

"And? Is it normal?"

"It says 'Normal Study.'"

"But does it look normal to you?" Ethan says.

I hesitate. Something isn't right. The waves alternate in size: big wave, little wave, big wave, little wave.

"Shock him again!" Ethan says. "Norah? Norah?"

"No, it's electrical alternans."

"Are you sure?"

"I think so."

"Norah, I'm going to tap him. Are you sure?"

My mouth goes dry. Ethan is preparing to put a needle into Dan's chest to drain the fluid that, presumably, is compressing his heart. If I'm wrong, the needle could puncture Dan's heart and kill him.

"Yes, I'm sure."

I hear him take a breath. "Okay."

I arrive back at the ICU, clutching the EKG, in time to see Ethan pull a syringe full of blood from Dan's chest. He smiles with relief as, a few moments later, the heart monitor resumes a sprightly rhythm. The nurses clap him on the back and file out of the room, rubbing their eyes.

"Get a Cardiology consult," Ethan says. "Why this guy bled into his pericardial sac, I have no idea."

The head nurse gives him a thumbs-up from the doorway. "Will do, boss." Then, thrusting his fists into the air triumphantly, he calls over his shoulder, "Fat Dan lives!"

"A normal blood pressure!" I say, grinning at Ethan over Dan's stomach.

"Yup, a normal blood pressure," he says. "Good work. Most interns wouldn't know what electrical alternans looks like. Where'd you learn that?"

"You," I say proudly. "You were talking about it at lunch a couple of weeks ago, so I read about it."

He laughs. "Do you always pay such close attention to what I say at lunch?"

I feel myself turning red and look at the floor. "I guess I do."

Ethan leans across the bed and there, above Fat Dan's fetid corpse of a foot, the incessant clacking of the ventilator in the background, he kisses me.

I've only been kissed once before. It was at the end of a party in medical school, a school-sponsored mixer for first-years at the Philadelphia Zoo. More specifically, in front of the bat habitat in the Small Mammal House at the Philadelphia Zoo. Why the Small Mammal House is a party venue, I'm not sure. It's dark and smells like bat feces—a smell reminiscent of basement mold and spoiled produce—and just under the pounding bass beat played by the DJ is the constant sound of flapping wings pounding against the glass of the bat enclosure. There was no alcohol served at the party, but a drunken classmate cornered me to profess, "My mother would love it if I brought home someone like you, Norah," and planted a sloppy, beer-infused kiss half on my mouth and half on my chin before staggering off into the darkness, never to speak to me again. The experience, wholly underwhelming, made me feel dull and insignificant. Not unlike a small mammal.

Ethan's kiss is quick, deliberate, and perfect. As he pulls away, he glances into my eyes and grins mischievously, then turns his attention back to Fat Dan's heart monitor.

My heart explodes.

It's like fireworks. Like a lightning strike.

It's like being defibrillated and brought back to life.

* * *

I awake the next morning with a start. I flail about frantically for my glasses, then for my pager. No, I haven't missed any calls. I've been asleep in a call room for forty blissfully quiet minutes. The last time I saw Ethan, he was headed to the ED. I wonder if he got a chance to sleep at all. I think about his lips on mine and marvel that anyone could be expected to work and carry on as usual when something so momentous transpired just a few hours ago. What I feel in my chest can't be contained. I want to pry open the rusted call room window and shout from it, to let the rollicking joy come tumbling out of my mouth. But I'm also sleep-deprived and exhausted, and it's all I can do to lift my head off the pillow.

As I stretch my legs, the ancient mattress springs creak beneath me. I pull off my sneakers and rifle through my duffel bag for flip-flops. I grab a tiny bar of hospital soap from the sink in the corner, pull the door shut behind me, and make my way down the silent hallway, rubbing the sleep out of my eyes.

Entering the ladies' washroom, I encounter a blast of steam. Elle, naked in a shower missing a curtain, says, "Oh, hi, Norah. I didn't realize there was another girl here today. I'm almost done."

I avert my eyes. "Take your time," I say. I am acutely aware of the diminutive size of my breasts. "Are there any towels in here?" I focus my attention on a linen cart.

"I think so. How was call last night?" she asks.

"Busy. Fat Dan's circling the drain."

"Again? I'm sorry, but that guy needs to die already."

"He needs to make it another six months. Ethan has a thousand dollars riding on him."

She laughs and shakes her head. "Ethan. He's crazy."

"How was your night?" I ask. "Busy?"

"Oh, I'm just getting started. Hopefully it'll be a quiet day.

Sundays sometimes are." She turns off the water and wraps herself in a towel.

"Do you always shower at work?"

"Not always. Just when I sleep here."

"But you weren't on call last night?"

"No."

"But you slept here?"

She smiles at me over her shoulder. "Uh-huh." Any sheepishness she might have felt the last time we met seems to be gone now.

I have so many questions. How long has she been sleeping with Dr. V? Does anyone else know about this? Does she feel like being Dr. V's mistress is the only way to get ahead as a Surgery resident? Doesn't the wrongness of it all bother her? Or is this a necessary evil for a greater good? After all, she's in training to save lives. I stay quiet. It's none of my business, and I'm not sure I really want to know the answers.

Elle slips into a pair of scrubs, quickly outlines her eyes with gray eyeliner, and pulls her hair into a high ponytail.

"Bye, Norah," she says with a wave, and is gone.

I shower quickly and put on a fresh pair of scrubs. I pull my hair into a high ponytail. I debate whether I should start wearing eyeliner.

Stuart springs up from the orange sofa in the residents' lounge when I enter. "Hi!" he says, wound with energy. "Anything interesting going on? What's up? Need help?" There are three empty coffee cups on the table in front of him. I sift through the throng of white coats hanging from pegs on the wall.

"Good morning," I say. "No, just looking for my coat, thanks."

"Right. But I mean, after that, what are you going to do?"

"Round. You know, just like every day."

"Right. Need help? I can come with you."

"Come with me to round? Don't you need to round on your own patients?"

"Oh, I finished that hours ago."

"Weren't you on call last night, too?"

"Yeah, yeah." He cracks his neck and bounces from one foot to the other.

"Aren't you tired? Don't you want to get some sleep?"

"No, no, I'm good."

"Stuart, is everything okay?"

He nods rapidly, as if his head is on a spring. His eyes dart about. I notice that his once pristine white coat is dingy around the cuffs. It probably hasn't been laundered in weeks. "I don't want to go in the call room."

"Why not?"

"They have me bunking with Blake, the Emergency Medicine resident." He rubs his temples.

"And he snores?"

"He's into watching some weird sci-fi porn on the computer in there."

"Sci-fi porn? As in people dressed up as—"

"Aliens. Yeah."

"But it's five o'clock in the—"

"Yeah."

"And he'll watch it even if there's someone else—"

"Yeah."

"I have to draw a blood gas."

"Great! Let's go."

Minutes later, holding a needle and test tube, I stare at the steady pulsing of an artery in a patient's wrist, my mouth dry.

"Got this?" Stuart says. "Or you want me to do it?"

I pass the needle to him and step away. "I'll do the next one."

The patient regards me doubtfully.

"I'm just going to draw some blood from the artery in your wrist. It hurts a little, but it's quick," Stuart says calmly. He jabs the needle through the man's skin. The man winces and grabs my hand as if he might arm-wrestle me. The test tube fills with blood, and Stuart withdraws the needle.

"Damn! You're good. That wasn't as bad as I thought," the man says. He wipes the corners of his eyes. One would never guess that the patient, sixty-five and tawny with barely a wrinkle, has stage-four renal cancer if it wasn't for the fact that he's lost his hair and, therefore, has no eyebrows. Stuart presses a square of gauze over the man's wrist. His pager sounds, and he frowns in my direction. "It's Francesca. Gotta run. Can you hold pressure?"

We've been trained that, after puncturing a patient's artery, pressure should be held over the site for at least two minutes. "Sure. Thanks, Stuart," I say, taking his place at the bedside. Stuart waves and is gone, and I can't help but feel decidedly inadequate compared to him. He makes everything look so easy.

The patient interrupts my thoughts. "Let me ask you something, Doc."

"Sure, okay. Ask away." I smile down at him.

"This chemo I'm on"—he points to the IV bag dangling from the pole next to the bed—"you know anything about it?"

"I've read about it."

"And you've read my chart?"

I nod.

"So, what are my chances of getting better?"

"Well, there's a study in the *New England Journal*," I say, proud to have some useful, current information. I might be developing some sort of phobia of needles, but I can still memorize facts just as well as Stuart can. "It just came out six months ago. It says that, for your type of kidney cancer, with the treatment you're having, the average five-year survival is forty-five percent."

"Forty-five?" the patient says. He takes a long breath. Then he says slowly, "You mean to tell me that I'm going through all this—the tubes, throwing up, peeing in a bag—for worse odds than flipping a coin?"

I hesitate. I hadn't anticipated that sharing this information would upset him. "I can get you a copy of the article . . . ," I say, my voice trailing off.

"Why didn't anyone tell me? Why didn't my doctor, Dr. Portnoy, tell me this?"

"I don't . . . I'm not sure," I say.

"Do you know when Dr. Portnoy told me I had cancer, he just said the word 'cancer' and left the room?" The man's face reddens. "He had his student, the resident or whatever, explain the treatment to me. Can you believe that? That made me furious. I know the guy's supposed to be the best, but he's an ass when it comes to bedside manner."

"I know he can come off a little uncaring," I say, trying to course correct, "but he's really a great doctor. You're in excellent hands. And we can help you with the side effects of the chemo."

The patient shakes his head and indicates his surroundings. "This isn't what I want. This isn't living. You're barely human in here. And I think, according to your study, that I've been in this goddamn hospital for three weeks when I should have been at home enjoying what quality of life I have left."

"I just . . . know what the study says," I reply, shifting uncomfortably.

The patient says nothing for a moment. Then, he extends his hand. "What was your name again, Doc?"

"Kapadia."

"Thank you, Dr. Kapadia. And I think I would like a copy of that article."

My pager sounds later that morning, just after I've poured milk over my cereal. A resident at another table smiles at me sympathetically, shrugging her shoulders as if to say, *Isn't that always the way?* I cram as many Frosted Flakes into my mouth as possible while dialing the callback number from the wall phone in the cafeteria.

"We have another patient who fell out of bed," the nurse on the other end says.

I groan. "How many does that make since yesterday?"

Her voice weary, the nurse says with a sigh, "Six. Although this is a repeat offender."

Rounding a corner on the Oncology floor five minutes later, I see Clark, standing before an audience of nubile student nurses, dip his pinky into a stool sample and taste it as if it were a bit of exotic caviar. I smirk as the girls erupt in shrieks of horror. Clark's melted-chocolate-looks-like-stool routine never fails to cheer me up.

It's 9:45 a.m., and my weekend call shift is almost over. *Only fifteen more minutes.*

I enter a room to find the Tallys with their arms crossed, glaring.

"Why are there so many electrical cords in here? She could have broken a bone!" Mr. Tally says. I've stopped expecting from him the formal greeting that accompanies most normal human interaction.

"Mrs. Tally, once again, you are not supposed to get out of bed," I say. "The nurse reviewed the falls precautions with you, right?"

Mrs. Tally sighs in frustration, folding and unfolding the bedsheet on top of her. "Yes, she did, practically a hundred times. But how am I supposed to go to the bathroom?"

"You ring the call button and your nurse will take you," I say.

"I don't want to bother someone every time I need to use the hopper. I birthed four children; I pee all the time." She offers her arm. "It's just a scrape."

"Your chemotherapy is affecting the nerves in your feet that control your balance. Relax your arm for me." I flex and extend her elbow and press into the springy fat of her forearm. "Does this hurt? No? Good. Call your nurse next time. I promise they won't mind."

"Oh, okay, okay," she says, her eyes on the television high on the far wall.

I hurriedly scribble in the chart *Called to see patient status post fall out of bed with complaint of left upper limb trauma. Patient examined. No tenderness to palpation of the limb. Full range of motion*. I sign my name and note the time, then head for the elevator. Just as the door is sliding shut, a hand appears to stop it. Mr. Tally steps inside and turns to face forward, his hands clasped over his abdomen.

"Cafeteria?" I say.

He nods. I push the "2" button and notice a text message from Ethan: Movie today?

I grin and struggle briefly to compose a clever reply before finally typing: Sure. Where? When?

Matinee? Ritz? They're showing some old movie, he sends back. The elevator lurches. Mr. Tally has pushed the Emergency button and we are stopped between floors. I glance at him, my pulse quickening.

"No one in this place gives you a straight answer," he says, his eyes on the floor. I reach into my pocket to arm myself with keys. I wish I still had that mini pepper spray key chain Ma gave me when I went to college.

"Doc, I need to know. Is my wife going to die?" Shoulders sagging, eyebrows overgrown, and a button-down shirt that barely closes over his rotund midsection, he is harmless, I realize.

"She's in excellent hands," I say brightly.

"But what she has, it's very dangerous, right?"

"Oh, she has one of the most treatable forms of lung cancer, and Dr. Portnoy is the best oncologist in the country. She's going to be fine."

"What will she be like after all this? The side effects of the chemo, I've heard, can last forever. She's losing her balance, and her personality. . . . She's so depressed. Will she be the woman I married? I'm already losing her, bit by bit."

"Well, it's best to take this sort of thing one day at a time," I say, reaching past him to push the Emergency button, starting the elevator moving again. "But I can order a Psychiatry consult for her. They can help her with the depression." The doors slide open on the second floor, and he steps out.

"Okay, sure. That may help. Sorry I stopped the elevator. Thanks, Doc."

I wonder momentarily if I should get out, too, offer to sit with him for coffee. I sense he himself could use someone to talk to. But I'm exhausted, and I remember what Ethan said about the importance of having boundaries. So instead I smile, nod, and press the button for the ground floor.

Sure! See you there! I text to Ethan as I cross the towering, sunny lobby lined on either side by leather armchairs and pass under a sprawling fresco of Hippocrates swearing his oath painted over the threshold.

"So, he just stopped the elevator? Without any explanation?"

We are the lone patrons at the Sunday 11:45 a.m. showing of *Casablanca*. On the screen, Rick and Ilsa drive through Paris in a montage of pre–World War II reverie.

"Yeah, but it wasn't creepy or anything," I say, yawning. "Not really."

He reaches into the box of popcorn on my lap. "That guy's a

prick. Everything's your fault, no matter what." He scrunches his forehead and says in a gruff voice, "'The TV's not working and I'm constipated. And you call yourself a doctor!'"

I laugh so hard I snort. I am both startled and ashamed. Ethan grins.

"I can't take you anywhere." He puts his hand on my knee, and an effervescent rush of butterflies shoots through my body and out the tips of my fingers and toes, taking my fatigue with it. His warm breath on my bare shoulder draws me toward him. As his lips move toward mine, I am vaguely aware of the box of popcorn slipping from my grasp, spilling kernels all over the floor.

It's curious that a culture that created the Kama Sutra is so buttoned up about sex. If you asked Ma if she would rather that one of her children engaged in premarital sex versus became a cocaine addict, she'd struggle to choose the lesser of the evils. Sex is so taboo a topic in my family, it was simply never spoken of, in any way, by anyone. If it came up on a television show, Ma immediately switched the channel. If I insisted on asking where babies came from and wasn't satisfied that they came from God or were delivered via FedEx, she sent me to my room. Ma wasn't only actively discouraging me from learning anything about sex, she was trying to fashion a reality in which it didn't exist.

I was twelve before the mechanics of human reproduction suddenly became clear to me while watching an animated video in Health class titled *Sexual Intercourse: It's a Natural Thing to Do!* A cartoon man inserted his penis into a cartoon woman's vagina, and I was so horrified that I wrote a strongly worded letter of complaint to the principal that I never worked up the nerve to send.

In medical school, the Reproductive Physiology course—which I, admittedly, found fascinating—covered, among other topics, genital anatomy, the microbiology of sperm, venereal diseases, and the landmark 1957 study by the gynecologist William Masters and his research assistant, Virginia Johnson. Masters and Johnson were the first to identify and name the four phases of the human sexual response cycle—excitement, plateau, orgasm, and resolution—and the changes in heart rate and blood pressure that occur with each. Their research techniques were unorthodox and included randomly pairing volunteers into "assigned couples" and observing them having intercourse in a laboratory. They were scientific visionaries, trailblazers in a burgeoning field. They were also, in my opinion, abjectly perverted.

Personally, I can barely stand to look at the word "Sex!" printed on seemingly every magazine cover in the grocery checkout aisle ("How to have great sex! Also, recipes for cheesecake!"). My prudence is deeply rooted, my id squashed firmly under the thumb of thousands of years of Indian tradition and disapproving, tongue-clicking aunties.

But kissing. There's something unexpectedly freeing about kissing. The thumbs and the aunties disappear, and I estimate I could make out with Ethan in this empty movie theater, Humphrey Bogart's voice in the background, my heart pounding in my ears, our arms and legs and lips intertwined, for hours, days, maybe forever. At a paltry one hour and forty-two minutes, *Casablanca* is far too short. Suddenly, the credits are rolling and Ethan breaks our embrace and murmurs into my ear, "Want to come over to my place?"

We hold hands, walk fast, and say nothing. I tell myself to calm down. Humans, after all, have been engaging in sexual intercourse since, literally, the origin of our species. Entire civilizations have been launched solely because two people decided to comingle their genitalia. Which, when I look at it that way, underscores the fact that sex is both critical to the survival of mankind and, at the same time, no big deal. I should stop overthinking this. *Confident and breezy. Fun and spontaneous.* I'm that uninhibited girl in country songs who dances on the roof of the hunky singer's pickup truck in the rain in cutoff shorts. Country songs love that girl. Everyone loves that girl. I mean, she's obviously someone who doesn't make decisions with personal safety in mind, and she might have a problem with impulse control but, regardless, they write songs about her. No one writes songs about people like me, virginal twenty-six-year-old risk-averse nerds with closets full of yoga pants.

What I'm feeling—heart skipping, breath fast, skin flushed—is, obviously, the result of a raucous jumble of emotionally triggered neurotransmitters and hormones bombarding my nerve endings. I don't think I've ever felt anything this intensely before. And I don't want it to end.

It's fourteen floors up to Ethan's apartment. I follow him into the elevator. He smiles and kisses my hair. I push the button for the fourteenth floor. The doors slide shut, we rise, and without looking back, I leave the old me behind.

CHAPTER ELEVEN

It's ironic. I've spent the better part of the last decade studying the human body, dissecting it, poring over diagrams of it, memorizing the names of every crook, divot, and fleshy hanging nubbin of it, yet I'm still *so* uncomfortable being naked. I get dressed immediately.

"You're not leaving?" Ethan asks from the other side of the bed.

I freeze. "Um . . . did you want me to leave?"

He laughs. "Of course not." He glances at his watch. "I mean, I have to go in to work at five, but I thought I'd order us some Chinese and we could hang out." He folds his arms under his head and looks at the ceiling. His clothes are in a pile on the nightstand. "You're probably the coolest girl I've ever met, do you know that?"

I grin. Poor Jeremy Corkie from sixth grade is somewhere right now, probably eating a sandwich that doesn't belong to him, with no idea that he once rejected this insanely cool girl. "You're cool, too," I say, then cringe inwardly at how awkward that sounds. I sit on the edge of the bed.

"This might sound weird," Ethan says, lifting his head off the pillow, "but can I just ask: Have you had a lot of experience with . . . this sort of thing?"

I clear my throat. "Um, you know, 'a lot' is a relative term." Good lord, how would he react if I told him he just took my virginity? I imagine him leaping out of bed and running, naked and horrified, from the room. "I've had *some* experience, you could say." Was it that obvious? I've studied the anatomy and physiology enough to know how it should go, but what if I somehow got it all wrong?

Ethan raises his eyebrows and smiles. "So, are the rumors true?"

"Rumors?"

"You know, about you and Clark?"

I hesitate, sensing an opportunity to cast myself in a less naïve light. Having an on-again, off-again relationship with a fellow resident is just the type of thing a spontaneous, non–socially awkward woman would do. "Well, actually, that rumor might be true. But that's all I'm going to say about it." Leave a little mystery. That's what they say, right?

Grinning, Ethan reaches over and slips my glasses off the bridge of my nose. Everything around me dissolves into blurry background, leaving only his smiling face in focus. "Dr. Shocks-a-lot, you are nothing like what I expected when I first met you." He kisses my neck, and I surrender to a dizzy, delicious haze before I can wonder what exactly he means.

As afternoon turns to evening, we finish off the Chinese food, taking turns reaching our chopsticks into each other's takeout containers.

"Someday we should watch the rest of that movie," Ethan says.

"You've never seen *Casablanca*?" I crack open a fortune cookie.

He stands at the refrigerator, staring at the mostly bare shelves. "Not until today. I wish I'd known you were coming over. I would have straightened the place up. And bought groceries."

I laugh and cross my legs, attempting nonchalance. "It's fine, really. I love Chinese."

He gazes at me over his shoulder for a long moment. "I really wish I wasn't on call tonight."

I shrug in a way that underscores my confident breeziness. "Duty calls, right?"

He smiles and places a can of soda on the counter before me. "See you at work tomorrow?" He slings a backpack over his shoulder, grabs his keys from the hall table, and waves sheepishly. "Stay as long as you want, okay?"

I grin and wave. As soon as the door shuts, I stifle a high-pitched squeal of delight. Do I feel different? I think I feel different. More worldly, maybe. Or just slightly less awkward. Whatever it is, it's exhilarating. For all the talk in popular culture about losing one's virginity, I don't feel like I've *lost* anything. Aside from a brief moment of pelvic soreness, the experience was entirely enjoyable. First-class, as far as I'm concerned.

I feel as if I've crossed some invisible threshold of life experience, and I have no regrets or second thoughts about it whatsoever. To think, all those years the aunties were subtly brainwashing us, shaming us about the evils of sexuality, it was all an elaborate lie. Not unlike Santa Claus.

I jump up and call Meryl.

"Thank goodness you called!" she says.

"Yes, I— Wait, what? What's wrong?"

"I don't know what's going on with Gabe."

I open the soda and walk around the apartment.

"What do you mean?" I say. "I thought you were breaking up with him."

"Breaking up with him? When did I say that?"

"After he told you his SAT scores, remember?"

In the living room, books are arranged on a shelf in height order. Pens and opened mail sit neatly in a caddy on a desk. The television and DVD remote controls are aligned in parallel on the coffee table. Hanging above the couch is a framed photograph of the Mediterranean Sea behind a hillside of white stucco buildings topped with azure domes. Ethan told me that he went to Santorini two years ago with his ex-fiancée. They were supposed to go back there for their honeymoon.

Meryl says, "Right, that. No, recently things were going so well; we were planning to go to his sister's wedding together, and I already bought my dress. Then all of a sudden, yesterday, he says he needs to 'take a step back.'"

"That doesn't sound good." I go into the bedroom. The sheets are still in disarray. I bite my bottom lip and smile. After a moment's hesitation, I open the top drawer of the bureau.

"He uninvited me! He said he finds me exhausting," she says. "What does that mean? I mean, am I exhausting?"

T-shirts and boxer shorts are folded into neat little rectangles and lined up in perfect, symmetrical rows.

"No, of course not," I say.

"Well, I was so upset, I had to pay a visit to the Three P's." The Three P's are Meryl's psychologist, her pedicurist, and her palm reader. "And, of course, the only one who made me feel any better was Adrianna." The palm reader. "She says my sun goddess is rising. So, that's a relief."

"Have you tried talking to Gabe?" I say.

"I have nothing to say to him. Who uninvites someone from a wedding that they've already bought a dress for? Let's just get on a plane and go to Hawaii now. Why wait another six months?"

"Because we're supposed to be going to celebrate you passing the bar and me surviving my internship. If we go now, we'll be admitting defeat."

"I feel pretty defeated." She sighs. "How's your guy?"

"I think he has a little obsessive-compulsive disorder. I'm in his place, and it's like beyond clean."

"Ugh, Gabe is such a slob. I'd be happy if he even made his side of the bed. Maybe this is for the best. It just needs to be over with him, you know? I can't deal with immaturity."

In the bathroom, I open the medicine cabinet and find Band-Aids, a razor, a bottle of Tylenol, and a can of shaving gel. Next to the shaving gel is a gray eyeliner pencil. Meryl's voice suddenly sounds far away, like I've just plunged underwater.

"Wait, there he is on the other line," she says. "Crap, I'll have to call you back."

I mumble goodbye after she's already hung up. I stare at the eyeliner pencil on its little glass shelf. It could be his ex-fiancée's, of course. But there, outside the bathroom, is a perfectly kept apartment, the apartment of someone who wouldn't store old personal-care items belonging to someone else in his medicine cabinet. I shake the thought away. It's illogical to jump to conclusions based on insufficient data. And it would be foolish to let speculation ruin what should be a happy moment.

I close the medicine cabinet and put the eyeliner out of my mind.

"I . . . can't . . . breathe!" A panicked man with several scraggly strands of gray hair protruding from each ear wheezes and clutches at his chest.

"Shhh!" I say. In between the steady thumping of his heart I hear a distant crackling, like bursts of faint static. I pull my stethoscope from my ears and loop it around my neck. "Can I get a stat chest X-ray, and may I please see his latest labs?" I say to the nurse as my pager sounds.

"It's the intern," I say, my cell phone wedged between my ear and shoulder, my fingers pressed into the patient's wrist, counting his pulse.

"You need to come to room 541," the voice on the other end says. "We have a patient with gangrene who's bleeding through his PEG tube."

"Fat Dan? I'll be right there," I say. I hang up as the nurse hands me the elderly man's chart. According to his laboratory results, the level of oxygen in his blood is critically, but not dangerously, low.

"You should intubate him," the nurse says, her arms folded across her chest.

"What does that mean?" The patient looks at her, his eyes wide.

"Mr. Worthington, the doctor needs to put a tube down your throat and connect you to a ventilator to help you breathe better," the nurse says.

"But I'd like to find out what's wrong with you first," I say, handing the chart back to her with a pointed look. "Please page me when you have the X-ray."

The patient gasps. "Please, call me Gerald." He gasps again. "Mr. Worthington was my father."

The nurse and I exchange a glance. I pat the patient on the shoulder. "Try not to speak, Mr. Worthington. It'll worsen your breathing."

My cell phone rings in my pocket. It's Paul. I answer while jogging up the stairwell.

"Norah, I'm over at Ma's house, and her blood pressure is two hundred over ninety-five."

"Did you check it in both arms?"

"Yeah. She's saying her chest hurts."

"She needs to go to the emergency room."

"That's what I told her, but she doesn't want to go. She thinks her blood pressure cuff isn't working."

"She has a manual cuff, the kind you inflate and listen to with a stethoscope. Those are more accurate."

"But I don't know how to use that."

"You could take her to CVS and use the blood pressure cuff there."

"I can't right now. Kai is sick with an ear infection. He won't stop crying, and Reena is losing her mind. I've been over here for an hour already; I have to get back home."

"I'm on call. I can't just leave and come check on her. Has she already taken a Valium?"

"She said she did, yeah. Can she take another one?"

I consider this. "Yeah, it's probably fine. She can take another one."

"It's *probably* fine? Are you sure?"

"Yes, I'm sure. I have to go. I'll call you back." I hang up.

Fat Dan survived multiple surgeries and, just this week, was taken off his ventilator and moved out of the Intensive Care Unit. When I arrive at his new room, the nurses look ashen.

"This guy is too sick to be here," one of them says. As evidence, she hoists onto the counter a plastic basin full of bright red blood thick with dusky clots. "He's bleeding to death!"

Blood, presumably from his stomach, is flowing at a steady pace from Fat Dan's feeding tube, collecting in a plastic bag hanging from the side of the bed. I review his laboratory results—his hemoglobin is dropping quickly, hour by hour. The nurse says, "It was a slow drip earlier in the day. It just started pouring out of him like this."

I use the phone in the hallway outside the room to page the senior resident on call.

"That sounds bad," he says. I can hear, in the background, the tinny sound of the ancient television in the residents' lounge. "You should definitely page the attending. Sounds like he needs to be transferred back to the ICU, or maybe to the surgery service. Good luck."

I call the operator and have the attending paged. He calls back fifteen minutes later. "Dr. Herring! This is Dr. Herring!" a familiar British voice booms.

"Hi, Dr. Herring, it's the intern. Sorry to bother you," I say. I describe the situation. I talk fast. Then I say, "I think he needs to go back to the ICU."

I hear the clatter of silverware, then the sound of his chewing. "No, this has been an ongoing situation," Dr. Herring says. "Just get a Gastroenterology consult. They'll take care of it."

"Okay, but his hemoglobin is six," I say.

He swallows and burps. "Transfuse." He hangs up.

I relay the order for a blood transfusion to the nurse.

"Okay, but are we transferring him?" Her voice is hopeful.

I shake my head. "Herring says no."

She swears under her breath as I page the Gastroenterology fellow on call.

"Gastroenterology," a female voice says.

I talk faster.

"Oh . . . yeah, I already saw that patient this morning," she says. "If he's bleeding like that, he needs General Surgery. There's nothing I can do for him."

I page the General Surgery resident on call. "Will you come look at this patient?" I plead.

"That sounds pretty bad," the resident says. "If he's that unstable, he needs to go to the ICU to be stabilized before we could even think about doing surgery. Don't want to have him croak on the table, you know? Maybe you could try calling Gastroenterology."

I page Dr. Herring again.

"Bloody fucking hell. Who is this?"

"It's . . . the intern," I say, closing my eyes and resting my forehead against the wall.

"Well, what do you want?"

I explain what has happened over the past hour. "And his latest hemoglobin is five-point-two," I say.

"Well, transfer him to the ICU. What are you waiting for?" He hangs up.

I page the ICU head nurse and wait for a call back.

My pager beeps. I dial the callback number. "It's the intern. Someone paged me?"

"That chest X-ray you wanted is ready," Mr. Worthington's nurse says. "It looks like pneumonia."

I find the nearest computer, stretching the phone cord down the hallway, and bring up the X-ray. What should be black airspace in each lung is completely obscured by wispy white puffs, like clouds in a dark sky. "It's not pneumonia," I say into the phone. "He's in heart failure. Give him forty of Lasix, please." Due to his weak heart, fluid has accumulated in Mr. Worthington's lungs, making it difficult for him to breathe. The medication will cause him to quickly excrete the fluid as urine.

"His blood pressure is already kind of low," the nurse says. "You sure you want to risk dropping it even more?"

My cell phone rings. It's Paul again. "Yes. I have to go," I tell the nurse. I hang up the hall phone and answer my cell.

"Her chest pain is getting worse, Nor. She took the extra Valium, but it's not helping. Now she's saying she has trouble breathing."

"Put her on."

"Norah?" Ma's voice is weak and quavering, the way it always sounds during her episodes.

"Ma, you have to calm down. You're fine. You've had an extensive cardiology workup, and there's nothing wrong with your heart."

"I feel light-headed," she says. She makes a distressed, high-pitched moaning sound. It's like nails on a chalkboard.

"Then let Paul take you to the emergency room," I snap.

"Why are you yelling at me? Is this how you talk to your mother?" Her tone is suddenly less frail.

Paul is on the line again. "Jeez, Nor. You're just getting her more worked up."

The hall phone is ringing.

"Paul, I have to go."

"Wait, Nor, what do I do?"

"Take her to the hospital."

"But—"

"I'll call you back." I hang up my cell phone and grab the hall phone receiver.

"ICU Head Nurse." His voice is gravelly and fatigued.

"Hi, it's the Medicine intern. I need to transfer Fat Dan back to you guys. Sorry."

There is a groan. "No. Nooo! He *just* left."

"I know. I'm sorry." I press the dull end of my pen into my chin until it's painful.

"What's wrong with him?" he asks.

"GI bleed. Hemoglobin five-point-two. We're transfusing," I say.

"Oh, no way," he says. "That is *not* an ICU case. Give me a break."

For a moment I consider that he may be joking. Then he says, "You can't just dump that patient here because you're too lazy to manage him down there."

I throw my pen to the floor. "Excuse me?" I say, immediately recognizing that my tone sounds less like an assertive leader and more like a whiny eight-year-old than I intended. I retrieve my pen. "Look, this wasn't my idea. Herring wants the patient sent back up there." I try for passive-aggressive and hit it square on the head. "If you want to page Dr. Herring so you can talk to him directly about it, I have the number right here."

The ICU head nurse grumbles something unintelligible that ends with, "Fine. But I'm not happy about this."

"I hear you. Me neither. Have a super evening!" I hang up before he can reply.

My pager sounds. It's Mr. Worthington's nurse again.

"You need to get back up here," she says.

When I return to Mr. Worthington's room, he looks clammy and lethargic.

His nurse says, "The forty didn't touch him."

"Give him another eighty," I say.

"A hundred and twenty of Lasix?" She looks at me, wide-eyed. "You'll kill him."

"Do it, please." There's slightly less whine in my voice. I put my hands on my hips and square my shoulders.

She draws up the medication and injects it into the IV.

Five minutes pass. Mr. Worthington's breathing begins to ease. The lines between her eyebrows disappearing, the nurse says, "Well, that's better, isn't it?"

My pager sounds.

"We need you to put an EJ line in this patient. She's a drug addict who won't eat or drink anything. She's dehydrated and has no veins. Room 420."

My cell phone rings again.

"What if I gave her a third Valium?" Paul's voice is strained, both genuinely worried and exceedingly annoyed.

"No, that's too much," I say. "Have you tried herbal tea? That sometimes works."

"I'll try that. When will you be able to get here?"

"Not for a few hours at least. I'm sorry, Paul. But there's nothing medically wrong with her. She's gotten herself worked up, that's all. Like usual."

"I believe you, since she just asked me to watch a movie with her. But she won't let me leave. I'll be here, sitting with her, all night."

"Can't you tell her that Kai is sick?"

"I did. It doesn't matter. She just keeps crying and bringing the conversation back to how terrible *she* feels."

"I'm really sorry. I have to go. I have patients."

He sighs. "Yeah. So much for being here when we need you, huh?"

The pressure behind my eyeballs is intolerable. "Paul—"

"It's okay, Nor. I get it. Bye." He hangs up.

When I arrive at room 420, a gaunt young woman with dirt under her fingernails, fighting to keep her eyes open, leans forward in the bed. "I'm in so much goddamn pain," she says, her head rolling from side to side. "You fuckers won't give me anything. All I want is two fucking Percocet."

"Ma'am, I have to put this IV in your neck," I say. "You need to lie down." She throws herself back onto the pillow, moaning. I wipe the side of her neck with alcohol, and she swats my hand away. "Jesus, that's too cold." She moans again. "You're all fuckers."

I steady the IV needle in my hand and bring it to her skin. "Here's the pinch," I say. Before I can stick her, she flinches, pulling away.

I will not get stuck again. Not because of you. Rage pulses through me, turning my breath shallow and quick. I know, intellectually, that this patient is not my adversary. She's not trying to compound my stress. But I can't help it. My fatigue and adrenaline and anxiety need an outlet, and they find a conduit in her. In this moment, I hate this patient, as much as I've ever hated anyone.

I grab her chin with my free hand, forcing her head into the pillow. "Hold still!" I dig my fingertips into her cheeks.

"Ouch! Is this . . ." Her voice fades away into a stuporous mumble. "Gonna hurt?"

I tighten my grip. "Yes."

CHAPTER TWELVE

Mrs. Tally is seated in a wheelchair, her handbag in her lap, her husband behind her. Her face is pink and glowing. She doesn't smile, but something about her looks triumphant.

"Good morning," I say, entering her room. "All set? Have you scheduled your first chemotherapy treatment at the outpatient center?"

"Sure did," Mr. Tally replies.

My phone beeps. A text message from Ethan reads, Come to the library conference room ASAP.

"I just signed your discharge paperwork," I say. "Good luck, Mrs. Tally."

"Doctor, thank you," she says, clasping my hand in both of hers.

Mr. Tally nods at me. "No offense, but I hope we don't see you again."

I smile and watch him wheel his wife down the corridor. Then I step into the bathroom in her room and check my makeup in the mirror. I've started wearing eyeliner and mascara to work, and I find it endlessly distracting. I'm always worrying it'll smudge and leave unsightly dark lines under my eyebrows. Satisfied, for the moment, with my reflection, I text Ethan: On my way.

The library is, as always at this hour, empty. As I pass the tall book stacks crammed with aging medical journals, I straighten my skirt and unsnap the top button of my blouse. I pull open the door of the conference room.

"Dr. Kapadia, sit down." A man with a thick black mustache that blends seamlessly into his beard is seated at a long table with all three chief residents—Francesca, Terry, and Ethan. Behind them hangs a portrait of a wizened gentleman wearing a white coat and an enormous monocle.

"I'm sorry that we're seeing each other again under these circumstances," the bearded man says. I recognize him as Dr. Stanton Forks, the director of medical education, in charge of all the hospital residency programs. He wears a perfectly tailored three-piece suit with a magenta ascot and a Burberry tie clip. Now I understand why the residents call him Fancy Forks. He opens a manila folder. "I called this meeting to address a complaint raised by one of your attendings."

"A complaint?" I steal a glance at Ethan while trying to discreetly refasten the top button of my blouse. He twirls a pen between his thumb and index finger and keeps his eyes fixed on the table.

"Did you tell one of Dr. Portnoy's patients that he should stop his chemotherapy?" Dr. Forks asks.

"No." A panicky tightness seizes my chest.

"The patient says you told him about a study from the *New England Journal*," Francesca says. "And that you gave him a copy of the study."

"Well, yes, but why is that—"

Terry snorts. "Nadine, how stupid are you?"

"Hey!" Ethan says. "Terry, come on." He turns to me, his eyebrows drawn together. "Norah, the patient left AMA this morning."

"That's right." Dr. Forks taps a pen against the manila folder. "The patient discharged himself from the hospital against medical advice because he had—as he put it—lost confidence in Dr. Portnoy."

I look around the table helplessly and am met with blank expressions.

"Portnoy is pretty upset," Ethan says. "He wants you off his service and placed on administrative leave for the next two weeks."

"Actually, he wants you fired, but we've convinced him to settle for administrative leave," Terry says, aggressively adjusting his glasses.

I try to control my escalating panic. "But I didn't do anything wrong," I say.

Terry squints at me, as if he's blinded by my incompetence. "You subverted an attending, and it led to the hospital losing a patient."

"But all I did was have a conversation with him. A two-minute conversation."

"Did you tell the patient that Dr. Portnoy is *uncaring*?" Francesca demands.

"What? Of course not!" I hesitate as I replay the conversation in my mind. "I mean, that's not what I meant to say."

Dr. Forks sighs and clears his throat. "Dr. Kapadia, you are a member of the house staff. That means your job—your *only* job—is to support your attending. In exchange, you get an education. That's how this works. You do not go around sharing your opinion, or what you think you read in the *New England Journal*, with the patients."

I grip the arms of the worn leather chair. Even the monocled painting seems to have assumed a disappointed expression. Dr. Forks continues. "You'll keep your position, for now. But you'll be on administrative leave for two weeks while this matter is reviewed, effective immediately. Understood?"

My mouth goes dry. *He can't be serious. I'm being reprimanded?* I'm not someone who gets reprimanded. I'm someone who gets nominated for hall monitor, someone with perfect attendance, someone who shushes other people in libraries. *This can't be happening.*

Dr. Forks looks at me expectantly.

I swallow, a feeling like hot sand in my throat. "Yes, sir."

* * *

A frigid rain is falling steadily outside. I pull my white coat closed and walk into it. *I just need to get out of here.* I am two blocks from the hospital when I hear Ethan yell, "Norah, wait!" He opens his umbrella as he runs. "Are you okay?" He holds the umbrella over me while raindrops pelt his face.

"Well, I almost lost my job and I'm totally humiliated, so . . ."

He wipes a tear from my chin. "What happened wasn't your fault."

My chest is so tight it's hard to speak. "The patient asked me a question, and I answered it. I don't understand why I'm being punished for that."

"Because it was a Portnoy patient. If it were any other attending . . . sometimes you can't just answer a patient's question."

"What in the world does that mean?"

He takes my arm. "Let's get out of the rain."

A few minutes later, we are seated at one of two tables in a tiny coffee shop that sells a slice of American cheese melted over a soft pretzel as a breakfast item. After a few deep breaths I've collected myself enough to focus.

"Okay. Explain, please. What do you mean, you can't just answer a patient's questions? What's wrong with answering questions? How can facts be wrong?"

Ethan sighs. "It's about how you *present* the facts. Look, Norah, there aren't enough hours in the day for Portnoy or me or you to sit down with every patient and hypothesize about what might happen if they don't follow our advice. No one has time for that. We have evidence-based treatments based on years of disciplined research. They have a Google search. And we can share statistics and studies with the patient, but only if it helps support what we've recommended. Our responsibility is to guide the patient into what we know is the best decision for them."

"By withholding information?" I'm thrown. I've never considered presenting a patient with half-truths regarding their care, even if I thought it would be for their own good.

"The information is our tool, not theirs. We're the scientists. Telling the patients everything is like giving a hammer to a toddler."

I shake my head. "But don't we have an obligation to tell the truth? All of it?"

"The oath says to do no harm. Not to tell the whole truth and nothing but the truth—that's a different oath. Listen, when I was a kid, my aunt died of uterine cancer. She was thirty-three, and her son, my cousin, was eight. It sucked. It was a fucking nightmare." His eyes are suddenly focused somewhere else, as if the ghost of the memory were seated at the other table.

"I'm so sorry. That's awful," I say. I reach across the table and put my fingertips on the back of his hand. He pulls away and lifts his coffee cup to his lips.

"After that," he says, clearing his throat, "I wanted to grow up to find a cure for cancer. That's what's happening on Portnoy's service. He's curing cancer."

"But if the chances of getting better with treatment are only forty-five percent—"

"You take it," he says. "Forty-five percent is pretty good."

"Not to the patient. He said it was worse odds than flipping a coin. Shouldn't he get to make his own decision?"

"What's his alternative?" Ethan asks. "To just do nothing? To use essential oils and pomegranate juice to treat his stage-four renal cancer? Throwing away the only real opportunity to treat his cancer isn't a good decision, whether he realizes that or not."

My shoulders sag. Maybe Ethan has a point. Maybe I should have kept my mouth shut, instead of being so eager to show off what I knew.

"I see what you're saying," I admit. "But it feels like I'm expected to be loyal to Portnoy no matter what, when what I should really be doing is putting the patients first. I mean, isn't that the point? Isn't that why we became doctors?"

"Careful, Norah. Or you'll bite the hand that feeds you."

"Meaning what?"

"Meaning there's a food chain in medicine," Ethan says. "The insurance companies are at the top; they're like the T. rexes. After them are the hospital administrators—the CEO and CFO and the rest of them, none of whom know how to practice medicine, by the way—only slightly smaller carnivores. Insurance and the admins fight constantly, each one basically trying to take the other's money. Next in line is Portnoy, who answers to the admins—if the admins don't eat, neither does he. After Portnoy comes the residents—we exist to make Portnoy's life easier, and if we do a good job, he throws us some scraps, and maybe we can eventually graduate and move up the chain. And after us, way down at the bottom, paying their insurance premiums and holding the entire ecosystem together like the plankton of the healthcare system, are the patients."

"So we agree, I should be putting the patients first. They're the most important."

Ethan shakes his head. "Fuck it, everyone should be putting the patients first, but that's not how a food chain works. Unless you want to be a bottom-dweller forever, your loyalty needs to be to Portnoy."

I am pensive for a moment, then say, "That food chain analogy was even worse than your sportfishing one."

Ethan grins and shrugs. His pager sounds. "Come on," he says, standing. "We'd better get back. You'll need to sign out your patients to one of the other residents on Portnoy's service so they can take over care."

As we walk, my chest starts to get tight again. "There has to be something I can do. I made a mistake. Maybe if I talk to Portnoy."

"Unfortunately, talking to Portnoy won't get you anywhere,"

Ethan says. "He has a zero-tolerance policy when it comes to mistakes."

"What if I call the patient? I could apologize and—"

"Portnoy's already called the patient and convinced him to come back into the hospital for treatment."

I nod, resigned. "Do you think they'll fire me after their review?" I ask.

He shakes his head. "Nah. I doubt that'll happen. They just have to punish you in some way to appease Portnoy. Think of it as a two-week vacation. And when you get back, I'll try to get you on an easy rotation, like outpatient clinic." He grabs my hand, his warm fingers intertwining with mine, and squeezes reassuringly. "It's going to be fine, Norah. I promise."

My shoulders relax until I remember the stack of bills on my kitchen table with a fluorescent-pink Post-it note stuck on top: *Norah, these are due in TWO WEEKS. Please put in your check ASAP! B*. "Is the leave unpaid?"

Ethan sighs. "Yeah, unfortunately."

My heart races, panic setting in. "I won't be able to pay my bills without a job for two weeks."

"Is there anywhere you could work, just short-term?" Ethan asks. "I mean, a two-week gig is hard to come by, but I can help you look for something. I'm guessing minimum wage isn't going to cut it?"

"No." But the answer is right there, budding from my subconscious and threatening to bloom in the frontal cortex of my brain. I try with all my might to stamp it down, beat it back, bury it before it becomes a coherent and viable thought.

Too late. There it is, an idea, a solution to my predicament, fully formed in my mind and impossible to deny.

Damn it. Damn it damn it damn it.

CHAPTER THIRTEEN

I move back in with Ma for two weeks. Paul and Reena, once they hear I'll be in town, book a last-minute trip to Disney World with Kai. On the first night, I return the latest of Ma's purchases (a $400 trench coat and a $650 pair of Jimmy Choo sandals that weren't even her size), watch *Dance India Dance* on television with her for two hours, discuss her blurry vision for forty-five minutes, boil rice and listen to her tell me I'm doing it incorrectly, dose her insulin, eat dinner with her while she checks her blood pressure, and hold her hand while she cries about how terrible her in-laws in India have always been to her, well into the night.

The next morning, I stand beside a humorless woman with a graying, frizzy ponytail and a dingy lab coat in a room filled with dozens of mice in cages. The cages, each of which contains a tiny food dish, a water dispenser, and one white-haired, red-eyed mouse, are lined up neatly on long tables. Against one wall is a counter covered with glass canisters of mouse food, tiny brown pellets with numbers etched into them. The room smells overwhelmingly of sawdust and rodent excrement, and the only sound is the cacophonous scratching of mice feet, punctuated by the occasional forlorn squeak.

"What are we supposed to be doing?" I whisper.

"Shhhh!" The woman with the ponytail doesn't look at me. She's intently watching the hands of a stopwatch she holds in her palm while also staring at a lone mouse, asleep in the corner of one of the cages. The mouse stirs. The woman clicks a button on the stopwatch and makes some notes on a clipboard.

Ketan enters the laboratory through a metal door that clicks shut softly behind him. *Shastri BioLabs* is embroidered on the sleeve of his white lab coat. His voice a whisper, he says, "Hey, Norah. How is training with Hester going?"

I've spent the last forty minutes with Hester, but she hasn't said more than two words to me, and she certainly hasn't trained me to do anything. I've ascertained that we're keeping our voices down so as not to wake the sleeping mice and that we're timing something, but that's all I know at this point. I shrug at Ketan, and he frowns sympathetically, as if he's unsurprised by Hester's aloofness.

He waves me aside and hands me a clipboard and a stopwatch. "Here's the deal. We're testing different sleep meds in this room. The meds are mixed into the food. Just follow the clipboard. You put the food pellet from the designated container in the food bowl. The mouse eats the food. You wait until the mouse falls asleep. You time how long it sleeps with the stopwatch. That's it. Pretty easy."

"I thought you said this job was awesome," I whisper.

"*My* job is awesome," he says. "I'm a lab manager. I've been here six years and worked my way up. I mostly just play on my phone at this point. *This* job sucks."

"How long would I have to do this to work my way up?"

"Three to four years."

I stare at him. "You're kidding. I might not make it two weeks."

"I find it's helpful to focus on the lunch breaks. You get a thirty-minute lunch break at noon every day. Something to look forward to." He gives me an encouraging thumbs-up and leaves.

I glance at my watch. It's 11:45. I approach Hester and whisper, "Hey, Hester, it's almost time for lunch. Do you want to stop early and we can eat in the break room together?"

She looks up from her clipboard. "Why?"

"Just, you know, to have someone to eat lunch with. . . ."

She looks at me skeptically for a moment. "No. I eat here in the lab, so as not to interrupt my workflow." She turns back to her clipboard.

"Oh, okay. See you in thirty minutes then."

She doesn't acknowledge me. I tiptoe out of the lab and into a stark, windowless hallway lined on both sides with brown metal doors, each labeled with a number. I find a door marked *Employee Kitchen*. Inside are several cafeteria-style tables, a kitchenette with a microwave and coffee maker, a row of lockers, and an aging vending machine selling snacks. A sign on the wall reading *Absolutely no cellular phones in the laboratories!* hangs above a sign that reads *Teamwork Makes the Team Work!*

I find my locker and punch in the key code. The door clicks open, and I retrieve my phone and my brown-paper lunch sack. I slide into a seat and rest my head in my hands. I've only been here two hours, but it feels like a lifetime. A long, meaningless lifetime.

"Are you the new mouse girl?"

I look up, and a man about my age wearing a mesh bonnet over his hair is smiling at me from a few chairs away.

"Mouse girl?"

"Lab 7?" he asks.

"Oh. Yeah. That's me. Mouse girl."

"How's it going?"

I unwrap my peanut butter sandwich. "Honestly, it's not the best job I've ever had. But I'm just here for two weeks."

The man laughs, a deep-throated guffaw that tapers to a high-pitched giggle. "Yeah, Lab 7 is a rough one to start on. I'm in Lab 12. I test shampoo on hair samples. It's pretty interesting."

"Sounds interesting," I say, though I find my sandwich more compelling than anything he's telling me.

"There are a lot of fumes, though," he says, his gaze becoming distant. "All those years inhaling formalin and bromine and who knows what else?" He looks at me and starts giggling again.

I'm wondering if I should distance myself from this clearly unhinged man when the break room door opens, and several people in lab coats and gowns enter. The tables fill, and a line forms for the microwave. No one, save my delirious friend a few seats down, is smiling.

I look at my phone: no text messages, not even from Meryl. I send Ethan a smiley-face emoji, but there's no reply. Clearly, everyone else is busy doing things of consequence today, while I'm watching rodents sleep.

"You the new mouse girl?" A woman in her sixties with electric-blue hair slides into the seat across from me. She opens a Tupperware container filled with something unsettlingly gelatinous.

I nod.

"I heard you're Vikram's niece," she says.

"Niece?"

"Yeah." My giggling friend a few seats down leans over to join our conversation. "I heard he's your uncle."

"He's just a family friend," I say. "Indian people call everyone our parents' age 'uncle' or 'auntie.'"

The blue-haired woman frowns. She seems disappointed. "Well, that's confusing. I should have figured he wouldn't make his *actual* niece a mouse girl. He'd probably find something better for her." She laughs, a throaty wheezing that suggests decades of cigarette use.

"Is it true it takes years to get promoted?" I ask.

The woman nods, coughing. "Oh, four years at least. I've been here twelve. Started in the mouse lab, like you, then moved up to rat lab, and now I'm in egg and sperm."

Moved up to rat lab? I'm trying to decide how rats are an improvement over mice when another question comes to mind. "How long has Hester been here?"

The blue-haired woman and the giggling man exchange a glance. "I dunno." The man counts on his fingers. "She's been here longer than most of us. Probably fifteen years?"

The woman nods her agreement. Then she leans toward me with raised eyebrows. "But Hester's not . . . right."

"What do you—"

She raises a hand to silence me. "Just. She's not right."

The man nods cryptically. They both turn back to their food.

Unnerved, I fish around my pockets for change. I urgently need a baked good. "I'm going to get something from the vending machine. Want anything?"

The man and woman shake their heads.

I deposit the change into the vending machine and look through the Plexiglas window at my choices: potato chips, Doritos, two different brands of pretzels, and Pop-Tarts. I punch in the number for Pop-Tarts and the machine hums to life, the metal spirals of row 4B spinning to push the shiny foil packet toward me. The bag plummets into the dispensing tray, revealing a dead white mouse as the next item to be vended. Its red eyes are open, and a fragment of strawberry Pop-Tart is wedged between its jaws. I scream and stagger backward into a nearby table. The group of people seated there looks up briefly, then turns back to its conversation, disinterested.

The giggling man lumbers over. "Yeah. Happens sometimes. At least it died happy, eh?" He pounds on the glass with the side of his fist. "Stuck in there pretty good. Do you have any more change?"

Reflexively, I hand him the rest of the change from my pocket. He deposits the coins in the machine, presses the button for 4B, and the limp mouse is dispensed into the tray below with a dull, metallic thud. The man reaches through the push-door and retrieves the packet of Pop-Tarts. "You still want these?"

I think I may be sick. I shake my head, throw my things back into my locker, and rush to the ladies' room. I splash water on my face and stare into the mirror. *Come on, Norah. It's only two weeks.*

When I return to Lab 7, Hester is sitting on a stool with her back to the door, her lunch box open on the counter in front of her, a mouse wriggling between her cupped hands.

As she feeds the mouse a bit of lettuce, she coos at it as though it were a beloved pet. "There's a good little girl. Aren't you a good little girl? Yes, you are." Then she draws her tongue over the mouse's fur, as if she were a cat grooming its young.

I squawk, horrified, and clamp a hand over my mouth. Hester glances over her shoulder at me. Rolling her eyes, she lumbers over to an empty cage and deposits the mouse inside.

I wait for her to explain, but she wordlessly zips up her lunch box, tosses it into a cabinet under the counter, and turns back to her clipboard. I clear my throat. "Were you—"

She waves her hand to silence me, her expression stern. "Shhh!"

I spend the rest of my first day at Shastri BioLabs in silence, drugging the mice with their tainted food pellets and timing their naps while trying not to fall asleep myself.

When I get to Ma's house that evening, Nimisha Auntie is at the kitchen table, a selection of pill bottles in front of her. I clench my jaw.

"Hello, Norah *beti*!" Nimisha Auntie grins and sips her tea. She knows I despise her and, I'm almost certain, relishes the fact.

I'm tempted to ignore her completely and go upstairs, but Ma waves me over enthusiastically. "Norah, listen to this! Nimisha is consultant for—what's it called?"

"Rapidly Fast Systems." Nimisha Auntie motions proudly to the assortment of products in front of her. "I was telling your ma all about it. It helps you lose weight in only one week, and you have so much more energy. I've been taking it and look!" She stands and turns this way and that so that I might appreciate her slender profile from all angles. "Your ma could stand to lose those extra pounds she's been putting on lately. Too much shrikhand, right, Rupali?" She gives Ma a teasing look, her eyebrows raised. "I have the willpower to stick to a diet, but your ma"—she shakes her head—"she likes all the sweets! Right, Rupali? Right?" She cackles and smacks the table with her palm.

Ma laughs weakly, a shadow of embarrassment flitting across her face. She tugs at the hem of her shirt, making sure it's tucked firmly over her slightly protruding belly.

The hair on my arms stands on end. "Auntie, Ma doesn't need to go on a diet."

"I do," Ma says. "Nimisha is telling truth."

"Of course I am!" Nimisha Auntie lifts her chin righteously. "What kind of friend would I be if I didn't tell you the honest truth? Listen, Rupali, you used to be nice and slim, and over the past few years you . . . you know"—she puffs out her cheeks—"a little. But I have just the thing for you." She holds out a white plastic pill bottle with the word "TurboLoss" printed in neon letters on the label.

Ma inspects the bottle. "How many pills are you supposed to take?"

"Six a day. You'd better buy it now, because all the ladies at the community center take this and I'm running out of my supply. If you don't order now, you'll have to wait another month."

"Oh, really? Even Smita takes it?"

Nimisha Auntie cackles again. "Of course she does! You should see her prancing around the community center these days. In skinny jeans!"

Ma gasps, scandalized. "Skinny jeans? At her age?"

Nimisha Auntie produces an order form from her handbag. "I'll put you down for three bottles. Only thirty dollars per bottle."

Ma starts to agree, and I steady myself, pull out a chair, and sit down. In my most respectful voice, I say, "Nimisha Auntie, Ma needs to exercise and eat healthy. Not take diet pills."

"They're not diet pills, *beti*," Nimisha Auntie says. "These are weight-loss supplements."

I scan the TurboLoss label. "This has pseudoephedrine in it. The same stuff that's in cold medicine."

"See that?" Nimisha Auntie beams at Ma. "Lose weight *and* clear your sinuses!"

I shake my head at Ma. "You shouldn't take this. One of the side effects of pseudoephedrine is high blood pressure."

Ma's forehead creases with worry. "High blood pressure?" She indicates the automated blood pressure cuff on the table. "I already struggle with my blood pressure."

Nimisha Auntie glances at me, irked. Then she dumps all the pill bottles back into her handbag. "Yes, of course. Your blood pressure. Well, more for the ladies at the community center. I'm entering their *desi* cook-off at the end of the month, did I tell you?"

"Cooking contest? For Indian food?" Ma raises her eyebrows in interest.

"Yes, why not?" Nimisha Auntie says. "There are chili cook-offs and pie cook-offs. It's about time we had a *desi* cook-off for our food."

"You are excellent cook, Nimisha," Ma says. "I'm sure you will win."

Nimisha Auntie waggles her head in agreement. "I'm entering my malai kofta. My Dimple always says my malai kofta is first-class. The grandchildren are always begging me to make it for them."

"Ma, you're a great cook, too," I say. "Maybe you should enter."

There is a fleeting spark in Ma's eyes. "But I haven't made anything more complicated than rice and simple curry in years."

Nimisha Auntie guffaws. "Your carpal tunnel would flare up if you tried!" She holds out her teacup. "Norah *beti*, be a good girl and get Auntie some more tea."

I reflexively reach for her cup, then stop myself. I'd love nothing more than to turn on my heel and leave Nimisha Auntie with her arm outstretched, the cup dangling from her fingers. Then I catch Ma's eye. I wouldn't dare disrespect her oldest, dearest friend. I take the teacup, fill it, and return it to Nimisha Auntie without a word. Then I politely excuse myself.

Upstairs, I shut the door to my bedroom and collapse on the sunflower-print comforter. The walls are covered with the posters I tacked up in high school: several Monet prints featuring water lilies, a black-and-white photograph of Sting holding a violin, and a four-foot-long graphic print of a twisting DNA molecule. An enormous periodic table of the elements hangs behind the desk in the corner.

On a shelf behind the twin bed is a yellowed certificate with a gold star embossed in one corner: *Norah Kapadia, Second Place Hartford Middle School Science Fair*. Next to it is Dad's stethoscope.

I run the bell of the stethoscope between my fingers. Engraved around the rim is *S. Kapadia, MD.* I put the earbuds into my ears and press the bell to my chest. I hold my breath and listen to my heart beat until the pain between my ribs forces me to let go. The sound of air rushing out of my lungs is loud and echoing in my ears, a windstorm only I can hear. I wait for the dizziness to pass. Then I carefully put Dad's stethoscope back in its place on the shelf.

In a cabinet underneath the bedside table, I find a copy of my high school yearbook. I flip to the page with the O's. Meryl O'Neill, Best Personality. Underneath her picture is her signature: *Dear Nors,*

Can't wait to see what our future holds! You are the best friend anyone could ask for! OMG this autograph is already getting waaaay too sappy! Love you always and forever, Peace out, Your BFF, Meryl. PS: We're going to college, bitches!

I close the yearbook without finding my own photograph. I look essentially the same, I'm sure, but everything else is different. The past few months have changed me—altered me down to my core, scrambled and rearranged my DNA—and now it's as if I never lived here, and these mementos belong to someone else. I fall into a restless sleep on this other person's bed, staring at her science fair certificate in the dim light, thinking of the hospital with its bright, cold corridors and longing to be back there.

Ethan calls two days later, just as I park my car in Ma's driveway after work. Just the sound of his voice makes my ears go pink. I grin so widely my face hurts.

"How's the job with your uncle going?"

"He's not actually my uncle. And the job is a nightmare. I spend eight hours a day in a lab full of mice."

He chuckles. "Sounds fun, playing with mice all day. I miss you here. The place isn't the same without you."

"Thanks, but I doubt that."

"I have news."

I accidentally knock the gearshift into reverse, and the car lurches backward. I slam my foot on the brake. "What is it?" My heart races. "Did Dr. Forks say I can come back to work after leave?"

There is a pause. "Oh. No, not yet. But I'm sure you'll hear back about that soon. Like I said, it's really unlikely they'll fire you." His pager beeps in the background. "So, I got the Portnoy fellowship." I can hear his smile through the line.

"Oh my gosh, congratulations!" My head spins. Portnoy might have me fired any minute. "That's really great for you!"

"Thanks! I'm just relieved, you know? The next thing I'm doing is throwing a party. And I need you there!"

"I will be there!" I try to match the enthusiasm in his voice.

"Gotta run. I have this patient with sepsis who's trying to die on me."

"Okay, yes, go quickly. Congrats again!" My voice trails off to a high-pitched warble.

"Bye, beautiful. Talk to you soon!"

A few days later, a text from Ethan reads, Hey peanut butter! Forks says case was reviewed and you're ok to come back to work next week. Told you so! See you soon! Xo jelly.

CHAPTER FOURTEEN

A rhythmic, mechanical squeaking grows louder as I hurry down a long hallway on the ground floor of the hospital. I'm almost giddy. Even the familiar, noxious hospital smell is ambrosial. Whatever awaits me at the end of this corridor, I can be confident that it's not a roomful of mice. I open a door marked *Ambulatory Clinic*.

Inside a cubicle, seated before a computer screen with rapidly changing CT scan images, is a woman in her late thirties, straw-colored hair pulled back in a bun, oxford shirt unbuttoned, two clear plastic funnels pressed against her breasts. She looks up at me. Tiny streams of milk shoot out of her nipples.

"Um, I'm sorry," I say, frantically looking about for an escape. "I'll just—"

"No, no, come in," she says, her voice weary. She rubs her forehead with the back of her wrist. "What time is it?"

"Eight thirty," I say.

"Oh, good." A length of thin, flexible tubing runs from each funnel into a nondescript black shoulder bag on the table. The woman reaches inside the bag, there is a click, and the squeaking ceases. She pulls the funnels away from her chest and unscrews the little plastic bottle attached to each. She sighs as she empties the whitish fluid from one bottle into the other.

She glances at the computer briefly, then, while fastening her bra and buttoning her shirt, says into a slim silver Dictaphone, as if it were all one sentence, without taking a breath, "Impression next paragraph number one depression stable on Lexapro period number two normal CT scan of abdomen and pelvis period all questions were answered and the patient expressed understanding period signature end." She turns to me. "Do you have kids?"

"No," I say.

She laughs mirthlessly. "Don't. It's a pain in the ass."

"How old is your baby?"

"Three months," she says. "The American Academy of Pediatrics recommends all babies be fed breast milk for the first twelve months. Well, they can go fuck themselves." A framed photograph of a naked, cherubic infant in a kitchen sink sits on a shelf above the desk. "Are you an intern?"

I nod.

"Come with me." She screws a lid onto the bottle of milk and, as if it were a precious heirloom, gingerly places it in a little padded cooler bag that she zips shut.

I follow her past several other cubicles, each with a physician seated at a computer mumbling into a Dictaphone.

"Is this your first outpatient experience?"

I nod again, enthusiastically this time. I'm thrilled to be back in the hospital on any service, but the outpatient clinic has a reputation among the residents for being fairly relaxed and enjoyable compared to other assignments.

"Well," she says, "the most important thing is not to let the visit drag on too long. We book appointments in fifteen-minute intervals. It takes about seven minutes to check off all the required boxes in the electronic chart so the hospital can be compliant with insurance requirements and get paid. That leaves about eight minutes to actually interview and examine the patient, make a diagnosis, and come up with a treatment plan. If a patient takes ten minutes to say hello, you're going to have a problem. Redirect, redirect, redirect. But try not to come off as rude or rushed or condescending."

"How do you—"

"It's not easy." Her tone indicates that our conversation is over. We reach a nurses' station ringed by examination rooms. Several residents and medical students are milling about, most of them reading quietly.

"Hey, Dr. Hale," someone in a short white coat says. "How many ounces this morning?"

It's Gabe. I sigh more loudly than I intend to.

Dr. Hale indicates her cooler with a flourish of her hand. "Five."

"Not bad," he says, nodding. "Strong work."

"I know, right? I called in some domperidone for myself and now I'm like a dairy cow."

Gabe fishes his phone out of a pocket of his white coat. "I'm looking up what domperidone is."

"It's a dopamine receptor antagonist," Dr. Hale says. "And a galactagogue. Makes more milk. It's amazing stuff." She turns to me. "The nurses will let you know when a patient is ready to be seen. Once you're done and you think you have a diagnosis and treatment plan, come find me or one of the other attendings. You'll need to log in to the computer to see lab results and order X-rays." She opens a mini-fridge marked with an orange biohazard sign and carefully places the cooler inside. She yawns. "If you have any questions, ask Francesca. She's the senior resident here today."

Dr. Hale leaves, and I take a seat at a computer. A blinking cursor on the screen is asking for my password.

"How do I log in?" I wonder aloud.

Gabe leans over the counter. "Just use mine. It's 'Meryl,' all caps. How is she?"

I type "MERYL" into the computer, and a list of patients and appointment times appears.

"Aren't you dating her?" I ask without looking at him.

"We split up. She didn't tell you?"

"No offense, but it's kind of hard to keep track."

Gabe furrows his eyebrows. "Wow . . . that's a terrible thing to say about your best friend. That's really messed up."

I feel my face turn red. "I mean, she's just . . . I've known her a long time—"

"Easy, Sensitivity, I'm just messing with you," he says, grinning. "So, how's Jelly?"

He thinks he's so clever, needling his way under my skin like this. I refuse to give him the satisfaction of a response. "Fine," I say, staring at the computer.

"You could do better, you know that, right?"

Okay, I have to respond to *that*. "You don't know what you're talking about. What did Meryl tell you?"

"Just that you're in over your head."

"I'm not discussing this with you."

"Fine."

It's quiet for a moment. I could just let it go. I could just keep my thoughts to myself and let the conversation fizzle and die here. Maybe I've been a little confused about what's going on between me and Ethan. Maybe it has occurred to me that I might be in over my head, flailing around as I am in a disorienting, murky space between being my chief resident's mentee and being his romantic interest, an arrangement that doesn't seem ideal, especially for someone with little to no dating experience. But regardless, I certainly don't owe Gabe any sort of explanation. "It's not like some casual relationship," I say.

"Okay."

"The only reason we haven't told people about it is because we work together."

"Sure."

My voice exasperated, I say, "Of course I can't expect a child to understand an adult relationship."

"And how many of those have you been in? One?"

I bristle. "Meryl really needs to stop talking about me behind my back."

"I figured that last bit out for myself," he says. "Look, this guy is on the rebound, and you're just one of several available basketballs on the court. A naïve, sexy-librarian basketball."

I massage my temples. "Does the gift shop sell Tylenol? Why does talking to you always give me a headache?"

He shrugs. "The truth hurts."

A nurse hands me a chart. "Patient up," she says, pointing toward an examination room.

Happy to escape my conversation with Gabe, I jump up and knock on the door, not waiting for a reply before I enter the room. "Hi, I'm Dr. Kapadia," I say.

A woman pacing back and forth glances at her watch. "Are you always this late?"

"Um . . . it's my first day in this clinic, so . . . no."

She hands me a thick stack of manila envelopes and a piece of notebook paper with a cartoon drawing of a woman with overly long limbs and flames emanating from the crown of her head. Arrows point to different body parts and are neatly labeled with corresponding symptoms written in capital letters in red ink.

"I had an eight thirty appointment. Fortunately, I've brought all my old records and drawn a diagram of my complaints to save time. This has all been going on since about 1987. My left elbow aches and tingles. My index finger, that feels like there's a hot poker in it. My right leg feels like there's cold water running down it, but there's not. I mean, I look at my leg, and there's no water on it. None. But that's what it feels like. I get cramps in my pancreas and in my thorasis. My neck itches, and so do both of my breasts. My scalp literally feels like it's on fire about three to seven times a week. And also, sometimes my right eye feels like there's pressure in it, like it might explode."

I look at the diagram. An arrow points from the cartoon woman's right eye to the words "EXPLOSION EYE!"

I sigh. "Tell me more about that."

I make it to the conference room on the first floor ten minutes after the lunchtime lecture is scheduled to start. I quietly nudge the door open. The room is full of residents and interns sitting in the dark while the lecturer clicks through a PowerPoint presentation on the causes of infectious endocarditis. Imani is asleep at her desk, her head resting on her folded arms. I slide into the seat Bianca has saved for me in the back row.

"Welcome back," she whispers, smiling. "We missed you."

I'm awash in a flurry of warm feelings. It's good to be among friends again.

Clark leans over from the seat in front of me. "Yeah, while you were out playing with mice, we had to cover all your call shifts."

The warm feelings fade.

Bianca shoots Clark a harsh look, then turns to me. "Are you okay? We were worried about you. Portnoy is such a jerk for having you suspended over nothing."

I wave my hand. "I'm fine. I'm just happy I wasn't fired."

"Do you think it'll affect your record? Being suspended?" Bianca asks.

I cringe. It's like I have a rap sheet now. "Probably," I say. "My evaluation from Portnoy for that rotation is going to be pretty dismal, to say the least."

Bianca shakes her head in disgust. "Ugh, bunch of jerks. You should sue for workplace harassment."

Clark smirks at her. "Oh, look who's suddenly a fan of lawsuits. Very American of you, Bee."

Someone up front turns around to shush them, and they fall silent. A moment later, I whisper, "Where's Stuart?" It's unlike him to miss one of these mandatory lectures. It'd be unlike him to miss an optional lecture.

"I haven't seen him since early this morning," Bianca replies. "He was on call last night. Maybe he's asleep somewhere."

"No way. Dude never sleeps," Clark says. "He's probably at the coffee cart getting his ninth cup of coffee."

My pager sounds. I recognize the number as one of the ICU extensions. I step out of the room and return the call from a phone in the hallway.

"Norah?" Stuart's voice is thin.

"Hey, Stu. We were just talking about you. You're missing the lecture," I say.

There is a long pause. Then he says, "I have a patient."

"Oh. Okay. Do you need help with anything? I can come up to the ICU."

"No, just . . . when you were suspended, did Dr. Forks say anything about it going on your record? Like, how did that work? I just wanted . . . to know." He sounds scattered and breathless.

"What do you mean? What's going on?"

"Nothing. It's . . . never mind. Just tell Francesca, if she's looking for me, that I'm busy with a patient, okay?"

"Sure, okay."

He hangs up.

I stand there for a moment, staring at the phone. Whatever's going on, I'm not sure I want to get involved. But it's Stuart.

I run for the elevator.

* * *

Stuart is hunched over a computer in a narrow work cubby at the back of the ICU, his hand on the mouse, his expression distant.

"Stuart?"

He squints at me, a deep crease between his eyebrows. His eyes are red and sunken, and he has what I estimate is a week's worth of stubble. "Norah," he says. "Norah, I fucked up."

I lower my voice. "What happened?"

Stuart explains, his head in his hands, that early this morning, he was paged to reinsert a nasogastric tube that had slipped out of a comatose patient on a ventilator. He followed the usual protocol: he covered the end of the tube in viscous jelly and threaded it through the patient's nose until he was confident it had reached the stomach. Then he ordered an X-ray of the chest and abdomen to make sure the tube was not accidentally lodged in the patient's lung.

"And? Was it in the lung?" I say. "That's not a big deal. We've all done that before."

He sighs and points to the computer screen. On it is an X-ray—a front view of the chest and the abdomen—but no NG tube.

"Where is it? Curled up in the back of the throat?"

He shakes his head. "The patient . . . had a head trauma," he says, avoiding my gaze. "Motorcycle accident. He has a basilar skull fracture."

I brace myself against the wall. "Please tell me it's not—"

"It took me a while to figure it out," he says. "Most of the morning, actually. I ordered a stat CT scan. The radiologist called me. It's fascinating, really."

"Whom have you told?"

"No one, yet. But it should be about ninety minutes before the CT report hits the chart and the nurses page the attending. I should quit, right? Before they fire me, I should quit. Or do you think they'll put me on leave and give me a second chance, like they did for you?"

I have no idea what to say. Wordlessly, I do the only helpful thing I can think of: I page Ethan.

"So, let me get this straight," Ethan says, staring over Stuart's shoulder at the computer screen. A CT scan image shows a bright white line the width of a pencil cutting straight through a field of scalloped gray and white. "You just inserted a nasogastric tube into this patient's nose, through the fracture in the base of his skull, and into his brain. Is that correct?"

Francesca appears behind him and peers at the screen. "Ethan, I got your page. What's going—ohholyshit. . . ."

Ten minutes later, the Neurosurgery resident—an unusually tall fellow with a serene expression and a monotone voice—is seated at the computer, the four of us huddled behind him.

"Well, this is a fucktastrophe," he says. "It went straight through the left temporal lobe. Hope this guy isn't right-handed." He stands. "The attending's gonna shit his pants. Congratulations. This is definitely a first. We'll take him to surgery within the hour."

He leaves, and Francesca turns to Stuart, red-faced. Even in heels, she's half his height. She jabs her index finger into his chest. "You should have called ENT to put that tube back in using a scope for visualization. That's how they got it in the first time. Did you even read the chart beforehand?"

Stuart shakes his head. "I usually do. I know I should have. But it was a simple nasogastric tube. We put in, like, ten a day. I had so many other patients to see, I thought . . . I just thought I could do it really fast and . . ." His voice cracks.

"What do I always say about the weakest link?" Francesca demands. "This is the type of shit I'm talking about! You don't take shortcuts. You check the chart, *every time*!"

Ethan takes her arm. "Okay, deep breath. Stuart, you're going to have to talk to hospital Risk Management tomorrow. You also need to tell the family what happened."

"The only silver lining here," Francesca says, "is that the man was brain damaged and in a coma to begin with."

"Except now he needs surgery to take out the tube," I say.

"What you mean is, he needs a *procedure* to *extract* the tube," Ethan says. "It's all about how you present the facts, remember?"

Francesca massages her temples. "We have to limit the damage here," she says. "Make sure you point out that the guy was probably never going to wake up anyway. This won't change the course of his recovery—or his lack thereof." Then she adds, under her breath, "You'd just better hope he doesn't die on the table."

Stuart nods silently.

"Do you need me to go with you to talk to the family, or do you think you can manage to get that part right?" Francesca asks pointedly.

"I can do it," Stuart says, meeting her gaze. "I'll do it."

"Fine," Francesca replies. "I'll stay here and get your patient ready for surgery. And then you and I will take a walk down to Dr. Forks's office so he can help sort out this disaster."

We leave Ethan, Francesca, and the Neurosurgery resident at the patient's bedside. On the walk to the ICU waiting room, Stuart swears under his breath and wipes his forehead with his scrub shirt.

"Stu, it could have happened to anyone," I say.

He leans against the wall, trembling slightly, then sinks to a crouch. Cradling his head in his hands, he takes several gasping breaths. For a moment I think he might scream. I kneel beside him and put my hand on his shoulder.

"It's going to be okay."

"I'm so tired," he says into his palms.

"I know. Just get through this, and then you can rest in the call room. I'll cover your pager."

"What if he's paralyzed? What if he dies and it's my fault?"

I can feel the weight of his guilt and shame and fear. It rolls off him like a leaden fog. He adds, in a voice I can barely hear, "How do I live with that?"

"It was an accident, Stu," I say. "Any of us could have made the same mistake."

He looks up at me skeptically, then takes a deep breath and stands. His jaw is set, as if he's refocused on the task at hand and blocked out everything else. I'm reminded of pins at a bowling alley: the toppled ones are cleared away and a perfect, new set appears, at attention, ready to be toppled again.

We walk down the hallway to a glass door marked *ICU Family Waiting*. A woman in sweat pants and a man holding a cup of coffee with both hands are sitting in an otherwise empty room lined with chairs. I turn to go.

"Wait," Stuart says, his gaze fixed on the couple. "Do you want to go in with me? Please?"

The woman holds a magazine called *Healthy Life!*, the cover of which features a man jogging with a dog and the headline "Could it be your prostate? Take our quiz!"

We walk in together. "I'm Dr. Ness," Stuart says. "This is Dr. Kapadia. Are you . . . ?"

"I'm Craig Perkins." The man extends his hand without standing up. "This is my wife. How's my uncle?"

"Thank you for coming in," Stuart says. "I was on call last night taking care of the patient. Your uncle. I'm sorry to say, there's been a complication."

The woman's eyes flash angrily. "What kind of complication?"

"An NG tube—that's a tube inserted through the nose and into the stomach—well, it's supposed to go into the stomach—it passed through his skull fracture and into his brain."

"His . . . *brain*?" the woman says. "How is that even possible?"

"It's a very rare complication of this type of fracture," Stuart says. "A complication, in fact, that no one in this ICU has ever seen before."

"But . . ." The man holds his index finger to his nose. "I don't get how that happened."

"The fracture is through the cribriform plate," Stuart says, his tone becoming more relaxed, even confident. "That's the piece of the skull that separates the back of the nasopharynx from the base of the brain. Usually the tube hits the back of the nasopharyngeal cavity—the back of the throat, essentially—and curves downward to go into the esophagus and then into the stomach. Because of where the fracture is located, there was nothing to stop the tube from going straight through the bone and into the"—his voice catches, and he clears his throat—"brain."

The man leans back in his chair. "Wow. What do we do about this?"

"He'll need a procedure," Stuart says, "to extract the tube. That will happen tonight, under the direction of a neurosurgeon."

"Will there be brain damage because of this? I mean, what are the repercussions of this tube being in his brain?" the woman says.

Stuart clears his throat again. "Well, we don't really—"

"This is unlikely to change the course of his recovery," I say.

The man nods and, after a moment, says, "Okay. Well, do what you have to."

"We'll have someone bring you the consent forms to sign," Stuart says.

In the elevator on the way back to the ICU, Stuart is silent. His fists are clenched, and the veins on the backs of his hands stand out, blue and turgid, against his pale skin. I notice he's lost weight, making him even lankier than when I met him that first day at orientation. He looks brittle, like if you gently pressed your index finger into him in the right spot, he might crack into pieces.

"Hey, why don't you give me your pager, and you can get some sleep?" I say.

He shakes his head. "No, thanks, Norah. I'm fine. I just need a coffee."

"Stuart, you need—"

"I need to get back to work," he snaps, silencing me. "And so do you."

I stare straight ahead, feeling my stomach lurch into my chest as we descend.

CHAPTER FIFTEEN

In fact, Stuart's patient makes a remarkable recovery. Two weeks later, he awakens from his coma and is removed from the ventilator. He's so grateful to be alive that the fact that his right arm is paralyzed is of minimal concern to him.

The hospital gossip machine has been working overtime since the incident, and I've overheard some of the upperclassmen bruit about the story, snickering, calling Stuart "Dr. Piths." The Radiology department presented the case at the monthly hospital-wide Grand Rounds lecture, so that all the residents and attendings from various departments could marvel over the amazing CAT scan pictures of an NG tube spearing someone's brain. They didn't use Stuart's name in their presentation, referring to him only as "a member of the house staff," but by now everyone knows it was him.

Stuart has been withdrawn and subdued, reading even more than usual, avoiding conversation, sometimes avoiding eye contact. For weeks, even Clark hasn't been able to get him to crack a smile, and none of us have seen him in the cafeteria.

I'm sitting with Bianca and Imani at breakfast one morning when Stuart appears at our table, half a grapefruit and a cup of coffee on his tray. His white coat is still filthy and he hasn't shaved, but he looks a little less dejected today.

"Mind if I join?" he asks.

"Shut up, Stu," Bianca chides, smiling. "Since when are you so formal? Sit down and tell us everything. Are you okay? We've been worried about you."

Stuart sighs as he picks at the grapefruit with a slightly quivering hand. "That patient will never use his right arm again."

"You don't know that," I say, trying to sound buoyant. "He might recover better than you think."

"I heard they're not putting you on leave," Bianca says, trying to stress the positive.

"No, they're not putting me on leave," Stuart says, his expression flat. "Lucky for me."

I shouldn't be bitter. It's fortunate for Stuart that his patient's attending was more forgiving of his mistake than Portnoy was of mine.

I am, I admit to myself, a little bitter.

Stuart goes on to tell us that his meeting with the hospital Risk Management team—a husband and wife, both attorneys, who, apparently, hate each other—lasted seven minutes. The attorneys told him it would be two years before the statute of limitations expired and the patient would no longer be able to sue him or the hospital. They seemed tremendously pleased to learn that the patient is, in fact, left-handed.

"And they told me to stay away from the patient," he says. "I'm not allowed to set foot in his room. Which I guess I understand. I'm a menace."

"Stu, it was an accident," Imani says, while Bianca and I nod in agreement. "You can't beat yourself up over it."

He sighs again and taps his fork against the tray. "Yeah, I know. Dr. Forks and Francesca said I should look at this as a learning opportunity. Learn from it and move on, they said."

"Exactly," Bianca says. "Move forward. You have to shake off this funk you've been in. You're coming to Ethan's party at the Elemental tonight, right?"

He scratches his chin. "I don't know. Maybe."

"Come on!" Bianca lightly chucks him on the arm. "You need to loosen up for once. Come out with us. I think that cute Emergency Medicine resident you've been crushing on will be there."

He shakes his head, his face reddening. "What are you talking about?"

"Oh, please." Bianca rolls her eyes. "We've all noticed you staring at her in the ED."

Stuart looks to me and Imani for confirmation of this statement, and we nod, grinning. He laughs—probably for the first time in weeks—and shrugs. "Okay, if I go tonight, will you promise to introduce me to her?"

Bianca's face lights up. I suspect this is her secret purpose in life, to connect would-be lovers who also happen to be healthcare professionals. "I promise," she says, delighted.

I breathe in silent relief. *He's fine,* I reassure myself. *He's moving forward. We're all moving forward.*

I am contorting my midsection into a pair of Spanx when Meryl calls.

"Did you book your ticket?" she says.

"Just did this morning. You?"

"You bet your ass." She emits a shrill whooping noise. "Here we come! Aloha, bitches!"

I wince, pulling the phone away from my ear. "Yup. Here we come."

"So, Ethan's party is tonight? Gabe's going to that, too."

I rub my forehead, a sudden pain between my eyebrows. "Really?"

"Yeah, I think practically every resident and med student in the hospital is invited."

"Word gets around quick. Hey, sorry to hear you and Gabe split up."

"Please, we're constantly splitting up. We'll probably be back together next week."

"I think you should move on," I say. "You deserve better."

There is silence for a moment. "Well, he's a good guy."

"I know," I say, fastening the strap of a gold-sequined sandal with a three-inch heel. "I just think you deserve to be in a real relationship. Everything between me and Ethan is so . . . effortless."

I glance into the living room, where Beth is watching *Jeopardy!* with her head resting on Al's chest while he absentmindedly picks his teeth with a paper clip. They've grown on me, the two of them.

"So you guys are officially dating?" Meryl asks. "I didn't realize."

"Well, we haven't put a label on it, but we basically are." My shoes click loudly against the kitchen tile. "I gotta go meet my Uber. These heels are painful."

"Heels again? Wow, look at you. All grown up."

I laugh. "I'm trying not to think about how much I just spent on these shoes. Remind me to thank Michael Kors when I go in someday to get my bunionectomy and file for bankruptcy." I check my watch. "I'm running late. Can I call you tomorrow?" I'm pleased that I'm too busy to talk, not because of work but due to my bustling and enviable social life. *Have to go meet my boyfriend at his party. Must run. Ciao, darling.*

A disgruntled man in a Ford Escort drives me across town to Rittenhouse Square. The sun is beginning to set, and the Elemental, one of midtown's most stylish eateries, glows neon orange just beyond the northeast corner of the square. Above the restaurant, several stories up, is the rooftop lounge. I hurry through the swanky wood-paneled dining room to catch the elevator. "Could you hold that, please!"

In the sliding steel doors, I catch my reflection—in my shiny, pink, one-size-too-small strapless dress, I look as if I've wrapped myself in moist bubble gum, and my legs are so constricted it's as if I'm trying to hold an index card between my knees. A hand appears, and the doors joggle open.

"Having trouble walking?"

"Hello, Gabe." I lean against the back wall of the elevator and fix my gaze on the ceiling.

"That's a nice dress. What floor are we going to?"

"Five."

He pushes the button for the fifth floor and turns to me. "Correct me if I'm wrong, but I feel like you've been avoiding me for a couple of weeks."

"Can't imagine why," I reply without turning my head.

"Look, your relationship—or whatever it is—with Jelly is none of my business." He crosses his arms. "I didn't mean to upset you."

I cross mine. If that was supposed to be an apology, it was glaringly inadequate. "The only way you could upset me is if I respected you more."

We ride the rest of the way in silence. When the doors open again, he steps out and strides off down a hallway, disappearing past the coat check while I hobble after him like a rusty tin soldier. A raucous group of Podiatry residents pushes past me and piles into the elevator.

The long hallway leading to the lounge is lined with potted evergreens strung with fairy lights. The young woman standing behind the counter at the coat check closet, scrolling through Instagram, barely looks up as I hand her my coat. At the end of the hall, I adjust my glasses before pushing through a lacquered mahogany door with a porthole.

The rooftop is reminiscent of the deck of a swanky yacht in an eighties music video. A circular, blue-tiled bar is ringed with white tables and chairs, and the floor is covered in a plush red shag carpet.

Wicker basket chairs hang from iron beams overhead. A firepit flanked by orange leather sofas glows in one corner. All around, towering office and apartment buildings stretch into the sky, their neon signs and picture windows blinking to life as the darkness falls.

I maneuver through a throng of exuberant people and find Ethan near the firepit, cheeks flushed, grinning, shouting over the music to a group of Dermatology residents.

"Finally!" he says. "Three years of working my ass off and I finally got it."

I put my fingertips on his arm and smile. Before I can say anything, a girl I've never seen before nudges me aside and throws her arms around his neck. "Congratulations on getting the Portnoy fellowship!" she says before kissing him awkwardly on the chin and stumbling off into the crowd.

"Norah!" Ethan envelops me in a bear hug. "Norah, Norah. I was wondering where you were!" He introduces me to the dermatologists, all of whom are in varying states of inebriation, then says in a hushed tone, his face close to mine, "That dress is . . . *nice*."

"I'm going to get myself a drink," I say, and, attempting a coy smile over my shoulder, limp toward the bar. An anxious knot forms in my stomach as I eye the rows of varied, colorful bottles behind the bartender. I've never ordered from a bar before. How do I get the bartender's attention? What do I order? A wine? Any wine? Do they have Mendocino Coast?

Bianca appears near my elbow, swaying slightly, holding a martini glass containing something frothy and pink. "Norah! Where is Stuart? That cute EM resident wants to meet him."

"I just got here. I haven't seen him," I say. "What's that you're drinking?"

She looks at her glass as if she's just noticed it. "I don't know. Some girly drink. I actually want a beer. Do you want this?" She hands me the glass. "Clark and I are sitting over there," she says, pointing, then disappears into the crush of people around the bar.

I wander through the crowd, surprised to be enjoying the thrum of music and chatter. For the past several months, there's been a constant stream of patient names, diagnoses, and drug dosages running through my mind on a loop, like a grating song on repeat. It's how I make sure I don't forget or miss anything. It's how I guarantee the torrent of worries about Ma and money and Nimisha Auntie and bills and the fact that I might not be married before the time I'm thirty doesn't interfere with my work, with the care of my patients. But it's exhausting, and for a moment, it's nice to drown it all out with this ambient, happy noise.

I take a sip of Bianca's drink. It tastes like pomegranate. I drink the entire thing while looking for Clark. When I find him, he's tucked into one of the hanging basket chairs, smoking a cigar. Bianca reappears, having finally procured a beer, and we settle into basket chairs, too. I look around for Ethan but can't see past the dense wall of people surrounding the bar.

"Should we tell Norah?" Clark asks Bianca.

"Tell me what?" I ask, reclining in my chair and closing my eyes, my mind swirly and relaxed.

Bianca sighs. "We're worried about Stu. I found out he started taking Adderall a few months ago."

"Is that why he's been so jittery?" I ask. "I thought it was all the coffee."

Bianca drums her fingers against her beer bottle. "I found an empty pill bottle in the call room with his name on it. I think at first it was just to stay awake on call, you know? But lately . . . I think he's taking it all the time, and more than he should. I think . . . I think he might be crushing them."

I sit up straight. "What?"

Bianca and Clark exchange a glance. After a moment of hesitation, Clark says, "And I'm pretty sure I saw him steal blank prescriptions."

The idea is so outrageous, I laugh. Bianca and Clark are stone-faced. "You're not serious."

Clark stubs out his cigar and leans forward. "It was a week ago. One of the attendings left his white coat hanging on the back of a chair at the nurses' station. I saw Stuart go through the pockets and take a bunch of blank prescriptions and put them in his own coat pocket."

I shake my head in disbelief. Legally, residents can't prescribe controlled medications like narcotics or stimulants. Those prescriptions can come only from an attending and have to be written on an attending's prescription pad. "Come on, you guys. There is no way Stuart is stealing blank scripts so he can write himself prescriptions for Adderall."

Bianca takes a swig of her beer. "But what if he is?"

"We have to tell someone," I say, my mind reeling. "Dr. Forks, or—"

"He'd be fired," Clark says, shaking his head. "Forging prescriptions is a felony. I Googled it."

"He's been under extreme stress, they have to understand that," Bianca says. "The whole NG tube in the brain fiasco—"

"You know something?" Clark interrupts. "I think he was upset they didn't suspend him. He *wanted* to be punished. He keeps asking me to check on that patient for him. He wants to know if the patient can move his arm today or wiggle his fingers. The guilt is eating him alive. Everyone keeps telling him to move on, but I don't think he can."

"He needs help," I say. "What if he's addicted to Adderall?"

"I tried to talk to him about it already," Clark says. "He swore the Adderall was for ADHD and said he got the prescription from his

Primary Care doctor. I didn't tell him that I saw him take those blank scripts."

"So what do we do?" My heart races, and my chest starts to feel tight. The cigar smoke isn't helping. I claw through my purse for my inhaler and realize I must have left it in my coat pocket.

"What *can* we do?" Bianca asks in frustration. "He won't admit he has a problem, and we can't tell Dr. Forks or administration without risking his career. Did you know that, even after residency, your state medical license can be taken away because you have a history of substance abuse or mental health problems? We don't have this kind of stigma in Italy."

"Well, maybe Stuart can go practice in Italy, then," Clark grumbles, rolling his eyes.

The two of them sneer at each other, and I announce that I need to find my inhaler before I have a full-blown asthma attack.

The coat check attendant has vanished, so I squeeze behind the counter and frantically sift through racks of coats, looking for mine. My purse slips out of my hands, and its contents—including my inhaler, which apparently had been in there all along—spill onto the ground. As I lunge for the inhaler, there is a faint tearing sound. I freeze. Slowly, I reach around toward my rump and feel . . . underwear. My dress has come apart in the back. Terrific. Crouched behind the counter, I take a puff of my inhaler and consider how much worse this night could possibly get.

"Why are you leaving already?" Ethan's voice asks from the hallway, just steps away.

I stay hidden behind the counter, trying not to breathe too loudly.

"I told you I could only stay for a bit." Elle's voice is tired. "I have to drive up to New York tonight."

"Why don't you just skip New York?"

"Ethan, things are complicated right now."

"The other night was fun, though, right?"

Elle's smile is evident in the silence that follows.

"So, skip New York and whatever or whoever is waiting for you there."

Elle laughs. "You really hate being by yourself."

"Don't you?"

There is a pause. Then Elle says, "I don't mind it. I have to go. But I'll call you."

Their voices fade away down the hall.

Sitting on a bench in front of the Elemental ten minutes later, I pull a stranger's coat closed around me and rest my forehead on my knees.

"Are you going to throw up?"

I sigh into my lap. "Go away."

"What's the matter?"

"Nothing. Go away, Gabe."

He sits next to me, his legs stretching onto the sidewalk. A car speeds by.

"Saw the Surgery . . . Individual. The chick in the green dress, right? You're way hotter than her."

I look at him. "You really think—"

He recoils. "No! No, you're not. You have mascara everywhere. Here, wipe, before you scare young children." He hands me a tissue from his pocket.

Laughing, I dab my eyes. "Any better?"

"Yes, better." He smiles. I can see why Meryl keeps getting sucked back into their relationship. He's kind of charming in his own irksome way.

"All right, I gotta go," he says. "It's late, and if I don't get enough sleep, I get cranky. You staying?"

"I am definitely not staying."

He takes my hand and pulls me to my feet. "I'll walk you home, then." Half a block later, he says, "Seriously? You're going to break your ankles."

"They're actually really comfortable."

He shakes his head. "This is ridiculous." He grabs me around my waist and hoists me over his shoulder.

I shriek. "What are you doing?"

"I'd like to get home sometime tonight. Where do you live again?"

"Ninth and Sansom."

He stops midstride. "Okay, yeah. There is no way I'm carrying you all the way there. I'm getting you a cab."

He turns to look up the street. There are no cabs in sight.

"Okay, plan B," he says. He sets off again.

"Where are we going?"

"I live two blocks up. We can call you a cab or an Uber from my place."

"I can walk it."

"You cannot."

"Put me down. You'll throw your back out."

"I bench-press more than you weigh."

"Am I supposed to be impressed by that?"

"I'm just saying, I work out." He flexes the biceps of his free arm.

A woman on a bicycle looks over her shoulder at us as she glides past.

"People are staring."

"Which people? Those?" He spots a couple across the street and waves jauntily. The man and woman avert their eyes and hurry away.

We stop at an iron gate on a side street. It clicks open, and we are in a little cobblestone courtyard covered in vines.

"Wow, this is where you live?"

He sets me down. "It's been in the family. My grandparents and both my parents went to school in Philly. Come in."

He leads me up a flight of stairs to the side door of a colonial-style brick home.

"I can't believe Meryl never mentioned how nice your place was."

"Excuse the mess."

Plates and silverware are strewn about the kitchen. Gabe gathers them quickly and piles them in the sink. "When do you two leave for your trip to Hawaii?"

"The first week in July. Only four months to go." Under my breath I add, "As long as I don't get fired before then."

"I heard about your leave. What happened?"

"I had a conversation with one of Portnoy's patients. Apparently, I shared too much information." I wave my hand in frustration. "Don't ask. Anyway, if I get the ax, I'll end up back home working for Vikram Uncle, so there's no way I'm letting that happen."

"Vikram Uncle? From the Diwali party? He offered me a job, too. Promised in a few years I could buy a Mercedes. I turned him down, though."

"Yeah, trust me, that was the right move," I say. I run my hand over the stainless-steel countertop. The kitchen opens into a great room with a pair of brown leather sofas and bookshelves lining each wall. "Can I have a tour?"

In an upstairs hallway, a ladder stretches to a tiny door in the ceiling. "What's that?" I ask.

"Follow me." He climbs to the top, pushes the door open, and vanishes into the dark. "You coming?"

I stumble out of my shoes and follow. Whatever was in Bianca's pomegranate drink is definitely still with me, and my vision is a little off. I grip the ladder rungs tightly. Stepping out onto a tiny terrace tucked between the gables of the roof, I gasp. Millions of lights stretch out in every direction like a vast, glittering field. Gabe leans against the shingles and tucks his hands into his pockets. "This is my favorite spot," he says. "You can even see City Hall from here."

I spot Ethan's building and wonder how many passionate encounters he and Elle have had there. Then I consider what it would feel like to just step off this little platform into the shimmering void.

Gabe sweeps his arm across the horizon. "And behold, in the distance, Camden. Want to go back inside? It's freezing out here."

"It's not that bad." I reach out my hand and run one of his shirt buttons between my fingers.

It would be worse than a miscalculation to kiss Gabe. It would be a totally illogical, stupid thing to do with countless unpredictable, but likely negative, consequences.

I kiss Gabe. I do so with my eyes open and, as a result, catch the look of complete surprise and confusion on his face. After what seems like an eternity, he kisses me back. I close my eyes, and the world tilts, then levels out again. A storm rages inside my mind. It's as if my rational self is being tossed about in turbulent seas, trying desperately to stay afloat.

"I thought I make your head hurt," Gabe says quietly, his face close to mine.

I flinch. "I'm sorry about what I said."

His hands slide under the coat. "This is a man's coat. Did you wear someone else's coat home? Again?"

"I didn't know what to do. My dress came apart in the back."

He laughs. "Really?"

I shrug out of the stolen coat and press against him, my face buried in his collar.

"You've been drinking," he says.

My voice is muffled. "I'm spontaneous and breezy now."

"I don't know what that means."

"It means I'm a coat kleptomaniac and wear impractical shoes and"—I lift my chin, my gaze meets his, and the waves close over my head and pull me under—"want this."

"You're going to need something else to wear," he says as, with slow and careful precision, he tears the dress in half.

CHAPTER SIXTEEN

That night, I dream that I am lying naked on a frigid operating room table. Ethan, his mouth and nose concealed behind a surgical mask, spreads my ribs apart and gingerly probes my heart with a pair of forceps. Then he scoops my beating heart into his hands.

I wake suddenly to the smell of eggs and a wave of nausea. I'm wearing an oversize Phillies T-shirt and a pair of sweat pants. My pulse is pounding, maybe from the dream, maybe from awakening to a nightmare. *What have I done?* I don't remember anything beyond being on the roof last night. And I'm in Gabe's bed.

"Voilà. A classic French omelet," Gabe says as I come flying down the stairs. He tips the contents of a frying pan onto a plate. "Learned it on YouTube while you were asleep." He smiles.

"Gabe! What happened last night?"

He laughs sheepishly. "You know, we made out a little, and your dress . . . blew away off the roof."

I implode with embarrassment. I desperately wish a strong gust of wind had whisked me off the roof, too, never to be seen again. "But after that? Nothing else happened, right?"

Gabe shakes his head. "You slept in the bed, and I crashed on the couch down here. Nothing happened."

I nod in relief until another thought comes to mind and I exclaim, more loudly than I mean to, "Oh my God. You saw me in my underwear?"

Gabe puts both hands up in front of him. "Whoa, calm down. No underwear was visible. You were wearing this constrictive tube garment thing."

"Oh my God, where are my Spanx?"

He slides a little plastic bag toward me across the kitchen island. "In here. I also bought you flip-flops from the pharmacy across the street."

I rub my temples. "I'm never leaving my house again."

"You should probably eat something and take an anti-inflammatory. It'll help with the hangover."

"I'm not really hungry, but thanks," I say. "I should get home."

Gabe hesitates. "So, which one of us should tell Meryl about the kissing?"

I sigh. "We're not going to let her be the elephant in the room for even a little while?"

"Norah, Meryl and I split up weeks ago. I don't feel guilty about this."

"She's not your best friend."

"So, I'll tell her, then."

"I think neither of us should say anything." I fold up the ends of the sweat pants and wriggle my feet into the flip-flops.

"Not saying anything is the same as lying about it."

My hand on the doorknob, I look at him over my shoulder. We keep things from patients in the interest of doing no harm, don't we? It seems only logical that the same principle should apply here, too. "No, it isn't," I say. "It's not the same at all."

When I was in tenth grade, Cindy Mills—who lived in my neighborhood and who was, in all ways, the girl next door—asked me one afternoon if I wanted a ride to school the next morning. I was sixteen and, though I'd passed the school drivers' education course, still hadn't worked up the nerve to take my driver's license exam. This was, at least in part, due to the fact that my father died in a car accident, and my mother never quite recovered from the trauma of it. She was fond of quoting car accident fatality rates for teens and liked to recount stories like this one whenever I asked to borrow her car keys: "Bhumi Auntie's cousin's daughter's niece was killed last year when she forgot to stop at stop sign. She was just seventeen. Pickup truck hit her so hard she went through windshield, and when they found her one of her eyeballs was hanging out of her skull, attached only by long nerve."

I was one of the only sophomores at school to still ride the bus. Every day, Cindy Mills and her popular, perfectly coiffed best friend, Joellen, would race past in Cindy's dad's Ford Taurus as I made the several-block journey back and forth to the bus stop, often in inclement weather, always with a book bag at least twice my body weight strapped to my back. On that frigid winter morning, sitting in the back seat of the Taurus, Paramore on the radio, flying past the shivering freshmen at the bus stop, I wondered—was this how the popular kids felt every day? As we turned off the main road in front of the high school, we passed the auxiliary parking lot and dozens of students making the quarter-mile trek in the blustery wind across an athletic field to the school. Then we pulled past an administrator in a fur coat and hat—who peeked into the car and gave us a thumbs-up sign—and came to a stop in Parking Lot A. I smiled and thanked Cindy for the ride. We'd never been friends in all the years we'd been neighbors, but maybe this was her way of saying she wanted that to change. As we walked up the front steps to the school, past the circle driveway where buses were starting to pull in, I asked where I should meet her after school for the trip home. She smoothed her short dress and exchanged an awkward laugh with Joellen. That was when

I noticed the orange signs taped to the glass front doors of the school: *New parking policy: Only vehicles with 3 or more students will be permitted to park in Lot A.*

That afternoon, when I stepped off the bus, pulled my coat closed, and started toward home, I heard a car approaching behind me. There was no place to hide. I winced and waited. As the Taurus roared past, Joellen's boyfriend, Chris, gawked delightedly from the rear window and waved at me.

And now here I am, ten years later, walking home in too-small flip-flops and a too-big Phillies T-shirt, carrying my Spanx in a CVS bag and wearing a coat I stole from a bar, again abjectly humiliated by a girl more socially adept than me—one who has, evidently, ravaged Ethan with her pheromones. I'm jealous and angry, but I know I don't have a right to be; it's not Ethan's fault that I falsely assumed our relationship was exclusive. I should have clarified. Now that I think of it, this whole thing is probably, at its heart, a miscommunication, a by-product of my inexperience with romantic relationships.

And, analyzing this further, there are several other potential sources for error here: I overheard a conversation out of context. Ethan may well have been trying to talk Elle into going to a concert with him in lieu of her trip to New York because they had just been to a concert together—platonically—and "the other night was fun." And naturally, no one wants to go to a concert alone, if they can avoid it. Hence, Elle's "You really hate being by yourself" comment. I may have been making an assumption about Ethan and Elle sleeping together based on insufficient data and interpreter bias. The more I think about it, the more this explanation makes perfect sense.

What happened last night with Gabe was, clearly, a regrettable, alcohol-induced misstep. But Gabe doesn't feel guilty about it and, probably, neither should I. Certainly, there's no need to flagellate myself over it. What's done is done. If Cindy Mills had kissed Gabe, I bet she wouldn't even think twice about it. She'd probably have slept with Gabe and then offered Meryl a one-way ride to Gabe's house. Because that's how people like Cindy Mills are.

"You're late. And do you think I could have West Nile virus?" Paul asks when I arrive at Ma's house that night.

I push past him and hang up my coat. "No," I say.

"I got a mosquito bite last week and—"

"No."

The stove is overflowing with pots and pans and baking dishes, and the oven is on. I can't remember the last time the oven at Ma's house was used. The pungent smell of garam masala is tempered today by the heavy, sweet scent of cream and paneer. Ma, wearing an apron, arches an eyebrow at me reproachfully. "We've been waiting for you. That's short dress." She ushers us into the dining room.

Nimisha Auntie is seated at the head of the table, Kai in her lap. "Hello, *beti*!" She catches the glare I shoot Paul and says, "I just stopped by to say hello to your ma. I'm going to stay for dinner." She meets my gaze pointedly. I sink into a seat at the opposite end of the table, forcing my mouth into a smile.

The meal has already been laid out in covered CorningWare bowls. Reena appears from the living room, and, taking Kai from Nimisha Auntie, deposits him onto the floor, where he squeals and toddles about on his plump, jiggly legs. Ma carefully fills Paul's plate with pillow-soft naan, fragrant chicken biryani, malai kofta swimming in a rich creamy gravy, two types of spicy lentils, and a golden-brown samosa.

Paul looks up from his phone. "Ma, did you make all this? By yourself?"

Ma beams proudly. "I did. This afternoon."

"Wow." He inhales the steam wafting up from the food. "This looks delicious. It looks like the dinners we used— It looks like a restaurant dinner." He squeezes Ma's arm in appreciation, and she glows.

Paul and I exchange a glance. This looks like the dinners Ma used to make before Dad died.

The bowls are passed around the table, and we fill our plates. Ma insists we all try the lentils. With some trepidation, I put a forkful in my mouth. Instead of the usual eye-watering, tongue-curling reaction I have to spicy foods, what I experience is a wonderfully salty, tart, and robust burst on my palate, followed by a subtle, tingling hint of chili pepper as I swallow. It makes the buttered pasta I had for lunch seem as flavorful as balsa wood by comparison.

I pass the bowl of malai kofta to Reena.

"Are those made with milk? I'm lactose intolerant." Reena pushes the bowl away while chewing a mouthful of biryani.

My mother raises her eyebrows. "Really? I must have forgotten. I thought you couldn't eat—what's it called—gluten?"

Reena nods. "Well, I'm only gluten intolerant in large quantities. Like if I eat four slices of pizza, I get really tired."

"I think that's actually normal," I say. "And aren't you a vegetarian?"

"I am." She wipes mashed carrots from the baby's forehead. "But I eat organic poultry."

"Poultry is meat," Paul says. "You're not a vegetarian if you eat meat."

She places her fork on the table with more force than is necessary. "I know what a vegetarian is."

Nimisha Auntie takes the bowl from Reena. "Is this malai kofta?" She sniffs it. "Is that paprika? Whoever heard of putting paprika in malai kofta?"

Ma shifts in her seat, glancing at Nimisha Auntie. "I heard there are lot of hormones in meat. It was on *Dateline*."

Reena nods in agreement. "Animal products are just toxic. That's why we only buy certified organic and free-range. And why we're not letting them push vaccines on Kai."

I lose hold of my fork, and it clatters in my plate. "You haven't had Kai vaccinated?"

Nimisha Auntie tastes the malai kofta with the tip of her tongue. "It's missing something. Salt, I think."

Reena wipes her mouth on a napkin. "Vaccines are made from hormones that they get from sheep. And the sheep are raised on farms full of pesticides. So guess what ends up in the vaccines? That's literally pesticide that they want to inject into my son. They don't just cause autism; they also cause learning disabilities and ADD."

Kai topples over and bumps his head on her chair leg. He wails loudly.

"That's what happens when you don't watch where you're going," Reena says to him, her tone matter-of-fact.

The baby continues to shriek as Ma scoops him up and pats his back. My phone beeps. A text from Gabe reads, Hi. Hope you're feeling better. I think we should talk about last night. Not sure how you feel about it, but I'd like to see you again. You left your shoes here. Can I bring them over later? I turn off the ringer and drop the phone into my purse. Guilt squeezes my lungs like a vise. *Lots of people make poor decisions from time to time,* I reassure myself. I glance across the table at Reena. *Sometimes I feel like I'm surrounded by people making poor decisions.*

After a moment I say, "That's actually not true about vaccines causing autism."

"Well, there *actually* have been a lot of studies," Reena says. "It's a fact. I've done my research."

I breathe in, my nostrils flaring slightly. An image of Stuart, his head buried in an immunology textbook, flashes through my mind.

That's what research is, you twit. Not the random internet search you conducted on your phone while getting a pedicure. "Actually, it's the opposite of a fact. The *New England Journal*—"

"The *New England Journal*," Reena interrupts, "is funded by the drug companies that make vaccines. You need to understand that. There's a scientist who did studies that prove the link between vaccines and autism, and he was shut down by big pharma because they wanted to keep him quiet."

"He lost his license because he fabricated his data," I say. "The diseases that we vaccinate against are deadly, and way more dangerous than any vaccine side effect." I turn to Paul and say, under my breath, "Dad was a pediatrician."

Paul avoids my gaze but nods thoughtfully. "That makes sense. Maybe the benefits of the vaccine outweigh the risks."

Reena shrugs. "Well, that's your *perception*." She stresses the word as if she's not sure I grasp its meaning. "You need to understand that drug companies and doctors are covering up the truth because there are literally billions of dollars being made off of vaccines."

"It's not my perception. Measles and whooping cough are deadly, especially in kids."

Nimisha Auntie smiles at Ma. "When I make my malai kofta, the sauce comes out much smoother and creamier."

Reena puts down her fork again and folds her hands patronizingly. "Norah, not everything they teach you in medical school is true. You're a cog in a billion-dollar healthcare machine. You need to understand—"

"The biryani is dry," Nimisha Auntie announces.

I throw down my napkin. "Oh, for God's sake, Nimisha Auntie!" It flies out of my mouth before I realize what's happening. "WILL YOU SHUT UP!"

Nimisha Auntie's face freezes into a stunned mask.

I turn to Reena. "And *you* need to understand that the problem is, in fact, idiot conspiracy theorists like you who are willing to literally risk their child's life based on some nonsense they read on the internet. The next time Kai gets a fever, maybe you should try taking him to an aromatherapist and letting a magical unicorn take a gluten-free crap on him!"

There is slack-jawed silence around the table, other than the baby's blithe cooing. Ma's bottom lip quivers, her head cocked in bewilderment.

Paul clears his throat. "Norah—"

Without another word, I grab my coat and am gone.

"And then I told Reena to go crap herself or something," I say, my head in my hands.

Meryl grins and swirls a stick of celery in her Bloody Mary. A waitress places a stack of pancakes in front of me.

"Good," Meryl says. "I'm glad you finally told her off. And Nimisha Auntie. They both deserved it."

I smile, grateful to have someone to whom I can vent.

"Are you sure that's all you want?" I say, indicating her drink. "You always get the pancakes here. Do you want some of mine?"

She waves her hand. "You go ahead. I'm just not hungry. Did I tell you I like that coat? Is it new? It's the perfect winter white."

"I just got it," I say, shrugging out of the coat—a stress-induced purchase after my meltdown at Ma's house yesterday—and carefully smoothing it over the back of my chair. "And thank you for noticing."

"Lawyers notice everything." She smiles, and it makes the dark circles under her eyes more noticeable.

"Well, it'll probably be a while before I speak to Reena again," I say. "And I probably won't be going to family dinners for a bit."

"Someone had to put those two in their place. I'm sorry, but those bitches talk too much."

I laugh. "That they do."

I'd forgotten how easy it is to be around Meryl. In college, I could spend an entire afternoon lazing around our dorm room, listening to Meryl pontificate on topics ranging from the appalling lack of human rights in East Timor to the many superlative qualities of Justin Bieber, her musings always accented by the perfectly timed expletive.

I finally texted Gabe back after dinner last night. I said I wanted to forget about what happened between us and move on. It was a mistake, I said, and Meryl is too important to both of us. He texted back to say he was disappointed but understood.

"So how are things going with Ethan?" Meryl asks, biting off the end of the celery stalk.

"Not as well as I thought," I say. "I can't believe how I gushed on and on about him to you. I'm sorry about that. I just feel stupid about it."

"Are you still with him?"

"I don't know if I ever *was* with him. In a relationship, I mean. I was . . . with him."

Meryl raises her eyebrows. "You slept with him?"

I nod and shrug. She gapes at me for a long moment. "Well, well," she finally says. "At long last. So, are you going to tell me any more about it?"

I laugh, cringing, suddenly very uncomfortable. "You know I can't talk about that stuff out loud."

She claps her hands. "This is a big deal. Congratulations, honey, you finally hooked up with a man!"

There's just something about the way she says it.

"Two men, actually," I say. I regret it instantly.

"Really? Who's the other one?"

"He's just some guy I met at Ethan's party." I jab at my pancakes with a fork. "It was nothing. And I didn't sleep with him or anything, I just made out with him a little. For like a few minutes, probably, is all. I was upset, and it was a moment of weakness, I was drunk, it's a blur now."

"What happened?"

"I overheard Ethan say something, I got upset, my shoes were uncomfortable, one thing led to another."

"Must have been some pretty uncomfortable shoes. Michael Kors, right?"

"Wow, good memory."

"Sparkly gold? Stilettos?"

"Yes, actually. How did you know—"

"And, I'm wondering, while you were *making out for a few minutes* with Gabe, did you remember that I had just told you we were getting back together? Or did you just decide that wasn't important? Or did the shoes make you do it?"

My brain is suddenly no longer able to do anything except hyperfocus on my hand, frozen over the stack of pancakes, clutching a fork. Hand, pancakes, fork. Hand, pancakes, fork.

Meryl stands, holding her drink as if she might make a toast. "I went over to his place last night to apologize, and in the hall closet was a pair of Michael Kors stilettos. He didn't tell me whose they were, but they were your size, so . . ." She reaches over my shoulder and slowly pours her Bloody Mary onto my coat. It spreads over my back, dripping onto my chair and the floor. I stare straight ahead. Hand, pancakes, fork. Neighboring diners glance at us in confusion. The glass empty, Meryl places it on the table in front of me and says, "So you'll understand why this was all I wanted." She grabs her purse and strides off.

My head is a swirl of guilt and remorse. I close my eyes. When I open them, something shifts in me. Like bowling pins. A waitress with a stack of paper towels dabs at my coat, tomato juice and vodka still dripping from the sleeves, and says, her voice hopeful, "I'm sure this will come out." I murmur something nonsensical and grab my ruined coat, rushing past several bemused glances to the street outside. Meryl is gone.

As a cab passes, I catch my reflection in its window. I look like something out of a horror movie—stunned, disoriented, staggering down the sidewalk covered in red. I almost scream.

I've never lied to Meryl, in all the years I've known her. I would never intentionally hurt her. And I didn't. I didn't lie. I didn't intend to hurt anyone. But what Meryl just did, deliberately setting me up to humiliate me . . . this type of infantile drama is just so typical of her. If she was too flaky to decide if she wanted to date Gabe, I can't be held responsible for that. I can't believe I've tolerated her ridiculous, self-centered bullshit for so long.

I stuff the coat into a trash can. Then I walk back into the restaurant, return to my table, calmly ask for a napkin to wipe the Bloody Mary from my shirtsleeve, sit in Meryl's seat, pull my plate toward me, and finish my pancakes. Every last bite of them.

CHAPTER SEVENTEEN

I duck around a curtain in the Emergency Department.

"We've been waiting for over an hour."

I smile. Their cantankerousness has become, in a way, endearing. "Hi, Mr. and Mrs. Tally. It's nice to see you both again, although I wish it were under different circumstances."

Mr. Tally squints at me, his arms crossed. "When will she be moved to her room? And when will Dr. Portnoy see her?"

"A bed should be available soon," I say. "Dr. Portnoy will be rounding tomorrow morning, but I'll be here overnight."

Mrs. Tally looks gaunt and paler than I remember. "I don't feel well." She puts her hand to her forehead.

"Your lab tests show you have an infection," I say. "It's probably pneumonia that spread to your bloodstream."

"It's the chemo, isn't it? It destroys the immune system," Mr. Tally says.

"Yes, unfortunately," I say.

"We were told she would be getting some sort of permanent IV?"

"A PICC line," I say. "It's for long-term antibiotics. You'll need it for six to eight weeks. They'll do a minor surgical procedure to put it in."

"Is there a vomit bin?" Mrs. Tally says.

I look around frantically as she covers her mouth and leans forward.

"I'll go get one." I yank an emesis basin from under the sink in the hallway and place it in Mrs. Tally's lap just as she vomits over the side of the bed and onto my front. She looks at me with an irked but still apologetic expression.

"Oh, my goodness. You were just standing right there," she says.

I've had bodily fluids of all varieties splashed on, spilled on, or squirted at me more times in the past several months than I can count. It's become somewhat routine, really. This time, however, I look down at my scrubs and am suddenly overwhelmed with despair and frustration. Tears form at the corners of my eyes, and my nose starts to run. I look up, and Mr. Tally is staring at me as if he's not quite sure what he's seeing. *Whatever you do, don't cry in front of the patients.*

"Excuse me," I say, my voice hoarse. I flee to an empty ladies' room down the hall and scream into one of the stalls. The angry sound of my own voice echoing off the walls is jarring and a little frightening. I stand there for a few moments to collect myself. A nurse enters.

"Was that you? Everything okay, hon?"

I smile. It takes all my strength. "Yes. Yup. I thought I saw a mouse. But I didn't."

"Oh my God, I hope not. I once saw a rat in the parking deck that I swear, from far away, looked like a dog. I kid you not."

I push past her out the door.

Ethan is the senior resident on call today. I stand at the nurses' station and page him while mopping vomit from my thigh with an enormous stack of paper towels.

"Hey, you disappeared from the party the other night. Where have you been?" he asks.

"Just busy." I tuck the phone between my chin and shoulder and push away thoughts of the party and what happened with Gabe and Meryl. I've been meaning to call Stuart, and I owe Ma a phone call, too. But all of that will have to wait. "Mrs. Tally is back with pneumonia. Her blood cultures grew multi-drug-resistant strep. She also has nausea and vomiting and a fever of 102.5. The EM doc started her on Cipro."

"I remember her. Since she's on chemo she may need a second antibiotic," he says. "We'll wait and see how she does. Want to have dinner in the caf in like half an hour?" His voice is beguiling and familiar, like the first few notes of a favorite song.

"I can't. I'm covered in vomit, no time to shower."

"Ah, attractive. See you later, then?"

"Sure. Maybe."

I hang up and stare at the phone for a moment. *Everything will have to wait.*

Later that evening, I find Clark reclining on a couch in the residents' lounge.

"Hey, Norah," he says, yawning. "You hear about the ED? It's crazy down there. A bus got into an accident on I-95 and they just drove the whole bus over to the hospital and dropped off like fifty people, all whining about neck and lower back pain. It's like the ninth circle of hell down there."

"You're not going down there to help?"

He arches an eyebrow at me. "Why?" Then, "You look awful."

"A patient vomited on me hours ago, and this is the first chance I've had to get a shower."

"That's disgusting." As I walk away, he calls after me, "You should be autoclaved. You should be hosed down like a circus elephant."

In the ladies' washroom, I stand under the shower and rest my forehead against the tile. The water is lukewarm, as always. Clark is right: I'm disgusting. I can't stand myself. I've run out of patience for my own patheticness. I glimpse my reflection in the foggy mirror above the sink across the room. I want to grab myself by the shoulders, shake myself, and yell, *What is wrong with you? Get yourself together and stop being a ridiculous child!* But I'm so tired. Just so utterly, devastatingly tired that even self-loathing takes too much effort. My eyes drift closed, and for a moment, I fall asleep, the water pouring over my hair.

A drafty window somewhere lets in a sudden blast of cold air. Shocked back awake, I turn off the water. My pager sounds. I consider lobbing it into the toilet.

"Doc, that patient who's waiting for a bed, she tried to get up by herself and she fell," Mrs. Tally's nurse in the ED says. "She hit her head on a chair. I checked her out, and she's fine, but the husband is insisting a doctor examine her. I tried asking one of the ED attendings, but he said I should call you guys."

"Nice," I say, rolling my eyes. The ED attending is probably standing five feet from the patient right now.

"I told Ethan, but he's busy," she says, her voice weary. "Listen, I don't care who, but I just need someone to come down here and shut this man up. He's driving me crazy."

I groan and bury my face in a towel. "Okay."

In the ED, nurses and doctors are rushing about frantically. "We have too many damn patients!" a nurse says as she pushes past me. "This is not a Greyhound stop!"

Mrs. Tally has been moved to a corner in a back hallway. Elle emerges from behind the curtain surrounding her stretcher, saying, "We'll see you tomorrow morning for your PICC line placement."

Mr. Tally says something inaudible, and Elle replies, "I think they paged the intern to come check on that. I'm from surgery. I'm just here about the PICC line. Have a good night!" She rushes past me, her pager beeping. "Do those two belong to you?" she says, nodding toward the curtain. "Good luck with that!" She smiles at me sympathetically.

I watch her go. I still have so many questions, but there's no time for them now.

I step around the curtain. "What's going on, Mrs. Tally?"

The clock above her bed reads 10:00 p.m.

"I told them not to call you," she says. "I'm fine."

"She fell," Mr. Tally says, worry creasing his forehead. "Getting out of bed by herself. You know you're not supposed to do that, Lenore!"

Mrs. Tally crosses her arms and glares at him over her glasses. "I had to get my socks, and you were at the cafeteria!" She turns to me. "He always overreacts. I just tripped and bumped my head against that chair there."

I sweep her hair off her forehead to look for a bruise but don't notice one. Then I shine a penlight into her eyes and watch her pupils constrict.

"Stick your tongue out, please," I say.

She does so. "See? I'm fine."

I tap my reflex hammer against her knees and ankles. "You do seem fine." I am trying to maintain a pleasant tone of voice, but I can't help myself. I look at Mr. Tally and say pointedly, "You seem perfectly fine." I turn on my heel.

I write a quick note in Mrs. Tally's chart: *10:15pm Called to evaluate patient for fall out of bed. Patient examined, neurologic examination normal.* Fantasizing about the possibility of sleep, I head for the elevator. Before I make it there, I am paged for an order for sleeping pills, then regarding a patient with gas, then to check on two patients on different floors who are both having chest pain.

At 12:30 a.m., I am slouched on the bed in the call room, debating whether to take off my sneakers, when I hear a knock on the wall.

"Norah! You awake?" a distant voice says. Ethan is in the next room.

I sit up straight, my heart pounding in my ears.

"Can I help you with something?" I say, trying to sound nonchalant.

"No, just saying hi. What have you been up to?"

"Two congestive heart failures, one stroke, four falls out of bed, three migraine headaches, and one guy who hasn't pooped in three days," I say, stretching my stocking feet. "You?"

"Four heart arrhythmias, one intubation, two central lines, three heart attacks that were actually heartburn, a lady who suddenly lost vision in one eye . . . and a partridge in a pear tree."

I laugh.

"Good night," he says.

"Good night." I smile and put my fingertips on the wall. My pager sounds. *Serves me right for taking off my shoes.*

I dial the callback number, and a nurse answers. "That patient—who is still waiting for a bed, I might add—her husband is demanding that a doctor see his wife. Again." I'd swear her teeth are grinding together.

"What for?"

"He says she's confused."

"Does she seem confused to you?"

"She seems fine to me, but the husband is threatening to sue if no one comes to check on her. I paged Ethan a while ago, but he refused to come down here."

"He did?" I rap on the wall. "You refused to see Mrs. Tally?"

I hear him yawn. "The one in the ED? The nurse says she's fine. Tell her to tell the husband to go home."

"Doctor, I am begging you," the nurse says, her voice taut.

I sigh. "Fine. I'm on my way."

Silently, I lace up my sneakers. I am about to tap on the wall again, but instead I wash my face, pull on my white coat, and quietly shut the door behind me.

The ED is still buzzing with activity. I hear a patient moaning,

"I have low blood sugar! I need crackers!" from somewhere in the distance.

Mr. Tally is pacing back and forth. "It's about time!" he says.

"Howard, stop it," Mrs. Tally says. "You are being ridiculous."

"The Tylenol isn't helping her headache, and she's confused."

"Do I seem confused to you?" Mrs. Tally asks.

"I'm telling you, she's not herself," Mr. Tally says. "Maybe she needs a different antibiotic."

I notice a bruise the size of a quarter on her left temple, partially hidden by her hair.

"This wasn't here before," I say.

"What?" She winces as I touch the bruise. "It's just a bump."

"You have a headache?"

"I've had one all night. But it does seem to be getting worse."

I sit on the chair at the bedside. "Mrs. Tally, I'm going to ask you some questions. Is that okay?"

She nods. "I guess so."

"What's the name of this hospital?"

"Philadelphia General."

"What state are we in?"

"Pennsylvania. Although I'd rather be in Florida right now."

I smile. "Me too. I'm going to name three objects, and I'd like you to remember them for later, okay? Spoon, basket, potato."

"Spoon, basket, potato. Okay."

"What's your name and today's date?"

"Lenore Tally, March twenty-third."

"Can you spell the word 'world' backward?"

"D-L-R-O-W," she says. Under her breath she adds, "This is silly."

"What's this called?" I point to my watch.

"A wristwatch."

"And what were those three objects again?"

"Oh my." She purses her lips. "Spoon, basket, potato. Did I pass?"

"Yes." I smile. "You passed. You seem to be doing all right."

Mr. Tally sighs and crosses his arms.

"I'll have them get you some Motrin for the headache," I say. "Try to get some sleep."

As I am pulling the curtain closed, Mr. Tally turns to his wife, chuckling, "I forgot the three objects. I would have failed."

"Oh, it was easy for me," Mrs. Tally says. "I just thought: I store spoons in that wicker basket on the kitchen counter, and I'm allergic to potatoes."

I glance over my shoulder.

"Tomatoes," Mr. Tally says. "You're allergic to tomatoes."

"Right, potatoes," Mrs. Tally says. "Why are you both staring at me?"

"Mrs. Tally, what are you allergic to?"

"Potatoes."

"And what do you make with potatoes?"

"I don't know. Pasta sauce."

"Tomatoes, Lenore, those are tomatoes," Mr. Tally says. "See, it's this kind of thing. She's been doing this all night."

I shine my penlight into her eyes again. Her left pupil seems slightly larger than her right. Could I have missed that when I examined her earlier?

"I'll be right back." I duck around the curtain. I look for a quiet corner, but there are patients and nurses everywhere. I call Ethan from inside a supply closet.

"Norah?" Ethan's voice is gravelly. "You're still with that patient? What are you doing?"

"Ethan, I think you need to come down here," I say, pressing the phone to my ear. "Something's not right."

"Can't. I just got paged. I'm on my way to Cardiology. What's going on?"

"Mrs. Tally confused two words that she normally wouldn't have," I say. "And she has a headache."

"A lot of older patients in the hospital get confused at night," he says. "It's called sundowning."

"And she hit her head earlier."

"Yeah, I heard. Did she pass the mini mental status exam? She knows the date and the name of the hospital and all that?"

"Well, yes, but I think maybe one pupil is dilated."

"Are her reflexes normal?"

"Yes, but you don't think she needs a CT scan of her head, just in case? The way she mixed up those two words, it reminded me of a patient I had once who had a bleed in his brain from hitting his head in a car accident."

"Well, she wasn't in a car accident. Hold the elevator! What were the two words she mixed up?"

I clear my throat. "Potato and tomato."

He sighs. "Listen, if we order a stat CT scan we'll be pushing your patient ahead of all the ED patients, and right now they have a dozen traumas from the bus crash waiting for their CT scans. You're going to get hell from the attendings down there."

"But what if—"

"Norah, don't look for zebras. This one's clearly a horse. She's just a batty little old lady. Have you looked around? They're all over the hospital. She needs a sleeping pill, not a CT scan."

"I just . . . I see your point. I'll just monitor her."

"Sure. Knock yourself out," he says. "Gotta run. See you later."

When I step back into the hall, Mrs. Tally's nurse is waiting.

"So what did we decide?" she asks.

I see Mr. Tally's legs beneath the bedside curtain, still pacing back and forth. "Just give her eight hundred of Motrin every eight hours," I say. "She's fine."

I spend the next hour staring at the ceiling in the call room. My pager is silent. After ninety minutes, I suddenly sit upright. The second antibiotic. I call the ED.

"How's Mrs. Tally?"

"Who?"

"The woman waiting for a room. With the pneumonia."

There is silence on the other end.

"Her husband is annoying," I say.

"Oh, her. Her head still hurts, but otherwise she's fine. She vomited again like a half hour ago."

"Did Ethan start her on another antibiotic?"

"Yeah, now she's on Cipro and Zynexa."

Zynexa. Fat Dan had just been started on Zynexa when he bled into the sac around his heart. The old man with penile bleeding had just been started on it, too. *Bleeding after minor trauma is a side effect.*

"Stop. Stop the Zynexa."

"I have a dose running into her IV right now."

"Turn it off. And get a stat head CT on her."

The nurse sounds skeptical. "Stat?"

"Yes."

"As in, right now?"

"Right now."

"On the woman with the hypochondriac husband?"

"Yes, that's the one." I clear my throat. "Do you need me to clarify anything else?"

"No, Doctor."

"Page me the minute she gets back."

"You're the boss."

I pace up and down the steps in the stairwell, tapping my reflex hammer against the outside of my thigh. Did I just imagine that one pupil was bigger than the other? A nurse pages for an order for Pepto-Bismol. I glance at my watch: 3:15 a.m.

Then, from the crackling loudspeaker, "Code blue, Radiology. Code blue, Radiology."

The reflex hammer clatters away down the stairwell.

One one thousand, two one thousand, three one thousand.

One of the Surgery residents douses Mrs. Tally's groin with iodine before jabbing her skin with a thick needle.

Four one thousand, five one thousand, six one thousand.

An Anesthesia resident works her jaws apart with a steel tongue blade and angles a breathing tube down her throat.

Seven one thousand, eight—

"Who is this patient's nurse? Why wasn't I paged sooner?" Ethan, pacing back and forth at the foot of the table, breathes vigorously through his nose. We are all crammed into the tiny CT suite; the giant ring of the CT scanner takes up most of the room. Alarm bells sound from the portable heart monitor attached to Mrs. Tally's chest.

"Another amp of epinephrine!" Ethan says. "Norah, hold chest compressions."

I stop silently counting and step back from the table, my arms aching. The monitor shows a flat line.

"Twenty minutes and still asystole," the Anesthesia resident says.

"Resume compressions!" Ethan says.

"It's time to call it," someone grumbles.

A tall, muscular nurse taps me on the shoulder. "I'll take over," he says. "The husband is asking for you guys."

I step aside, and he laces his fingers together, squares his shoulders, and begins the forceful, rhythmic compressions of Mrs. Tally's chest. As I turn away, I hear the faint snapping sound of her ribs breaking.

In the hallway outside, Mr. Tally braces himself against the wall.

"Sir, your wife's heart isn't responding to the treatment," Ethan is saying. "We can keep trying to resuscitate her, but—"

"How did this happen?"

"We don't know. Her heart just stopped working suddenly. The team has been doing everything they can, but further treatment at this time will just prolong her suffering."

Mr. Tally straightens. Then he says, his voice low, "You do whatever it takes to save my wife."

"Sir, I assure you, everything *is* being done. Her heart isn't beating; it's not circulating blood to her organs. The medicines are keeping her alive right now, but without a functional heart, she won't survive."

"What about shocking her? The shock treatment they show on TV?"

"You can't shock a flat line. That won't work. Sir, I need your permission to stop treatment."

Mr. Tally takes a step toward Ethan. "Stop treatment? You don't get to decide anything! Who the hell are you?"

I put my hand on his arm. "Mr. Tally—"

He turns and grasps my shoulder, his expression relieved. "Doc, what's going on? I don't understand."

"I'm so sorry," I say, quietly meeting his gaze, "but we can't fix what's gone wrong with her heart."

"What should I do? I'm not ready. I'm not ready for her to go."

The words catch in my throat. "She's already gone."

He looks at me for a long moment. Then he says, "Stop. Tell them to stop."

Ethan goes back into the CT suite, and a moment later, the beeping and alarm bells cease.

A wound opens somewhere deep beneath my ribs, the pain so intense I'm afraid to take a breath. Guilt and shame coil themselves around me, like a pair of vipers, squeezing my lungs and hissing into my ears: *If you were a better doctor, this wouldn't have happened.*

Mr. Tally's voice is tenuous. "Can I see her?"

"Let me check," I say.

I pull the door open and step into the room. Where, just a moment ago, there was clamor and movement and chaos, now there's silence and stillness. A trickle of blood flows from the corner of Mrs. Tally's mouth. Her chest is bare and covered with bruises. Blood-soaked gauze pads litter the floor like strewn flower petals.

I take a breath through my mouth, so the smell of blood and iodine and urine won't make me nauseous. It's a coping strategy I first learned in dissection lab, where the smell of formaldehyde was so noxious it could linger in your nasal passages for days.

In my first year of medical school, I had a classmate, a friendly girl called Abby with ear-length curly blond hair and a penchant for baking, who would cry her way through dissection lab twice weekly. The rest of her lab group named their elderly male cadaver Mortimer and busied themselves with the painstaking work of cutting and teasing apart its tissues to locate this or that organ or nerve or blood vessel. Meanwhile, Abby would stand over their shoulders and weep, her tears occasionally falling onto the dead man's formaldehyde-soaked skin. She still managed to score well on every Anatomy exam, however, which irked her group members tremendously. Shortly before midterms, they confronted her, telling her they were tired of her emotional theatrics and insisting that she carry her own weight in the lab. When it came time to dissect Mortimer's eyes in order to study them for the Ophthalmology unit, Abby was given the unhappy task of coaxing the old man's eyeballs out of their sockets and then slicing them in half with a scalpel to study their insides. No one was surprised when she didn't return to school the following semester. Only the tenacious ones make it through. The ones who don't cry, at least not where anyone can see them.

Back in the hallway, I lay my hand on Mr. Tally's arm again. "Give them a moment. The nurses will come get you," I say gently. He nods.

His cell phone rings. His hands trembling, he presses the phone to his ear. "Mikey? She's gone. Mom's gone. You have to tell your sisters." He shakes, and it's like the wrenching sound that erupts from his throat has punched and thrashed its way up from the depth of his being. If pain could be distilled, if it were possible to concentrate and crystalize agony, to boil it down to its essence, this sound would remain. The sound of a heart being torn to pieces.

It's too wretched, too overwhelming to be here. The sound is sharp, jagged like a knife, and the wound under my ribs is too raw and too friable to withstand another blow.

Mr. Tally presses his hands to his eyes, sobbing, and reflexively I curl inward, trying to protect myself. I tell myself that it's presumptuous and intrusive to try to share his pain. I didn't just lose a loved one. This is my job, not my personal life, and I have no claim to his grief.

A nurse, speaking in low tones, wraps her arm around Mr. Tally's shoulders, and I walk away. He doesn't notice me go.

"Norah, come here." Ethan appears behind me, Mrs. Tally's chart tucked under his arm. He leads me down a long hallway and through a door marked *Radiology Reading Area*. The room is full of dark, empty cubicles.

"Where is everyone?" I ask.

"There are no radiologists on call overnight," Ethan says, logging in to a computer.

"So who reads the studies?"

"It's called NightHawk. It's usually a radiologist in India or Australia. The studies are emailed to them."

"We outsource our radiology?"

"Yup. Cheap-ass hospital administrators."

Black-and-white CT scan images appear on the screen. A large blotch of white has eliminated half of Mrs. Tally's brain. I gasp.

"I know. They were only able to get part of the study done before she coded," Ethan says, his voice hushed. "I've never seen a bleed this bad. We are so fucked."

He sinks into a chair. My mind spins.

Ethan pages through the chart. "How hard did this woman hit her head? She wasn't on any blood thinners, right?"

"She was on Zynexa."

"Holy shit. I put her on Zynexa."

I look over his shoulder at the chart.

9:35 pm Patient fell out of bed and sustained bump to head. Dr. Cantor notified. Intern to evaluate patient is written at the bottom of one page, followed by the nurse's scribbled signature. Below that is my note from when I checked on her: *10:15pm Called to evaluate patient for fall out of bed. Patient examined, neurologic examination normal.* The next line reads: *10:35pm Start Zynexa 75mg IV every 8 hours. Verbal order per resident* and another nurse's signature.

Ethan turns the page. *12:05am Patient's husband complaining she is confused. Vital signs stable. Called Dr. Cantor to come evaluate patient. He refuses. Called intern. Intern states she will come evaluate patient.* The rest of the page lists routine blood pressure and temperature checks, followed by *Start Motrin 800mg Q8 hours, verbal order per intern.*

"Shit. This looks bad." Ethan rubs his temples. "She said the patient looked fine, but the husband was being a dick. She didn't document *that*. Fucker." He stares at the images of Mrs. Tally's brain. "I have to call Portnoy. What am I going to say?"

"It was a mistake," I say. "He knows you. Maybe—"

"Maybe I put a patient with a documented head trauma on a known blood thinner, and then I refused to check on her, and then she bled into her brain and died? That's what this looks like. It looks like negligence. It looks like a lawsuit. He'll have me fired. Zero-tolerance for mistakes, remember? My ass is . . . done." He is silent for a moment. Then suddenly he swipes at an empty chair and sends it skidding across the floor. His eyes flash angrily. "Why the hell did you order that CT scan? I told you not to."

It's sharp and shaming, the realization of what I've done.

"You don't go behind your senior's back," he says, his voice quieter. "That's just not something you do."

"I didn't mean for this to happen," I say. I feel my face getting hot, that prickly feeling that always precedes tears. I turn away.

We sit, for what feels like a long time, in the darkness. Then: "Wait, maybe there's something we can do about this. Stay here," Ethan says as he jumps up and rushes out the door.

He returns a few moments later with a jovial-looking X-ray tech. "Ken, does this study have to be sent to NightHawk?" Ethan asks.

"It's incomplete, so it's up to you," Ken says. "If you want it read, I can send it. Otherwise we just mark it Incomplete." He points. "That is so freaking awesome, right? I mean, I feel bad for the patient, whoever they are, but I love how the blood just squashes the brain like that."

"Yeah, it's . . . awesome," Ethan says. "Don't send it. It's a waste of time. I'll just document the result in the chart."

"You got it, Chief. You guys have a good night." We listen to the squeaking of his sneakers in the hallway as he walks away.

"Jesus, that was close," Ethan says, relieved. "Listen, Norah, when Portnoy asks, we never saw these CT scan pictures. This woman's cause of death was cardiac arrest of unknown origin. Okay?" He grabs both of my shoulders, his expression pleading. "Okay?"

If I'd listened to him, if I hadn't ordered the CT scan, we would never have known what killed Mrs. Tally, and we wouldn't be in this situation. Ethan's career wouldn't be at risk. The truth here isn't useful or helpful in any way—nothing will bring Mrs. Tally back to life. Still, lying to an attending . . . the same attending who had me put on leave for no good reason. . . .

I nod. "Sure. Okay."

He exhales and leans back in his chair. He glances at Mrs. Tally's chart. "I wish there was a way to get rid of that line about me refusing to see the patient. Who documents something like that? It's like the medical equivalent of 'Fuck you, douchebag resident.' Nurses are the enemy."

I stare at the chart for a moment, then reach over, click open the binder clips, and remove the page with the 12:05 a.m. note. "There's nothing else on this page except blood pressure checks and the order to start Motrin."

Ethan rubs his eyes with the heels of his hands. "Of course there isn't. They only document what they feel like documenting. Because in the end, they're not the ones responsible when shit hits the fan. We are."

"But what if this page just wasn't in there? Would anyone miss it?"

He glances at me, then sits up straight. "You're a genius."

"If it isn't documented, it didn't happen, right?" I say.

He grins and envelops me in his arms. He still smells like cucumbers and apple cider. His pager beeps, and he releases me. "Damn, there's a guy in the ICU about to tank," he says. He points to the page of the chart in my hand. "Take that home and burn it or bury it or something, okay? Portnoy will probably page you in the morning. Remember, cardiac arrest." He cups my face in both his hands, and his eyes soften. "You are amazing. Thank you."

My pulse skips under his fingertips.

It's been shown in studies that falling in love causes changes in the immune system that are similar to those caused when you're fighting off a virus like the flu. Love sick. The racing heart, the sweaty palms, the loss of appetite. There's also evidence that the brain regions involved in decision-making and caution—the frontal cortex and the amygdala—become less active in a person in love. I know this, yet I feel completely clearheaded, maybe more so than I've ever felt. How I feel about Ethan—how we feel about each other—outweighs the burden of evidence. It's a thing as profound and indefinable as gravity. You can't see it, but it's impossible to doubt its existence.

"Of course," I say.

He kisses my cheek, grabs his phone, and is gone.

Mrs. Tally, her body covered up to the chin with a white sheet as if tucked in for bed, has been moved to an empty room. There is a picture on the wall of grizzly bears frolicking in a river. At the foot of the bed, a man stands trembling. With gasping breaths, he says, "Mom, you made me the man I am today. . . ." His voice trails off. Mr. Tally puts his hand on the younger man's shoulder.

I watch them, for a moment, from the doorway. Then a nurse motions from the nurses' station. "I need you to fill this out," she says, handing me a large index card with perforated edges. Mrs. Tally's death certificate. "I already did most of it. I just need the cause of death and your signature."

I hesitate, my pen hovering above the paper. The idea that a person can be suddenly gone—one moment blood pounding through their arteries, electricity crackling between their nerves, muscles flinching and straining, then abruptly all of that elaborate machinery comes to a halt—seems ludicrous. This focus of energy, this intricate collection of cells and organs and thoughts and passions and efforts, this flourishing plexus of things both tangible and intangible, it—

she—has simply ceased to be. It's madness. Yet this little, official-looking certificate proves it's so.

I realize I am still clutching the page from Mrs. Tally's chart. I cram it into the pocket of my white coat. Under *Cause of Death*, I write in *Cardiac Arrest*, followed by my signature. I hand the certificate to the nurse. She raises an eyebrow.

"You don't want to put the head bleed down as the cause of death?"

"No. The resident spoke to Dr. Portnoy. This is how he wants it filled out."

This is what Portnoy wants. It's the magical incantation I've heard the residents use, always with the same result: the nurse to whom the words are spoken shrinks away, nodding demurely.

Apparently, not this time.

"Who spoke to Portnoy? You?" the nurse says as I'm turning away.

"No, the resident. Ethan."

"Ethan talked to Portnoy, and they discussed how to fill out the death certificate?"

I wonder if she can see the pounding artery I feel in my neck. "Yes, I guess. That's what Ethan told me."

"Because most attendings don't care about the death certificate."

I fight a rising tide of panic. My voice exasperated, I say, "Listen, I just coded my patient and it's four a.m. and I don't want to keep discussing this, so if you want to page Portnoy and ask him yourself, you're welcome to."

"No, no, just checking," the nurse says, her expression apologetic. Like a jungle cat that has stalked its prey and changed its mind, she takes the death certificate and slinks off.

Relieved, I sit for a few moments and catch my breath. When I look up, Mr. Tally and his son are slowly making their way toward the elevators, shoulders hunched, leaning on each other. As they pass, I stand.

"I'm taking these home," Mr. Tally says, his gaze distant. He unwraps a paper towel and shows me Mrs. Tally's dentures, still shiny with her saliva. I nod. As he shuffles away, he carefully folds the paper towel and clutches the little parcel to his chest. Then he says, "Thank you, Doctor."

CHAPTER EIGHTEEN

When I pass the hallway outside the ICU at 5:30 a.m., on my way to the residents' lounge, a medical student is crying.

"You don't ever show up to rounds without a penlight!" Terry says, his nose inches from hers.

A throng of residents and interns stands nearby. They all avert their eyes while the pretty young student fumbles for a response.

"I didn't realize. . . ."

"You didn't realize you needed to be prepared for rounds? You just thought you'd show up and check the cranial nerves with your *magical powers*?" His voice sounds like air being let out of a balloon.

I stand discreetly at the back of the group, and Clark appears near my elbow. "How long has this been going on?" I whisper.

"A while," he says, glancing at his watch. "Terry has had the hots for her for weeks. He's been looking for an excuse to ream her."

I glance at him in alarm. "He's yelling at her because he thinks she's attractive? That's insane."

"Yeah. It's not the most effective dating strategy," Clark admits. Then he sighs in frustration and looks at his watch again. "If she wasn't so good-looking we'd be done with rounds by now."

Terry has launched into a lecture about professionalism in the workplace that includes the words "moral obligation" and makes several historical references to great surgeons of yore, the most notable of whom ended up working himself to the point of mental breakdown and being committed to a sanitorium. He adds, without irony, "That is the level of dedication we expect at PGH."

Gritting my teeth, I push my way to the front of the crowd as if I'm heading into the ICU. "Excuse me! I need to get through. Oh hey"—I struggle to read her name tag—"Brittany!" I grab the student by the arm, smiling like we're old friends. She looks at me in confusion as I barrel on. "There you are. I've been meaning to return this to you. Thanks for letting me borrow it. I keep losing mine." I dig my penlight out of my pocket and hand it to her. "Hey, Terry. How's it going?"

Terry's mouth twists into a scowl. He doesn't reply, but turns awkwardly to the group and barks, "Let's keep rounding! Why are you all standing around?"

"Have a great day!" I call after him as he stalks down the hallway, the other residents on his heels. The med student catches my eye and mouths *thank you* before rushing off to join them. Clark gives me a little salute over his shoulder, and I return it.

My pager sounds. It's a nurse from the Oncology floor. "Dr. Portnoy wants to see you. Right now."

Portnoy looks more perturbed than usual as he flips through Mrs. Tally's chart at the nurses' station. Ethan stands at the counter, watching, his brow furrowed.

"Sit down," Portnoy says, looking at me expectantly. "Well, whatever your name is, what happened?"

I am relieved he doesn't seem to remember me. I glance at Ethan.

Portnoy clears his throat and peers at me over his reading glasses. "My patient with non-small-cell lung cancer suddenly died last night. Do you recall that? You signed the death certificate. What in the hell happened?"

"She went into cardiac arrest," I say.

"In the CT scanner," Portnoy says.

"Yes. In the CT scanner . . ."

Portnoy drums his fingers on the table. He sighs in frustration. "And why was she in the CT scanner?"

"She was having a CT of her head," I say, then add quickly, "Because her husband told the nurse she was confused, but when I checked on her she seemed fine." An image of Mrs. Tally with a bewildered expression saying "Potato" will not leave my mind, no matter how much I will it to.

"Then why did you order the CT scan?"

"Because the patient's husband was insisting."

Portnoy flips to the tab labeled "Imaging Results" in Mrs. Tally's chart. "We don't practice medicine to appease patients, Doctor," he says. "The patient's husband may want you to inject cocaine into her eyeball, but you wouldn't do that either, would you?"

"No, sir," I say.

Portnoy's mood seems to brighten. "Have you heard about these women who give birth to their babies in their own bathtub at home? They're sitting in a tub of hot water, surrounded by feces and blood, and some acupuncturist or midwife or something is in there with them extracting the baby, who then aspirates that crap—literally, it's crap—and ends up in the NICU on a ventilator or dead. Wonder what moron thought of that. And the doctors, they're the bad guys, right? They're the ones pushing evil medications and C-sections on people."

He looks from Ethan to me, and we both smile and nod in reply. He hesitates as if he's waiting for a more enthusiastic reaction from us. Then he turns back to the chart. "So she had the CT scan and it was . . . where's the report?"

"They didn't get any pictures. She coded as soon as she got in there," Ethan says. "It was probably a cardiac event. She had a family history of heart attacks."

"Or a pulmonary embolus," Portnoy says. "These sudden-death cases usually are. Malignancy is a hypercoaguable state; people with cancer get blood clots. What else is a hypercoaguable state?"

It has just occurred to me that the chart still says that Mrs. Tally hit her head and that, one hour later, Ethan started her on Zynexa. All Portnoy has to do is flip to that page in the chart and question if she really was confused.

"You should know this. You're a woman," Portnoy says, and I realize he is talking to me. "I just mentioned it a second ago."

"I'm not sure," I say.

Portnoy shakes his head. "Maybe you fell asleep during that lecture in medical school. Pregnancy is a hypercoaguable state."

"Right. Of course," I say.

He takes a printed list of patients from his white coat pocket, finds Mrs. Tally's name, and crosses it off. "All right, Ethan, let's start rounding. I have a meeting at seven."

Ethan looks back at me as he follows Portnoy down the hallway. I let out my breath. A nurse jostles my chair as she pushes past me and, as if through a fog, I hear the distant squeaking of a wheel on a passing gurney. Time has slowed, and my thinking is fuzzy. Then, like a record realigning itself on a turntable, suddenly life resumes its frenetic pace. The loudspeaker overhead announces "Code blue, room 556. Code blue, room 556." I run toward the stairwell and am about to crash through the fire door when I remember that my white coat is hanging on the back of the chair at the nurses' station. I dash back, grab it, and am off again.

"You need to come down to Dr. Forks's office."

"Who is this?" I ask, even though I knew the minute I heard her tinny voice on the other end of the line.

"It's Barbara, his secretary."

"Okay. I can stop by there at noon."

"He wants to see you now."

"About what?"

"He didn't say."

"But I'm in the middle of seeing patients."

"That's nice. So, you'll be right down?"

My heart pounds in my ears as I jog down the stairwell to the Medical Education office on the first floor of the hospital. *I'm such an idiot*. I wonder if it was the nurse with the death certificate who told Portnoy about Mrs. Tally's real cause of death.

Barbara, in her late sixties with flawless makeup, waves me into Dr. Forks's tiny, closet-like office and closes the door behind me. I'm stunned to find Bianca, Imani, and Clark here, too. They're seated silently and so close to one another that their shoulders are touching. I cram into an empty chair in the corner.

"What's going on?" I mouth to them.

Bianca shrugs and mouths back, "No idea."

Dr. Forks, his beard so perfectly manicured I wonder if he has it professionally maintained, looks annoyed. He takes several pens out of a wire basket on his desk, shuffles them about in his hands so that their points all face the same direction, then carefully deposits them back in the basket. He clears his throat.

"I called you all here to inform you that your colleague Dr. Ness resigned this morning."

Imani gasps. We exchange glances.

"Why?" Bianca demands. "Why would he do that?"

"I was hoping you could tell me," Dr. Forks says, sighing. "He was a bright, hardworking young doctor. He made a mistake, as you all know, but he wasn't reprimanded for it, and the patient survived. I'm baffled, frankly, that he would walk away from PGH the way he did."

"He didn't give you a reason?" Clark asks.

Dr. Forks shakes his head. "Handed in his pager this morning without explanation. Shockingly unprofessional. Anyway, this being the case, you four will have to pick up the slack for the rest of the academic year. That means more frequent call shifts. I know it'll be difficult, but PGH—and especially our patients—are counting on you to rise to the occasion."

We sit in sullen, mournful silence.

Dr. Forks nods, then stands and is abruptly upbeat. "I told administration we have a great intern class this year, and they can handle anything that comes their way. Go get 'em." He ushers us out into the hallway and shoos us away.

"I'm calling Stu," Bianca says as we head for the elevators.

"Already ringing," Clark replies, his phone pressed to his ear. "Damn! Straight to voicemail."

"Do you think he's okay? Should we go check on him?" I ask.

We pile into the elevator.

"Does anyone know where he lives?" Imani asks.

We shake our heads. I know Stuart lives in a suburb of Philadelphia, with his parents, but I'm not sure where.

"His parents will make sure he's okay," Bianca reasons. "Right?"

"His dad's a surgeon, and his mom's a nurse. He's in good hands," Clark says. "But I'll keep trying to call him."

Bianca shakes her head. "I'm still worried about him."

Our silence echoes her concern. I lean my head back against the cold steel of the elevator. The walls feel as if they're pressing in on me. The past forty-eight hours have been the most stressful of my adult life, and I'm not sure how much more I can take.

My phone beeps.

It's a text message from Ethan: The Tally family is asking for an autopsy.

* * *

An Indian woman wearing a teardrop-shaped bindi and a yellow surgical gown is holding half of Mrs. Tally's spleen in her outstretched palm.

"I love spleens." Her thickly accented English is almost melodic. "You know why? Because of this beautiful fan pattern of arteries in the middle. It reminds me of the inside of a peach. Every time I eat peaches I think of spleens."

This was a terrible idea.

At a metal lab table in the middle of the room, an enormous man with a tattoo of a bare-chested woman on his forearm lifts one of Mrs. Tally's lungs from her chest. The organ, just like all the others I've watched him remove through the incision that stretches from the base of her neck to the top of her pelvis bone, is dark pink and dusky. A liver, gallbladder, pancreas, two kidneys, and a three-foot length of colon are neatly lined up in gray plastic bins next to the body.

"You're interested in pathology as a specialty?" the woman asks.

There is no way this is going to work. How am I supposed to stop her from opening the skull?

I hesitate. "Yes."

"Wonderful!" she says, smiling broadly. "I'm always happy to have student and resident observers."

"Dr. Sridhara?" the tattooed man says. "Are you ready for the heart?"

"Ready and waiting, my darling." The woman deposits the piece of spleen into an empty bin.

The man produces a huge pair of what look like garden shears from underneath the table. As he uses them to snap each one of Mrs. Tally's ribs in half, Dr. Sridhara says, "Benji is the best prosector in the world, right, Benji?"

The giant man replies, "That's right"—snap—"been working here ten years"—snap—"and love what I do"—snap—"Dr. Srid is the best pathologist"—snap—"she'll teach you a lot"—snap—"People don't realize how important"—snap—"our line of work is"—snap—"That's why I'm here at six p.m. on a Friday." He smiles.

"Is this your first time observing an autopsy?" Dr. Sridhara asks.

"I saw one, once, in medical school," I say.

"Of course. But this was *your* patient. You are following her from admission to death and, now, past death," she says, smiling encouragingly.

I return her smile and nod.

She seems pleased. "That's the best way to really understand disease. The only way. Have you heard of Ibn Zuhr?"

I shake my head.

"He was an Arab doctor in the twelfth century. The father of pathology. The first to dissect deceased patients. He believed in observation, not speculation. To truly understand disease, you have to see it, to hold it in your own hands. The pathologist is the doctor's doctor. Have you ever heard that saying?"

I shake my head again. The smell of feces drifts from the plastic bin containing the colon. Benji has seized Mrs. Tally's sternum with one hand and is jostling it. Abruptly, he yanks it out of her chest with the ribs attached to either side. Dr. Sridhara adjusts her glasses and peers into the chest cavity. "So here"—she pauses, I assume for dramatic effect—"is the heart, in situ." I lean over, quickly take a look, and nod. Mrs. Tally's heart and lungs are dull and still, nothing like the vibrant beating heart I held in my hand during Dr. V's surgery case a few months ago.

"You said the patient just suddenly went into cardiac arrest?"

"Yes."

"In the CT scanner?"

"Yes."

She shakes her head while making a clicking sound with her

tongue. "Too bad. Probably just your typical pulmonary embolus, right?"

"Probably."

"Benji, darling, hand me a scalpel, won't you?" She cuts into the pulmonary artery—a shiny, dark red cord the width of a sausage link—in several places. She pokes inside with her gloved finger and cleans out some dried blood. I hold my breath. *Please let there be a clot.*

"No blood clot here," she says, moments later. Benji helps her lift both lungs from the chest cavity. He places them, carefully, in one of the gray bins and carries them to an adjoining room.

"Okay, next we open the pericardial sac," Dr. Sridhara says. The pericardial sac is where blood collected in Fat Dan, the place Ethan inserted a needle to save his life.

Dr. Sridhara cuts into the wispy layer of tissue surrounding the heart, then lifts the heart out of the chest and places it on a metal tray. Within moments she has sliced the heart into two neat halves. She holds the pieces up to the light and turns them this way and that, then presses her thumb into the flesh like she's examining produce at a grocery store. "Looks good, actually. No signs of infarction or any damage. So . . . what happened to our lady?"

Through a glass partition, I catch sight of Benji using something that resembles a deli meat slicer to make sections of the lungs.

"Benji! How do the lungs look?"

"No blood clots, Doc. The tumor is pretty tiny."

"Should we open the cranium?"

"Up to you, Doc."

"She had lung cancer," I say.

Dr. Sridhara glances at me over her glasses. "Yes, I know."

The back of my neck is hot. "I mean, could it have just been the lung cancer that caused her death?"

"She had one small tumor in her lung. How would this have caused her to suddenly die?"

"I . . . don't know."

"What service did you say you were from?"

"Internal Medicine." I tug at the sleeves of my yellow gown.

She stares at me for a long moment, then smiles again. "Right. So, we open the cranium." She draws the scalpel from one of Mrs. Tally's ears, over the crown of her head, to the other ear. Then she turns the blade on its side and scrapes it back and forth, in quick, jerking movements, underneath the skin. "Hold up the head for me," she says. I cup my hands under the base of Mrs. Tally's head. Seizing a flap of skin with both hands, Dr. Sridhara tugs—gently at first, then with a vigor I would not have expected from such a diminutive woman—and peels the skin and hair off Mrs. Tally's skull, as if she were pulling up a carpet. The bone underneath is eggshell-white, dotted with drops of golden fat, and covered with lacy blue veins. The flap of skin and hair rests on my forearms.

"Benji, darling. We are ready for you," she says. Benji returns, holding a small electrical saw with a circular blade. I step away from the table and divert my eyes. There is a high-pitched screeching sound and a smell like burning popcorn. Powdery bits of bone spray out from the table. Then Dr. Sridhara says, "Thank you, Benji," and the screeching stops. A round piece of bone the size of a tea saucer sits on the table next to Mrs. Tally's arm. Her brain, glistening and pink, is visible through the hole in her skull.

Dr. Sridhara is using forceps to tease apart the folds of brain tissue when she says, "Look at this! Look at the size of this blood clot. This was a huge bleed. Did the patient have a trauma to her head?"

"I'm . . . not sure," I say.

She removes her gloves and pulls Mrs. Tally's chart from a shelf on the far wall. "Let's see, let's see." She flips through the pages with slow deliberation. Finally she says, "It looks like she was on Zynexa, which, as you know, can cause bleeding with minimal trauma. And it looks like she did fall and hit her head, at least once." She makes some notes on a clipboard. "There's the diagnosis. This is what killed her. That's a shame. Especially since her lung cancer might well have been cured someday."

I'm breathless, the wind knocked out of me to hear what I already knew, put so matter-of-factly. I reach toward the back pocket of my scrubs for my inhaler as the room sways.

Benji places the heart, liver, lungs, and colon into a clear plastic bag, then hoists the bag into the open stomach cavity. "All done, Doc? Sew her back up?"

"Yes, dear, thank you," she says.

All done. The sum of Mrs. Tally's existence has been reduced to a plastic bag full of organs.

"You can tell your attending, Dr. Portnoy, that I'll be calling him," Dr. Sridhara says. "Do you have any questions? I hope this was a good learning experience for you."

I murmur, "Yes, thank you," pull off my gloves and gown, throw them into the trash, and rush out. The heavy, metal door of the Pathology lab slams shut behind me, the sound reverberating up and down the damp basement hallway. Just steps away are the hospital morgue and laundry. A woman with a plastic bonnet over her hair is pushing a cart of cleaning supplies toward me. I duck around her and into the elevator. I press the Up button several times in a row. At last, the doors slide shut, and I sink into a crouch, gasping for breath.

A text from Ethan is waiting when I pull my phone from the back pocket of my scrubs: How's it going?

"She opened the skull. I couldn't stop her. She saw the bleed. She's calling Portnoy," I say before he can even say hello.

Ethan sighs. "Yeah, it was probably a long shot. Shit. I can't say I didn't know she fell and hit her head."

"No, you can't. The chart still says she hit her head, and Dr. Cantor was informed, and the intern would come examine her," I say.

The elevator stops at the third floor, and Dr. V enters, pulling off his surgical bonnet. He rubs his eyes and seems not to notice me. I shrink into a corner and lower the volume on my phone.

"Yeah, I know." Ethan's voice is defeated. "And the next line is the verbal order from 'the resident' for Zynexa. I'm probably screwed no matter what at this point."

"Maybe . . . ," I say. The elevator stops again, and Dr. V heads down a long hallway toward the operating rooms.

"Norah? You still there?"

"Ethan, I have to go." I hang up and follow Dr. V. He has disappeared into the men's locker room. I take a breath, turn the corner, and push open the door to the women's locker room. It's empty for a moment. Then Elle walks in wearing skinny jeans and a tank top.

"Hey, Norah," she says. She breezes past me to a locker and starts to change into scrubs. "I didn't know you were on call tonight."

"I'm not," I say. "I stayed late to watch an autopsy."

She raises her eyebrows. "Wow, that's impressive. Not many interns would voluntarily stay late for an anatomy lesson."

"Ethan thought it'd be a good learning experience for me," I say.

She closes the locker door and smiles. "He's a good senior resident."

"He's the best." I hesitate. "Are you operating with Dr. V?"

"I am. Mitral valve repair. Did you want in? I can ask if you can observe."

"No, thanks, but I do have a favor to ask. Something I need your help with." I catch a glimpse of myself in the mirror above the row of sinks on the far wall. I stand up straighter. I put my hands on my hips.

"Okay. What is it?"

"There was a case two days ago. A patient fell out of bed, had a head trauma, and bled into her brain. A patient you were going to put a PICC line in."

"The one that coded in the CT scanner? I heard about that." She starts to pull her hair into a ponytail. "She had a bleed?"

"That's what they found at the autopsy. Ethan admitted her earlier that night. He put her on Zynexa."

Elle freezes, her hands in her hair. "Before or after she fell and hit her head?"

"After. It was an honest mistake. And Ethan doesn't make mistakes."

Elle shakes her head and sighs. "It could have happened to anyone. Hopefully there won't be fallout for him."

"There will be. It was a Portnoy patient."

Elle winces. "Ouch. Yeah. That guy's a prick. I wouldn't be surprised if he took back Ethan's fellowship offer."

"He might even have him fired. Which is why I need your help," I say.

"My help?"

"You saw the patient right after she was admitted," I say. "She was still in the ED. The chart doesn't say which resident ordered the Zynexa."

Elle's mouth opens slightly. After a moment she says, "I'm sorry . . . you want me to say that *I* ordered the Zynexa?"

"Portnoy doesn't even know you. You're a Surgery resident. There's a whole different set of rules for you."

"You mean no one expects us stupid Surgery residents to know the risks of Zynexa?" She crosses her arms.

"I don't mean it that way," I say quickly. "It's just . . . I know that you care about Ethan, like I do, and I just thought you'd want to do what you could to protect him. He doesn't deserve to lose his career over this."

"Neither do I."

"But the consequences for you wouldn't be nearly as bad. You don't have a fellowship to lose—"

"But I have a reputation to lose. And I'm running for Chief." She looks at me for a moment. "He put you up to this."

"No," I say, my face reddening. "He has no idea I'm here."

A look of realization crosses Elle's face. "Oh, wow. Okay . . ." She frowns sympathetically. "Listen, I know what it's like to have feelings for someone and want a relationship with him, but this . . . is not the way. This isn't going to work."

It stings. "Don't patronize me," I say.

She looks me up and down. "Oh, hon. I'm not patronizing you."

"All I'm doing is asking for your help, for Ethan's sake. That's all."

"I'm sorry. I can't. I don't want Ethan to get screwed over, but I can't lie for him." She shrugs. "Ethics are kind of a bitch." She turns and heads for the door.

I take a deep breath. My voice shaking, I manage to croak out, "I'm sorry to say, then, that I can't keep that secret we talked about."

She stops and looks over her shoulder, her expression stunned.

"You're right," I say resolutely. "Ethics are kind of a bitch."

"I don't know what you're talking about," she says.

"Does Dr. V's wife know what kind of car you drive? It's a red Toyota Rav4, right? All she'd have to do is check the security camera footage to see how many times you've been to her house while she's away."

Elle's voice is low and steady as she turns to face me. "You need to stop talking. Because you have no idea what you're doing."

"I know that an attending sleeping with one of his residents is a reportable ethics violation that could result in both parties being fired. You spend the night in the hospital whenever he does. That's not hard to prove. Not to mention that all the nurses know, and you're not exactly popular with the nurses."

Her eyes flash angrily. "Are you kidding me right now?"

"I just want you to help Ethan. Tomorrow morning, the pathologist is going to tell Portnoy about the bleed and the Zynexa, and the first thing Portnoy's going to do is check the chart and ask which resident ordered the Zynexa. I'm going to tell him it was you. All you have to do is go along with it."

"You think you're being loyal, but he's just using you. You get that, right?"

"If Portnoy asks, just tell him it was you, Elle," I say, heading for the door.

In the elevator, descending toward the lobby, I draw in my breath. It's a very long time before I let it out again.

CHAPTER NINETEEN

The most notable thing about the medical student sitting across the table from me is that his suit pants are too short. He has unbuttoned his jacket and keeps alternately fidgeting with his pen and smoothing his hair off his forehead. He looks as though he's been accidentally separated from the rest of his boy band. He's been talking for what feels like an eternity, but I've stopped listening. Since the autopsy three days ago, I'm having trouble concentrating on anything for more than a few minutes at a time.

"And then, when I was eighteen, I sprained my ankle and had to wear an ACE wrap for like four weeks. And that's why I want to become an orthopedic surgeon," he says.

I glance down at the list of questions on the table. "So, question number five is 'What are your goals for your internship year?'"

"My goals? Well, it's been my dream to work at Philly General. There are so many goals I have. . . ."

There is a blank space underneath question 5, below which "Fill in the candidate's answer here" is printed.

"I'm sorry," I say, "it wants me to list some of your goals." I smile and hold my pen at the ready, nodding encouragingly.

The young man's brow is starting to sweat. I sense the answer that has come to his lips, the one he is trying to beat back. Silently, I will him to come up with something, anything else to say. He cannot. "I just want to help people," he says.

I stare at him for a long, disappointed moment. I write down *He just wants to help people.* Then I say, "Question number six: Do you have any questions about this internship program?"

The young man hesitates, then says, "Is it hard being an intern? I mean, as hard as everyone says it is?"

"Yes." I stand and extend my hand. After a moment's hesitation, he shakes it.

Barbara is sitting at her desk outside the conference room. I hand her the list of questions, turn to the young man, and say "Good luck."

In less than three months, my internship year will be over. Clark was finally able to reach Stuart, who didn't want to talk but confirmed he was doing okay. He told Clark he was considering applying to a graduate program for the upcoming academic year, maybe working toward a master's in Public Health or an MBA in Health Administration. He said he wasn't sure if he'd ever return to medicine but didn't explain why. Before hanging up, he promised to keep in touch and apologized for leaving the rest of us to cover his call shifts.

I haven't spoken to Meryl since that morning at brunch. I tried calling her once, but I didn't leave a message, and she never returned my call. I didn't try her again. I've debated going to Hawaii by myself, but there doesn't seem to be much point in that now. I make a mental note to call the airline and cancel my ticket.

Clark looks annoyed when I walk into the residents' lounge. "Where have you been? We're getting killed with admissions."

"Med student interviews," I say. "Dr. Forks asked for volunteers."

"No one asked me to volunteer," he says, frowning.

"Maybe that's because you would have told them that the Golden Age of Medicine is over and a physician assistant with less training will take their job and their money," Imani says from the sofa, where she's reclining with one arm draped over her eyes.

Clark sinks farther into his seat. "I would have, because it's the truth."

"Norah! I have a special one for you." Bianca waves the list of admissions in her hand. "For showing up late, you get a wrinkly old man with a urinary tract infection and possible scabies."

I relax all the muscles in my face, which gives my countenance a more unpleasant look than any I could assume voluntarily.

"Don't look at me like that," Bianca says, taken aback. "It was Clark's idea. And it might not really be scabies. It could just be, what do you call them in English . . . maggots or something."

I sigh and write down the patient's name and ED bed number. My phone chimes. A text message from Ethan reads, Could you come over later? Around 9? Important. Need to talk. Not safe at work.

I feel a knot forming in my core. I text back, Sure. Everything ok? while jogging down the stairwell to the ED. There's no reply. I haven't told Ethan what I said to Elle after the autopsy, and Portnoy has said nothing about Mrs. Tally's case to either Ethan or me since the morning after she died. By now, I'm sure, Portnoy has heard about the autopsy results and knows that someone ordered the Zynexa that caused Mrs. Tally to bleed into her brain.

My breath is quick and shallow as I walk to Ethan's apartment that evening. Elle really didn't leave me any other choice; I had to protect Ethan. If she truly cared about Ethan, she would have been eager to help him when I asked, and she wouldn't have forced my hand. I only did what was necessary and logical, given the situation.

By the time I reach Ethan's building, my heart is racing. I take the elevator up and hesitate in front of his door. I've gone over, countless times since this afternoon, what I'm going to say. I've decided that I'm finally going to admit my feelings for him. There's no point in dancing around the subject anymore, especially since it's obvious he feels the same way about me. I marvel at how far I've come: from someone awkward, self-conscious, and overly cautious—a doormat—to this bold young woman, speaking her mind, seizing the moment.

I knock. After a long moment, Elle answers.

"Oh, hi, Norah," she says, pleased but not smiling. She puts her hair up in a bun and secures it with a pen.

Ethan appears behind her. "Norah? What are you doing here?"

"You texted me," I say.

"I did?" He rubs his forehead. "When?"

"This afternoon," I fumble for my phone in my coat pocket.

"I was just leaving," Elle says, stepping past me with her jacket and purse in hand. I look at her, stunned, and she smirks. Leaning toward me, she says, "He really needs to lock his phone." Then she is gone.

"Um, come in, excuse the mess," Ethan says.

I step into the doorway and see two empty Chinese food containers on the counter in the kitchen.

"I got this text—" I start to say. "I'm sorry, what was Elle doing here?"

Ethan starts to clear the takeout containers. "She came over to tell me."

"Tell you what?"

"What she did." He stops and looks at me with a grateful expression. "She told Portnoy she ordered the Zynexa for that patient—"

"Lenore Tally. That was her name," I say curtly.

"Right. Her. Elle took the blame for that to save my ass. I don't even know what to say. She's amazing."

"That's . . . great," I say.

"Portnoy came down hard on her, but he can't have her fired since she's a Surgery resident."

"There's a whole different set of rules for her," I say.

"Exactly. Still, I can't get over that she would just fall on her sword like that for me. She's some girl."

"She did it because I asked her to." There is a rising shrill in my voice that I am finding impossible to control.

"She told me that, too." Ethan smiles over his shoulder as he pulls a soda from the refrigerator. "Do you want a soda?"

The door to the bedroom is open. I move toward it. "What exactly did she say?"

"That she ran into you, and you told her about the autopsy. And that you two discussed her taking the hit for me."

The bed is unmade. Both sides of it. "Did you—" My voice catches. I am at once in disbelief and furious at myself for being so glaringly naïve.

Ethan hurriedly closes the bedroom door. "Excuse the mess." His face reddens, and he laughs uncomfortably. "I know what you're thinking, and this is not some sort of rebound relationship to get over my failed engagement. I've been friends with Elle for a long time."

Whatever I thought I had with Ethan, this crystal palace painstakingly built from glances and moments, from conversations I've committed to memory and relived in rapturous detail, again and again, comes crashing down around me. It doesn't collapse neatly, folding in on itself like a house of cards, so that there's order to the destruction. It's obliterated. As if it were bombed. I stand dumbstruck, overwhelmed by the wreckage. Finally I say, "Relationship?"

"Well, you know," he says, "it's pretty new. We'll see how it goes."

"She's been sleeping with Dr. V for months," I say.

"What are you talking about?"

"Dr. V asked me to go to his house for some scut, and Elle was there. Half-naked. She asked me not to tell anyone."

Ethan takes a breath. He twists the cap off his soda. "Well, she's her own woman. If she was messing around with an attending, that's her business."

Any measure of reason has left me. My voice trembles, rage spilling out of me in fitful bursts. "Not was. Is. She's fucking you both. In fact, I'd say she's fucking all three of us."

"What's going on with you?" Ethan's expression is both stung and puzzled.

"With me? What's going on with *me*?" I laugh. "You slept with me, remember?"

"Yeah, once, and I thought. . . . You were so nonchalant about it. And the situation with you and Clark . . . I thought that's the type of thing you wanted."

"What situation with me and Clark?"

"You guys are in a no-strings relationship, right? Sex only when you're on call together?"

My mouth drops open. "With Clark? *With Clark? While on call?*"

"That's what you said."

I brace myself against the counter, the breath having been knocked out of me. Evidently, in aiming for confident and breezy, what I achieved was nonchalant and floozy. "Oh my God, no, I didn't. I never said that."

"You said the rumor was true."

"*That's* not the rumor I was talking about!"

Ethan runs both hands through his hair, bewildered. "Wow. Okay. I'm really sorry. I feel awful. I just totally read that wrong."

His remorse only makes me more scornful. "You're reading *this* wrong," I say. "You're crazy if you think Elle actually has feelings for you. She would have let Portnoy fire you if it wasn't for me."

Ethan stares at me. Then, opening the front door, his voice steady and stern, he says, "Good night, Norah. Thanks for stopping by."

I hesitate, then rush out, saying "See you around" over my shoulder. I hear the door shut behind me. The elevator call button glows on the wall. My insides tear apart slowly, as if millions of tiny threads that have been holding me together are all snapping at once. As if my ribs are cracking apart. I'm eviscerated, turned inside out.

How could I have been so wrong? How could I, someone who believes in the sanctity of logic, have been so foolish? It's like I've spent months confidently puzzling through a math equation, only to arrive at the wrong answer. I retrace my missteps, one at a time: humiliating myself in front of Ethan, blackmailing Elle, lying to a dead patient's family. I trace back the flawed chain of reasoning that led me to the conclusion that anyone, much less Ethan, could love me.

Reeling, unmoored, I grab onto an idea: letting my emotions get the best of me was my first mistake. It's where everything went wrong. What's needed now is a mental shift, a resetting, not hysteria or self-pity.

I push the button.

Resolutely, I ride the elevator down to the lobby and walk out to the sidewalk. My phone rings. It's Bianca.

Stuart's been taken to a suburban ED. It's an overdose. Adderall and cocaine, they're saying. He won't make it through the night. She's still talking, but the phone slips from my hand to the pavement, and I can't bear to pick it up again.

If I cried when my father died, I don't remember it. What I remember is that I went right back to reading my library book. And I kept my nose in a book for ten more years, reading away. I read away thoughts of what his last moments were like, alone on a dark stretch of highway, where he fell asleep behind the wheel after working forty hours straight at the hospital—did he know he was dying? I read away the birthdays and holidays and school concerts he missed.

I read away the gaping wound his disappearance from my life left behind.

I've been through worse than this. And I've learned I can read anything away.

And that's what I do for the next two years.

CHAPTER TWENTY

Two Years Later

The woman in the mirror behind the barista and the many rows of delicate-mouthed bottles of flavored syrups is wearing a red trench coat and a scowl. I press my lips together and try to force my mouth into a smile.

"Next up, the pretty young lady in the red coat," the barista says. "What'll it be, miss?"

"Medium dark roast in a large cup. A splash of whole milk, steamed, no sugar, and one and a half shots of espresso," I say.

"You work at the hospital?"

"Yes."

"In that case, three dollars even. Are you a nurse?"

I hand him the cash. "No."

"Physical therapist?"

A voice from the end of the line calls, "Dr. Kapadia!"

I turn, and a young woman with long red hair bounds over. Her eyes are huge and aquamarine, her nose tiny and pointed, like an adorable Disney character who lives in a glen and is friendly with forest animals. "Hi! Good morning! Can I ask you a question?" From the pocket of her short white coat she pulls a list of patients. "This patient, Gina Fromley, with the pancreatic—"

I yank her arm and pull her toward an empty corner near the trash bin. "First of all—what was your name again?"

"Traci."

"Traci, keep your voice down. You can't talk about a patient's information in a public place. You've heard of HIPAA, right?"

"Oh, right. I'm sorry."

I grab my coffee from the counter. "Jesus, you're going to get us both sued or fired."

She follows me across the street to the hospital. "Right, so you know that patient? The lady with the pancreatitis we admitted yesterday afternoon? And the radiologist thought her X-ray showed right lung pneumonia, but you thought she had fluid in her lung instead—I think that's what you said, right? Or you thought she had pneumonia and the radiologist thought she had fluid?"

She follows me across the lobby and into the elevator. "Anyway, when I came in this morning to round on her—it was probably around five a.m. or five fifteen—I checked her labs, and her sodium level was 124. Normal is 135, right? So, I wasn't sure if I should worry because her blood pressure was a little on the low side." She follows me off the elevator, down the hall, and to the residents' lounge. "So I checked her medication list, and I didn't see anything on there that would cause hyponatremia."

I sift through the rack of white coats on the wall. "Traci, did you have a question?"

"I was just wondering what the criteria are for transferring a patient to the ICU?"

I look at her over my shoulder. "Why do you ask?"

"Because that patient was transferred to the ICU. You know, after she coded this morning and they put her on a ventilator."

I am still pulling on my white coat as I crash through the doors of the ICU, Traci on my heels holding my coffee.

"What the hell happened to my pancreatitis?" I ask as I thunder into the room.

I recognize the patient by her shock of auburn hair with a blond streak on the left side. She was alert and talkative, funny even, when I admitted her yesterday. Now, she lies comatose on a ventilator, her face so swollen that her once-distinct features are completely obscured. She could be anybody. Or any body. That's the acidic power of disease: to dissolve us from people into amorphous collections of body parts. Not a woman, but a pancreatitis.

The resident at the bedside has bags under his eyes, and his white coat looks as though it hasn't been washed in months. "The nurse paged me this morning saying her blood pressure was seventy over forty and she was 'sleeping really soundly,'" he says.

"For fuck's sake." I try to rub away the sharp pain between my eyes.

"That's what I thought, too. When I got to the bedside, she wasn't breathing. Like, she was blue. We coded her and got her back, but . . ."

We watch the cardiac monitor overhead. The narrow, neat spikes of normal heart activity—the steady *beep beep beep*—slow gradually until one, then two, then several wide waveforms appear: ventricular fibrillation, a life-threatening arrhythmia.

My muscles tense like a runner in starting blocks. "Get a crash cart!" I say, my voice loud and an octave lower than its usual pitch. I've learned that the staff responds more readily to a lower tone of voice.

The resident and several nurses have been staring, transfixed, at the cardiac monitor. Now, the spell broken, they spring into action. "Code blue. ICU Bed 10" is announced from the loudspeaker. A defibrillator on a rolling cart appears, and the patient's chest is exposed. Standing over the bed, his fingers laced together, the resident hesitates and looks up at me. I nod, and he begins chest compressions. It's never spoken, just silently acknowledged, that all of what follows next will be futile.

"Charging!" someone says. A high-pitched whistle signals that the defibrillator is ready.

"Shock 100!" I say. "Clear!"

The resident steps back from the bed, bringing his hands into the air at the same time that a nurse places two electrical paddles on the patient's chest and shocks her. The body arches off the bed. Time is suspended. I glance at the monitor—there's been no change.

"An amp of epinephrine and an amp of bicarb!" I say. The resident begins chest compressions again. A nurse pushes a syringe of medication into one of the IV lines. I barely notice the crowd that has formed in the doorway.

"Shock 200! Clear!" I say. Again, the jolt lifts the patient off the bed.

"Dr. Kapadia, chief resident extraordinaire, where are we at?" A silver-haired woman wearing tortoise-rim glasses and a red blazer pushes her way into the room.

"Hey, Dr. Linberry," I say, my eyes on the monitor. "Six minutes in and still V-fib."

"Dr. Linberry, are you this patient's attending?" one of the nurses asks.

"So I was told," Dr. Linberry says. "I thought I was getting a pancreatitis patient. I come in this morning and find out she's a train wreck in the ICU. Any idea what went wrong?"

"Shock 300! Clear!" I say. Another surge of electricity tears through the body. "I'm guessing she had a pulmonary embolus or sudden heart failure."

Dr. Linberry nods. "The usual suspects. This is our second time at this party?"

I glance at her. "Yes. She coded earlier this morning."

She flips through the chart calmly while the resident resumes chest compressions. The alarm chimes from the heart monitor, the shrill whistle of the defibrillator, and the creaking of the bedsprings with every thrust against the patient's chest fill the room with a cacophony I've heard so many times I barely notice it.

Dr. Linberry says, "Hold compressions. How many minutes in are we now?"

"Ten minutes," a nurse says.

"Think we ought to call it?" Dr. Linberry asks.

The resident, his brow covered in sweat, glances at us. I look at the monitor. A flat line. "It's up to you, ma'am," I say.

Dr. Linberry sighs. "Yeah. It's over. Thank you, everyone."

"Time of death: eight fifteen a.m.," I say quietly to a nurse standing next to me. She writes it down on a clipboard. The crowd at the door melts away. The resident steps back from the bedside, rubbing his arms. A nurse switches off the cardiac monitor and peels the electrodes off the patient's chest.

"Did you meet the family, Norah?" Dr. Linberry asks, paging through the chart.

"No, I didn't."

"Me neither, obviously. I didn't even meet the patient." She sighs again. "But the least I can do is call them myself, right?"

"Sure. That would be nice," I say, shrugging. This is neither here nor there. The patient is already dead, and which one of us calls to tell her family this is irrelevant.

"It's why I get paid the big bucks," she says. "No, wait. I actually don't get paid the big bucks. Hospital administration gets the big bucks, and they never have to call the family." Reluctantly, she tucks the chart under her arm and heads for the door, calling over her shoulder, "Thanks for the help, everyone!"

A nurse appears near my elbow. "Norah, could you please talk to the medical student that was in here?"

I look around. Traci is gone. "Why?"

"I think she took this pretty hard," the nurse says. "Poor thing. She just looked devastated."

I sigh, annoyed. Med students. "Did you see where she went?"

"Conference room," the nurse says, pointing down the hall.

I pass the nurses' station where the resident is filling out the death certificate. "Your student needs a pep talk," I say. "You're coming."

"Whatever you say, Chief." He loops his stethoscope around his neck and follows me.

We find Traci sitting alone at a long conference table, her eyes puffy, staring into her lap.

"Hey, Traci. Everything okay?" I sit on the edge of the table. The resident stands in the doorway and glances at his pager.

"I didn't think she'd actually die," Traci says softly, without lifting her gaze. "I talked to her yesterday. About her kids. They were going on a trip to Alaska. I don't . . . I don't get what happened."

The resident and I exchange a glance.

"None of us get what happened," I say. "But it does happen. People die suddenly."

Traci shakes her head. "But they got her back. They got her back once."

"Most people that code once, code twice," the resident says, his tone impatient. "And most people that code twice don't survive. It's not like this was a surprise outcome."

Traci wipes a tear from the side of her nose. "Maybe we could have ordered another chest X-ray or a Pulmonology consult. . . ." Her voice fades away. Then, "How do you do this? Every day?"

The resident shrugs dismissively. "Well, you could just go into radiology or another specialty where you have minimal patient contact."

"These are always tough cases, Traci," I say, glaring at the resident. "But they're learning opportunities, too."

"Does it get easier?"

I consider this. "Your memory gets shorter. You'll forget this patient—"

"I don't want to forget her," she says, affronted.

I shrug. "But you will. It's not a bad thing. You'll remember this case, the facts, what you learned. That's what's important."

She nods, then says, with a vague wave of her hand, "Science."

"That's the idea. So, back to work, right?" I say.

She smiles weakly. "Right. You're right. Thanks, Dr. Kapadia."

As I head for the door, I glance at the resident. His bun is gone, his hair cut short, but otherwise he looks just the same as he did the day I met him three years ago. "You really do get cranky when you don't get enough sleep. Get some rest, Gabe."

He smiles. "Yes, ma'am."

It's nearly 9:00 p.m. by the time I pull into Ma's driveway. The garage is outlined in a string of blinking lights and an intricate, colored-rice *rangoli* decorates the front step along with a glowing jack-o'-lantern that was, clearly, carved by Kai.

"We weren't sure you were coming." Reena, her cheeks and hands dusted with flour, turns on her heel and leaves me in the doorway.

"And Happy Diwali to you, too," I say, under my breath.

Ma bustles in from the kitchen, wearing an apron. "Norah! You couldn't change out of your scrubs? Is that blood on your pants?" Her tone is somewhere between irked and sympathetic. "Have you been starving yourself? You're so skinny, and your hair is mess! Help us in kitchen. We have so much to do!"

I follow her into the kitchen, where serving trays of food are everywhere—covering the table and counters, stacked on top of the microwave. Trays of onion-stuffed naan, mustard-yellow rolls of khandvi garnished with bright green coriander, two different kinds of fried pakoras, a huge stockpot of golden brown gulab jamun bobbing in warm sugary syrup. Reena is at the stove, stirring a different pot with each arm.

Ma notices my stunned expression and swells with pride. "Our biggest order yet. One hundred and fifty people for Diwali party tomorrow! Did you see our new business cards?" She pulls a stack of glossy cards from the pocket of her apron. Over a background of orange, green, and white stripes (the colors of the Indian flag) are the words *Rupali & Reena's Catering, Your One Stop for Indian Delights!* and, in smaller print below that, *Twice winner of the Paramus Community Center Desi Cook-off!* and Ma's phone number. She hands me the cards and a box of Saran wrap. "Put one of these in each tray and wrap with plastic." I marvel at her buzzing energy, something she attributes to switching to a gluten-free diet a year ago. Since then, she and Reena have bonded over their shared business venture and dietary restrictions. It seems the role of Ma's Good Indian Daughter was always meant to be filled by Reena after all.

The front door opens, and Paul comes in holding Kai, who is wearing a Spider-Man costume and—despite being fast asleep on Paul's shoulder—clutching an orange bucket of candy in one hand.

"Hey, Nor. You made it! Happy Diwal-oween," he whispers. He holds out his fist for me to bump, and I tap my knuckles against his.

Reena motions to him. "You stir. I'll take Kai up to bed. He can sleep in Norah's old room." She gathers the limp Kai into her arms and turns to me. "I assume you're not staying overnight."

I smile regretfully. "I have to work tomorrow—"

"Of course you do." She turns and heads upstairs, leaving an awkward silence behind her.

After a moment, Paul clears his throat. "I'll go get more trays from the garage."

He leaves, and Ma calls after him, "Bring yellow box for Norah!" She shrugs and shakes her head. "She never liked you," she says with a sigh, while stirring the two pots on the stove. One of them is chai coming to boil.

I struggle to tear a piece of plastic wrap from the roll. "I've apologized. Many times. But I'm never going to think it's okay not to vaccinate Kai."

"It's not that." Ma hesitates, staring at the bubbles of milk swelling and bursting on the surface of the chai, struggling for the right words. "Reena is young, but she's old-fashioned. Family and tradition are everything to her. You don't speak our language, you don't cook our food, you don't drop everything for us. Your world doesn't revolve around us. She doesn't understand you."

It's impossible not to hear judgment in Ma's voice. I always hear judgment in her voice. I make a noise to defend myself, but she stops me.

"But I do. Your life is about something else." She smiles simply and shrugs. "Reena was asking me if you were going to come to Kai's birthday at Legoland. She's reserving rooms at hotel."

"I won't make it to that. I have to work." Still stung, I say it without apology.

"That's what I told her."

"What did you tell who?" Paul enters with a yellow cardboard box that used to hold an economy-size quantity of baby wipes, but now has *Norah* written across one side in Ma's handwriting. He sets it down on the floor.

"Norah can't come to Kai's birthday," Ma says.

"Oh. Sure. No problem." Paul gives me a reassuring nod, though the way he avoids looking directly at me hints that he's disappointed, if not surprised. He peeks into the box. "Hey, this is all of Nor's old stuff." He fishes out a CD case. "Justin Bieber's Christmas album? Really?"

I roll my eyes at him while kneeling by the box. "Shut up, Paul. You had the Spice Girls CD."

He recoils in mock offense. "They were very underappreciated.

Ma, why are you throwing out Nor's old junk? She needs this"—he pulls out a heart-shaped pink plastic box—"Hello Kitty stationery set."

Ma swats Paul's arm and kneels down next to us. "I'm not throwing it out. Now that Norah has her own apartment, I thought she may want her things."

Paul regards her suspiciously.

"And it's about time I cleaned up around here. I was thinking of making Norah's room into office." She looks at me guiltily. "If that's okay with you, *beti*."

"That's fine with me. It's a great idea," I say, exchanging a glance with Paul. First the catering business, now this interest in home redecorating. There's a palpable sense that the tide of grief is turning, that the tight grasp our family tragedy has held on Ma all these years might finally be loosening. Her automated blood pressure cuff has been on a high shelf in the garage for the past few months, and she hasn't spoken to Nimisha Auntie—who was banned from the community center after it was determined that she had violated center policy by trying to sell diet pills on the premises—in over a year.

A smile flits across Ma's face as she pulls Dad's stethoscope from the box. "I think, *beti*, this is most important thing in here. It's time you took this home with you, don't you think?" She drapes the stethoscope around my neck and gently cups my face in her hands. "You are like me little bit, but you are more like him." She sighs, a bittersweet sound. "He would be proud. *I* am proud."

I wrap my arms around Ma; then Paul envelops us both in a bear hug. We stay like that, the three of us, for a long time.

CHAPTER TWENTY-ONE

There are several drunk people, two of whom are drinking coffee from enormous Dunkin' Donuts cups, gathered in the Intensive Care Unit and waiting for the man in bed 5 to die. Every twenty minutes or so, the most inebriated of them goes to the patient, who has been comatose for days, leans in so that his face is just next to the patient's ear, and says in a loud, passionate voice, "You can fight this, man. Come on, buddy, you can fight this."

A woman in their party clutches the counter at the nurses' station to steady herself. "Excuse me, he's bleeding," she says.

I glance up from the chart I'm reading. "Yes, ma'am. We know."

An endogastric tube snakes from the patient's stomach, up his esophagus, and out his nose. Blood drips steadily from the end of the tube and into a huge clear plastic collection bin attached to the side rail of the bed. Two hours ago, the bin was empty. Now, the level of blood hovers just under the one-liter mark.

"Why isn't anyone trying to help him?"

I squint. I've already explained this to four other family members. "I'm so sorry, but his liver has failed. It's stopped making the proteins that help his blood clot. He has varices in his esophagus—"

"He has *what* in his esophagus?"

"Big veins. They are friable and bleed easily. That's where the blood is coming from. But, unfortunately, there's nothing more we can do at this point to stop it."

She stares at me blankly. "What do you mean there's nothing you can do? Give him a blood transfusion!"

"We did. We've been transfusing him for the past three days. We also had interventional radiology try to burn the veins to stop them from bleeding. They also tried to put a balloon called a Sengstaken-Blakemore tube down his esophagus to stop the bleeding. Nothing we've tried has worked, and the bleeding is just getting worse. I'm so sorry."

"What about an operation?"

"Unfortunately, surgery won't fix this. The problem is too extensive. Even if there was an option for surgery, he wouldn't survive the procedure."

"Why not?"

"Because his blood doesn't clot."

"Because he has liver failure?"

"Yes."

"Because he's an alcoholic?"

"Well, yes, probably."

"So, what, we just watch him bleed to death?"

"I wish there was more we could do."

"Well"—she straightens and breathes in through her nose—"that is unacceptable." She stumbles away.

I check my pager and my phone—no messages. For a moment I consider going to the call room to try to sleep for a bit; I've been awake all night. Then I consider the idea that I might be asleep when this patient finally goes into cardiac arrest, and I will be paged out of my near-comatose slumber and forced to try to resuscitate him because his family refuses to make him DNR. No matter what I say, they will not accept that he cannot be saved, that he is a shell, a carcass with the life—quite literally—draining out of him before their eyes. Their refusal to understand the inevitability of his death annoys me; it's so self-indulgently, moronically, unrealistically optimistic. I sigh, thinking of the perfectly made bed in the call room. My pager sounds.

"Hi, Dr. Kapadia. It's Traci, the medical student. Sorry to wake you."

"I wasn't sleeping."

"Oh. Okay. Sorry to bother you. Gabe and I have a patient to admit down here in the ED, and we paged Dr. Herring, but he's refusing to accept the patient onto his service."

"I'll come down there."

Traci is sitting at the nurses' station making notes in a chart, her red hair in a long braid over one shoulder. Gabe sits next to her, his arm draped over the back of her chair.

"What's going on?" I ask.

"Herring is refusing to admit the patient," Gabe says. "He thinks Orthopedic Surgery should take her."

"Let me guess," I say. "Ortho won't take her either."

Gabe frowns and nods.

I sigh. "What's broken?"

"Her hip," Traci says. "Left femoral neck."

Gabe leans back in his chair. "Ortho is more than happy to operate on her—the Neanderthal resident was all 'Bone broke. Me fix.'—but they'll kill her. She's diabetic with a fever of 102, cellulitis of her right foot, and she's in kidney failure."

"And why is Herring refusing to admit her?" I ask.

"We have no idea," Gabe says. "Because he's a dick who enjoys making our lives harder than they need to be?"

Traci giggles, and she and Gabe exchange impish grins.

"Get him on the phone," I say.

Traci dials the hospital operator.

"Norah, are you going to the NASIM conference this year?"

Gabe asks as we wait for the call back from Dr. Herring. "Chiefs usually get time off to go, right?"

I nod. "It's a good place to start your job search. I still have to book my flight, though."

"Where is it this year?"

"Maui."

"Nice. Lucky. Ever been to Hawaii?"

"No."

Fifteen minutes later, the hospital operator calls back. "I have Dr. Herring on the line. Go ahead."

"Dr. Herring, this is Norah Kapadia," I say.

"Okay."

"The chief resident."

"Okay."

"Sir, the patient with the hip fracture is a medical train wreck. Please reconsider admitting her to your service."

"No. Ortho can take her, and we will consult."

"Sir, I don't think—"

"She needs surgery. They'll fix the hip."

Gabe and Traci look at me expectantly.

"Sir, she's ninety-four years old with cellulitis and kidney failure," I say. "We're not going to recommend hip surgery."

Silence. Then, a faint tinkling in the background.

He's peeing.

"What'd he say?" Gabe asks.

The sound of flushing.

I press my lips together. "Dr. Herring?" I wait a moment. "Dr. Herring!" I slap my open palm onto the counter in front of me, causing Traci and Gabe to flinch in surprise.

"Stop shouting," Dr. Herring grumbles, along with something else unintelligible.

"Dr. Herring," I say, my voice decidedly louder than what would be considered appropriate in a professional setting, "who the fuck do you think you're talking to?"

Several nurses and a patient on a nearby gurney take notice.

"You are admitting this patient to your service because *that is your job*," I continue. "I am done discussing this with you. And if you have a problem with that, you can zip your fly, drive over to the hospital, and deal with this shit show yourself. Those, sir, are your options."

"Wait," Dr. Herring says, almost immediately, "she has cellulitis?"

"Yes." I'm so exasperated I can barely get out the word.

"Oh. Then she can't have surgery. Admit her to my service."

The dial tone hums in my ear. I hang up. Traci's cartoon-princess eyes have expanded to twice their usual size.

"Damn." Gabe raises his eyebrows. "That was fun to watch."

I hand the chart to him. "Herring says he'll take her," I say. I turn to go, adding, "If you need me, I'll be in the call room. Sleeping."

Early the next morning, I stop by the grill station in the cafeteria.

"Good morning," I say. "I don't mean to pry, but you don't by any chance happen to have six fingers on your right hand?"

"Do you always begin conversations this way?" Lionel turns around with a broad grin. "How's it going, Dr. Kapadia?"

"Fine, Lionel. You making waffles today?"

"I am for you." He waggles his eyebrows flirtatiously. "Be about ten minutes."

The Princess Bride. Never misses.

"You're the man," I say, winking at him.

As I step away, a man behind me asks, "Can I get a waffle, too?"

Lionel busies himself with the grill. "Sorry, buddy, just ran out."

I haven't spoken to Ethan since the end of my internship year. His oncology fellowship was mostly outpatient, at Dr. Portnoy's clinic across town, and I rarely saw him. I saw Elle around the hospital for another year—she did become a chief—and managed, for the most part, to steer clear of her. We once shared an excruciatingly long elevator ride together, each of us shifting our weight and crossing and uncrossing our arms, Elle sighing angrily every time the elevator stopped to let someone on or off, from the fourteenth floor to the lobby. I frequented the stairs much more after that. The last I heard, she had moved across the country for a competitive transplant fellowship. In the end, I had been right—taking the blame for Ethan's mistake hadn't cost her anything in terms of her career. This, however, doesn't make me feel any better about what I did, about damaging her reputation in the final year of her training (word got around that she had accidentally killed a patient by starting Zynexa after a head trauma) and making the other residents question, even after she was elected, if she was truly competent enough to be chief.

I'm the only one in my class who stayed on at PGH. The other interns scattered to the wind at the end of that year—Bianca to her dermatology residency in Denver, Clark to a radiology residency in Miami, and Imani to ophthalmology at Mass General. We keep in touch, occasionally, on Facebook, but everyone's busy. I miss their company, though things were never the same after Stuart.

I try not to think too often about Stuart.

The cafeteria dining room is empty. I drop into a seat near the window, in the Staff Only section. Dr. Forks appears across the table from me, a cup of coffee in hand. Since I became a chief resident, my relationship with him has improved from icy and distant to lukewarm and occasionally cordial.

"I'm glad I caught you, Dr. Kapadia. May I?"

I nod, and he sits, clears his throat, and says apologetically, "Norah, you're going to have to meet with the hospital legal team."

"What? Why?"

He plays with the lid of his coffee cup. "The truth is, it happens to most physicians at some point."

"What happens?"

"A lawsuit. The family of one of your patients is suing the hospital over a bad outcome that happened two years ago."

I ask, although I know the answer, "Who is it?"

"The patient was Lenore Tally."

"This is because Zynexa was just recalled," I say.

"You remember the case?"

I nod. "She fell, was put on Zynexa, and had an intracranial bleed."

"With that history of falling and hitting her head, she shouldn't have been started on Zynexa." Dr. Forks sighs. "We think this is just the first of many Zynexa-related lawsuits to come. We had no way of knowing how bad the risk of bleeding was. Hell, I put my own mother on Zynexa for pneumonia last Christmas. She did great, incidentally."

I sit back in my chair. "So, the Tallys are suing me?"

"Not you personally, no. They're suing Dr. Portnoy and the hospital as a whole. As the intern, you had minimal responsibility in this case. Your supervisors are the ones they go after."

"So, Ethan, too."

"Yes, him, too. We've contacted him to let him know. He's practicing down in Baltimore."

"I know," I say. Then I add, "Social media."

Dr. Forks smiles and shakes his head. "You younger generation and social media. I still type with my two pointer fingers." He clears his throat. "Anyway, the legal team will be here tomorrow morning at nine thirty."

"I have clinic in the morning."

"One of the other residents will cover you. The meeting shouldn't take long. They just want to ask you what you remember about the case, I think. I don't get too involved in this legal mumbo jumbo."

"Okay." I nod.

"You'll meet them in the executive conference room on the fifteenth floor. Make sure to check out the painting while you're up there. It's really something."

"Painting?"

"You'll see."

We exchange nods, and he leaves.

I bury my head in my hands. After Mrs. Tally died, I tucked the memory of that night into a neat little box that I shoved into a back corner of my mind. I'm always aware of the box, never able to ignore it, but I've never opened it, never unpacked it, never taken out all the pieces and tried to make sense of it. There's no point in dwelling on that type of thing. Bad outcomes happen.

I'll have to lie again. There's no way I can reveal that Ethan was the resident responsible for ordering the Zynexa without admitting my part in trying to cover up the truth. With only months left in my residency, I can't risk my career.

Lionel appears. "Everything okay, Doc?" He places a waffle in front of me, a warm pat of butter melting into its crevices.

I smile at him gratefully. "Thanks, Lionel. This waffle is about all I have going for me at the moment."

His normally harsh eyes soften slightly. "Hey, when you're at the end of your rope, the only way to go is up, right?"

"Maybe." *Or, more likely, this is the beginning of the free fall.*

The stout middle-aged woman lying in the fetal position on the exam table in the outpatient clinic looks furious.

"I've had this pain for three days! It's excruciating!"

Seated at the computer in the corner of the room, I click the box in the electronic medical record labeled PAIN, and a menu of body parts appears, along with the command ENTER LOCATION OF PAIN.

"I'm sorry to hear that," I say. "Where is the pain?"

"I mean, it's like a knife. It's stabbing. It's worse than labor. Can you give me something for it? A shot? Anything?" She tries to adjust her position and moans.

I click a box labeled QUALITY and type in PAIN IS STABBING, and a blinking text box appears admonishing me to ENTER LOCATION OF PAIN.

"Can you point for me where the pain is located?"

"It's like, I can't even get off the toilet without crying. It's horrendous. On a scale of one to ten, it's a twelve. It's two hundred."

I type "10/10" in the box marked PAIN INTENSITY, and another angrier, flashing text box, superimposed on the previous text box, demands ENTER LOCATION OF PAIN.

I raise one hand, fingers splayed apart. "I want to try to help you. Let's start with you telling me what body part we're talking about."

"On a scale of one to ten, it's four thousand." Her phone rings. "Hello? Oh, hi, thanks for calling back." She covers the receiver with her hand. "I'm sorry, I have to take this. Can you just let me know when a doctor is ready to see me?" She tucks her purse under her head like a pillow.

"I *am* a doctor." I indicate my white coat and point to my identification badge. The word DOCTOR is printed below my name in capital letters.

"It's fine, I can talk," the woman says into the phone. She glances up at me impatiently. "That'll be all, Nurse, thank you."

I hesitate, then leave, pulling the door closed behind me. I peek at my watch—twenty more minutes until my meeting with the legal team. "She's on the phone," I say to the nurse at the desk.

The nurse rolls his eyes. "With who? The cable guy? People drive me crazy. Do you want to see someone else?" He hands me a chart. "Young guy with headaches. He's kinda cute."

"Hi, I'm Dr. Kapadia, one of the residents," I say when I enter the room.

The patient frowns. This does nothing to diminish his attractiveness. Square jaw, high cheekbones, a pleasant amount of stubble. "A resident? Will I be seeing a real doctor, too?" he asks.

And suddenly he's less attractive.

"As opposed to an imaginary one?"

He looks embarrassed. "I mean, no, a supervisor."

"An attending? Yes, Dr. Hale will come in after I get some information and do a physical examination."

"Oh, okay. Sure, that's fine." His shoulders relax, and he pulls at his examination gown. "I just started this new job, and my health insurance doesn't kick in for another three weeks. I've never used a hospital free clinic before. It's just like a real doctor's office, surprisingly. I mean, not real, but nice. It's nice. You look real. I mean, that's a nice lab coat. Very . . . science-y." His voice trails off.

I smile in a way that conveys that I will remain silent to make this as awkward for him as possible.

He clears his throat. "I just got a job at a law firm. I'm a junior attorney. We do a lot of pro bono work, so I'm down with the whole free clinic idea. It's not like you're just learning how to be a doctor by practicing on people who can't afford health insurance." He laughs weakly.

For a moment, I weigh the pros and cons of throwing a chart at a patient.

"I'm actually helping depose one of the doctors here later today.

I haven't prepared at all. It's my first real deposition. I'm not sure what to expect."

I nod while raising my eyebrows and glance at my watch. Five of our fifteen minutes have already elapsed. "Mr. Kwan, what brings you in today?"

"Nate," he says. "Call me Nate."

I force myself to smile politely. "Okay, Nate. What brings you in today?"

"Right. Sorry. I get nervous at doctor's appointments. And chatty. Sometimes I get all clammy and I feel like I'm . . . going to pass . . . out." Suddenly pale and sweaty, he leans forward. His eyes drift closed.

"Whoa, are you okay?" I grab his shoulders and hold him upright. He's twice my size and like dead weight in my arms. "Help!" I struggle to keep him from falling off the exam table. "Help!"

A nurse opens the door. "Did you need something? Oh, looks like a fainter." With no urgency at all, she wraps her tiny, twig-like arm around Nate's waist, grabs his ankles, and swings him onto the table so that he is lying on his back. She tucks a pillow under his knees.

"I'll go get the blood pressure cuff and some juice," she says, and is gone before I can say anything.

"Did I pass out?" Nate mumbles, his eyes still closed.

"You did. But you're going to be fine in a few minutes."

"This is embarrassing."

The nurse returns and takes his blood pressure.

"I feel better," he says. "Can I sit up?"

"Not yet." The nurse pats his head sweetly. "You just lay here and relax for a few minutes, and we'll wait for your blood pressure to go back to normal. I'll get you some crackers, too." She leaves again.

"I'm really sorry about this," Nate says, staring at the ceiling.

"No need to apologize." I pick up his hand and press two fingers into his wrist to feel his pulse. "Does this ever happen to you in other stressful situations?"

"Nope. It's not often, but it only ever happens at the doctor's office. They call this a vasovagal response, right?"

"Yes. How did you know that?" I count his heartbeats while looking at my watch.

"I listen to this science podcast. I forget the name of it, but anyway, there was an episode recently about fainting and how it's your sympathetic nervous system's reaction to stress."

"*Justin Beakers*?"

"You know it?"

"I love that podcast!" I say, dropping his wrist before I finish counting. "Did you hear the episode about Nigerian bush mice?"

"And how they're smarter than humans?" he says. "And their language system is more complicated than ours?"

"And you can train them to do complex tasks like puzzles? Wasn't that amazing?"

"All I could think was, I'm trading in my dog for a Nigerian bush mouse," he says. "Like, this bush mouse is going to drive me to work and pick up my dry cleaning. And help me with my crossword puzzle."

I laugh so hard I have to gasp for breath. "I'm never going to be able to do a crossword again without thinking about bush mice."

He grins. "I've ruined crosswords for you forever."

He really is kind of cute. Not that I would ever think that, because he's a patient and that would be creepy and weird of me. An objective third party who was not involved in his healthcare might find him kind of cute.

"I like the episodes about tumors and nerves and stuff like that," he says. "That stuff is fascinating. I think I would've tried to go to medical school if it weren't for, well, my tendency to pass out in doctors' offices. Speaking of which, can I sit up now?"

"Sure. Feel okay?"

He sits up. "Yeah, I'm fine. Thanks, Doctor."

"So, you never said what brought you in today."

"Don't laugh, but I actually just came in for a refill on my migraine medication."

"You're kidding."

"I only take it like twice a year, whenever I get a migraine. But the pills I had expired, and my old doctor's office wouldn't refill it because I hadn't been there in like two years. Again, because my sympathetic nervous system doesn't like doctors' offices."

"So your choices were either pass out in the office or risk going through a migraine without medication? That's awful."

He shrugs. "It sucks. But it's not my doctor's fault I have a weak constitution."

"It's not your fault either. Anyone can have a vasovagal response to anything. It has nothing to do with how weak or strong you are."

"That makes me feel better. You're going to laugh at me when I leave here, though, right?"

"Oh, definitely." I grin. "You take Maxalt for your headaches? We can refill that. But let me just check you out, as long as you're here."

I check his reflexes, ask him to walk in a straight line, and make sure his eyes track normally by having him follow my moving index finger without turning his head.

"Did you go to law school in Philadelphia?" I ask.

"I did. Temple."

I hesitate, then say, "You wouldn't happen to know Meryl O'Neill, would you?" A look of consternation flashes across his face and, embarrassed by my failed attempt at small talk, I quickly add, "I know. It was a long shot. She's the only Temple Law alum I know."

"She's a good friend of mine," he says in amazement. "How do you know Meryl?"

"We're, I mean, she used to be . . . we went to camp together in sixth grade."

"Are you serious? Meryl was in the class one year ahead of mine at Temple. It's been a few months since I saw her. She throws this yearly Halloween party, the Booze-o-Rama—"

"I know."

"I heard she just made junior partner at her firm."

My breath catches on its way through my vocal cords. *She passed the bar!* "That's wonderful," I say. It's bittersweet—the thought of Meryl opening her results envelope without me. But I'm overjoyed for her.

"Jeez, what a small world," Nate says. "What was Meryl like in sixth grade?"

I consider this. "Frizzy hair, braces."

"She was a geek? That's hard to picture."

"We were both geeks back then. She grew out of it."

"*She* grew out of it? Just her?" he asks skeptically.

I raise one hand. "Lifelong member of the Geek Federation, unfortunately."

He smiles. "You could have fooled me. Although"—he raises one hand, too—"I salute you as a former member of my high school Dungeons and Dragons team."

"There was a *team*?"

"Absolutely. And it was competitive as hell."

"Really?"

"No. There were like three other people on the team and there were no opposing teams so we just made matching T-shirts and called it a day. We were all Korean, and I think the rest of the school thought we were some sort of Korean language club or something."

I laugh. "Look straight ahead, please." I shine a penlight into his eyes, watching as his pupils flinch and shrink in response. Black pinpoints in amber disks. *One of Mrs. Tally's pupils was bigger than the other.* "You pass," I say, forcing my thoughts back to the present. "I'll let the attending, Dr. Hale, know and we'll get you a prescription for the Maxalt."

"Great, thanks." He fidgets and pushes his hair out of his eyes. "Can I ask you a question?"

"Sure."

"Would you maybe want to grab coffee sometime? With me? You're probably not allowed to do that, though, right?"

I hesitate. "Right. I wish I could. I mean, thank you, that's flattering, but I can't."

"That's what I figured. It was nice meeting you." His cheeks are turning progressively redder. "And sorry for passing out. And then asking you out. Yeah, I'm just really sorry. For all of that."

"No apology needed."

He extends his hand, and I half shake and half high-five it.

"Nice meeting you, Mr. Kwan. Nate. Bye, Nate."

"Bye, Dr. Kapadia."

I rush out, mortified and slightly pleased at the same time. "That patient just asked me out," I say to a nurse in the hallway.

She looks me up and down and shrugs. "Good for you."

I print out Nate's prescription and hand the chart off to Dr. Hale. Then I head for the elevator, a gnawing feeling in my stomach. In a hallway on the fifteenth floor, encased behind thick glass and hanging just outside the executive conference room, I find the painting Dr. Forks was talking about: *The Gross Clinic*, painted in 1875 by Thomas Eakins. In the center of the floor-to-ceiling canvas, the white-haired, waistcoated Dr. Gross stands over a comatose patient in an amphitheater while an audience of male students looks on. Dr. Gross, his expression pedantic, holds a scalpel in his ungloved hand and addresses the crowd. Only the patient's buttock and leg, a bleeding incision just above the knee, is visible; the rest of him is draped with white sheets. In a corner, a woman has collapsed to her knees, weeping. Neither Dr. Gross, nor anyone else, seems to take any notice of her.

I'm transfixed, my eyes drawn to the looming figure of Dr. Gross. Bathed in light, stern and certain, blood dripping from his scalpel and his hand. He commands the room. *This is how it's done,* he seems to say.

This is how it's always been done.

CHAPTER TWENTY-TWO

"Did you know that painting in the hallway is worth something like $80 million?"

I turn my attention back to the conference table. "It is?"

Georgia Pitman is in her early fifties, tall, broad-shouldered, wearing a meticulously tailored purple suit, with her hair in a neat bun at the nape of her neck and noticeably perfect diction. Her husband, Joe Pitman, is short, wiry, and has a very conspicuous coffee stain on his tie. Together, Georgia and Joe are the Philadelphia General Hospital legal team. Their disdain for each other is obvious, even to a casual observer.

"Yup," Georgia says, smiling cheerfully. "This hospital has so much money, you wouldn't believe it."

"That's why everyone tries to sue it," Joe grumbles. "Did you want to get started? It's nine forty-five."

Georgia glares at him pointedly, then opens a thick manila folder. Mrs. Tally's chart.

"Yes, let's get started," she says. "Do you recall this case, Dr. Kapadia?"

"You can just call me Norah."

Joe adjusts a pair of reading glasses on the bridge of his nose. "We'll address you as Doctor, just as we will during your deposition."

"Deposition?" I look from husband to wife in confusion.

Georgia raises her eyebrows. "They didn't tell you that you were going to be deposed?"

I shake my head anxiously. "Dr. Forks told me that you were going to ask me some questions about the case. About what I remember."

Joe looks at me expectantly. "Right. A deposition. That's what a deposition is."

"Is this the first time you've been deposed?" Georgia asks, her tone like a grandmother asking how I prefer my tea.

"Yes."

"Well, don't worry. You're going to do great," she says. "Just answer their questions as briefly as possible, and if you can't remember, you can reference the chart."

"*Their* questions? Someone else is going to be asking me questions?"

Joe taps his pen on the table impatiently. "Yes, of course. The Tallys have their own lawyers." He glances at his watch. "Who are probably in the lobby right now."

"They're going to try to make a big deal about the patient falling out of bed and hitting her head," Georgia says. "But I'll just ask you if you examined the patient after she fell, which you did, and if the examination was normal, which it was. So you'll say 'yes' to both those questions. Then I'll ask if it is possible to have bleeding in the brain"—she references her notes—"an intracranial hematoma, without falling and hitting your head. And you'll say, of course, that yes, it is possible."

"And hopefully that'll be it," Joe says.

"Short and sweet," Georgia says. She smiles and folds her glasses onto Mrs. Tally's chart.

I relax, slightly, into my chair. There is a knock at the door.

"Come in!" Georgia says.

A harried older woman with short gray hair parted down the

middle enters, pulling a suitcase and panting. She waves hello and pulls out the chair next to me. From the suitcase, she produces a keyboard attached to a tiny monitor, a voice recorder, a Bible, a notebook, and a pen. She places all of these on the table in front of her, then looks at me and smiles.

The door opens again, and a striking young woman in a gray suit and lace-trimmed high heels enters, followed by a dark-haired young man who carries her attaché case.

"Aubrey!" Georgia springs up to give her a hug and a kiss on both cheeks. "I didn't know you were opposing counsel."

"I'm filling in for Mike. His wife had the baby," Aubrey says.

"Speaking of which, how's yours?" Georgia asks.

"Oh my God." Aubrey takes the seat across the table from me. "He's the most amazing little human. The other day he grabbed his little walker and pulled to a stand."

"No! He didn't!" Georgia claps her hands giddily.

Joe sighs loudly and glares at them while adjusting his tie.

"He did! I was like, wow, this is the most transformative experience, you know? I've just grown so much since having him."

Georgia nods. "You do. You do grow."

The young man with Aubrey has been glancing at me while he pulls papers from the attaché case. I suddenly notice him.

"Nate?"

"Oh, do you two know each other?" Aubrey asks.

"She's . . . my doctor," Nate says, pulling awkwardly at his suit jacket while avoiding eye contact with everyone.

The woman with the keyboard says, "Are we ready, ladies?"

This seems to annoy Joe even more. "Can we please have social hour another time? This isn't your book club."

I exchange a glance with Nate, whose ears are going flame red.

Aubrey shows Georgia a photograph on her phone. "Here he is eating spaghetti."

Georgia coos in delight as Joe rests his forehead on the table. Then Aubrey takes a manila folder from Nate, readies her pen, and looks at me.

"I think we're ready," she says, her tone pleasant.

"Doctor, would you please place your right hand on the Bible?" the woman with the keyboard says. I do so, and she continues. "Do you swear that the testimony you are about to give is true?"

I glance at Georgia. I nod. "Yes."

Georgia says, "Okay, this is the deposition of Dr. Norah Kapadia in the case of *Tally versus Philadelphia General Hospital*. Dr. Kapadia, were you the medical intern assigned to Lenore Tally's care on the date in question?"

The woman with the keyboard types in a manner that resembles playing a piano.

"Yes."

Georgia smiles encouragingly. "And what was the diagnosis for which Mrs. Tally was admitted to the hospital?"

"Lung cancer. Well, she had chemo because of lung cancer and probably due to that she developed pneumonia."

"And by 'chemo,' you mean 'chemotherapy'?"

"Yes, chemotherapy."

"And how did the medical team treat her pneumonia?"

"We started her on an antibiotic."

"Which one?"

"Ciprofloxacin. But that wasn't working, so we added Zynexa."

"And why was that particular antibiotic chosen?"

"It's broad-spectrum."

"Can you explain what broad-spectrum means?"

I fumble for the right nonmedical words. "You know. It means it kills a lot of bacteria."

"In other words, it would be effective against a wide variety of different bacteria or viruses?"

"Not viruses. Just bacteria. Antibiotics don't kill viruses. Antivirals kill viruses. Zynexa is an antibiotic."

The woman plays her piano keyboard furiously.

"And who ordered the Zynexa?" Georgia asks. She shows me the chart. *10:35pm Start Zynexa 75mg IV every 8 hours. Verbal order per resident.*

"The resident," I say.

"Which resident?"

There's a rising tightness in my chest. "I don't know."

Georgia nods. "Doctor, prior to the patient being started on Zynexa by the resident, did she have a fall out of bed?"

"Yes."

"And did you go examine the patient?"

"Yes."

"And did she, in your opinion, have any neurological problems at that time?"

"No."

"No. And you, in fact, wrote a note in the chart stating that the patient's neurological examination was normal, correct?"

"Correct."

"Later that evening, the patient went into cardiac arrest. On autopsy, she was found to have an intracranial hematoma—bleeding in her brain. Could this type of bleeding occur without a trauma to the head?"

"Yes."

Georgia smiles at Aubrey. "Those are all my questions."

Aubrey, who has been taking notes, clicks her pen. "Dr. Kapadia, if a patient fell and hit their head, could that cause bleeding in their brain?"

"Yes."

"And would there always be obvious signs, on the physical examination, of this bleeding?"

"No, not always."

"Would some of those signs be subtle?"

"They can be."

"It might take years of experience to really know how to identify those signs."

Georgia's eyes narrow. "Is there a question in there, Counselor?"

Aubrey smiles. "Pardon me. I'll rephrase that. Would you agree that even an experienced doctor could miss the subtle signs of bleeding in the brain? That the diagnosis can be challenging?"

"Yes, I agree."

Aubrey nods. "How many years have you been practicing medicine?"

"Three."

"So, as of the date in question, you'd been practicing medicine for . . . six months? Less than a year?"

I shift in my seat. "A little less than a year, yes. I was an intern."

"So, it would be safe to assume that an intern might miss the subtle signs of a brain bleed, correct?"

"That's very leading, Aubrey." Georgia's smile has faded.

"I don't think it is." Aubrey looks at her. "But I'll rephrase it. Doctor, could someone with less than a year of experience in the practice of medicine be reasonably expected to detect the subtle physical examination findings associated with bleeding in the brain? You just said that even someone with experience could miss them."

"No," I say. "Probably not."

"Doctor, would you please read aloud the nurse's note timed nine thirty-five p.m.?" Aubrey slides the manila folder across the table.

I hesitate.

"It's right there. It's highlighted," she coaxes.

My voice irritated, I say, "Yes, I see it. Nine thirty-five p.m., Patient fell out of bed and sustained bump to head. Dr. Cantor notified. Intern to evaluate patient."

"Ethan Cantor, who was at that time the chief resident, your supervising resident, correct?" Aubrey says.

"Yes."

"Did Dr. Cantor ask you to evaluate the patient?"

"Yes."

"And Dr. Cantor would have known that you were an intern and, therefore, inexperienced?"

"Um. I guess."

"But he still sent you to perform a neurological evaluation on this patient, instead of going himself?"

"Counselor," Georgia says, "Dr. Kapadia can't be expected to know what her supervising resident's reasons were for—"

"There were a million other things going on that night," I say. "I'm a chief resident now, and I can't examine every patient myself. We can't be everywhere at once."

"And, as a chief resident," Aubrey says, "would you start a patient who had, just an hour before, fallen and hit her head on a chair, on a blood thinner without examining him or her yourself? You said yourself that an intern might miss the signs of a brain bleed, right? Would you trust the intern to detect this potentially life-threatening problem?"

"Zynexa's not a blood thinner," I say.

"Is bleeding a possible side effect of Zynexa? Could it cause a small brain bleed to become catastrophic?"

"Theoretically, yes. But Dr. Cantor wasn't the one who ordered it."

"You previously said you didn't remember who ordered it."

"I remember it wasn't Dr. Cantor," I say pointedly. I briefly consider how my dislike of Aubrey has grown exponentially over the past ten minutes.

"So," she says, "you remember who it wasn't, but you don't remember who it was?"

"No."

"In his deposition, Dr. Portnoy indicated that one of the Surgery residents wrote the order for the Zynexa, Elle Chambers. Do you remember Dr. Chambers being involved in this case?"

"She was consulted to put a PICC line in."

"So, isn't that unusual, for a resident from another team to write an antibiotic order for one of your patients without your knowledge?"

"It happens sometimes."

"What that would really suggest is a lack of communication between members of different teams, right?"

"Oh, objection," Joe says, throwing up his hands. "Objections all over the place."

"Fine." Aubrey shuts the manila folder. "Those are all of my questions. Thank you, Doctor."

"I have a few follow-up questions, Dr. Kapadia," Georgia says, her tone saccharine. "You wrote the admission orders for Mrs. Tally, correct? The instructions for the nurses about how often to take the patient's vital signs, what kind of food she should be given, that sort of thing?"

"Yes."

She shows me the chart again. "Are these the orders that you wrote for Lenore Tally?"

I recognize my handwriting. It all seems like such a long time ago. "Yes."

"Would you read the first few orders?"

Aubrey rolls her eyes and flashes a steely smile.

I read, "Vital signs Q4 hours—"

Georgia interrupts, "That's every four hours?"

"Yes. Low-sodium diet . . ." My voice fades away for a moment. "No tomatoes. Falls precautions. Bedside commode—"

"Ah," says Georgia, as if she's just now had a revelation, "so you ordered falls precautions—what are those?"

"It's a protocol the nurses follow. The patient has to call the nurse for help if they want to get out of bed."

"This, of course, is to make sure the patient doesn't fall?"

"Yes."

"And why were you concerned about her falling?"

"Patients who get chemo—chemotherapy—are often unsteady on their feet."

"Uh-huh." Georgia nods. "Now, the patient's husband has stated"—she looks at Aubrey—"on the record that the patient fell because she was getting out of bed on her own, without calling for help, to get her socks. Would she have been told when she was admitted to the hospital that she was at risk of falling and shouldn't try to get out of bed by herself?"

"Yes. She said she didn't want to bother the nurses," I say.

"So the patient," Georgia says, "knowingly went against your orders, which resulted in her falling and hitting her head. Would you agree with that, Dr. Kapadia?"

I stare at her. "Well, wait a minute."

Joe interrupts me. "It's a yes-or-no question, Doctor."

He and Georgia glare at me over their respective glasses.

"Okay, then, yes, sure," I say, shrugging my shoulders in exasperation.

"Thank you. That's all I have," Georgia says.

The lawyers all begin to pack up their things.

"Aubrey," Georgia says, "we have to get together. I want to meet your little man."

"Oh my gosh, I would love that!" Aubrey's voice is effervescent. "Do you want to have lunch at Nordstrom's on Wednesday?"

"Perfect! I'll text you," Georgia says, giving her a little wave as Aubrey and Nate head for the door.

"Wait, are we done?" I ask.

"Yes, thank you so much, Doctor," Aubrey says.

Nate catches my eye and smiles sympathetically; then they are gone. The woman with the keyboard zips up her suitcase and follows them out.

"What just happened?" I look around the room, my mind spinning.

"You survived your first deposition!" Georgia extends her hand. "You're finally all grown up!" She laughs buoyantly.

As she pumps my arm up and down, I say, "That was horrible. That was so horrible."

Georgia laughs with even more mirth.

Pushing past us toward the door, Joe gives his wife a scornful look. "She's not making a joke, Georgia." Then, heaving a sigh and rubbing his forehead, he leaves.

Georgia stares at me for a moment before releasing my hand. "You are such a pretty girl," she says. "You look too young to be a doctor. What you need to do is bottle your secret beauty routine and sell it!"

"You can't blame Mrs. Tally for what happened," I say.

Georgia blinks. She folds her hands on her waist. "Young lady, my advice to you is that you learn to stay in your own lane." She places Mrs. Tally's chart in a leather briefcase and starts toward the door. She smiles cheerfully. "Thank you, Doctor!"

The shiny, seaweed-wrapped little packages of sushi arrive on a cobalt blue plate that looks like the sea.

"Anything else, miss?" The bartender hands me a pair of chopsticks.

"A Mount Fujiyama."

"Oh, we stopped making those. Liability issues. I could make you a mai tai, like a normal-size one."

"Sure. Whatever." Then I say, "I'm going to need two mai tais."

I stare at the bits of fish swimming on their ocean-plate. I bat them around a bit and finally manage to spear one on the end of my chopstick. I put it in my mouth, bite down, and immediately spit it out into a napkin. I am still reeling when Gabe appears.

"Norah? Are you okay?"

The bartender places two orange drinks garnished with pineapple wedges in front of me. I snatch the tiny paper umbrella from one of them and immediately drink half of it without taking a breath.

Gabe raises his eyebrows. "How's it going?"

"Fine. Fine. Great," I say, gasping.

"I thought you hated sushi. Like, you find it revolting."

"Yeah. Yup, I still do. Not everything has changed."

He looks at me quizzically. Then he takes the seat next to me and says, "So, are you gonna eat that?"

I laugh and slide the plate over to him. "Be my guest."

As he adds soy sauce, he says, "I'm guessing it was a rough day?"

"What are you doing here?" I ask.

"I'm supposed to meet Traci."

"Traci?"

"The med student. Red hair?"

"Right. Traci. So, like a date?"

"I don't think we've given it a formal title, but kind of a date, sure. Your turn."

"I had to do a deposition on a patient I had two years ago. She bled into her brain and died after being started on Zynexa. Her family is suing."

"Jesus. How'd it go?"

"Not unlike that plate of sushi, it was hard to take."

"Norah, I'm sorry. That sucks." He points his chopsticks at the plate. "These are killer, though. Thank you for them. Little bites of nautical heaven."

"I'm glad for you."

"I still don't understand why you would order something you know you hate."

I shrug. "I don't know. Everyone loves sushi."

"You're not everyone." After a moment, he says, "You're different now, you know? Compared to when we first met."

I smile ruefully. Gabe always had that way of noticing things about me. "I guess I'm all grown up."

I stare into my drink. When I look up, Gabe is regarding me as if I were a challenging math problem. Finally he says, "You adapted. I guess we all have to. I've changed since back then, too."

"We all evolve," I say. "But I'm not sure that's always a good thing."

"I miss talking to you. I mean, about something other than patient care."

I look at him for a moment. Seeing him always reminds me of Meryl.

"Traci," I say.

He looks confused. "What?"

"Hi, Gabe! Hi, Dr. Kapadia!" Traci bounds over, barely able to contain her exuberance. "Sorry I'm late. I was in the ICU and one of the attendings taught me how to put in a bedside pacemaker. He let me push the catheter into the patient's heart through his jugular vein. It was amazing!" She tugs at her slightly-too-short dress.

"No worries," Gabe says. "We can still catch the movie if we head over now." He smiles at me with a reluctant expression.

"Have fun, you guys," I say. Once they are out of sight, I let out my breath and press my forehead into my palms. *I miss talking to him, too.*

The bartender appears. "More sushi, miss?"

I can't help but laugh. "No, thanks. But I'll take a chocolate volcano, please."

CHAPTER TWENTY-THREE

"That is some bullshit!"

A group of nurses, interns, and residents are crowded around a computer in the clinic a few days later. At the center of the throng is Dr. Hale.

"I cannot believe this shit!" she says, scrolling furiously.

"Oh my God, did you get to this part yet?" A nurse points to the screen. She reads, "'Dr. Hale tried to force me to take IV antibiotics for my heart infection, instead of taking the time to explain holistic treatment options like tea-tree oil and cosmic meditation.'"

"What the flying fuck is cosmic meditation?" Dr. Hale asks.

"It's how she goes back to her home planet," someone answers.

I stand on tiptoe to try to see the screen. "What's going on?"

"Some nut job posted a one-star review about Dr. Hale on that Healthgrades website," a resident says.

I pull my father's stethoscope from my bag. I run my thumb over the engraving—*S. Kapadia, MD*—and loop it around my neck. "Do people actually believe what's written on those websites?"

"Norah, are you kidding? Everyone believes it," Dr. Hale says, still scrolling. "Including insurance companies. Mother of God."

"What?"

Dr. Hale's nostrils flare as she reads, "'I would strongly recommend that people not go to her for their medical care. Dr. Hale is the worst chiropractor I've ever been to, and I should know because I've been to over twenty chiropractors in the past six months.'"

Several of us burst out laughing.

Dr. Hale grimaces as she struggles to her feet, one hand on her protuberant belly. She's seven months pregnant with twins, but that seems to be a minor annoyance compared to the stress of online physician rating sites. "It's not actually funny, you guys," she says. "Hospital administration takes this crap very seriously, and this loony tune just took my score from a perfect five—which I worked very hard for, by the way—to a two-point-five. And Healthgrades won't get rid of a bad review, no matter how ludicrous it is." She slams some charts around on her desk. "You guys keep laughing it up. All you residents, this is your future. Did you take a Hippocratic oath? Because you may as well have memorized the Burger King menu instead. Have it your way. Side of fries with your Percocet? Pull up to the next window and I'll hand you your antidepressants."

"Sorry, Dr. Hale," I say, trying not to grin.

"Fine. Whatever." She waddles away from the computer. "Does anyone have a fucking patient that will actually take my fucking advice—you know, as opposed to Dr. Google's—that they want to discuss?"

One of the residents raises his hand and meekly offers her a chart, as if he's afraid she may tear his arm off.

"Dr. Kapadia, the next patient to be seen is in room 4," a nurse says, pointing.

I pull on my white coat, grab the chart from her, and knock on the exam room door.

"Come in!" The patient is a genial, slightly sunburned man who looks like he's worked at the beach his whole life. He is fit, sinewy to the point where most of his arm muscles are easily distinguishable from one another; a living study in anatomy. He wears a *Life is Good* T-shirt with the sleeves cut off and cargo pants.

"How you doing, Doc?" He grabs my hand and shakes it enthusiastically.

"Hi. It's Mr. Flynn, right? I'm Dr. Kapadia, one of the residents. The attending today is Dr. Hale. She'll be in to see you after I get some information and do a physical examination."

"Whatever you say, Doc."

"So, what brings you in today?"

"I work down the shore, in Stone Harbor. I run one of those aerial billboard companies. You ever seen those planes pulling the banners that fly over the beach?"

"Yes, I have. You do that?"

"I can't fly the planes anymore because of this." He lifts his pant leg to reveal a prosthetic foot and lower leg. "But I maintain the airplanes and do just about everything else. It's a family business."

"Very interesting. So, what's going on today?"

"Like two weeks ago I was leaning into the engine of the plane and I felt a pop in my neck. Then I started to have shooting pain into my arm, and my hand went numb, like totally dead."

"Tell me more about that."

"Well, I shook it around a little, and the feeling came back. The pain lasted a week or so, then it went away, too. I feel fine now, but my sister told me I should get it checked out, just to be safe. Is that stupid?"

"Not at all. Do you have any weakness in the arm?"

"No."

"Any bowel or bladder problems?"

"Nope."

"Okay if I examine you?"

I ask him to move his neck and shoulders. I check his reflexes and test his arm strength by asking him to push and pull against me. I spend several minutes silently entering the information into the electronic medical record.

"I don't think this is anything dangerous," I say finally, "but I'll give you a prescription for an MRI of your neck. It could be a pinched nerve."

"Is that pretty common?"

"Very."

He nods. "That's a relief. So, I get the MRI and come back here so you can look at it?"

"You could come back here for your follow-up visit, or you could see a doctor closer to home. Stone Harbor is like two hours from here, right?"

"It is, but I like to come to Philly General for all my medical stuff. I just have a lot of faith in the doctors here."

I smile. "That's nice of you to say."

"I'm not just saying it. This hospital saved my life."

"Really?" I glance at my watch. Only a few minutes left before I have to move on to the next patient.

"Yeah, I was messed up. I had kidney failure and heart problems. I lost a piece of my colon. My leg was even paralyzed for a while. I was in and out of Intensive Care for, like, over a year. I almost died three or four times, but they kept bringing me back."

I stare at him. A memory starts to take shape, like a ship sailing out of a fog. "How long ago was this?"

He purses his lips. "Like two and a half, maybe three years? It's been a while now."

My voice is almost a whisper. "What was your name again?"

"Daniel Flynn."

Fat Dan.

"I thought you died."

"Wait, were you one of my doctors?"

"But you were like four hundred pounds."

He nods sheepishly. "I was retaining all this fluid. Plus, I was always a husky kid growing up. Whoa, Doctor, you okay?"

I am crying, quietly at first, then with loud, heaving sobs that leave the lapel of my white coat soaked in tears and render the room a blurry haze.

There is a knock at the door. The patient hands me a crumpled tissue from his pocket as Dr. Hale peeks into the room.

"I heard— What the hell is going on in here?"

I press the tissue to my eyes, and my vision clears.

When I look up, I see things in sharper focus than I have in years.

Dr. Portnoy stares at the creased piece of paper for a long time. His office is sprawling; a sitting area with a brocade couch is at one end, a huge mahogany desk at the other. A rocking chair with the Philadelphia General Hospital logo painted on the seat back sits in front of a wall of bookshelves lined with textbooks and framed certificates. I count five copies of the massive *Principles of Oncology* by Portnoy et al.

My father's stethoscope is heavy around my neck. I've draped my white coat, frayed after many years of use, over the arm of my chair.

Portnoy leans back in his desk chair with his coffee cup in one hand. Finally he says, "What is this?"

"It's what really happened to Lenore Tally," I say.

"You took this page out of the chart? And kept it?"

I nod.

"First of all, that's against hospital policy." He's becoming increasingly flummoxed. "This says Ethan refused to go examine the patient after she fell."

"He started her on Zynexa. It wasn't Elle Chambers. I missed the signs. By the time I ordered the CT scan, her bleed was massive."

"You saw the bleed on the CT scan? So there were, in fact, CT pictures that night."

"Yes."

Portnoy puts his coffee cup on the desk and removes his glasses. "Christsakes, they did an autopsy on her. For no reason."

There was a sound when Mrs. Tally's skin was being pulled away from her skull. It was like paper tearing.

"Do you have any idea?" Portnoy says, stunned. "The debacle you've created?"

"Sir, that's why I'm here. I've thought about the Tallys every day for the last two years. I'm here to take responsibility for what happened."

"Do you have any idea how this looks? We are three months into a lawsuit and about to go to trial."

"I can go to Georgia and Joe Pitman and tell them what—"

"You'll do no such thing," Portnoy says. "Jesus, the blowback on me—on the entire hospital—if it were public knowledge that a doctor tried to cover up the cause of death in a Zynexa case. It'd be national news." He glares at me. "No, you'll do no such thing."

"This should never have happened. It's my fault, but I can at least try to make it right. I have to try. It's changed everything about me, everything I thought I knew about me."

Portnoy looks at me in bewilderment. His voice scornful, he says, "This isn't about *you*, Dr. Kapadia. It's not about your guilty conscience. You don't get to have some Hallmark moment of sentimentality for the patient—two years later—and drag me and your colleagues down with you."

"I wasn't trying to—"

"You have a responsibility to this institution. We trained you. *I* trained you. This hospital is where your loyalty should lie."

You don't go behind your senior's back. That's just not something you do.

Portnoy crumples the page from Mrs. Tally's chart. "You never should have taken this, but since you did, you'll accept responsibility for making sure this doesn't turn into a nightmare for the hospital. You'll say and do nothing, understand?"

My hands tremble, but my voice is steady. "Sir, respectfully, I don't think I can do that. Mrs. Tally's family deserves to know what really happened."

Portnoy regards me. "How many months do you have until you graduate from residency? Four?"

"Two."

"Do you want to graduate from residency? Do you want a future in medicine? You're very close. And you have, potentially, a long career in front of you, if you put aside your own agenda here."

"My agenda?"

"I'm going to ask you one more time, Dr. Kapadia. Do you want a future in medicine?"

The Team rises and falls together and is only as strong as its weakest link. What if the weakest link has been, all along, the tiny man behind this massive desk?

I don't bother answering Portnoy's question. I stand and walk out of his office, leaving my white coat on the chair.

Nate is waiting at a table when I arrive at the Starbucks.

"Hi. It's nice to see you." He pulls out my chair. "Can I get you something? Coffee?"

"No, thanks," I say.

He grins. "I'm glad you called. How'd you find my number?"

"Your patient chart."

"That's kind of a HIPAA violation, isn't it?"

"Not really, since technically I'm your doctor. How are the migraines?"

He laughs. "You know, I really was surprised to hear from you. What made you change your mind?"

I hesitate. "I haven't, exactly. Changed my mind, that is."

He shakes his head, confused.

"I called because I need to ask you to do something for me," I say. "Something you probably shouldn't tell Aubrey about."

"What is it?"

I pull an envelope from my bag and hand it to him. "It's not sealed. You can read it. Just promise me you'll try to deliver it?"

He opens the envelope, pulls out a typed page, and reads it. His eyes wide, he looks up and says, "Okay. I'll try."

I stand. "Thank you, Nate."

"What about you? What are you going to do now?"

"Me?" I consider this for a moment. "I'm going to do something I've never done before."

CHAPTER TWENTY-FOUR

Even at this altitude, the air smells like mangoes. I close my eyes and imagine I'm floating away, carried off by the warm, sticky breeze.

A van with the words *Banana Bungalow Hostel Excursions* stenciled in fading yellow paint across the side waits, idling.

"Last call! Everyone in who doesn't want to walk down the mountain," says the driver, a bald man crusted with sand.

I look over my shoulder at the pink sky one more time, the sun dropping into a thick layer of clouds like a coin tossed into a fountain. Then I climb the embankment up to the road. Under my feet, pockmarked gray volcanic stones make tinny, hollow sounds as they knock against one another. As the van pitches and shudders around every curve, I let my head sink back into the worn leather seat that smells like brine and sweat.

"You're new at the hostel?" A young woman with blond, almost white, hair pulled back in a long braid smiles at me from the window seat. "Hi, I'm Alice. How long are you staying?" Her accent sounds Australian, maybe South African.

"I don't know," I say.

"I've got another two weeks at the Banana Bungalow," she says, despite the fact that I'm looking out my window. "Then I'm off to Japan for another month, then . . . who knows? Wherever I find work. I teach surfing or sailing, usually. You traveling alone, too?"

"Yes."

"What do you do for work?"

I stare over the driver's shoulder to where the van's headlights are swallowed by the interminable dark road ahead. "I work in a lab."

"Aloha, welcome to the Grand Maui Hotel. Are you checking in?" The doorman struggles to hold the towering lobby door open against a strong wind.

"I'm here for the conference."

"Ah yes." He points. "The convention center can be reached down that breezeway there."

A sign on a tripod reads, "North American Society of Internal Medicine Annual Conference. Proudly sponsored by Pfizer." In front of it, several women at a desk are registering attendees. I get in line behind a group of residents all wearing matching Cleveland Clinic hoodies.

One of them is saying, "It's like a junket for politicians. Only with fewer hookers and less booze."

"Actually, it's more like a middle school science fair, but with free stuff," one of the others corrects him.

I give my name to one of the women at the desk, and she hands me a name tag and a green fabric tote bag containing a pair of cheap sunglasses, a travel mug, and a mini flashlight, each of which is emblazoned with the logo of a different pharmaceutical company.

"Is this a vibrator?" One of the residents holds a device shaped like a tiny hockey stick. *Cialis for erectile dysfunction* is printed on the handle. She presses a button, and the device trembles and hums frenetically.

"It's a back massager," her colleague says.

She switches it off. "Sure it is."

We are directed toward the cavernous exhibition hall. Stretching out in every direction are elaborate displays, each representing a different pharmaceutical or medical device company. The atmosphere is carnival-like. I pass a tent with plush red carpet and white lounge chairs where a woman in bright lipstick and a tight suit is handing out stress balls with *Ritunda, #1 for Anxiety* printed across them and a small man in a tracksuit with a massage table is offering free ten-minute neck and shoulder rubs. At another tent, a man dressed like a hypodermic needle is handing out informational brochures for "Flantis, a new injectable for type 1 diabetes!" as well as insulated grocery bags. A waiter passes by with a tray of hot hors d'oeuvres and is immediately set upon by a throng of elderly gentlemen with name tags that nearly knocks him over and clears the tray within seconds.

I make my way past several stands selling textbooks for medical students: titles like *Microbiology Made Ridiculously Simple*, *Crush the Clinic!*, and the Everything You Ever Wanted to Know About . . . But Were Afraid to Ask series (featuring volumes *The Thymus*, *The Spleen*, and *The Lymphatic System*, among others).

At the far end of the exhibition hall is a maze of cubicles, each labeled with the name of a recruiting company or hospital. I find the one marked *SEEK*.

"Hi, do you have an appointment?" a smartly dressed man behind a desk asks.

I nod. "Norah Kapadia."

He extends his hand. "Nice to meet you. Please, sit." He hands me a shiny brochure with a smiling woman in a suit pictured on its front, underneath the words "SEEK: A Better Option."

"Have you had a chance to look at our website and read over the many nonclinical job opportunities we have?" he asks.

I nod.

"Great," he says. "Did anything pique your interest?"

"Well, I won't be graduating from residency, so I think that limits my options, right?"

The man winces a little. "Yeah, yeah, it does limit them a bit. How much longer do you have until you could graduate? There's no way you could finish?"

"Two months," I say. "But no, there's no way I can finish." I adjust the lapel of my navy-blue suit jacket.

"That's too bad. But still, there are options. For example, a job with pharma. Have you ever considered pharmaceutical sales?"

I lean forward to hear him over the din that has erupted from the floor of the exhibition hall. The Flantis booth is blasting peppy music, and the hypodermic needle is performing a break-dance routine.

"No. I don't think that's for me," I say.

"Well, what about a job in research? Or medicolegal review?"

"Sure, those sound fine, I guess."

"Do you have a copy of your résumé?"

I open my purse and hand him a sheet of paper. My credentials and work experience fill only half the page.

"All right, Dr. Kapadia, thank you. I'll email you some options over the next few days and maybe we can schedule some interviews for you. Are you interested in looking only in the Philadelphia area?"

"I'm open to anywhere at this point. Thanks." I shake his hand again and stand to leave. I squeeze the brochure into my purse.

As I make my way out, I count six other SEEK cubicles, each with a line of interviewees of varying ages. I am passing the Ritunda tent when I notice a young woman wearing a floral summer dress, sunglasses holding back her long hair.

"Bianca?"

Ten minutes later we are reminiscing over piña coladas at the hotel lobby bar.

"Remember that time I had to start an IV on Clark because he drank too much the night before and started having heart palpitations while on call?" Bianca chuckles. "We had to steal bags of normal saline from the ED?"

"What? No," I say, taken aback. "Where was I during that?"

"Probably studying." She smiles. "You always had your nose in a book."

"Funny, the way I remember it, it was Stuart who always had his nose in a book."

Bianca looks down at her hands, shaken by the mention of Stuart. "I knew about the cocaine, you know," she says quietly. "At least, I suspected it. I've never told anyone that."

My mouth drops open. "What do you mean?"

"That night I found the empty pill bottle, I also found a little mirror and a bit of a plastic straw under the bed. I never told anyone, because I wasn't sure they were his, and I didn't want to get him in trouble. . . ." Tears form at the corners of her eyes, but she blinks them away. "I'll never forgive myself for that."

"It wasn't your fault, Bee. If you'd told me at the time, I'd never have believed it. I remember when I first met him, back at the beginning of that year, being so jealous of him. He made being an intern look easy."

She shakes her head. "After that accident with the NG tube, he wasn't the same."

"Something like that can change you." I stare at my shoes. "More than people realize."

Bianca regards me and points to my purse. "You have a SEEK brochure."

I fidget.

"I heard what happened," she says, her smile sympathetic.

"You did? How? You live in Denver."

She smirks. "I still have my sources." Then she says, "Portnoy is beyond horrible to have you fired two months before graduation."

"I resigned, actually."

"You did? Why on earth would you do that?"

I sigh. "It's a long story. But in the end, I just didn't want to do it anymore, you know? I didn't want . . . to be at the center of it." An image of the painting of Dr. Gross flashes through my mind. "I didn't want the blood on my hands."

Bianca smiles ruefully. "We all have a little blood on our hands. It's a part of the job. And sometimes it's our own blood."

"I was sitting in Portnoy's office, and I just kept thinking, this can't be right." I struggle to find the words, to define the shape and limits of what has been, for months, a vague but unshakable feeling. "I don't care if this is how it's always been done. We can't be expected to take care of human beings by becoming less human. They tell us it's weakness if we can't handle it, but that's a lie. It's a lie everyone plays along with. I can't be a part of that anymore."

"But all of those years of school and training . . . and all the loans. What will you do next?"

"I'm still figuring that out." Smiling thinly, I say, "Marry rich and never work again?"

Bianca shrugs. "Like Elle Chambers?"

"What do you mean?"

"You didn't hear? And you work at Philly General?"

"What didn't I hear?"

"Dr. V left his wife for Elle like a year ago. She hasn't worked a day since."

"Wait. What?" I almost knock over my drink. "I thought she moved to California for a transplant fellowship."

"She did. And then she quit and married Dr. V. She's a trophy wife now. And she's pregnant with his kid."

"Wow." I picture Elle lounging by the pool at Le Cœur. "I heard Dr. V got remarried, but I had no idea it was to Elle. She quit surgery?"

"Right? I was shocked, too. But I guess there's life outside of medicine."

I consider this for a moment. "I guess there is."

Bianca orders another drink. "Are you staying here at the hotel?"

I shake my head. "I'm actually staying at a youth hostel."

She raises her eyebrows disapprovingly. "Why?"

"I meant to take this trip years ago. I'm finally doing it. It's been pretty amazing so far. Plus, I just quit my job and have no real prospects of finding a new one for a while, and the Banana Bungalow is like thirty-five bucks a night, so there's that."

"It's not all weird college drifters?"

"Oh, that's all it is. But I don't mind them. They kind of remind me of us as interns: idealistic, no idea what the future holds, sharing shower and bathroom facilities. It feels like home."

Bianca laughs. "When do you fly back to Philly?"

"I haven't actually bought my return ticket yet. I'm not sure how long I'm staying. Maybe in a week."

We promise to keep in touch, and she walks me out to the doorman. I give her a quick hug goodbye and settle into the back seat of a taxi. We pass a long line of elegant, towering hotels that all face the shoreline, then turn to head inland. The scenery outside the window changes from manicured lawns and expensive boutiques to straggly banyan trees and strip malls. The road becomes muddy and rough. We pass a tiny roadside stand where a man is selling papayas from the trunk of a car. We turn into a short driveway and stop at a one-story concrete structure with an overgrown garden in front.

A young man at the front desk is asleep, his baseball hat covering his face, his arms crossed.

I am passing the communal kitchen on my way to my room when I hear, "Philadelphia! Want to come to our wine tasting? We're about to open this bottle of pineapple wine from the ABC Store."

"Cheap wine? Count me in," I say.

They are a group of five, including Alice, all strangers to one another until check-in this morning. They look as if they've all just come from a long afternoon at the beach. We stand around a lime-green tile island in a kitchen that looks like it hasn't been updated since the 1970s.

"Nice suit." A girl in a tankini hands me a coffee mug with a chip in the rim.

A young man with an Irish accent is fishing through the kitchen drawers. "Is there a corkscrew in here anywhere?"

Alice examines the bottle, then twists the cap off it. "There's no cork, my friend," she says. Smiling, she fills each of our coffee cups with a tiny bit of fragrant, mawkish wine.

"To Maui. Welcome to the Bungalow," someone says. We raise our cups and clink them together.

"That's not the *worst* wine I've ever had," Alice says thoughtfully, swirling her cup.

We spend the evening sampling several other dollar-store wines and exchanging stories. The girl in the tankini, Jin, is from Ohio. She's planning to spend two months hiking around the Hawaiian Islands while doing odd jobs before making her way to Japan to visit her ancestral home. The young man, Ian, recently dropped out of college in Dublin in favor of traveling to tropical destinations and writing short stories. His parents, both of them successful professionals, are livid with him, which is why he hasn't called or emailed them in over three months. Alice is, indeed, from South Africa and comes from a long line of world travelers. There's a young woman from Barcelona who speaks minimal English but, clearly, hates the wine, and an Israeli man hoping to make enough money waiting tables in Lahaina to afford a plane ticket to his next destination, Tibet.

I enjoy the hazy, muddled state of consciousness induced by so much third-rate wine. As I listen to the easy laughter of my new friends, it occurs to me that I want, more than anything, to be one of them. I can't remember ever being this blithely unconcerned about the future, unburdened by responsibility. Free. I've always been so preoccupied with what comes next—the next exam, the next semester, the next rotation, the next patient, the next month, the next year, the next four years. The steps required to carry on my father's legacy. I've been dragging around the weight of my self-imposed expectations for years, blind to the fact that there's this whole other, open-ended, joyously rambling way to live. I've been trying so hard to know who my father was, I never stopped to wonder who I am.

They're planning a trip to a different beach tomorrow, they say, and invite me to join them. I pack away my blue suit and, the next morning, dress in a bikini and cover-up and cram into Ian's rented, ramshackle Dodge Intrepid for the ride to the coast. We spend the day swimming and listening to Jin complain about Ohio. It's wonderful and pointless.

As the sun sets, we climb over an embankment and make our way to the hidden Little Beach where the locals gather to beat on drums, dance, and smoke marijuana. Nudity, we're told, is encouraged. Jin and Alice immediately take off their tops and disappear into the crowd. The other three spread out a blanket and buy pineapple slices on skewers from a little shirtless boy wearing a shell necklace.

"I'm going to take a walk," I tell them, and set off down the shoreline, the surf rushing over my feet. All around are smiling faces and dancing naked bodies—of all types—cast in orange and pink hues. I take off my cover-up and toss it onto the sand. After a moment, I unsnap the top of my bathing suit and toss it aside, too. Finally, laughing, I wriggle out of the bottoms as well. Then, with the rapturous, rhythmic sound of drums behind me, I walk into the sea, toward the kaleidoscope of the sun.

CHAPTER TWENTY-FIVE

Dear Dr. Kapadia,

Thank you for your letter. My father remembers you well, and he asked me to write back to you on his behalf. He's recently had a stroke and has trouble using his right hand for fine motor tasks such as holding a pen.

My father and our family appreciate your letter. My mother was a warm, wonderful person. In the face of her cancer diagnosis, she was brave and steadfastly optimistic. If she ever had doubts that she would survive, she never let that show to my father or her children.

Knowing the truth about how she passed has brought long-overdue closure to us all. We still grieve for my mother every day, but please know that your words brought comfort and healing to our broken family. To feel that someone who cared for her in her final days and moments shares our profound sadness somehow makes our burden easier to bear. I hope that knowing this will help ease your own burden. Thank you for reminding us that everyone who cared for my mother during her illness suffered a loss that night as well. On behalf of my family, and in memory of my mother, thank you.

"It's signed Michael Tally."

I am quiet for a long moment, the phone pressed to my ear. Then I say, "Thank you, Nate."

"Aubrey says they're probably going to drop the lawsuit. She's pretty pissed."

"Not at you, though, right?"

"No. She doesn't know I connected you with them. Michael Tally said that all they wanted were answers. They wanted someone to acknowledge that a mistake was made, and they wanted an apology. It was never about money."

"I know. I didn't think it was."

"Now boarding Flight 435 to Orlando," a voice announces overhead. A silver-haired grandmother in a Mickey Mouse T-shirt shepherding four young children through the airport terminal smiles at me as she passes. Mrs. Tally in another life.

"Wait, did they say Orlando?" Nate asks. "Where are you going?"

"It's my nephew's fourth birthday tomorrow. My family is meeting up at Legoland."

"How long will you be there?"

"Two days. Then I'm flying to Dublin."

"Why Dublin?"

"I've never had a chance to travel. And I met a guy in Maui who was born and raised there. He made it sound amazing. We'll see, I guess."

"But you'll be coming back to Philly at some point, right?"

"At some point. I still have an apartment. And all my stuff is still there."

"Okay, at the risk of sounding pathetic and desperate, I'm going to point out that I, Nate Kwan, am also in Philadelphia, and you're no longer my doctor. So . . . just in case that's of interest to you."

I laugh. "I will keep that in mind. It's definitely of interest to me."

"It is? Good. That's good. By the way, I ran into Meryl last week. I told her that you said she used to be a geek."

My voice catches. "You did? What did she say?"

"She said it was true. And she said to tell you that she just got engaged."

"She did? To who?"

The final boarding call announcement comes over the loudspeaker.

"To this guy at her firm," Nate says. "She had an engagement ring the size of a baseball. She said something about the decision being so easy she didn't even have to ask the Three P's, whatever that means. She said you'd understand."

I grin. "Yeah, I do. Tell her . . ." There are so many things I want to say to Meryl. "That I said congratulations. I couldn't be happier for her."

"Sure. I'll tell her."

The gate agent, a man wearing a floral shirt and a lei, waves urgently and calls, "Final boarding, miss!"

"I have to go. Thanks again, Nate."

"Talk to you soon, Norah. Safe travels."

As he scans my boarding pass, the gate agent says, "Aloha. Welcome aboard."

I settle into my seat and leaf through the magazine in the seat-back pocket, the cover of which promises an article about destination weddings. *Meryl, engaged?* I smile as the plane thunders down the runway and we ascend, an unfamiliar feeling of lightness filling my chest.

I skim an article about restaurants in Palm Beach and then come to a full-page advertisement from the Law Firm of Strand, Spear, and Polanski that reads, *Have you or a loved one suffered catastrophic bleeding after being treated with Zynexa? Get the compensation you deserve! Call now for a free consultation!*

I close the magazine and decide on headphones, music, and staring out the window instead.

We are three hours into our flight when a distressed flight attendant rushes past, nearly tripping over a man whose feet are protruding into the aisle. A moment later, two other flight attendants follow. Then, a pleasant but anxious voice announces, "Ladies and gentleman, if there is a doctor onboard the flight, would you kindly make yourself known to the cabin crew by turning on your overhead call light?"

I look up. A dull red button with a picture of a lightbulb glows in the ceiling panel overhead. The woman in the aisle seat next to me was awakened by the announcement. She yawns and stretches, then falls back to sleep.

I stare straight ahead, listening to the blood pulsing in my ears and feeling my fingertips on the vinyl arms of the seat. I let my lungs fill with air. I breathe into my bones. Into my muscles and tendons. Into my nerve endings and arteries and skin.

Then I breathe out. And I push the button.

ACKNOWLEDGMENTS

First, to the hundreds of thousands of doctors, nurses, physician assistants, medical assistants, and other medical staff members who tend to patients across our country every day, often at great personal sacrifice, thank you. You are undervalued and overworked in our broken healthcare system.

Thank you to the thousands of patients I've had the privilege to know over my years of training and practice. Your generosity of spirit humbles and inspires me every day.

Thank you to my wonderful agent, Jessica Watterson, and the entire team at SDLA. Jess, thank you for believing in this story and in me.

To the brilliant Kristine Swartz, thank you, from the bottom of my heart, for your guidance and patience.

To the genius team at Berkley—Lindsey Tulloch, Vikki Chu, and Rita Frangie—who turned my random Microsoft Word document into a real book, thank you. It's so beautiful.

To Diana Franco and Fareeda Bullert, thank you for being amazing at what you do. You make it look easy.

Thank you to Andrea Monagle, Kayley Hoffman, and Megha Jain for their meticulous copyediting and proofreading. You have my most heartfelt admiration and apologies.

To Katie McCoach and the team of editors at RevPit. I will always be grateful. Katie, thank you for teaching me how to tell a story.

For editing and beta reading and commiserating, thank you to my wonderful friend SS.

For her thoughtful beta reading and feedback, thank you a million times over to Dr. Kimi Chernoby.

To the #RevPit2018Winners, especially Gayle Gillespie, Liselle Sambury, Ellen Mulholland, Sarah Hawley, Loretta Chefchaouni, Rachael Edwards, and Raquel Miotto E. Thank you for sharing this journey with me.

To the Real Divas: SS, VSV, NA, GT, PO, and KH. Thank you for the many years of friendship and support. You girls get me.

For being honest readers of an early draft, thank you to my friends VSV and JS. JS, thank you for the advice regarding legal issues discussed in the book.

To my family, thank you for your support. Mom and Dad, sorry for all the curse words. Love you guys.

To AS, thank you for literally everything. We finally published a book. I love you, and also you're extremely good-looking.

To my girls. Thank you for understanding that sometimes mommy spaces out because she's thinking about her stories. L, no, you're still not old enough to read mommy's book. K, yes, we can have pizza for dinner. I love you both beyond words.

The White Coat Diaries

MADI SINHA

Questions for Discussion

1. Impostor syndrome is when an individual suffers from self-doubt and feelings of fraudulence, in spite of being qualified to handle the situation. Discuss Norah's experience with impostor syndrome and whether you have ever felt similarly.

2. Norah struggles to balance her career expectations with her family's expectations. When do these expectations clash? Does she handle the situations the right way? Have you had to balance conflicting expectations in your own life?

3. Recurring emotional stress can lead to "compassion fatigue," the experience of becoming emotionally numb and disconnected from the suffering of others. In the medical field, compassion fatigue is recognized as a factor in burnout. Discuss which characters show signs of compassion fatigue and what factors you think contribute to its development.

4. Norah and her sister-in-law, Reena, have a rocky relationship. Why do you think that is? How is this relationship different from Norah's friendship with Meryl? Reena is Indian American and Meryl is not—do cultural factors play a role in how Norah relates to both women?

5. *The White Coat Diaries* is written by a doctor and shows what it's like to work in a hospital. Does it match your expectations of how a hospital is run? Why or why not? Did this novel change the way you think about the medical system?

6. Where do you think Norah will be five years after the end of the novel? Will she be practicing medicine? Why or why not?

7. At the beginning of *The White Coat Diaries*, Norah reflects that she's spent so much time caring for Ma and studying to become a doctor that "for a person in my midtwenties, there are a lot of things I've never done." Discuss how this relative inexperience shapes her decisions. How does Norah change over the course of the novel as she experiences various firsts (first night on call, first real kiss, first group of friends, first sexual experience, etc.)?

8. Norah tries to adopt a "confident and breezy" persona around Ethan, essentially trying to remake herself into someone she thinks he'd find attractive. Have you ever tried to change yourself for someone? Looking back, do you wish you'd made a different decision?

9. At the end of *The White Coat Diaries*, Gabe remarks on how different Norah seems compared to when he first met her, and Norah replies that "We all evolve." How does Norah's person-

Photo by Ashley Walsh Photography

MADI SINHA is a physician and writer who loves the nervous system, bookshops, tea with milk, and snarky conversation (but not necessarily in that order). She lives in New Jersey with her husband and two children.

CONNECT ONLINE

MadiSinha.com

MadiSinha

MadiSinha

ality change from the beginning of the novel to the end? How has your own personality changed over the course of your life? Are our personalities ever fixed, or do we keep evolving? In what ways do you think you will be different ten years from now? In what ways will you be the same?